PRAISE FOR *FORGED BY FATE*, AND FATE OF THE GODS

"This story was absolutely amazing! It's like nothing I've read before… a complete game changer. You won't be able to deny that Miss Dillin is a genius."

—Parajunkee Reviews

"A fascinating and artful blend of myth and legend that makes for a rich story of transcendent courage and hope. Not to be missed!"

— Saranna DeWylde, author of the *10 Days s*eries

"Inspired! An amazing fantasy world."

—Book Chick City

"I was hooked! I can't wait until the second book comes out so I can find out what happens next."

—Jeep Diva Reviews

"A beautiful, sweeping story that puts on display the power of every interpretation of love, and the truth of what can be accomplished when people choose peace over strife. I couldn't put it out of my mind for days."

—Trisha Leigh, author of *The Last Year* series

"A unique, hauntingly beautiful story."

—JC Andrijeski, author of the *Allie's War* series

Also by Amalia Dillin

Fate of the Gods
Forged by Fate
Tempting Fate (Novella)
Fate Forgotten
Taming Fate (Novella)
Beyond Fate

Anthology
A Winter's Enchantment

BEYOND FATE

Fate of the Gods Trilogy
Book Three

AMALIA DILLIN

World Weaver Press

BEYOND FATE

Published by World Weaver Press
Alpena, Michigan
www.WorldWeaverPress.com

Edited by Eileen Wiedbrauk
Cover designed by World Weaver Press

First Edition: September 2014

ISBN: 0692278834
ISBN-13: 978-0692278833

Also available as an ebook.

For Karen—
Thank you for reading and rereading and re-rereading,
but most importantly, thank you for being my friend.

ACKNOWLEDGMENTS

I must begin with the people who supported me from the first words—Karen, Dan, Sarah, Tom, and Mom, thank you so much for encouraging me to write on while also providing constructive and thoughtful feedback. And thank you also for reading and then reading again, when I reworked whole chapters or an entire book along the way.

Thank you also to my extended family: Uncle Joey, Uncle Johnny, Aunt Tommi Lou, Aunt Rose, and Aunt Debbie, for all your early reading. I know I've thanked you before, but I can't tell you how much I appreciate the time you spent in helping me to be a better and stronger writer. Your feedback was invaluable, and I consider myself incredibly fortunate to have such a wonderful (and well-read!) family, willing to take the time to invest in me and my books.

Thanks to all my early alphas and betas, too (for this project and others!), including Cait Greer, Diana Paz, Zak Tringali, L.T. Host, Katie M. Stout, Trisha Leigh, Valerie Valdes, Nick Mohoric, Stephanie Thornton, Mia Hayson, Wendy Sparrow, Tessa, Tina, Emi, Con, Gina, Becky, Laurie and Seth, Biz, D., Meg, Justin, Cassie, John, Kevin, Andrew, and the entirety of our old Writers' Group at UND—most especially Brandon, Emily, Gilad Elbom, Nick, Nikki, Josh and Jess—I would not be the writer I am today if not for your interest in reading and critiquing!

And to my friends and family who didn't read, but provided moral (and other!) support, particularly Drew the Third (who I suspect I will owe even more thanks to before this adventure is over) and Zan (thank you for putting a roof over my head and letting me write beneath it! I can't promise I'll ever be able to repay you, but I'll certainly keep trying.)

Finally, thank you times infinity plus one to Adam: you made all of this possible, by giving me the love and support to chase after my dreams and always believing I would succeed. You're the best husband I could ever have asked for, and I'm so glad to share this journey with you!

I really hope that over the course of these five titles I haven't missed anyone—but I also need to thank every single one of you who are reading this now. Thank you for reading. Thank you for thinking Fate of the Gods sounded interesting. Thank you SO MUCH for writing reviews and giving copies to your friends and family. Thank you, thank you, thank you!

Fate of the Gods has been an incredible adventure, and I hope its conclusion doesn't disappoint!

FATE FORGOTTEN

PROLOGUE

Michael

He had waited an eternity for this. Michael hovered above the campus, watching Thor so near to self-destruction. He could only hold his breath and pray. *Reveal yourself to her. Reveal yourself, and let me stand in witness. Let me see you fall with my own eyes!*

Elah had sent him to fetch the Odinson, and how perfect it would be to bring back not only the interloper, but also the proof of his betrayal. Michael had been waiting for it. Ever since Elah had forbidden Thor from Eve near a century ago, he had kept watch for any sign, any evidence of his disobedience.

But when Eve appeared at the entrance of her dorm and stepped out on the sidewalk, Thor shifted back behind a wide oak tree. As Eve continued past, he remained hidden, and when she turned the corner of the building, leaving his line of sight, he did not follow. Thor's shoulders drooped, his head bowed, and Michael, hand closed tight upon the sword at his hip, was left with only bitter disappointment.

The weak fool.

Odin had made the right choice in leaving such a pathetic creature behind. It would be a kindness to put him out of his misery.

One-eye will meet his own doom, soon enough. Let the Odinson suffer.

Michael bared his teeth, anticipation pricking down his spine. Thor would suffer. Lifetime after lifetime, forbidden from Eve, forgotten and alone. When this world burned, everything he loved lost, perhaps he would even go mad. But Michael still hoped to see him trip before then. Let him be forbidden even the sight of Eve, from breathing the same air, from walking the same earth. Let him be exiled to the void, with no one and nothing, to waste away in eternal wretchedness, never knowing her fate. Never knowing.

A fitting end for the Odinson. But I would torture Elohim's heir with my own hands, my own fire.

Michael shook his head to clear it, forcing himself to release the sword. Elah waited, and he must serve. Perhaps if he were very fortunate, he might provoke the Odinson into violence, and Elah would give him leave to strike. He'd never agreed with Her decision to offer a new Covenant. Every god that remained was a threat, even if She refused to see it. Thor, worst of all.

If Elah knew the truth, allowed Thor the freedom he desired, it would destroy everything Michael had built, everything he had nurtured so carefully.

He would not allow it.

Elah, this world—it was *his*, and he would do everything in his power to see that it remained so.

She had not told Michael why she wished to speak to Thor, but he knew it related to the god's frequent trips to earth. To Eve. He had made sure Elah knew of them, delivering the news himself when called for, or allowing word to reach Her ear through the lesser angels, as if he had not noticed those occasions himself. Elah may have been young, but She was not nearly as foolish as he might have wished—distractible, to be sure, naive as only a daughter of Eve could be, but not foolish—and he did not dare press Her further than he already had on the subject of Thor Odinson.

Even so, when Thor was welcomed into the Redwood Hall and dropped to one knee before Elah's throne, Michael could not help but sneer from his place at Her right hand. His fingers closed upon the pommel of his sword. How easy it would be with his head bowed to bring the sword down upon his neck and watch his startled face roll away through the mulch.

Let them all burn.

"Lady," Thor said, all respect and reverence. "I am at your service."

Elah leaned forward, rainbow black hair cascading over Her shoulder. Michael's nostrils flared, taking in the scent of Her, mingled with his own. She was wildflowers and ocean air, geranium and pine, and sometimes, in Her anger, the merest hint of woodsmoke on a crisp autumn night. He could not say She was not beautiful. His greatest prize, now that he'd won Her.

"I am honored to be so served by you, Thor of the North," Elah said, Her voice rich and warm. Too warm. "You may rise."

Michael's eyes narrowed, his gaze shifting to Raphael. His brother looked far too pleased with himself. Far too at ease for one who stood in witness to the punishment of his friend.

"Near a century ago, you asked a favor of me," Elah said. "My refusal was . . . shortsighted."

No. The hilt of the sword warmed beneath his hand, begging to be drawn, whispering of fire and need. *He must suffer. He must burn!*

"As you know, my mother languishes. She refuses all comfort, all companionship."

Her sorrow serves, her pain well-earned.

Michael shuddered, fury snaking through his core.

"You asked me once if you might go to her, to reveal yourself and your love. If you are still willing, I would grant you that freedom now, for her sake."

"My lady," Michael growled, his jaw tight. "You cannot mean this."

She did not look at him, though Her head turned, just slightly. "If Thor is what she desires, I will not withhold the means to my mother's happiness. If he is not, I have lost nothing in the trying."

"And if he is, you would risk everything!"

"I have heard your counsel and your warnings," Elah said, steel behind Her words. "This is Our will, Archangel."

She would displace you. Destroy you. Take the world from your grasp and hand it to another, less worthy. She will ruin everything.

Michael hissed, spreading his wings and launching himself into the air. The branches parted, making way, and he barreled through them. His fingers itched, his arm aching to draw the blade of the God-Killer, to act, to claim what was his, at last, at last, at last.

He had earned it. He had waited so long, suffering in silence, trapped in the dark. He had waited and it was his time. Elohim's heirs would not stand in his way, now. Not the Goddess, not the Thunder God, not the Archangels, all blinded to the true threat. He would drain them all dry, and he would rise.

Rise up for his vengeance, spilling blood and fire across this green world, with an army of the dead.

And he would not be defeated again.

CHAPTER ONE

Eve

Eve had forgotten how loud the campus could be. All she'd wanted when she settled down in the grass beneath the oak tree, acorns digging into her spine, was a little bit of peace and quiet. But all the quiet did, even interrupted by the chirping of chipmunks and the bird song, was focus her mind on the things she didn't want to feel. So much mental noise when she had been alone for so long—too much, and all of it connected to her daughter. All of it Elah's.

"Anna!"

She blew out a breath of frustration. Marcus, of course, and now that they were away at school together, he hovered over her with a mix of almost parental concern and decidedly possessive romantic interest. When they were younger, when this life had been new, it hadn't bothered her so much. He'd just been the boy next door, protective of her and friendly, refusing to let her isolate herself from the others. A welcome warmth after the cold of Elah's punishment. Five years ago, the worst thing about Marcus was how much that protectiveness had reminded her of Garrit DeLeon, another husband lost at the end of another lifetime, and all the heartsickness that came with the remembering how completely she had been forgotten.

Three hundred years ago, Marcus would have been exactly the kind of man she might have loved and married, even if she couldn't ever tell him the truth.

But now?

She'd spent a summer helping to build houses for the homeless in China—a volunteer program associated with the child of what had once been known as the Peace Corps—in order to escape him. Not that it had done her much good, it seemed.

Eve opened her eyes to find Marcus standing over her, grinning. "Still recovering from your indentured servitude, I see."

"Not exactly."

Marcus offered a hand up, and she took it. There was something about lying flat on her back that left her feeling exposed around him. Not that he'd pounce on her stomach, but it was certainly an invitation to intimacy she didn't want to make.

"Your parents said you were back, but I almost didn't believe them. You don't call, you don't text—I would even have settled for some old fashioned paper and ink, since I know you're so obsessed with it."

She smiled in spite of herself. It was impossible to stay irritated with Marcus for long, which was maybe half the reason she hadn't quite been able to rid herself of him. "I'm not sure I could have afforded to mail it. I definitely couldn't afford an international call."

"The Free West isn't that far from China, in the grand scheme of things."

Eve snorted. The Free West—the result of the ideological fault lines within the once United States—wasn't any different from The United East, as far as she could tell. The Republic of Texas was the real outlier, founded a solid century ago and taking a good portion of the dustbowl-center of the country and the south with it. But whatever the United States had become, it was still very, very far from China. Plague had struck in the overcrowded cities just two decades ago, a superbug evolved from drug resistant strains of Scarlet Fever. Eve remembered hearing the reports of devastation before she'd died, and the nation was still recovering, which was why they'd allowed the Peace Corps to provide aid, and why Eve had signed herself up.

"All right, fine," Marcus said, throwing a wave to one of his other friends as a group of boys clowned past them, showing off for the handful of girls sunbathing nearby. The quad was all sun at this time of day, and the brick buildings around the edges offered a strange illusion of privacy, or at least security. "But now you're back, and I'm on my way to a picnic, to which you are now invited. Come as my date and make me look attentive and sweet and hard to get."

"Um, no," Eve said, though she couldn't quite keep from a laugh for the absolute absurdity. "Not a chance."

"Please, Anna. The first party of the year sets the tone for every chance meeting thereafter. I need you to make me shine. And without a roommate this year, you need all the help you can get finding opportunities for socialization."

"How does having a date help you to meet other girls?" she asked, then shook her head, holding up a hand to stop him from explaining. "Don't. Don't answer that. I'm not getting sucked into this scheme or any other. No. Go to your picnic and leave me to my jetlag."

"Then I believe we have a longstanding arrangement regarding dinner—don't even think about arguing, Anna, I'm not going to let you hermit yourself away completely, this semester or any other. Your room or mine?"

"I should really get a jump on my reading . . ."

"Classes haven't started. You don't even know what you have to read yet. And don't think I don't know your habits. You always wait until you get the syllabus to decide what books you're buying as archaic physical references, and which books you'll suffer to read as scans."

"Not this year," she said. "Now that I'm taking mostly sciences I've already ordered all of them in both formats. In fact—" she glanced at the sun "—I should go pick them up before it gets any later. Unless you want to come with me and play packhorse?"

"Honestly, Anna. Where do you get these expressions?" But he was already backing away. "You ordered those doorstops, and you get to haul them. I'm certainly not going to encourage your bad habits by helping. Dinner at eighteen hundred, and no excuses!"

She rolled her eyes. He could be so absurd about modern technology. Though she supposed it made her equally as absurd to him. Eve sighed and collected her bag from where she'd been using it for a pillow. Honestly, she hadn't really ordered them all in hardcover. It just didn't make sense when the scans were updated quarterly with new research and findings. The books would be out of date again in three months, and she'd have wasted the trees it took to print, as well as her money.

It was just that one mythology book—her last humanities course to fulfill the general education requirements before she could focus on her major. Those stories certainly weren't going to change now if they hadn't already.

She turned toward the library—they'd become bookstores as well, sometime before her last life, in Montreal—and walked face first into a wall of flesh.

"Excuse me," she mumbled, stumbling back. "So sorry. I didn't realize you were there."

A broad palm reached out, catching her by the elbow with a steadying hand. "My mistake, I assure you. I couldn't help but overhear you say something about real books? I didn't even realize they still sold them."

The voice, affectionate and throaty and richly masculine, froze her completely. Worse, it was familiar. She stared at the hand on her elbow, followed it to the wrist, then the well-muscled forearm and the even more defined bicep. Wide shoulders, broad chest, and mountainously tall. Her breath caught when she finally forced herself to look at his face. She tore her arm free, tripping backwards until her back hit the oak tree and her hands clutched rough bark.

Familiar blue eyes, warm enough to make her shiver, that nose with its bump in the arch from an old break, a strong, square jaw and red-gold hair pulled neatly back from his face. But she didn't need him to let it down to know how long it would be, how it would rest just perfectly against his shoulders. She'd seen it before. Seen him before.

"You should be dead."

"I hope that isn't wishful thinking, Eve."

She blinked, absorbing the sound of her name—her real name—from his lips. Soft, as if he savored the saying of it as much as her ears delighted in the listening. Her eyes devoured the shape of it on his lips. Blinding hope speared through her, sudden and intense. "If the DeLeons sent you—"

"They didn't."

She swallowed her disappointment, blinked back the pressure behind her eyes that heralded tears. Of course they didn't. Of course. "But you must be one of Owen's line?"

He pressed his lips together. "It would not be entirely untrue to say so, but I'm afraid I had to mislead you as to our exact relationship the last time we met."

"The last time!" she half-choked on the words. "The last time we met, you were—I was—"

"Married," he supplied. "To Garrit DeLeon, two hundred years ago."

She shook her head, closed her eyes. Was she this desperate for connection, for family, that she'd invented him completely? It was just a hallucination. A memory. She'd done her fair share of that during her last life, but now? It made no sense.

He laughed lowly. "Why are you always so certain I'm a ghost? Tell me there isn't some small part of you that doesn't wish otherwise. That hopes desperately for the opposite?"

Eve pressed the heels of her hands against her eyes, a strangled sound escaping before she could stop it. "If you were in my head, some hallucination, you'd already know the answer to that question. You'd know without even the smallest doubt. But it doesn't matter. It isn't possible. Medicine has advanced, but no one lives 200 years. Even the oldest, healthiest people don't live beyond 120. Not without—without some kind of cybernetics and that much modification sends the body into shock. It doesn't work, and I couldn't bear it if you were some android. I just. I can't. You can't be here."

"Eve." His voice was so gentle, so sympathetic, and then his hand had closed around her wrist, warm and calloused and so familiar. "Look at me, I beg of you, and then I will go, if you wish it."

"No!" She clutched at his shirt, at his hand, her heart constricting at the thought that she might never see him again. Even if he wasn't real. She hadn't realized how much she still wanted it, to be herself, to be free of all the lies, but it hit her like a punch to the gut. And all the more precious for what Elah had taken from her.

He was smiling when she met his eyes, gently, kindly, as if he knew how difficult this must be for her. And how could he know? How could he know what looking at him, seeing him in the flesh did to her? The memories it brought to the surface of her thoughts so perfectly clear, all joy and happiness and the bittersweet knowledge that it would end. That it always ended. And that was why it couldn't matter, now, and she wouldn't have any part of it, of him, of any of it.

Love wasn't enough. Love didn't stop them all from dying, and it made the grief of it, the loss, so much more difficult to face. Even more so when the person she lost knew her and loved her as Eve.

And he couldn't know any of that.

"My name isn't Thorgrim," he said firmly, catching hold of her chin when she would have looked away, forcing her to face him, to see *him*. "Nor is it Lars Owen, no matter what Garrit might have told you."

His eyes. Had his eyes always burned that way? Not in that first life, so long ago, when she had been his wife. She would have remembered. Just like she remembered, now, staring up at him, that he was the only husband who had outlived her. His face had been the last thing she had seen, his hand on hers the last comfort she had felt. She swallowed hard, then did it again, because her throat was so thick, and just the memory made her eyes mist. But she couldn't look away.

She didn't want to look away.
"My name is Thor, Eve, and like you, my father is a god."

CHAPTER TWO
Adam, 93 Years Before

"You worthless, filthy *rakki.*" Thor held Adam by the collar, lifting him up off his feet and shaking him until his limbs went boneless. Adam gripped the god's wrists and hung on, doing his best to keep himself in one piece under the circumstances. It wouldn't be anything serious—Thor wouldn't risk doing Eve any real harm—but the god's eyes were burning blue-white, and the shiver of static over his skin meant very shortly the circumstances might change drastically.

In Asgard, Thor could beat him bloody, and Eve wouldn't feel a thing. Something about the distances and time being stopped. Adam hadn't exactly been paying attention the last time he'd experienced it, too busy trying to keep himself from bleeding all over his second-best suit.

"Thor," Athena caught his arm, and even with his brain rattling inside his skull, Adam could see the strength of her grip, the sharp press of her nails against the god's skin. Clouds had darkened the sky, flashes of lightning still too high up to reach him. But for how long? "Eve might not know you've done him harm, but the baby is certain to reach for her father. And if she ascends, believing us to be her enemy…"

Thor growled, thunder rumbling in sympathy, and suddenly, Adam was falling. *Do not twist an ankle*, he ordered his body, because Thor hadn't simply dropped him, he'd thrown him back several paces, and

Adam landed hard on his backside in the grass to avoid any greater injury. To leave Eve with bruises she couldn't explain now, after he'd abandoned her to raise their daughter alone . . .

He picked himself up from the neat, carefully manicured lawn of his own back yard, and brushed himself off, his stomach twisted into knots again. He almost could have used a beating to straighten himself out. A fitting punishment for what he'd done.

"I promise you, Thor, no one regrets this more than me," he said quietly. "But I had no choice. Gabriel made that clear."

"No choice!" Thor roared, the war hammer appearing in his fist as if it had been there from the start. Adam knew it hadn't. A moment ago, both the god's hands had been on him. "From the start, you had nothing but choice! You could have left her alone, never gone in search of her to begin with!"

"God's Will is not so easily thwarted as that, Thor," Ra said, and where he'd come from, Adam wasn't sure. One moment it had been the three of them—Thor had nearly broken down his door while he had been packing, and Athena had been fast on his heels—and the next, the old raisin of a god had shimmered into being on his patio.

Teleportation. There were men in startlingly white clean rooms trying to figure out how to make it possible, and these gods just thought themselves somewhere else, and appeared without a moment's consideration for the fact that they had defied all science, even the laws of physics themselves. But then, if they could stop time, physics became much less of a law, and a lot more of a guideline.

Thor snarled at Ra. "If you knew this was coming—"

Ra held up one brown hand, permanently creased. "After so long in exile, I knew little for certain. What Elohim's plan was, once, long ago, and what He hoped for in the present might well have been two different things."

Athena's expression had altered, her eyes narrowing, and Adam frowned. At her, at the Egyptian who had captured her attention so entirely with his few words. Ra had taken him in once, after his memory had been returned, cared for him when he was so broken in mind he couldn't even feed himself without help. He hadn't thought much of it until now, and it appeared Athena hadn't either.

But he couldn't be in league with Michael. It didn't make sense. Michael never would have been part of returning his memory, or allowed it to come to pass had he been given any say, any influence in the matter. That much was more than clear.

But in league with Elohim, Himself?

Or.

Or.

"Raphael," Adam murmured.

Three sets of eyes snapped to him, with the weight of three divine minds boring into his, and Adam swore, stumbling back another step, clutching his skull. It was all he could do to keep from spilling every memory, every thought he'd ever had into the open, and Eve—he could not let Eve hear him now, when he had gone to so much trouble to hide himself.

"Stop!" he gasped. These gods. They had no consideration, and his mind felt as though it was exploding. Drills through the bone, into the soft matter beneath, spinning out wisps of memories. "Before she feels it, too!"

"What has the Archangel to do with this?" Thor demanded, the pressure of his insistence fading first. "He has not been seen or heard from for as long as I've walked the earth."

Athena's gaze shifted from Adam to Ra, then, her forehead furrowed. "You could have trusted me."

The Egyptian's mouth was a thin line of pain and regret. "I didn't dare risk the others learning of it. No matter what my heart yearned for. Could you have really kept it from your father, had he commanded otherwise?"

Not so Egyptian after all, perhaps. Adam shook his head. "All this time, you were working with them. Did Michael realize it?"

Ra looked even more ancient, as though he'd been carved from stone and worn away again, scoured by the wind and the rain. "When I realized the threat to this world, after Bhagavan's arrival, I tried to reason with him. Michael would have been happy to fight every god who appeared, one by one, uncaring if mankind suffered because of it. To thwart him, I left, taking a portion of Elohim's host with me into exile. Enough to weaken my brother, to make the outcome of any battle waged unclear. Of course, Michael did not forgive me for it, and to save my own head, I remade myself into a god, hiding in plain sight. What he knows of my accomplishments since, of what I forged with Bhagavan and the others, I cannot say. Gabriel still came to me, now and again, keeping my secret, as he has Lucifer's, but he never spoke openly with me, after that. I was not to know what Michael chose to accomplish in God's name."

Thor was staring at them, all of them, the hammer long forgotten in his hand and the blaze of lightning gone from his eyes. "You're the third Archangel. Raphael, the healer."

"Forgive me," Raphael said, his shoulders bowed. "I beg you both to forgive me. I did not see another way. When Bhagavan arrived, I knew it would only be a matter of time before others sought us out. This world, Elohim's creation, shone like a beacon in the void."

"But you helped us," Thor said, the words confident. "You protected us from being cast out again, from the rise of the third prophet . . ."

Ra opened his hand, staring into his empty palm as if it held some secret. "Better the world be left in your hands, Thor, and Bhagavan's, than given up into Michael's keeping. Of course I helped you, to protect Adam and Eve, to protect all the innocent who would have suffered under Michael's rule. And Adam had suffered his punishment long enough. Until it was lifted, Elohim could never truly rise again. The world would never be free."

"The trees," Athena murmured, her eyes widening as they shifted to Thor. "It was not just idle talk, was it? No coincidence at all."

Raphael shook his head just once, his gaze sharp on the goddess. Athena pressed her lips together and turned her face away. Whatever answer she sought lost to Adam. And the way she had said it, the shape of the words felt like a kick to his gut. Familiar and strange, all at once, as if she had stolen them from his own mouth.

"What trees?" Adam asked. A snake around Athena's wrist hissed, and her hand closed on his forearm, all but crushing. He met her gray eyes and clenched his jaw against the discomfort. "If you speak of the Garden—"

"Hera's garden only," Athena snapped, releasing him. "And none of your concern."

A glance at Raphael's haggard face proved the lie, but the old god—the old Archangel—was more concerned with Thor's response, judging by the way his gaze didn't leave the younger god's expression. And if it were the Garden, what could it have to do with Thor? Adam shook his head. There was only so much he could discern when half of what these gods said to one another was communicated in complete silence and the privacy of their own minds.

"If you are Raphael," Thor said at last, "then go to her. Ease her sorrows. None of this would have happened if it weren't for our interference. If we hadn't returned Adam's memory, Eve would never have thought him changed. Had he given her a child still, she would not be so heartbroken as she is now when he proved himself false. Neither Michael nor my father will allow me to stand by her side, but you could!"

Adam looked away, swallowing his own bitterness. *It is not Eve we cannot trust.* That was what Gabriel had told him, what had driven him away. And if he was gone, if Eve raised the child by herself, perhaps she'd have just that much more time with their daughter. And maybe the world would be kept whole, because of it.

Eve could teach her love, and what could Adam give his daughter, this new goddess, but pain? That was all he'd ever given to Eve, after all. Heartbreak and suffering and struggle. Betrayal heaped upon betrayal, even when he hadn't meant to give her anything but some kind of peace, some kind of future. But neither one of them would have a future if Elah wasn't raised by Eve, protected by Eve, loved by Eve. That was all that mattered now, and it was the only thing he had left to give them, this one last act of love laced with sorrow. As long as he stayed away, the world could go on turning.

"If she'd known you lived, still," Adam said to Thor, the words like broken glass in his mouth. "If she'd known you lived, her Thorgrim, she never would have had me. And maybe you're right. Maybe she would have been better off, for it."

And then Adam left them, the two gods and the Archangel, cluttering up his patio. He took his bag, hastily packed with a change of clothes and the documentation he'd need to start over somewhere as far away from Eve and Elah as he could get, and he left them all behind.

Once, maybe, he would have let the world be destroyed because it wasn't his, because it could never be his. But not anymore. Because if the world didn't survive, neither would Eve. And finally, after all this time, he was starting to really understand what love meant.

What loving her meant.

He was beginning to wonder how she'd survived so long, so beautifully, now that he knew how much it hurt to lose.

CHAPTER THREE

Thor, 93 Years Later

"No," Eve said again, shaking her head and dropping her hand from his shirt. "No, that isn't—it can't be. Unless—unless your father is Elohim?"

Thor stepped closer, catching her hand. She was so different. He'd known it, but somehow he'd thought if he only revealed himself, if she only knew he lived . . . "Not Elohim. Odin. My father is Odin, and I am Thor of the North, Thor of the Aesir, Thor of Asgard."

"Asgard!"

Behind her, a handful of girls broke into titters. Another group of students turned to look at her as they walked by, and Eve shrank in upon herself, her shoulders curving.

"Asgard is a fairy tale," she said lowly. "And none of those gods are real. I would have known. I should have known."

"Unless they had a reason to keep themselves from you," he said, searching her face, willing her to understand, to open to him. It would be so much easier to explain, then, but she was so withdrawn, so determinedly distant. "And then you would know nothing, see nothing, remember nothing they did not want you to see."

She rubbed her forehead, pressed two fingers against her temple, and that small crease between her eyebrows formed.

"What are you saying? Exactly. What are you—how are you here, now, if that's true. You kept your secret for so long, why reveal yourself now? Today?"

He smiled. "Because you remade the world, Eve. You and Elah. You set me free, at last to come to you, to tell you everything, with Elah's blessing, of course."

"And what does all this mean for her, for my daughter?" Eve demanded, and even while she straightened, somehow she withdrew even further, as if even the question pained her.

"It means she allowed me to come to you. That I am sworn to her service, or I would not be here at all. But she has granted me freedom, at long last, and Eve—" he squeezed her hand, still caught against his chest, his heart. "*Hjartað mitt,* I had begun to fear this day would never come. That you would never know me, never realize my love."

She froze, staring up at him for a heartbeat, two, and he couldn't even begin to imagine her thoughts. Gods Above, but he'd never seen her this way before. Her aura was so dim he doubted any other god would have recognized her, and he was beginning to fear it was worse than those months she'd spent in the ward. At least then she'd wanted to love, wanted to believe in him. Now . . .

"I don't even know you," she said, jerking her hand free, herself free. "Everything before now, it's all been a lie, and I'm supposed to believe you, to swallow all of this whole."

"I do not doubt this must be difficult for you," he said slowly. "And I do not ask you to believe me without proof. I can show you all that you need to know, prove myself completely, if you will let me."

"And if I don't?" she hugged herself, pressing back against the oak tree. As if she couldn't get far enough away.

"I never left you, Eve. From the moment I first saw you, from the birth of Moses on, I reached for you. And that small life we shared, I have treasured every moment of it in memory, as I will always. Tell me you did not love me then, and I will go. Tell me you did not love me then, when I lived as Thorgrim, and I will never reach for you again, even—" he swallowed, his throat too thick with emotion. If she rejected him now, after everything he'd given up . . . But it was her choice. Her right. "I'll even help you to forget all of this, if you wish it."

She turned her face away, stared at the girls who still half-watched them. Tears filled her eyes, glistening, and Eve blinked, letting them fall. Something shifted then, just for a moment. He saw himself in her memories, coming out of the woods with an elk across his shoulders, felt the leap of her heart at the sight of him, the hunger as she searched his body, reassuring herself that none of the blood was his. And love, shared between them, filling her with so much peace. He felt her soften, and his whole heart lurched with need, with desire to give her the same again, to give her everything. He'd never lie to her again. Never mistrust her.

"Let me show you," he said gently, brushing her tears away with his thumb. He wanted to draw her into his arms, but he didn't dare. She was so wary. "Let me prove myself, now."

She shook her head, her eyes focusing again on him, and as suddenly as that moment of openness had come, she was gone again, leaving an ache where her presence had filled him for so many, many years.

"I'm tired of love," she said. "So tired of the loss that follows on its heels, wearing me thinner and thinner with grief. Every child I've borne but Elah, every husband I've loved, every family I've made mine. I won't do it anymore, whether you're Thorgrim or not. I'm too tired to do it again."

"What if it didn't have to end, this time?" He was begging, he knew, but he didn't care. He would humble himself a thousand times if that was what it took. "What if it could be forever? No death, no rebirth, no sorrow, no grief."

"It's impossible," she said, and stepped aside, not meeting his eyes. His heart tightened. But he couldn't believe it. He couldn't believe she had changed so much as this. "But if you want to stay, then stay. If you're a god, I can hardly stop you."

And then she was gone. So entirely withdrawn he lost her among the other students between one breath and the next. By the time her aura flickered with gold again, she'd reached the library, and he watched her disappear through the wide, double doors, her challenge still echoing in his ears.

"That could have gone better," Ra said, appearing beside him with a ruffle of feathers. Looking back, it seemed he'd always been accompanied by such a sound, but because he had kept his wings so well hidden, Thor had never recognized it for what it was. Or maybe he'd thought it some element of his power as Horus.

"As changed as she is, it could have gone much worse, too."

"She was alone for a long time, Thor. None of this will be easy for her, even with your help. This isn't like the ward, where we had only to wait and hope the poison might leave her body. She may not ever recover from her isolation, not truly. "

"We both remember what happened before. War after war after war, and she was not nearly so lost, then. So detached. If she continues on this way . . ." He couldn't think that way. He had to believe she would recover, that she would love him again, and give her Grace to the world. He pressed his lips together, tearing his gaze from the library to look at his friend. "She has never needed me more, and I have no intention of abandoning her, now, regardless. I only wish I might have come to her sooner. That Elah might have permitted me this freedom to see to her before now."

Ra sighed, his face no longer so lined, so aged, but for his eyes. Golden, sharp, and burdened with ancient grief. "Even Adam argued on your behalf, you know. Gabriel and I, as well. But Elah . . . She was so young. Too young to be burdened with so much power."

"I fear in some ways she still is."

"No," Ra said, frowning. "It isn't Her youth that worries me now. It's all the rest."

Michael.

He influences Her more than he should, Ra agreed. *But allow me to worry over Michael and the Goddess. Concern yourself with Eve, for she has the greater need, by far.*

Thor gave him a sharp glance, hearing a tension beneath the angel's words, left unspoken. *What is it you fear, Raphael?*

But Ra only shook his head, peeling his lips back in a poor imitation of a smile. *Nothing that cannot fix itself, I hope, with a little bit of good fortune.*

Thor studied his profile, searching his strange youthful face, so much more difficult to read than the old, wrinkled form he'd known for so long. *I used to be able to tell when you were lying.*

Ra snorted. *Or so I would have you believe.*

Do you keep so many more secrets from us now, Raphael?

Not more, no, but no fewer either. Much of what I keep, it is not my place to tell. But this—I wonder if it is simply that I have been away for so long. Michael was always argumentative, polarized and aggressive in his views, but after the Purge . . .

You fear he does his work too well. That he has gone Berserk.

It's as though the sword in his hand has made him that much thirstier for bloodshed.

He is a soldier. The sword of God. It is in his nature to desire to test himself in battle. But he is loyal to Elah.

He has guarded Her too well, at times. And you saw for yourself how he responds when She acts without his counsel. Even when it is an action blessed by Elohim, he bridles.

Elohim altered the seas in punishment of my love for Eve, Ra. I cannot believe He would have blessed Elah's decision to let me go to her, now.

His amber eyes crinkled in the corners, his smile warm. *Elohim would have been pleased beyond measure to know you cared so much for His daughter. That it was your love for her which caused Him to stir, I have no doubt, but not to punish you. Your father, perhaps, or Loki, or Sif, but never you.*

Thor lifted his eyebrows. *You're so certain?*

Ra chuckled. *Of that more than anything. But I have lingered long enough, and I will not burden you further with my troubles when you have work of your own. Give Eve my love, my friend. And I grant you all the Grace it is within my power to give, for whatever good it will do you.*

Thor bowed, humbled by the gift, but when he lifted his head, all that remained of Raphael was the flutter of his disappearance and the impression of two feet in the grass.

And he was left with only one thought, one small reassurance.

Eve had not sent him away.

And until she did, until she told him to go, he wasn't giving up, and whether she would admit it or not, she hadn't either.

Not completely.

CHAPTER FOUR

Eve

❧

She unpacked her books, organizing them by subject, alphabetically on the long shelf that she'd built over her desk. After constructing houses all summer, a shelf had been easy, and it felt good to work with her hands, to *make* something in a world where everything came pre-made and pre-packaged, manufactured in robotic plants without a single fingertip of human contact. Maybe she would take up weaving again, if she could get what she needed to make a loom.

Her fingers lingered on the spine of her new Mythology textbook, and Eve frowned. She drew the textbook back down off the shelf, and paged through the index.

Thor, see also Donar. She snorted. Like Zeus, see also Jupiter. They weren't that substantially different, only reflections of the same god, and she should know. She'd lived under the rule of both, Greek and Roman, and Greek again. Not that there had been such a thing as Greek for much of the time she'd spent among them.

She flipped to the right page and wrinkled her nose at the accompanying artwork. Thor battling Jormungand, the World Serpent. Had he really run around with no pants and a belt? It seemed an impractical wardrobe for slaying a venom-spraying snake large enough to encircle the earth. Though—her eyes narrowed, but the memory still eluded her. Just the impression of a kiss she hadn't meant to solicit, and a meadow.

She turned the page, skimming through the information it presented. Nothing she didn't already know. Thor was the god of thunder, though to the Sami people he had been something more, a god of health and the sea, an archer and a warrior. He was also loyal to a fault, and far too trusting. The god of the common man, as opposed to his father, who was the god of kings and nobles and war.

She turned the page again, and her stomach dropped. The image of a flaming sword, fire blazing from the eyes of the monster who carried it. Dark lips peeled back in unholy joy at the destruction raining down around him. He was a giant of some kind, judging by the army of corpses in his wake, none of them taller than his waist. She tore her eyes from the imagery and looked for the heading. Surt. Bringer of Ragnarok. The end of days and the destruction of the gods. And far, far, far too familiar in the strangest way. Something about the sword, and his smile . . .

Eve shut the book, shaking off her discomfort. Surt wasn't her concern, and whatever the book said, it wouldn't give her the information she wanted about Thor. Subtlety and nuance was often lost in translation, if any of it had survived at all through the oral retellings, generation to generation, before it reached that point. She'd read enough interpretations of the Book of Genesis to know that much. No one got Adam even close to right, and as for herself . . .

Well, she had taken the fruit, and she had eaten it first. But it wasn't because she had been tricked by the serpent, and the last thing she would have done was encourage Adam to eat it, too. And the Book of Genesis didn't say anything about the others. Reu and Lilith and Hannah and Lamech, and the rest of the men and women God had made before her.

There was only one way she would know the truth of who Thor was, and that was by talking to him, asking him about his past, seeing the world through his eyes. It would be easy enough to find the lies, then. Whatever they were. And once she knew him, she was confident nothing else would matter. His promises would be empty, just like

Adam's, and even if he didn't die, she would. What would he want with an infant, or a toddler, or for that matter, an old woman, wrinkled and stooped with age?

"Anna?"

She swore. Marcus, of course, and she had been too distracted to hear him coming, or his knock, which sounded again.

"Enter!" she called, and the door hissed open at the command. There were plenty of technological advances she couldn't complain about. Voiceprints and voice recognition, for example, were certainly convenient.

"For a moment I thought you'd stood me up," Marcus said, leaning against the doorframe. "I suppose you're not interested in going to the dining hall?"

"And why do you suppose that?"

He pulled a bottle of wine out from behind his back. "For one, we won't be able to drink this. And for another, you have that look about you. The angry at the world, I hate people glower. What happened? Did they not have your books in or something?"

"No," she said, stepping away from her desk to accept the wine. She almost wished he hadn't brought it, and they could have gone to the cafeteria instead. Anything to keep temptation to a minimum—his and her own. "Nothing like that. It's fine. I'm fine. Just thinking about how much work I'll have this semester."

In reality, hardly any. Oh, there were advancements in medical science since her last life, but she did all her learning by lifting it from her professors' minds whenever possible. It was so much more complete that way, especially when she really wasn't a fast learner otherwise. Mind reading gave her a full understanding as opposed to partial interpretation. No failures to communicate, no struggling to read through dry passages in a scan. That was what she went to class for, to read their minds, and in the service of contributing all that knowledge toward saving lives, she didn't regret it for a moment.

"I've never in my life seen you read a book for anything but pleasure," Marcus said, crossing the room. His hand rested on the mythology textbook, and then he lifted his gaze to the rest of the books on her shelf. "But you keep collecting them, anyway. What do you do with them all?"

"Hoard them for the future," she said, though she hadn't quite figured out how to accomplish that now that she couldn't send her things to the DeLeon vault. "And just because you don't see me reading, doesn't mean I'm not."

He arched an eyebrow and she shrugged, suddenly impatient with this boy who thought he knew her so well—so well, when all he knew were the lies, and the truths would send him running.

"As much as you'd like it if we spent every waking moment in one another's company, we don't. How do you know I'm not reading at night while you're sleeping half your life away?"

"That's an easy enough theory to test, Anna. You might recall I'm a big fan of co-ed sleepovers."

She pressed her lips together, wishing she'd never said anything at all. Getting a single had been a mistake. A roommate would have offered her more protection, or at least more pretext. Of course, then the poor girl would have fallen in love with Marcus, the way Ashley had last year, and it would be another heart bruised, and more psychic noise she didn't want to deal with. "I think I have a cork screw somewhere . . ."

"Cork screw? Really?" He took the bottle from her hands and twisted. The cap came off with a soft crack. "Sometimes I think you were born in the wrong century. Who uses corks anymore?"

"And you all wonder why the cork oak is going extinct," she mumbled, getting cups from a crate under the bed. "Perfectly good renewable resources thrown away because no one can be bothered to learn to use a corkscrew anymore."

"What was that?"

"Nothing." She passed him the cups, and sat back on her heels, watching him pour. Much as she might like to get drunk enough to drown out the gnawing, green emptiness in her belly, she didn't dare risk it with Marcus on the hunt. And she had no doubt that was what this all was, as many times as she'd seen him pull it over on other women. "You were planning on more than just wine tonight, I hope."

"I ordered pizza," he said, flashing her a smile. The smile he used on the unsuspecting subject of his passing interests. "The real kind, even, not the printed stuff you hate. After all those months in China, I thought you might like some comfort food."

Ordering for her. And he thought *she* had been born in the wrong century. If he thought she was going to fall into his trap, he was more hopeless than she'd realized. "A little bit presumptuous, isn't it?"

"Are you really going to tell me you wouldn't have suggested the same thing?"

Just like Thor, asking if she hadn't loved him, once. She climbed to her feet and pushed the window open wider, making the screen spark when she opened it too quickly and the static field couldn't adjust fast enough. She let her hand hover close enough to feel the thrum of the screen against her palm, and stared at the space where it stretched across the window, invisibly repelling bugs, and bouncing debris, like two magnets with like poles. She could force her hand through it, if she really wanted to, could feel the strange pressure like a too-tight rubber band stretched around her finger, her hand, her arm.

The screen sparked again and she jerked her hand back inside, rubbing the place where the current had zapped her wrist.

Marcus laughed, catching her hand and brushing his thumb gently along the red stripe. "How many times are you going to do that before you learn that it bites?"

"A few more, I'm sure." She pulled her hand free and reached for her wine cup as an excuse to put some space between them. He was too close, and his thoughts, when she skimmed them, were too determined. She couldn't do this tonight. "So when is this pizza supposed to get here?"

He was staring at her, searching her face, his expression so soft. It hurt to look at him when he studied her like that, and she knew what was coming, could hear the words he rehearsed in his mind. Phrases she didn't want to hear, like *we need to talk,* and *I'm in love with you.* Eve took another step back.

"Anna, listen—" A knock on the door made him swallow the rest, and Eve let out a breath of relief, even while Marcus frowned at the door. "Were you expecting someone?"

She slithered by him to reach the manual door release, brushing her palm across the panel. *Let it be Ashley. Let it be Ashley. Let it be Ashley.* Then she could throw her between them and problem solved. For one night at least. "Probably just some floor activity or something, you know how they like to round us up for that kind of . . ."

But it wasn't one of their fellow students.

It was Thor.

CHAPTER FIVE

Eve

"Hello, Anna," he said, his voice pooling somewhere in her center, all comfort and warmth.

And the smell of him, like rain after a drought, and thunderstorms rolling in. It was all so familiar, so easy to remember how it felt to be in his arms, and all it took was that look in his eyes, that subtle curve to his lips, as if he knew her from the inside out. And why was it, when Marcus looked at her that way, she wanted to disappear, but from Thor, for the first time in ages, she felt something inside her flicker back to life.

"I hope I'm not interrupting anything?"

"No," she said, the word rasping against her suddenly dry throat. Ashley would have been a lot easier to negotiate. "Not at all. I just wasn't expecting . . ."

"I know," he said, though she wasn't even sure how she'd meant to finish the sentence herself. "And I apologize. I hadn't meant to confess myself quite so completely."

"I'm sorry," Marcus said from behind her. Too close behind her, she realized belatedly. He was hovering over her shoulder as if he belonged there. "I didn't catch your name."

"Thor." He offered his hand. "You must be Marcus."

Marcus's jaw tightened as they shook hands, and Eve couldn't help but notice the way he flexed his hand afterward. Gorillas, the both of them. No. That was insulting to the Gorillas. Their keepers trained them better, and there weren't any left in the wild at all.

"And how do you know Anna?" Marcus asked, the unmistakable flavor of possession in his tone. She could hear the *my* he'd omitted before her name, still floating about in the air around them.

"We met overseas," Thor said, smiling at her with so much warmth Marcus couldn't fail to recognize it. The kind of warmth that spoke of intimacy, and quiet moments, and so much history shared between them. And it wasn't a lie, his explanation. She appreciated that, almost as much as she appreciated his timing. Though the rest—she wasn't at all sure how she felt about the rest.

"Ah," Marcus replied, giving her a sidelong glance which she ignored. "Of course you did."

"We're just waiting for our pizza to arrive," Eve said, feeling vaguely light-headed. She'd barely even sipped her wine, but she was floating, all the same. "Have you eaten?"

It was rude of her, she knew, to invite another man to eat the food which Marcus had paid for, but she couldn't quite help herself. And not only because the alternative was spending an awkward dinner dodging his advances. Thor winked at her, and she blinked.

Had he come for her sake?

If you'd rather I go . . .

She strangled a gasp at the richness of his voice in her thoughts, like so many memories of whispers in her ear, husky with need and desire. Eve flushed at the realization and forced herself to breathe.

If you don't mind my using you? she answered, once she was sure nothing else would leak out with it.

His smile widened. *I wouldn't have come otherwise.*

"I haven't eaten, no," he said aloud. "But I don't want to impose..."

"Of course not," Marcus muttered, turning away. "No imposition at all."

"Allow me to pay for my share, at the least," Thor said, offering a gold coin, the center struck with an eagle. Paper money had been given up as a lost cause, too easily forged, and the Free West had shifted back to a commodity based currency. Gold was gold, after all, still as limited—or unlimited—as ever. Though there were always rumors that someone had learned to print it. Uproars about debased currency. It was never true. At least it hadn't been yet.

But Marcus shook his head, smiling politely. "Really. It's no trouble." He'd always made good recoveries in these kinds of situations, turning awkwardness into warmth. A gift she seemed to have lost somewhere in the last two lifetimes. "Any friend of Anna's, right? You just caught me by surprise, that's all. I hadn't realized Anna had made any friends—I'm sure you realize how prickly she can be, if you were with her all summer."

"I've never found her to be so," Thor said, stepping inside. "Though I cannot say she does not have reason enough if she chooses to be."

Marc laughed. "You're kidding, right? I've never known anyone who had things as easy as Anna. The perfect parents with the happy family, the brains, the body, and then the sponsorship to get into the medical program here . . ."

"She's lost more than you'll ever have," Thor said quietly. "Though of course, I can hardly expect you to realize it."

"Really." But Marcus's voice was flat, and his gaze cut to her, questioning, almost betrayed. Though how he could feel that way when it was her life, her story, she didn't know. She gave him just the barest shake of her head. She hadn't told Thor. It was still their secret. Her secret. Not that he had a right to be at all upset about it, either way. "I have to say, I almost can't believe we're talking about the same girl."

"Woman," Thor corrected him absently, he had wandered across the room, past her small, raggedy, red loveseat, and was staring at the mythology book on her desk. "Have you been reading about any gods in particular, Anna?"

"I'm not sure a book like that would have any of the answers I was looking for, if I were," she said, grateful for the change of subject.

Thor met her eyes and smiled. "I'm relieved to hear it."

And that was when the pizza arrived.

❦

It was still an awkward meal, though in a very different way than it might have been. Marcus had temporarily given up his planned romantic overtures, evidently believing that Thor had gotten to her first, and neither Eve nor Thor dissuaded him of the notion. Not that it had stopped Marcus from showing off.

"Anna can't stand to be around children," he said at one point. "Didn't you ever notice the way she recoils? I'm sure you must have run across packs of them during your adventures, overseas."

Thor had just refilled her wine cup, and if Marcus didn't notice the way he hesitated, his hand hovering frozen with the bottle for just a heartbeat longer than it should have, Eve certainly did. She could feel his gaze on her, searching, and the gentle nudge of his curiosity against her mind. Not an invasion, just a question, unspoken, unformed. She didn't answer it, or even look up, because Marcus may not have realized the significance of what he was saying, but if Thor had watched her all this time, he surely did.

"The elderly, too," Marcus went on. "We tried to get her to volunteer at a retirement community during our Twelves, and she had an anxiety attack. Head between her knees, trouble breathing, the whole works. Lucky for her, I was there. But she was always odd about large groups of people, anyway, growing up. The most introverted of introverts." He smiled. "Good thing I was friends with everyone for her or she'd never have made it through grade school. Don't you remember, Anna?"

She remembered. She remembered Marcus's encouragement and kindness on their first day of school, his hand wrapped tightly around hers, lending her the strength to face their classroom when she'd been overwhelmed by even the thought of so many minds. He'd never understood. How could he? Marcus loved people so easily. And they loved him back. Because he never judged, never faulted. Hadn't she been that way, once? Before she'd learned her lesson. Before Adam had left her. Before Elah had drowned her in silence. She couldn't even remember how she'd managed in her past lives, not when the noise of it stretched her so thin, now. So brittle. She'd been devastatingly lonely in her last life, walking a fine line on the edge of sanity, but this? The way the world felt to her now, all yawning green pits of despair and starvation. In its own ways, it was worse.

"First day of our Nines, when we got off the bus, I thought she was going to faint," Marcus said, laughing far too lightly for a friend treading much too near to truths they'd sworn never to speak of in company. "Her face went whiter than snow when she saw how many of us there were. My poor, socially stunted girl. Her parents tried to put her on medication for the anxiety, but she was having none of it, even then. And now? Forget it."

"Enough, Marcus," she said. The weight of Thor's curiosity had shifted toward concern and she was fast losing what was left of her patience. Marcus had never understood, but he had promised not to tell anyone about the severity of her troubles, as a child. Not her parents. Not their few mutual friends. Certainly not Thor.

It had been difficult for her to readjust to living within the world. Difficult to live. And maybe Marcus hadn't understood, but he'd been there, always, to help her through. Crawled in through her window to keep the nightmares away, when they were children. Locked the other girls out of the bathroom for her at school when she'd been crippled by migraines and had to get away from all the noise of undisciplined minds and furious hunger. Cut school to take her home for the same reasons, when they were both older. And she'd never been certain if he'd done everything he'd done because she'd called to him, manipulated him, or because he'd just . . . known.

But they weren't children anymore. And he wasn't looking to take up residence in her bed just because he was worried about her. Not this time. Though she couldn't honestly say it wasn't *part* of what contributed to his overprotective habits.

Marcus shrugged. "I'm surprised it never came up while you were working together. Even in spite of the plague, overpopulation in China is a serious concern."

Eve? Thor asked, his tone gentle, nothing more than a prompt, an opening she didn't want to take.

She poured herself more wine, and locked Thor completely out of her mind. She wasn't doing this now, and every brush of his mind against hers only reminded her how different she'd become. How out of character it all was. But she just couldn't stand it. The way death and despair hung so near to the elderly, eating them from the inside out, dragging at her soul. All the potential and innocence of a child, poisoned more and more every day by greed and lust and selfishness. To say nothing of their minds. Loud and raucous and needy.

"And you know," Marcus went on, oblivious—or perhaps not, she didn't dare open herself enough to find out. "I never did understand why you wanted to go into medicine if you were so messed up about that stuff. Odds are, you'll see a lot of everything. What are you going to do when you have to perform emergency bypass surgery on an octogenarian? Or some kid comes in with a broken leg?"

"As I don't have any intention of becoming a surgeon, I don't foresee that being an issue," she said, keeping her tone light. But her stomach roiled, and Thor's interest had only intensified. Marcus was pushing her, and she didn't like it. Not one bit. "Internal medicine is more about preventative care, and children see pediatricians, anyway."

"Yes, but if you're going to some rural, war-torn back of beyond, they probably won't have pediatricians or surgeons," Marcus said. "You'll be doing some of everything, on some of everyone."

She shook her head. "Treating them once and moving on—that's different. And I don't want to talk about it anymore, if you don't mind."

He cocked his head at her, one eyebrow raised, and she knew exactly what he meant by it. If she was going to be in a relationship with someone else, if she was going to push him away and wall him out, she needed to be honest with that someone, for her own sake. It was just that it was so easy for him to say, for him to think, and he'd never understand how it was so completely impossible for her to do. But Marcus didn't press her any further, and Eve drank wine until she stopped noticing Thor's curiosity.

Because maybe he had been her husband once, maybe he'd known her better than anyone three thousand years ago, but she wasn't the woman he had married.

Not anymore.

ꕥ

When Marcus began yawning, smothering it behind a hand and pretending as if it hadn't happened at all, Eve sent him to bed with the barest of nudges. A suggestion that he would embarrass himself if he stayed any longer, and he was excusing himself, finally, with one last grudging frown in Thor's direction. He'd been trying to outstay him, she knew, but it was for the best if he left, and saw that Thor didn't. To say nothing of the tension he took with him when the door whisked shut again, and she was alone with Thor.

Eve sighed, falling back against the sofa and relaxing into the cushions. The room rocked just slightly, but it was more comforting than disturbing. Too much wine, but it had felt so good to have some quiet in her own head, especially the way Marcus had been broadcasting.

"He won't give up."

She opened her eyes to see Thor standing at her window, probably watching Marcus as he crossed the street to return to his own dorm. But she didn't want to think about Marcus.

"Will you?"

Thor glanced at her over his shoulder, that half-smile tugging at his lips. "I don't believe that's what you want of me, not truly. Those stories of Marcus's, about how you can't stand to be near children, the way you refuse to form relationships with the people around you, they might fool a man, all those things you say. But Marcus can't see the wounds you carry."

"There is nothing in that book that says anything about mind reading," she said.

"And there is nothing in the Bible about the man you married at Creation, or the burning of the Garden, or the tyranny of Adam."

"You couldn't read my mind before." She rubbed the furrow from her forehead, and struggled to focus on the memories, even as she said it. That was the other benefit of alcohol. When she wanted to, she could forget sometimes. Or lose herself completely, if she liked. Just for a moment, for the length of a memory. She'd made good use of it in her last life.

"Not as Thorgrim, no," he said, turning from the window to study her. "But later, forever after, and before as well."

"You grew old, then."

"Yes," he agreed.

"And now?"

"Now it is different. Everything is different. You could come with me to Asgard. See what I would offer you, at the least."

"It doesn't matter," she said, closing her eyes again, to keep from falling into his. Blue and warm and overfull of affection she couldn't, wouldn't return. "None of it matters, if I die, and you live, and then what? You won't even know where to find me when I'm born again."

He laughed. "Is that what you think? That you're so easily lost to me? Even when you smother the flame of your love, I need only close my eyes to feel your presence in the world, drawing me, your sorrow tugging at my heart."

The sofa was still rocking beneath her, like the little fishing boat, and Thorgrim sitting across from her, watching her as he pulled the oars. She reached out to touch him, to stroke the memory of his cheek, rough with stubble. Oh, she had loved him. So much. So, so much. Life after life after life afterward, she'd longed for him. Dreamed of him. Like she wanted to, now. Dreaming was so much safer than reality.

"Your hair," she heard herself say. "It's never the right color."

If he said anything in response, she didn't hear it.

All she heard was the sea.

CHAPTER SIX

Eve

❧

She didn't leave her dorm until supper the next day, and when she finally showed up in the dining hall, Marcus practically pounced on her. He'd left her at least four messages during the course of the day, all of which she'd ignored, and now, she placed her order on the tabletop menu while he vibrated impatiently, waiting for her to tell him why.

"Hungover," she said finally. "And your hovering is aggravating my headache."

"I was worried sick that something had happened."

Eve sighed, sidestepping him to reach the fruit and salad bar. "What on earth could possibly have happened to me?"

"Anything. You could have been assaulted, for all I knew. How well do you really know this Thor guy? He obviously doesn't know everything about *you*."

"Well enough, or I wouldn't have invited him into my room at all," she said, refusing to rise to the bait. How could she explain that he'd been in her life for eternity, and she'd never known it. He probably already knew everything about her life as Anna. He'd probably been watching her for years, waiting for her to grow up enough . . . "Nothing happened. I fell asleep and he tucked me in, perfect gentleman-style. Then I slept. And woke up feeling vile. You do realize that I took care of myself without your mothering for the whole summer, right? Nobody assaulted me when your back was turned, then, either, and I came back in the same perfect health that I left."

"Honestly, Anna, no, I have no idea what you did all summer," he snapped. "Apparently it involved cozying up to some Icelandic bodybuilder, though. Which, I might add, makes absolutely no sense. You won't be provoked into making a friend even if you trip over one for as long as I've known you, even fighting against sitting anywhere but alone for lunch when we were younger, and now you bring this guy home with you from China?"

"I didn't bring him home with me from China." Asgard. She'd brought him home from Asgard. And hadn't he said something about taking her there? The more Marcus talked, the more appealing it sounded. He could leave a thousand messages and it wouldn't matter. He'd never reach her. She'd be free of him, even if it was just for a few hours, a few days. But then there'd be Thor to face. Thor, who had even less of a reason to give up. Thor, who was offering so much more than Marcus ever could.

"So he just happens to go to school with us, too, then?"

She shook her head, refocusing on the conversation with an effort. "Is it so impossible that alone, in a strange place, I might form a relationship with someone?"

"No, of course not." Marcus raked his fingers through his hair. "But did it have to be him?"

"Did you have to date that gorgeous model from Sweden? Or what was her name? The transfer student when we were in our tens? Come on, Marcus. I never once stood in your way in all the years we've known each other. I don't know why you're getting in my face now."

"You know *exactly* why, Anna. And even if you expect me to believe you don't—you can't compare this with any of that. You need me."

She sat down with her fruit, and found her cheeseburger and fries already waiting for her, spit out by the printer. All she'd had to eat was some mint tea to help settle her stomach so she didn't have to fake interest in her food to avoid engaging any further down that line of reasoning. It was too much to hope she wouldn't have to engage any further at all, and Marcus plopped down across from her, looking absolutely miserable.

"Did you sleep at all last night?" she asked, frowning.

"I was too busy agonizing over having left you alone with an unknown quantity when I knew you'd had too much to drink. And the way you were acting—I know you haven't had an attack in years, but after China, and coming back to school, for all I knew it might have been a perfect storm for a comeback tour of crippling brain-fail."

"I'm fine, Marc."

"But you're different," he said, scrubbing his face with the heels of his hand. "Every year, you push me further away. You push everyone away, and what are you going to do the next time you need help getting out of a situation that's sending you down the rabbit hole? Or do you really want to be alone that badly? Because that's where this is going if you keep this up, and I'm not even sure you realize it."

She picked at her fries and said nothing. Of course she realized it. She'd been trying to shed him almost since he'd befriended her, and no one else had ever stood even half a chance. It wasn't his fault he was exactly what she was hoping to avoid—a romance she couldn't afford emotionally. If she'd met him before Adam, before Elah's birth, before Thor . . .

But she hadn't. And she was done with love. Done with these relationships that only ended in pain and loss, and that yawning green pit beneath her feet.

"Anna, I'm really trying here."

"I know."

"Can you help me out? Give me something."

She shook her head. "That's just it, Marc. I don't have anything left."

"Because you gave it all to that—that Viking Neanderthal?" he demanded. "Is that why? Because I'm not buying what you're selling, Anna. You have plenty, you just don't want to give it up."

She flinched at his tone, and the lash of his frustration. But this was an opportunity. Thor had given her an opportunity. She'd be lying if she said she wasn't more than tempted by it, by the escape of Asgard. By him. And Marcus had to realize the truth.

"To you."

He stared at her. "What?"

She hadn't ever had the excuse before, or the proof to back it up, but with Thor's presence, for the first time, it was believable.

"I don't want to give it up to you. And that's what you've been hanging around for, all this time. Why none of the girls you date ever last for more than a month or two, and somehow you're always knocking on my door for that great party on Saturday night when you have your pick of any other woman on campus for a date. But it isn't going to happen." She met his eyes. "And it isn't Thor's fault he's the one and you aren't."

Marcus sat back so hard, his chair scraped across the thin carpeting. "Are you being serious with me right now?"

She didn't say anything, but she didn't look away, either. Not a blink, or he'd pounce on the weakness, the regret, hold it as hope that she didn't mean what she'd said. Because obviously she cared about him. And that wasn't untrue, she did, but she didn't want to watch him die, either, and feel as though she lost a limb in the process. She didn't have the strength for it. Not anymore. Honestly, she was beginning to wonder how she'd ever managed the emotional drain in any lifetime, as sick as she felt about everything now.

"Shit," he said. And whether it was an accusation or an exclamation, she wasn't entirely sure. "Just—shit."

And then he got up and left her alone at the table.

She slumped over her plate, hiding her face in her hands. *I will not cry in the cafeteria,* she told herself sternly. So she picked up her tray and made the dining hall watch-guard look the other way as she walked out with the fruit and the cheeseburger.

Next time, she just wasn't going to leave her dorm at all. It would work out so much better that way.

But of course Thor was waiting for her at her building. Because that was the kind of day she was having. And worse than that, her cheeseburger and fries were cold. She stared at the tray so she didn't have to look at him, and wondered why she hadn't just stopped to eat in the quad somewhere. Cold fries were terrible, no matter what century it was, but cold *printed* food was even worse.

"I confess I thought humanity might do away with food altogether, for a time," Thor said, "turning it into pills and supplements and nothing more. But I can hardly imagine a world where that was so. There is so much pleasure in the eating of it, the sharing it with friends and family."

Family. The one thing she no longer had. Could never get back. It struck her like a punch to the gut, and suddenly she wasn't hungry at all anymore. She dumped the food into the garbage just outside the door, and sighed. "What do you want, Thor?"

"I'd like to show you something, if you have the time."

"I've got nothing but." She rubbed her face and looked up. Thor's expression was polite, the concern she felt brushing against her thoughts hidden from his eyes. "Don't," she said, tapping the tray against her thigh. "Please. I'm not looking for another babysitter right now, if it's all the same to you."

Creases formed at the corners of his eyes, but he withdrew the tentative touch of his mind and extended his hand instead. "I know you said it didn't matter, but I'd like to show you Asgard all the same. And I'm afraid there isn't any way to get there but through my power, if you'll trust me to return you home."

"My reservations were never about trust, exactly." She set the tray on top of the garbage can, hesitating. "If you meant to kidnap me, I think you had plenty of time before now to accomplish it."

He smiled. "Less than you might realize. And Elah would hardly let me survive the offense."

"Did Adam know?" she asked, not meeting his eyes. A lot of things made a lot more sense if Adam had known, all along. "Elah does, of course, and the Archangels, I assume. But was I the only one who didn't know about the rest of you?"

Thor dropped his hand, closing it into a fist, and the sun disappeared behind a cloud, bringing a chill with it. She frowned, looking up just in time to see the cloud disperse completely. One moment there, the next gone, as if it had never existed at all.

"Was that you?"

"Yes." He cleared his throat. "Forgive me."

"Adam would have that affect, I suppose." She pressed her lips together. "And he never said a word to me about it. Not really. At least tell me it wasn't his idea?"

"His silence was part of the price he paid."

"For what?"

"His memory."

"His . . ." Eve stared. Thor's jaw was tight, and his gaze slipped from hers. "That was you?"

He grimaced, but didn't answer, and she laughed. For the first time in how long? She didn't remember, but it felt so good. And then she laughed again, because Thor's distaste was so clear and she couldn't even blame him. If he'd known Adam before, when he had still been so insufferable—she laughed harder.

"Is that why he's so afraid of thunderstorms and lightning?" she finally gasped, her stomach aching. It had been so long, but the look on his face! She knew it so well, the emotion behind it, the frustration and disgust. "Oh, but that's funny. What did you really think it would accomplish?"

Thor twitched a shoulder. "It distracted Michael for a time, and I am told the world is better off in Elah's hands than it might have been in his. Perhaps that's enough."

"My brother is still trying to conquer the world, you know. I thought he could change, but . . ." She shrugged.

"But he only changed you, instead," Thor said quietly, searching her face. "Anything else, I might have been willing to forgive, given time. But not this."

"It wasn't out of malice, and it wasn't—it wasn't only him."

He offered his hand again, palm up. "Come with me. Please."

She hesitated, still. It was dangerous, every moment she spent with him, every touch, every gesture, every kindness. He knew so much. *Knew.* And she didn't have to lie about a thing. Even worse, part of her still remembered, no matter what he was, no matter what lies he had told so long ago, exactly how it felt to love him, to be loved by him. And it was a part of herself she had spent a lifetime burying, from the moment she had realized that Adam had left her, after Elah's birth. And again when Elah showed her how completely her love could be twisted into crippling pain.

But then she caught a glimpse of Marcus, coming around the corner from the dining hall, and the decision was made for her, because the last thing she wanted was to face him again. Not yet.

She gave Thor her hand, trying not to think about how much comfort it brought her, like sunlight after a dark, dreary winter. "Let's go."

His fingers closed tightly around hers and static skated across her skin where they touched, then rippled up her arm, every hair standing on end. She looked up at him, her eyes widening, but he only smiled.

"Hold tight."

And then the static turned to spider-webs, spinning around and around and around until she was wrapped from head to toe in a cocoon of lightning. The thick scent of ozone filled her head, her lungs to bursting, and she was liquid, and wind, and rain, melting into puddles on the ground of blinding white.

CHAPTER SEVEN

Eve, Before

Adam wasn't coming back.

It was hours before she realized it. Hours longer before she really understood it, before she could admit it to herself at all.

Elah was sleeping on her chest, and Eve struggled up, fought her way out of bed with sore, abused muscles, all the while conscious of her daughter's weight and warmth and the soft hum of her dreams. Sitting upright, on the edge of the bed, Eve panted, exhausted by even that much movement. Exhausted in every way.

What kind of man left his wife and child, still covered in blood, still aching from the labor of delivery? It didn't seem possible, or real, but it had happened.

Adam wasn't coming back.

Thinking it again didn't make it easier to wrap her mind around, not at all. She reached for him, searched for him with her thoughts, but there was no response. Nothing at all, and she didn't have the strength to try again, just then. It was all she had in her just to stay upright with Elah.

Her daughter. Their daughter. Eve closed her eyes and focused on the soft sound of her breathing, the peaceful little twitches of her dreaming body.

Maybe he had been delayed somehow. By Michael, or Gabriel, or God. Maybe he was shopping for something to surprise her, a gift for the baby and he didn't want her to know. Maybe he'd been caught in traffic. It was possible. Certainly it made more sense than anything else, and it was a long drive to anywhere from the mountains.

He had to be coming back. If not for Eve, for his daughter. Even at his most selfish, he had always wanted this child. Now that he had her, he wouldn't just abandon the power she promised. The power he had always lusted for.

Adam had to come back.

But what did it mean that she was hoping his most despicable compulsions would make it so?

§

Days later, after she had recovered from the worst of the shock, and she and Elah had found a rhythm together, and Eve had begun sleeping beside her daughter's bassinet, one hand draped over the side for Elah to grip with her tiny, impossibly strong fingers, even then, she found herself reaching for some excuse or another. He was preparing some getaway, where they would go into hiding with the baby, where no angel could ever reach them. He was fighting with Michael over their daughter, negotiating terms for the Archangel's surrender, because the world was his, now, and Elah's.

It made more sense that way, and gave her an odd, small sense of comfort in those strange, quiet days, and with the distraction of Elah, who smiled long before she should smile, and laughed long before she should ever be capable of more than a coo or a cry, Eve sometimes forgot that Adam wasn't just away on some kind of business. Though when they had been apart for those five years, she had always been able to reach him, and he had opened himself to her completely when she touched his mind. Now, when she reached for him, there was only silence, a blankness as complete as death. It wasn't long before she broke the habit of it, too disconcerted to try, and too absorbed in caring for Elah. She only had so much power, so much strength, and she needed it for their daughter.

But then, Adam would have known that, too. He would have known she wouldn't be free to follow him, to search for him, that she would refocus her life around her daughter without any conscious thought. Mothering was what she did, what she had always done, and Elah required more of her attention than any other child she'd ever raised, needed more from Eve than she was certain she could give. It was those moments when she missed Adam the most, when she doubted herself and looked out into the world, praying to God that these would not be its last days.

She couldn't even take the time to cry, afraid that any real grief or sorrow she shared would influence her daughter, and if Elah believed the world were anything but good . . .

Eve wouldn't let herself think of that, either. She didn't dare give the baby any ideas. The way Elah reached into her mind when she was hungry, into her thoughts when she needed to be changed, she was already powerful enough to cause trouble, if not destruction, and Eve had no intention of testing her.

With or without Adam, the world must go on turning, and Eve would not let her daughter become the reason it stopped.

Two weeks after Elah's birth, the doorbell rang, Eve was certain it was the police, come to tell her Adam had been in some accident. Except she would have felt it, if he had. She would have known. And even that small hope died, too.

She opened the door, her hair seven days unwashed, and Elah in her arms, staring up at her with such utter adoration that Eve couldn't bring herself to care. But the pure white wings of the man who stood on the other side gave her pause. An Archangel, for in Eve's experience, only they had wings of white. Not Michael, thank God for that small mercy, or Gabriel, whom she would have been relieved to see, just for the kindness of his eyes, and the knowledge she might trust him with Elah for long enough to take a shower, but a third winged-man, with ancient, golden eyes, and the weight of the world on his thin shoulders.

"May I?" he asked, the words accented strangely—but strange in a familiar way that wouldn't quite surface through the molasses of her memories.

He wore no sword on his hip, and his face was lined with a strange grief, half-compassion and half-pity.

Elah gurgled with delight, reaching for him, and Eve stepped back, giving him space to enter the cottage. Her cottage, according to the DeLeons, though she could not quite remember how it had come to be so, either. But then, something about having a baby to feed and wash and care for grounded her in the present the way nothing else ever could. Particularly when she faced it alone.

Perhaps after the Archangel left her, she would call on her great-grandson, and ask him to watch his newest auntie just long enough for her to wash her hair. After all, what good was it to live so near her family if she couldn't ask them for a favor now and again. And she didn't have to tell them that Adam had gone. She didn't have to tell them anything, except that she required a babysitter. Then again, considering how easily Elah willed her way, even with Eve, it was probably better that she just go unwashed.

"You look as though you could use a nap, my dear." The angel held out his hands, and Elah strained to go to him, much more agile than a two week old child ever should be. Eve handed him her baby, her godling daughter, and suddenly the old angel, with his lined face, and his stooped shoulders, and his knotted joints was fresh-faced and startlingly beautiful. Every year of his too long life faded into a straight-backed young man of no more than twenty-three.

He sighed, his eyes fluttering shut. "I hadn't realized how much I had withered until now, standing apart from the Host for so long."

"Raphael?" she asked.

"I am." He smiled, though the look he slanted at her over Elah's head was more knowing than it should have been, considering she hadn't seen him since she had left the Garden. "And I thank you for the gift of your daughter to the world."

"Is there something I can do for you?"

He laughed. "You've done it already, and more than I had any right to ask for. Please, allow me to return the favor. If you will not take the time to sleep, do feel free to wash, at the least. I believe Elah and I can keep ourselves occupied in the meantime."

She hesitated. It wasn't that she didn't trust him, for there was nothing in his mind that she could see beyond his desire to help her, and none of the malice or resentment of Michael's presence. But it was strange, all the same.

"She's strong-minded," she warned him. "And no matter what she tells you, she isn't to have any solid food, yet."

He laughed again. "Go, Eve. Before she's hungry again and you have another delay. I promise, you'll miss nothing, and we'll be waiting here the same as you left us."

Eve frowned, taking a few steps back, and then another few after that, before tearing her gaze from Elah and turning away.

Even so, she showered quickly.

When she returned, hair still wet and heart-anxious, Elah was in her high-chair, tucked neatly up against the table, and Raphael, his white wings folded tightly against his back, was making tea.

"Sit down, Eve," he said, not bothering to look up from the water he was pouring. "Peppermint or chamomile?"

"I suppose that depends." She stroked Elah's sparse hair, reassuring herself that she was well. Elah cooed, waving a spoon, and sharing her pleasure at Eve's reappearance. She remained standing. "What have you come for, Archangel?"

Raphael tapped his spoon against the edge of his mug and frowned into the steam. "Chamomile, then."

"Will I be in need of soothing?"

He dropped the tea bag into her cup, and handed it to her with a spoon. "You realize the danger of losing control, I hope."

"I realize the danger of my daughter losing control," Eve said slowly, accepting the mug. "If I had any intention of modeling a poor example, I believe you would have found me in my bed, and Elah wailing beside it."

"Indeed," he said, leaning back against the counter. Then he grunted, rolling his shoulders, and the wings disappeared, one lonely feather floating up, and then down, to teeter on the lip of the sink. He caught it up, and used it to tickle Elah's nose.

She laughed, like wind chimes and tinkling bells, and grabbed at it. Once she closed her small fist around the delicate vane, Raphael let her keep it.

"Gently, now," he said, hunkering down to her level. "Feathers are fragile things, grip them too tightly and they lose all their beauty, even if they bend instead of break. Not so different from the world itself, really. Creation requires a light touch, after the making, just a nudge here, or a spring rain there. I'm sure your mother will agree."

Elah loosened her hold, then held the feather out to Eve.

"Very wise," Raphael said as Eve accepted the gift, running the feather between her fingers, soft as down. It smelled like cinnamon and snakes. "Your mother will keep it safe, and I hope you'll let her keep the world safe, as well. You must always obey her, Elah! Even when you are grown, trust in her judgment, and your father's as well."

Eve sucked in a breath at the mention of Adam; even so indirectly, it still felt as though she had been struck. Raphael was watching her, his gaze steady.

"You should know he only left for your sake, both your sakes. That you might have one another for awhile longer." Eve wasn't sure anymore if he was talking to Elah or herself, but she turned her face away, swallowing back a sob.

"He asked me to send his love, Eve."

She shook her head, blinking back tears she didn't dare let Elah see. And if she gave in to them and wept, she wasn't sure she'd ever stop. Another breath, careful and controlled, and another after that before she dared to even think about how she would respond.

Eve stirred her tea, rang the teabag out against her spoon.

"He should have come himself, if he wanted me to believe him." Her throat had thickened again, and she cleared it, fighting against the pain in her heart. "Excuse me," she managed. "I just need to get some air."

She took the tea with her—she needed all the help she could get.

CHAPTER EIGHT

Eve, Later

§

Eve felt as though she hung suspended in the roar of a storm, and then she felt Thor's hand squeeze hers, and the white light became gray stone and soft, green grass. The return to her own feet tripped her, and Thor's other hand fit against the curve of her waist, steadying her before she fell.

"Forgive me," he said. "I ought to have warned you, but I forget what affect traveling by lightning can have on those unused to it. Are you well?"

But Eve couldn't respond. She couldn't do anything but stare at the tree in front of them, with its broad, red leaves and golden fruit. If it hadn't been for Thor's hand at her waist, she would have fallen to her knees before it. As it was, she stumbled back, directly into Thor's chest behind her.

"What's the matter?" he asked, gathering her against him, soothing her with soft words and gentler hands, even as her body shuddered. She needed to be away. Away from here, away from that, but Thor was rock-solid, and he swept her up, taking three steps to a stone bench and settling her in his lap. "Eve, I beg of you."

She shook her head, unable to tear her eyes away from it. That tree. The tree that should have been nothing but ash, long turned into earth and buried beneath stardust. She had seen the Garden burn with her own eyes, the tree lost with all its fruit.

"It can't be," she said. "It shouldn't be here."

Wherever here was. And that realization, finally, broke the spell. Her gaze swept over the immense stone buildings set around the courtyard, all with a view of this tree. The tree that shouldn't exist and drew her eye again barely a heartbeat later. This couldn't be Asgard. Not with that tree at its heart.

Her hands turned to fists in Thor's shirt. "Please, I can't—"

"Shh," he said, tucking her head beneath his chin, as everything around them melted away into white and heat and rumbling ozone. "You're safe," she heard him say, an echo in the storm, even as it faded to more stone.

The lightning sizzled against four new walls, a floor, a ceiling resolving above her head. It scorched the edge of a chest and smoked the hem of a cloak hanging on a bedpost just beside her. She recoiled from the sparks, but Thor only flicked a finger at the cloth, and they died, smothered by his will.

"I will always keep you safe," he said again. "You've nothing to fear from me, or anything in Asgard, I promise you."

Eve closed her eyes, breathing in the scent of storm from the curve of his shoulder, and soaking up the comfort of his heartbeat, steady beneath her palm. He was always steady, that much she remembered well, and didn't begin to doubt. Steady, and warm, and resolute. What he believed, he believed, and that faith was never shaken.

"I'm sorry," she said, once she had matched her heartbeat to his, and the tightness in her chest had eased. "I wasn't expecting—how did you find it?"

"Find what?" His hand had tangled in her curls, the gentle pull of his fingers through her hair calming her as easily in this life as it had three thousand years ago.

"The tree, from the Garden," she said, lifting her head.

"The tree in the courtyard came with us from the Old Worlds." Thor was watching her guardedly, his expression carefully neutral, though he couldn't quite hide his longing from her thoughts, or his pleasure at having her so near. "It belonged to my mother, her last gift before she left us."

If she stayed in his arms any longer, she'd never have the strength to leave. But the moment she pushed against him, he helped her to rise, not even the barest flicker of emotion reaching his face as she left his hold. She swallowed and turned away from him, taking in the rest of the room beyond the immense bed, covered by a quilt of furs. The chest at its foot had clearly been scorched before, the edges of the wood and the silver fittings blackened with soot to varying degrees. Another chest stood open in a far corner of the room, overflowing with clothing from a mish-mash of time periods. Her forehead furrowed at the sight of a brown suit, oddly familiar, before she was distracted by the leather breaches beside it, and the blue mechanics jumpsuit with Donar spelled across the breast pocket.

"This is your bedroom?" There was so much to take in. So much she never knew. But there were small familiar things, too. The haphazard treatment of his clothing, never folded neatly. The side of the bed he obviously slept on, judging by the small corked jug on the floor within a lazy arm's reach. Filled with wine, from her experience, to help him sleep. She'd cut it with water when they were married, teasing him for it, but now she wondered if he hadn't had good reason for the drinking he'd done. The drinking he still did.

"Mm," he agreed, rising. "Forgive me, it was simply the first place I thought of, and it was clear you did not wish to remain in the courtyard. If it makes you uncomfortable . . ."

"No," she said, trailing her fingers along the edge of the side table where a stub-handled war-hammer sat within reach of the bed. He'd kept a blade, in their life together, but in the same place. She traced the worn leather wrapping of the shaft, phantom fingers showing where his hand most often gripped it. She closed her own hand around the impressions, meaning to lift it, but the hammer didn't budge.

Thor's hand covered hers, helping her, and the weapon had no weight at all when he put his arm to it. Immense strength, she noted absently. But she'd already known that.

"*Mjölnir,*" Thor said. The wood beneath it was as scorched as the chest.

She slipped her hand free from under his. "And did you run around swinging her wearing nothing but a belt at your waist?"

He laughed, tossing the hammer up, end over end, and catching it before he set it back down. The hammer hummed and sizzled, making her fingers itch to try to lift it again. "I'm familiar with the images, but I fear it is not so. I did ride a chariot pulled by goats, however, and to some, that is equally as strange."

She snorted. "They'd have to be big goats to pull someone your size."

"And large enough to terrify my enemy, as well. They pulled my chariot into battle."

"You can't be serious." She spun to look at him, trying to imagine him being pulled anywhere by goats, least of all into a warzone, but then she was imagining him in nothing but that belt again, and she had to look away just as quickly to hide her blush.

Because she knew much too well what he looked like naked, every centimeter of his body bared for her pleasure. Her fingers itched again, and she smoothed her hands against her thighs to keep from imagining the feeling of his skin beneath them.

"Completely," he said, and if he knew her thoughts, he spared her the embarrassment of commenting on them. "Would you like to see them?"

She shook her head, not in answer to his question, but to clear it, because the memories of his touch, his body beneath hers, weren't so easily forgotten. And it had been a very long time since she'd been loved. Since Adam. Her thoughts shied away from her last experience out of habit, and she found herself skipping back to the life before

Elah's birth, when she had lived as Eve among the House of Lions, and Thor had come . . .

"Garrit knew you were a god, didn't he?"

He'd come, and he'd kissed her, and she had ached for more, her body remembering even if her mind made excuses, grasped at explanations. How could she have ever believed he wasn't Thorgrim? At least she knew better how she could have been so confused by his presence. She only wished . . .

But it didn't matter what she wished. Her Lions weren't hers anymore.

"He was sworn to secrecy as well, for your own protection. My father didn't care for my preoccupation, you see, forbidding me from revealing myself to you. And more than once, he tried to have you killed, through some agent or another."

"Strange," she said, forcing herself to focus on the present, on Thor. To be the cause of so much trouble, and not ever have known it. How had she never known it? If he had wanted her dead, she should have felt something, recognized some danger. But she hadn't. Not even the tiniest bit. "So strange, to think about it all. You cloaked yourselves so well from my sight, but I don't think you ever explained why. What was so dangerous about me? I don't have anywhere near your power, that's obvious. I can't even read your mind if you don't want me to, but you seem to have no such trouble with mine."

Thor grunted. "Power is a difficult thing to measure, god to god. Yours is more subtle, but no less impressive. Most of what you think makes me stronger is just a question of practice. I spent far more time with meddlesome Olympian goddesses attempting to dig through my thoughts."

One god at a time, Eve told herself. Thor was enough to handle just then. But. "How many are there?" she heard herself ask.

"I suppose that depends," he said slowly. "Now, we are far, far fewer. Bhagavan remains with his multitude of aspects, though he is no more counted as hundreds of thousands, millions, perhaps, than Elah should be, with her Host."

Eve laughed, the sound edging toward hysteria even to her own ears. "Is that all? Far fewer, and you still number in the millions."

"We number in the handful, now. Myself and Athena, Bhagavan and Buddha. Others tried to stay, thinking they might remain beneath Elah's notice, but Michael hunted them. If Elah happened to be watching, she exiled them into the void. If she was distracted elsewhere, he struck them down with the God-Killer."

"She let him kill them?" Eve's stomach lurched, her heart twisting. She'd thought she'd raised her better during those brief years, to be compassionate, to love. But it was a familiar disappointment, one she'd revisited far too often. And Michael had been given far more influence over her life than Eve had ever had. "For what offense?"

But Thor shook his head. "Michael serves Creation, as he was made to, and owes allegiance to Elah only through Elohim's command. As long as Elah guards Creation, Michael will guard her. Beyond that, she does not control him."

She let out a breath, not realizing she'd held it, and sat on the edge of the bed, suddenly weak, though whether it was relief or fear she wasn't sure. She'd always known what Michael was. From the day that Adam had burned the Garden and the Archangel had beaten him in body, then in mind. The sword he carried had always hung over her head, over Adam's, and Elah's, too, before her birth, haunting Eve's steps, burning through her nightmares. She'd tried to warn Elah, once. Tried, and failed so completely.

"Sometimes I wonder if anyone ever controlled him."

Thor crouched before her, searching her face. "He is a danger, Eve. To all of us. You and your brother, most especially. Elah will not hear a word against him from me, or even from Raphael, but perhaps if you spoke to her—"

"You'd be better off asking it of her father."

"Adam didn't raise her."

"No. He didn't," Eve said, her voice sharp.

Even his name cut through her, and she hated it. She hated that he could still make her hurt this way, nearly a hundred years after he'd left. She hated that Elah had forgiven him so easily, when they'd struggled together, alone for so long. And she hated that her daughter hadn't forgiven her for not immediately wanting him back.

"He never had to tell her no, never had to punish her when she threw a tantrum that caused an earthquake. He didn't lie awake at night searching her dreaming mind to be certain she wasn't going to remold the world the next time she played with her blocks. He wasn't part of her life until she knew better, and she's always loved him for it."

More. Loved him more, but that part she managed to keep to herself, despite the tears pricking her eyes.

"I should never have asked it of you at all." Thor rose, offering his hand. "Allow me to show you the rest of Asgard. As a peace offering."

She slid her hands between her thighs, looking away. That she'd said any of that—she hadn't been able to say any of it to anyone. Until now. Until he'd come into her life, and suddenly the world was so strange, and she was sitting in Asgard, a place that shouldn't exist, kvetching about her brother and her daughter and all the things she couldn't change and wished so much had happened differently. She wished so much that Adam had stayed, no matter what he feared, no matter what Gabriel had said. If he'd only trusted her with the truth.

But he never had. Nor had Elohim, or Elah, and here was Thor, offering her everything revealed at last, telling her he had always wanted to confess himself, to walk beside her. He'd wanted her to know, but hadn't been free to make that choice.

"Please, Eve. Let me make things right between us."

But there was nothing wrong, not really. That's what made it so much harder. She wanted to say yes. She wanted to take his hand and let him pull her into his arms, and never think of any of it ever again. Until she grew old and died, or Elah came and took it all back, and she had to begin all over again, alone and empty and drowning in grief.

It was too easy to love him, but the rest?
She wasn't sure she could survive it, when it ended.

CHAPTER NINE

Adam

❧

Tyrant hadn't always been synonymous with evil, Adam reminded himself, frowning at the headlines. Of course, that didn't mean he cared for the sight of the word attached to his own name—or the name he'd assumed for this lifetime, anyway. He tossed his scanner away and rubbed his jaw. If Eve was paying attention to the news, she'd be congratulating herself by now, drinking in every word they said and telling herself she'd made the right choice in turning him away.

But that couldn't matter. Or at least he couldn't let it stop him. At twenty-one, he'd had two options, the long road or the short road, and the world couldn't afford to wait another fourteen years before someone did something about the encroaching deserts and the shifting grain belts. The rainforests were all but evaporated, and the exodus of the starving was putting too much pressure on the northern food supply.

In fourteen years, they would be facing famine on a scale previously unheard of, and all because politics had been kicking the can down the road for the last two centuries.

So Adam had taken the short road, the meteoric rise to power by virtue of his natural talents. And by talent, he mostly meant manipulation. Turning parliaments into puppets had been a challenge, and he had no doubt he wouldn't have been able to come even half so far if Elah hadn't given her blessing to the whole affair. But eventually he had nudged and bullied enough minds of enough politicians to create a united nation in the North, from the center stronghold of Denmark. And eventually, he had convinced them they needed one firm hand at the wheel, if they were going to make the most of their resources and build a lasting union. Through some sleight of hand and an exhaustively rigged election, during which he'd had no other choice but to commandeer the free will of an outrageous number of citizens in order to grant himself a victory that would appear just legitimate enough, Adam had elected himself President of the Scandinavian Union and Canadian North.

For life, naturally.

His first order of business had been to send ten thousand refugees off to Greenland, where he desperately needed more labor. And now he was being punished for it.

Well, as punished as one could be by foreign press with little in the way of proof or information. All they knew was that he had somehow made ten thousand refugees disappear, and of course they assumed the worst. Never mind that the price of food worldwide had dropped by ten percent since he'd come into power. Never mind that the refugees themselves weren't complaining at all about having honest work and on-the-job training. Never mind that the citizens of the North Country (as they preferred to call themselves) had no complaints whatsoever about their new President, who had taken over the running of their great conglomerate without passing one, single, solitary law which infringed on their liberties.

No. They insisted on believing he was some dictator out of the twentieth century, oppressing his people and amassing a fortune off their backs, simply because he had raised a few taxes (most of which related to the use of fossil fuels, for reasons which should have been self-evident to anyone paying attention), and instituted a state religion (worshipping the Great Goddess, of course, though religious freedoms were still protected).

"You shouldn't read those rags, Mr. President," Hilda said. "They only upset you, and Goddess knows why they should talk at all. Half the Free West would be starving by now if you hadn't allowed the export of Canadian foodstuffs, and that much only because you've been able to supplement the Canadian supply chain from what's being produced in Greenland."

"Off the backs of my slave labor force, you mean?" He leaned back in his chair, and put his feet up on his only marginally oversized desk. After seeing the size of President Washington's desk in the United East, he'd decided it was best for all parties if he didn't attempt to compete. That man's office was nothing *but* desk.

Hilda sniffed. "Let them lie all they want, it doesn't change the truth."

"Only the perception of what is true, Hilda. Which is in itself dangerous enough." And Eve would never give him the chance to explain if they kept on this way. He'd be lucky if she let him near enough to even call out her name. She'd already shut him completely out of her head. Not that he'd honestly expected anything else.

"You and the Goddess both know you're doing good in this world, sir. I think that's what matters most."

Adam smiled, reaching for Elah. His daughter, at least, always responded. A soft wave of love and affection washed through him from her presence in the back of his mind. It would just have to do for the time being.

"Thank you, Hilda. That will be all for today."

"Yes, sir," she said, gathering her things.

He watched his secretary go, and sighed. It helped to remind himself that he wasn't doing any of this to impress Eve.

Until he remembered how much more they could be accomplishing together, for the world, for Elah. Evey hated being looked to, hated being made into a leader of any kind, and he understood that she needed space, he did, especially after everything that had happened with Elah, but if she would only help him—

For someone who hated war, he couldn't understand why she refused to do everything in her power to spread peace. And together, that was what they could accomplish. Peace and prosperity for all, or at the very least a better chance at it. Instead, what was she doing?

He didn't know, and it drove him demented.

But surely as the leader of one of the most powerful nations in the world, he ought to be able to find out the old fashioned way. A spy of some kind, set on her trail, and it wouldn't hurt to learn what kind of things set them both apart from the general populace. Neither one of them had ever been under any kind of observation previously, and as carefully as they both covered their tracks, they were bound to leave evidence of their not-quite-mortal selves all the same. It would give him an idea of where he needed to be more vigilant in his own behaviors.

He just needed to figure out where to send them.

Elah?

There was a pause, longer than usual, and then bewilderment came back. *She isn't there.*

He was on his feet and calling for a driver—no, a pilot. If she were in the North Country, he would have known it. She would never have let him take the presidency if she'd been part of his constituency.

Where? he demanded. *Where should she be?*

The Free West. She should be in the Free West, but she isn't.

What do you mean she isn't?

I can't find her. Another pause, with Elah's confusion carrying through the silence. His daughter was many things, but confused was rarely one of them. Not since her ascendance. *Wait.*

Adam waited, his blood roaring in his ears. If something had happened to Eve—

But he would have known it, he was sure. He would have felt it. She couldn't be hurt, not really, not without his feeling it, too, and Elah would have whoever had done it unmade in less than a heartbeat. This was supposed to be their retirement, now. The good life. That's why he'd been born with money, why Eve had been born into a loving family for a peaceful life, given everything she could possibly want. Eve and Elah weren't exactly on speaking terms, but it was only a matter of time until Eve found the grace to forgive her. Just like she'd forgive him, someday. He hoped.

I've found her.

Adam let out a breath, pinching the bridge of his nose. *Is she all right?*

Yes, I think so. She's exhausted, more than anything. Perhaps that was all it was. Or she was hiding herself from us both. Sometimes I think . . . But Elah stopped herself. *She won't want to see you, Father.*

He fell back into his chair behind the desk. *She'll never want to see me, Elah. But she can't isolate herself this way forever. And when I think of all the good she could be doing, all the things we could be doing together—*

I had hoped that he might reach her somehow, coax her back into the world more fully before any more damage was done. She wouldn't listen to me, and I didn't see why she would listen to you, either, all things considered. Not while you were king-making.

Adam frowned. *He?*

Elah hesitated, the silence stretching, filled with a bitter tang that he could not quite place. Guilt? Regret? Embarrassment?

He who, Elah?

She sighed in the back of his mind, and then: *I sent her Thor.*

Thor. Adam's jaw clenched, but he reached forward to the intercom on his desk. "Hilda, cancel that request. I'll need to do a bit more planning before I go anywhere."

"Of course, Mr. President."

He told himself he should be happy for her, if she found any kind of peace with the god. He told himself she was better off, loving Thor over him. He made all the same familiar arguments he'd been making since he'd left her to mother Elah alone.

But the lies didn't change the truth. The truth was, in the deepest part of his heart, he still wanted Eve to be his. He always would.

And if Thor was with her, the thunder god was standing in his way.

"Ah, Hilda?" Adam said, touching the intercom again. A misnomer, really. Or perhaps he just had the wrong associations for the word. It buzzed right into her ear, all completely private. And thank Elah he was the president, and didn't have to keep one of those contraptions in his own ear. They'd wanted to implant one, all the better to monitor his safety, but Adam didn't particularly care for the way they tracked his brainwaves. Whatever power he had, better if it didn't show up on something like that. After all, if science developed telepathy for the common man, they might also develop a way to block it, and Adam rather preferred not to have to resort to remedial brainwashing to get his way. Manipulating a person's thoughts from the inside was so much easier.

"Yes, sir?"

"Get me the director of intelligence, would you, please? I have a small new project for him."

And he'd go ahead and codename it Eve.

Mostly just because he could.

CHAPTER TEN

Eve

Asgard was empty. By and large, that was what Thor showed her. Incredible stone halls, echoing with their silence and muted by layers of dust. In one, they found an overgrown greenhouse, trees and flowers and bushes in shapes and sizes and colors beyond her wildest dreams. She touched her finger to a star-shaped bloom, seemingly grown from crystal and ice. It shattered into snowflakes and stardust, hazy in the sunlight.

"This was Freyr's garden," Thor said, and a soft rain began to fall around them, pattering against leaves and singing against glass. Mist swirled around her ankles, and she shivered at its touch. "I've done my best to keep it watered, but I fear I have not the patience for much more. I could not stand to see his plants wither and fail when there is so little life left within these halls."

"Why didn't he take it with him?" she asked, stepping closer to another bed, filled with iridescent vines and electrum flowers. The rain moved around her. When she held out her hand, palm up, the drops puffed into steam before they reached her skin, ozone tickling her senses. Thor, shielding her.

She glanced back over her shoulder, but he hadn't done himself the same service. Rain trickled down the bridge of his nose, and he stood unflinching, as if he belonged to the storm.

"He took the seeds he wanted." Thor plucked a rose of paper-thin gold, offering it to her. "The only plant Odin would allow us to bring whole was Yggdrasil, the world-tree."

"The tree in the court yard." She took the flower, bringing it to her nose. Sweetened cream and marshmallow and something else she couldn't identify. Eve closed her eyes, pulling the memory from the deepest part of her mind. Broad, red leaves, the golden apples winking between the branches. "My father's tree."

"My mother's tree," Thor said. "Is it really so similar?"

"Not just similar." Eve opened her mind to his, sharing the memory. The ache of her heart, the despair. All she had wanted in that moment in the Garden, hidden from Adam beneath the tree's red canopy, was the void, the peace from which she'd been torn. "It's all the same."

"Eve." His voice was hoarse, and his fingers brushed along her jaw, gentle as rainfall and warming her to her toes. "My heart, it doesn't have to be. It never has to be that way again."

She turned her face away, and slipped from his grasp, her heart tripping with longing. The memory of his fingers tracing the shape of her lips, his breath against her ear and his mouth—her chest felt too tight, just thinking of it, her body alight with want. And if she gave in, what then? More of the same. It was always the same, from the moment she'd opened her eyes and been blinded by the light.

"You mentioned goats."

She didn't have to look at him to know he was smiling, that familiar confidence curving his lips. It was part of what she had loved about him, how sure of himself he'd always been. How sure of her he'd always been, and content to wait until she was ready, until she was sure, too.

"Not just any goats," he said, guiding her back the way they'd come. "*Magic* goats."

She laughed. The way he said it, and even the very idea. That was probably why he'd said it at all. To make her laugh. It felt so good to laugh. "And what exactly makes them magic?"

"There's their size," Thor said. "And their strength, of course."

"That sounds like breeding, not magic."

"Perhaps that is so. But breeding does not account for their resurrection, after they've been eaten."

She glanced at him sidelong, but his expression was perfectly serious. "You're teasing me, now."

"Admittedly, I found them while we lived in Jotunheim." His lips twitched, but she wasn't in on the joke. "My father had another which could be milked for mead, but he took it with him when my people left. Fortunately, there is still gold enough for me to buy all I require. For as long as the bees last, anyway. I've been thinking of starting a hive of my own, here, to ensure their survival."

"Wait," she said, ducking beneath his arm as he held the greenhouse door open. The way he talked about these other worlds, as if he had been some army brat. "What was Jotunheim? How many times have you done this—the moving from world to world."

The smile faded from his face, and his gaze slid away. "You said you wanted to see the goats?"

"Thor."

He grunted, his hand falling to the small of her back, then dropping away. They were in the courtyard again. Or a quad, she supposed, not so different from the campus, with its manicured lawns and carefully planted trees. Except the only tree was Yggdrasil and Eve tried not to look at it. Thankfully, Thor was guiding them in the other direction, back toward his own fortress of brilliant gray-green granite, shining with flecks of gold in the sun.

It was oddly Greek to her eyes, or maybe Roman. More a monument than anything else, from the outside, and half-museum inside, except for the rooms where Thor actually seemed to live. The kitchen, oversized but cozy, and filled with sun; his own bedroom, of course; and a third room he seemed to have co-opted as a study of some kind, books stacked precariously, and mixed with odds and ends that had nothing to do with one another. Drinking horns next to samurai swords, next to Civil War era rifles complete with bayonets, and small pieces of tile or pottery, bolts of cloth, coins of every size and shape and color filling empty oak casks, which had once held some sort of wine . . .

Now that she thought about it, she was sure there had been a lion head on them, but the DeLeons hadn't used casks of that size in ages.

"The Aesir came from a world we called Niflheim," Thor said finally. "But it was before I was born, and I know little of our history there, but that we were driven from it by Surt. It was his invasion from the firelands of Muspelheim which brought the destruction of Ragnarok to our world. The battle was terrible and long, and many of our people died before my mother arrived. She stole Surt's sword, which had made him invulnerable to our blades, and struck him down, but it was too late to salvage anything from the flames that demon had wrought. My mother showed us how to light the Bifrost and travel between the worlds, helped us to escape as our own home burned upon our heels. Surt has been trapped there ever since, along with the dead, below, in Hel."

Eve tipped her head, watching him. His face was lined with grief before he fell silent, and she could feel the way his thoughts churned, even if she could not hear them. It was a miserable story, she couldn't deny that.

"But you lived. Your people lived."

Thor snorted. "Yes, we lived. To offer others the same fate. The Jotuns, the Vanir, the Álfar, and the Dverger, too. I have lived through five cycles of Ragnarok, Eve, and there is an old legend that we will see our own doom at the ninth. Nine worlds, all ruined, before we are stopped. Before we destroy ourselves, too."

She understood, now, why he hadn't wanted to answer, the bitterness behind his words cutting through her heart. She almost wished she hadn't asked, not because it was horrible—so many lives wasted, so much war and death and pain she couldn't even imagine the scope—but because it was clear it was something he hated, something which twisted him with regret.

Eve slipped her hand into his, just for a moment. Because she could never know what he'd lived through, what he'd lost, what he'd given up to live here in this empty city, with its echoing, cavernous halls. Alone and apart, because the alternative was death and destruction and despair, repeated again and again. It made her own pain feel so small, so selfishly unimportant.

"You didn't ruin this one," she said softly.

He squeezed her hand, and said nothing.

Eve didn't let go.

§

"Where have you been?" Ashley asked, peeking out of the lounge. Then her eyes widened as she realized Eve wasn't alone. "Oh! Well. That explains that."

Eve rolled her eyes, wishing, not for the first time, that her room wasn't right across from the floor lounge. Not that it mattered most of the time. And Ashley was the most harmless of the other girls. The only reason she poked her nose into Eve's business was because Marcus had practically deputized her—and it gave her an excuse to call him.

Everyone loved Marcus.

"Goodnight, Ashley," Eve said, pressing her palm against the doorplate.

She would have preferred an old fashioned lock and key, but she couldn't say biometrics weren't convenient. Thor touched a hand to the small of her back as the door whooshed open, and Eve swallowed a hum of pleasure before it escaped.

"Wait!" Ashley called.

Eve turned, touching her hand to the door sensor to keep it from closing, even as Thor slipped past her inside. It had been a long day, and she just wanted to collapse on her sofa and accidentally let her leg brush against Thor's for a moment or two before kicking him out and going to bed alone.

She hadn't realized how much she'd missed being touched. Marcus was always trying to close the distance between them, but she'd never let him, and when he'd managed it, she'd just felt crowded. But with Thor—he wasn't trying. Every intimacy was like an old friend rediscovered. His hand on her back was a natural extension of her own body, his arms around her just a jacket she'd forgotten. There was no hesitation in his touch, no question or nervousness, and it helped, she was sure, that she didn't get any stray thoughts along with the contact, either.

"Marcus was looking for you, earlier. He said to call him."

Eve rubbed her eyes. "It's kind of late for that, don't you think?"

"He said the *minute* you got back. And he didn't care how late it was. Or early, at this point."

So Ashley hadn't just been in the lounge. She'd been waiting for Eve, specifically. At Marcus's request. For the whole, entire night. Eve pressed her lips together and counted to ten. He had no right. None, to keep tabs on her. And after dinner earlier, he should have been too angry to care, maybe taking someone like Ashley to bed with him instead of setting her on Eve as some kind of watchdog. It really wasn't his business how she spent her evening or when she came home.

I told you he wouldn't give up, Thor said in the back of her mind.

You'd think telling the man in no uncertain terms that he wasn't what I wanted would have done the job.

From behind her, Thor chuckled. *Wishful thinking. For that matter...*

"Thanks," Eve said to Ashley. She prodded at what Thor had thought better of saying and got nothing but blank innocence in response. "But tell Marcus to do his own waiting around next time, all right? You're better than this, and if he can't see it, you should find someone who does."

Ashley raised her eyebrows. "Are you kidding? Now that you're involved with someone else, the field is wide open." She grinned. "Goodnight, Anna!"

Eve let the door slide shut and turned. Thor was already taking up more than half of her loveseat, seemingly counting the tiles on the ceiling. A god, sitting on a sofa, counting ceiling tiles. No. She didn't buy it for a minute. He might have lived as a human for a lifetime, but no one who had seen as much of the world as they had would be that absorbed by tiles, no matter how detailed. And these were as utilitarian as they came.

"For that matter, what?"

He shook his head. "Just an idle thought. Are you going to call Marcus?"

"Are you going to tell me what that idle thought was?"

He grimaced. "You won't like it."

Eve crossed her arms. "There are a lot of things I don't like right now, Thor. Are you trying to add yourself to that list?"

"Hm." His gaze met hers, that familiar concern flickering through his eyes, drawing crow's feet at the corners. "I had thought perhaps it was just your frustration with Marcus mingling with the heartache of your last life, but I suppose I should have known better, all things considered. Just as I should have considered that Elah might have tried other methods of softening you before giving me her blessing."

"In plain language, Thor." She didn't like it, what he was suggesting. *Don't be saying what I think you're saying . . .*

He rose, coming to stand before her, near enough that she could feel his warmth. When his hand found her cheek, she closed her eyes, leaning into the caress. Just for a moment. For a last moment of comfort.

"Marcus won't give up until your daughter does. She's sent him to you, just as she sent me," he said after a moment, and she could feel the bitterness in his thoughts, the heartache. He dropped his hand and stepped back. "I hadn't realized until now what she meant to accomplish with her sudden change of heart. That she meant to accomplish anything at all but your happiness. More the fool, me."

Eve shook her head, her stomach going sour and her heart twisting. She'd worried it was all a trick from the start, that Elah would take it all back before she was ready, use it somehow in punishment, just as she had before. But this was worse. So much worse, to realize how easily she was being manipulated. Used.

"Elah may rule, but Creation still requires your Grace, Eve," Thor said, his words rough with pain, even resentment. "And it appears with Marcus's failure, I'm meant to seduce it from you."

CHAPTER ELEVEN

Eve, Before

When Eve returned to the cottage, Raphael greeted her with dinner. A casserole on the table, and Elah fighting with a bottle—and how the Archangel had found everything he needed, she wasn't quite certain.

"Feeling better?" he asked.

Eve shook her head. "Trying not to feel at all, if I can help it."

"Hm," he said, giving her a long look, accompanied by the brush of his mind against hers, soothing more than questioning. "I suppose that's the best we can hope for, isn't it?"

"For the moment," Eve agreed, joining him at the table. "Thank you for this."

Raphael smiled, somehow the expression made him look almost grandfatherly, even with his impossibly young face. "It's my pleasure, truly. Much preferable to the last time we shared this cottage together."

"The last time?" Eve frowned, looking up from the plate he set in front of her. "I'm sorry, I don't remember . . ."

"No, of course not," he murmured, and his gaze flicked to Elah, who was much too young to hold her own head up, never mind a bottle, but seemed to be having no trouble with it at all. "Perhaps now isn't the best time to discuss it."

"She'll sleep, after she's finished. Especially if she didn't nap while I was gone."

"Hm," Raphael said again. "It didn't even occur to me to put her down."

Eve sighed. "I don't imagine it did, if she wasn't interested. She has a habit of making a person forget what she doesn't want done. It took me a week to realize it, and then I had to build a wall around my own mind to stop her, but I don't know how long it will last."

"Indeed." The angel served his own plate and sat down across from her. "And can you make her do as you ask? Sleep when you'd like her to sleep, eat when you're ready to feed her?"

Eve shrugged. "She seems to understand some things are mutually beneficial. Now she's found her schedule, and as long as I keep to it, she doesn't give me too much trouble. But putting her to sleep against her will is . . . challenging."

"You haven't called upon your DeLeon family for help."

"No," Eve agreed, pushing the casserole around her plate. Spinach and cheese and ham, with rosemary and potatoes. She hadn't realized she even had potatoes.

"Because she's a goddess?" he asked. "Or because you fear what their response will be when they learn of your circumstances?"

Eve pressed her lips together. "Does it matter?"

"It matters if you fear she'll manipulate them."

"She won't," Eve said, her voice firm. "Not as long as I stand beside her."

"I meant no disrespect, my dear," he said mildly. "I'm fully aware of how capable you are as a mother. I only wonder how best I might be of service, and how carefully I must guard myself."

Eve flushed, poking at her casserole again. She wasn't sure she had the energy to eat, never mind to defend herself. If this was some kind of test, she was going to fail it. But it wasn't as though this was a truth he wouldn't discover on his own, soon enough.

"Completely," she said quietly. "As completely as you know how."

For once, Elah went to bed without a fuss, and Eve returned to the living room, where the wingless Archangel waited for her, his hands behind his back as he stared out the window. The last rays of sunlight gilded him with red-gold, the color so exactly familiar . . .

She couldn't quite remember what it reminded her of. A person, maybe? The blanks in her memory were starting to become disconcerting.

"My fault, I'm afraid," Raphael said, without so much as glancing in her direction. "And now is hardly the time to begin undoing it. Too great a risk, with Elah plumbing the depths of your mind when you're not looking."

"I don't understand," she said, dropping to a seat on the edge of the couch. She rubbed her forehead. "But I feel like I should. All of this feels strangely familiar."

"It isn't the first time you've stayed here, no. Nor the first time I've come to you, to give you my help. But you have never known me by my proper name, if that makes you feel any better."

She gave a strangled laugh. "None of that is particularly reassuring."

"And if I say I'd like to stay? To help you care for your little goddess in her father's absence? Not to take his place, of course. Only to provide an extra set of hands, another pair of eyes, another mind she cannot so easily alter to suit her whims. You will not have much time together, but the longer she can be controlled, the longer you're likely to keep her."

"What exactly do you mean?" Eve asked, looking up sharply. He'd said something similar before. About why Adam had gone. "What does that mean, that we won't have much time together?"

"Ah," Raphael said, his shoulders drooping. "It's part of why he left, you see. You'll have two years, maybe three. He believed it would be much less if he stayed, and he did not trust himself not to influence her negatively. To make her a force of chaos, rather than order. Something Gabriel said, the fool."

The fool. Not Gabriel, but Adam. Or maybe both of them, together. The fools. And Adam had just run off, not even granting her the respect of an explanation. Not even pausing to consult with her. But that was always his way, wasn't it? He always decided. He'd decided he wanted her. He'd decided he would stay with her until Elah was born. He'd decided they could have a life together—that it didn't have to be heartbreak and loneliness. And now he'd decided to take it all back. She should have expected it. She should have known it was too good to be true.

"What happens after?" she asked, closing her eyes. She squeezed the bridge of her nose, trying to keep the tears back, because if she started crying now . . . "Two years from now, three, what happens to her then?"

"She'll go to God," he said. "In communion with Him, she's unlikely to do much harm, and Elohim will use her power to set His house in order before her ascension. He will not last beyond her eighteenth year, if even that long, and then she will have everything. All of Creation, all of God's power, made Hers, to do as She wills."

"She already has so much," Eve whispered, hiding her face in her hands. "She could kill us with a thought, if she realized—wrap her fingers through my hair and tell my heart to stop beating, just because she didn't care for the sound."

"And if you fear her, she will know it. She'll wonder why. She'll act out, because of it. She must love you, Eve, and be loved by you. She must trust you, or it is all for nothing."

"Adam knew all this." The coward. The gutless jellyfish. The worthless, filthy cur. "He knew all this and he left me without even a hint. He didn't even warn me!"

Raphael sighed. "If it makes a difference, I believe he acted out of love."

"It doesn't," Eve said, rising. She was exhausted, and she needed—she didn't know what she needed. Nothing that this Archangel could ever give. "It doesn't make any difference at all."

And then she went to her room. While Elah slept, she could at least stop pretending it didn't hurt.

❧

Raphael stayed, and Elah grew. Faster than any child had a right to. At just one month, she was sleeping through the night, and Eve wasn't alone in her relief. A full eight hours a night when they could both relax their guard. Because the older Elah grew, the more insistently she pushed against Eve's mind. Questions, mostly, in the shapes of what and why. What was the animal that Elah had seen out the window? Why did it run away?

And then they stopped running away. Squirrels and birds lined the windowsills, looking in, half-dazed. Songbirds would sing themselves hoarse outside Elah's bedroom window, and wolves howled in harmony at dusk. Again and again, they would have to intervene, setting the birds free of Elah's influence, or encouraging the squirrels to go back to gathering their nuts.

"We ask for their help," Eve explained after she had sent the wolves back into the woods again, and not for the first time. "We don't command it."

Want, Elah responded, straining to reach them as they ran away. *Want!*

"They're meant to be free," Eve said, pushing her hands down. "And we can't always have what we want, besides. You must never take what isn't yours, and free will is the most precious possession of all."

At least it was only wolves, Eve thought very privately, and not stray children from the village. And she would have, too young to understand that it was wrong, if Eve hadn't kept her in the cottage, where she wouldn't see them to call to them. But Eve wasn't certain how much longer they would have before Elah started hearing their minds in the distance. She only hoped by then, she'd understand they weren't hers to play with.

Not yet, Raphael said from the kitchen, and Eve stiffened. The angel had an uncanny ability to read her thoughts, even when she buried them. *But one day, they'll all belong to her, to do with as she pleases, and she'll need to know that too.*

Having the power doesn't mean she must always use it. It's no different than asking her to keep the world whole, that we might live on.

Are you so certain God would not have done more, had he been strong enough to act? It is the prerogative of gods to engage with their creations, to interfere, if they desire it, for good or ill.

Eve shot a glare at him through the kitchen window. *Maybe it is, or maybe it doesn't have to be.*

Would you have her stand by while her people suffered, then? Let them languish, when she had the power to save them?

If it was their choice to suffer, their desire. But if they called for her, begged for her help, no, of course not.

Is that not a similar sort of interference?

It isn't the same as claiming their minds and walking them off a cliff. Toying with them just for the pleasure of watching them squirm.

Then perhaps you ought to teach her simply to do no harm. To help the wolves to find game or shelter, to help the squirrels collect their nuts and the birds to find worms. Teach her to use her power to nurture what surrounds her, Eve, and she will be that much more interested in the learning.

"Tomorrow we'll leave bread crumbs for the birds and the squirrels on the windowsill," Eve said to her daughter. "And you can tell them where to find it. If we do it every day, they'll remember, and in time, you'll only need to open yourself to them, and when they hear you, they'll come out of friendship."

Want, Elah repeated, reaching again in the direction the wolves had run.

Eve smiled to keep from frowning. "Why don't we start with the birds and squirrels first."

CHAPTER TWELVE

Eve, Later

❦

"I swear to you, I didn't know," Thor said lowly. "If I had—"

"If you had, you would have come anyway and done your duty with pleasure." He flinched, but didn't deny it, and she pointed at the door. "Go. And if you see Marcus on your way out, tell him I don't want to see him, either. Ever again."

"Eve—"

"Get. Out." She slammed her palm against the door release, which only served to jam it. But since Thor was only staring, looking as though she'd slapped him, it was probably for the best that he had a little bit more time to make it through the doorway.

"Eve, please."

"Anna," she snapped. "My name is Anna. To you. To everyone. Whatever I was before now, none of it matters. If it did, my daughter wouldn't be trying to manipulate me."

"Do you not see that it is *because* of how much it matters? How important you are to the world? Elah has treated you wrongly, yes, and to realize so belatedly how she meant to use us both does not please me, either. But it isn't because you and everything you've done, from Creation to this day, doesn't matter. It is because when you are ill, when you will have no part of the world, when you refuse to love, it *suffers.* We all do."

"I am not her *plaything,* Thor. I won't be thrown away when it doesn't suit her and then picked up again when she's bored of the mess she's made of everything else!" And how was she supposed to believe any of what he'd told her now? For all she knew it was just an elaborate lie.

What would it have taken for Elah to shape a man into Thorgrim, give him memories of their life together, and set him in her path? The man claiming to be a god could just be another one of her Host, with the powers to match and a story that broke her heart. Eve could just imagine them, Adam and Elah, hatching this scheme behind her back, determined to trick her into—into giving them whatever it was they needed to complete their plans for world domination.

Eve wanted no part of it. She'd already lived a life manipulated by her daughter, torn from everything she loved in the blink of an eye just to suit her preference, and she wasn't interested in doing the same again, even if the circumstances were different.

"Nothing I told you was a lie, Eve."

"You can believe that with every fiber of your being but it doesn't make it true."

Whatever Elah and Adam had worked out between them, it wasn't his fault he'd been caught up in it, she reminded herself, rubbing her forehead to stave off the headache building behind her eyes. It was always this way when she lost control. An outburst of anger, or bitterness, or despair, followed by a crippling migraine and exhaustion so bone deep even sleep didn't help.

"Just go, please. I can't think clearly when you're here and I need to have my head straight."

He hesitated for another heartbeat, then nodded. "Of course you would need time to yourself. But I beg you not to banish me utterly. Whatever proof you require that I am who I say I am, you need only whisper it and it will be yours. I would turn my soul inside out, if you would only believe me."

She looked away from his begging eyes, her gaze falling belatedly on the audience gathering across the hall in the lounge. Ashley among them, her finger pressed behind her ear to activate her earpiece, and whispering to whoever was listening. Marcus, probably. And if Thor was right, that meant Elah would know, too, before long. If she didn't already. Every one of these people was her tool, her eyes and ears when she chose to employ them. Walking recordings of everything Eve did or didn't do. She had to get him out and shut the door. Preferably before everything started taking on a greenish cast and she had no choice but to assume the fetal position.

"Give me three days," she said at last. "And I don't want to see even a glimpse of anything that looks like you or Marcus in the meantime. Do you understand me?" she raised her voice for the benefit of her audience. For Elah's benefit, though it made her head throb harder. "I need to think!"

"Three days," Thor agreed, and at his glower, the girls scattered. "And you may leave Marcus to me."

Then he left, ignoring Ashley's too-interested stare, and Eve jimmied the door plate until it finally hissed close again, shutting all of them out. Just for good measure, she tinted the windows to full reflection, too.

Not that it mattered. None of it would keep Elah out of her life. As long as Eve lived in Her world, she'd never escape.

Only this life hadn't felt quite so much like a prison until now.

Eve hid in her room the next day, the last day before her classes began, doing her best to remember to breathe, no matter how nauseated it made her feel. Ashley knocked on her door at one point, but she ignored it, just like she'd ignored the ten messages from Marcus, ranging from apologies to accusations to pleas that she just let him know she was alive. He could worry himself sick, for all she cared.

He was just Elah's tool, another piece on Elah's game board. Like Thor. Like Eve was, herself.

Every motion in the corner of her eye made her freeze, searching the room for any sign of Elah's shimmer. She could appear with a thought, with less effort than even Thor traveled through lightning. But worse, she could stand in the center of the room, a silent, invisible ghost, and Eve would never even know she was there. The first time she'd done it, Eve's heart had been in her throat, terrified that somehow she'd lost her daughter, that she had escaped into the woods, while her back was turned. Elah had always been fascinated by the wolves, calling them to her from miles and miles away, no matter how many times Eve tried to stop her. And once she'd realized there were people on the other side of the trees, living in the village and the manor, Eve had been running herself ragged trying to keep her daughter out of their minds. She hadn't realized that Elah had slipped inside hers.

It was only part of how she did it, slipping inside someone's mind and erasing herself altogether from their sight. Eve had caused people to overlook herself in the same way often enough. But in order to keep herself out of sight, Eve had to remain in their heads, constantly focused on misdirecting them. It was exhausting work, even with one person, never mind a crowd.

Not so, for Elah. Once a person forgot she was there, or mistook her for someone else, her very appearance altered to match. She became invisible, or more beautiful, or hooked-nosed, taller or shorter, thinner or fatter. Whatever a person wanted to see, Elah became, until and unless she wanted to be something else. And all of it was effortless.

Eve had found her daughter that first time when she laughed, and she'd winked into existence in her crib, standing up with her hands on the bars, bouncing herself with a wide grin. But Eve wasn't so fortunate now. As an adult, Elah knew perfectly well how to make herself silent as well as unseeable, and she didn't even have to be in a room to know what happened inside it.

All she had to do was look, and roofs and walls fell away, exposing everything inside. It had never bothered Eve before, knowing that her daughter could see her. She had been happy to know it, after she'd been forced to give her up. Because it meant Elah wouldn't forget her, that Eve would always be a part of her life, no matter the distances that separated them.

Now, all Eve wanted was the privacy to weep, to rail and scream, to have just one moment she could be sure was hers alone. But if Elah had sent Thor to seduce her, to manipulate her, she couldn't convince herself that her daughter wasn't watching.

She couldn't convince herself that she would ever have any kind of privacy or freedom again.

At four in the morning, when the worst of her migraine had subsided and the white walls of her dorm no longer looked green, she went to the gymnasium. At that hour, it was all but empty, and the artificial lights and sterile rows of exercise equipment, tucked deep underground, felt safer, somehow, than her own room, isolated enough to ease the pressure behind her eyes. Maybe it was the lack of windows, giving the illusion that no one could see her from the outside, or maybe just knowing she had three meters of dirt over her head. It didn't matter. She could breathe again.

Eve took to the track. Until this last life, she had preferred to run outside, barefoot whenever possible, with the sun on her face and shoulders and wind wicking away the sweat from her body. She'd liked to feel the world around her and be part of it. But now it just made her ache, dull and throbbing and too tight around her heart. And after everything else with Elah, and Thor, the last thing she wanted was to be part of anything greater than herself. She wasn't certain she wanted to *be* at all.

She still ran barefoot, though the texture of the track left her soles feeling raw. The sting and burn of each step distracted her the way digging a fingernail into a mosquito bite stops it from itching. Such a small physical discomfort enough to trump her emotions, and even the ebbing ache of her head. But not her thoughts. Not the question which had been nagging at her all night long, keeping her from sleep. The person, really, and the pain in his eyes when he spoke of the worlds that had been lost.

Everything about Thor had felt real, and if Elah had hoped to manipulate her, to trick her into loving, a god who had been part of the destruction of five worlds through war was the last person she should have sent. Why not just resurrect Thorgrim himself from among the dead, and skip the rest altogether. Why make Thorgrim into a god, and send him with this story?

But Thor had said himself that he served Elah now, and even if he'd told the truth about who he was, it didn't change that he was on a mission. That everything between them was tainted by Elah's will, and whatever she hoped to gain from bringing Eve back into communion with the world after she had driven her out of it. Even if Thor hadn't been lying, it didn't mean she could trust him.

And that was what stung the most. Because she wanted to. Because that night, when they'd returned from Asgard, all she had wanted was to give in, to let him whisk her away into that strange, empty piece of the world, and just be with him for as long as he'd have her.

It would end, of course. She'd grow old and die, and be born again, but he wouldn't. He would lose her, but that didn't mean she had to lose him, and even if it meant just forty years in each life that they might spend together, it could still extend, on and on and on into forever. Maybe it wasn't perfect. Maybe it wasn't exact. But maybe, too, it didn't have to be. Maybe it could be enough.

But if this, all of this, was just about Elah getting her way. If Thor had returned to her not because he loved her, but because her daughter had made it so, it never would be.

Without love, it didn't matter who he was, or why he'd come. She never wanted to see him again.

CHAPTER THIRTEEN

Thor

Not even Thor could reach the Redwood Hall without invitation, but when he arrived at the edge of its borders, the entrance stood open, shimmering between two lean saplings, their branches weaving together in a delicate arch of knotwork above his head. Another time, he might have admired the beauty of it, the simplicity, for he was normally struck with a sense of awe and peace when he entered the grove of tall Redwoods, the branches of which formed incredible buttressed ceilings and domes over his head. A cathedral built of living trees in the heart of a forest. Normally, it felt like home—more so, at times, than Asgard, empty as it had become.

But not today. There was nothing peaceful about his feelings for what Elah had done to Eve, and even the scent of rich earth and the crunch of the leaves beneath his feet did nothing to soften him. He'd waited so long, and he should have realized Elah would not change her mind so swiftly without reason.

"Thor." Athena waited for him inside, taking both his hands in greeting, and searching his face. "Ra warned her this would happen, I promise you."

"And yet, she chose not to listen."

Athena sighed. "She is young yet, but none of it is done out of malice, now. She only wants her mother's happiness, and peace for her world."

"Peace for her world, first," Thor said. "Her mother's happiness only after, if it will not interfere."

"Do not be cruel to her, Thor. It will serve nothing but the loss of her goodwill, and if you wish to see Eve again . . ."

He pulled away, his hands itching for *Mjölnir*. "A threat?"

"No," Athena said, her face paling. "Of course not. Only a warning."

"Just as Ra warned Elah?" he asked. "You tell me not to be cruel to her, but her mother weeps now. After everything Eve has sacrificed, she deserves better from her daughter!"

"Come, Thor." And it was Raphael himself who called to him now, standing before the greater entrance to the throne room, another doorway of living trees. "Elah will see you."

Thor followed, averting his gaze from the broad white wings that seemed so out of place upon Ra's back. The Archangel had been old even before Thor had arrived to this world, and to see him so young, so altered in form by his angel's wings only underscored how immensely the world had changed.

Not that many beyond the gods had noticed the difference when Elah had come to power. Outside of a repression of religious conflict between nations, and the glorification of her own name, little had affected humanity. Eve's withdrawal, on the other hand, was something else entirely. It was worse than the wars from her time in the ward, for at least then she had still been struggling to act, to serve and protect, and what she did, she did out of love for the world itself.

Her complete disaffection now, after everything she had triumphed over, made him heartsick. He wanted more than anything to understand, to lend her the strength she needed to overcome. She had more than earned her peace, and he would grant it to her if he could, or offer the love and support of his presence at the least, if he could not.

Elah sat upon a throne formed from the roots of a redwood, bark worn smooth with age and use. She rose as Thor entered the hall, her expression sweet with grief and confusion. A child's face, innocent, even afraid.

"What word do you bring of my mother?" she asked, coming down from the dais of raised earth. Roots formed the treads of stairs, surfacing beneath her feet where she required them, before disappearing again beneath the mulch of leaves and needles.

"She wants her freedom, Lady," Thor said. "And I come to ask it of you. Call Marcus off, and leave her in peace to find her own way."

Angels with all shade of wing and feather came in and out of the hall, descending from above and departing the same way, weaving their way through the branches parting before them. With each arrival, Elah's appearance shimmered, her light growing brighter, then darker again as they left. She was not overly tall, not even of a height with Athena, but her power and presence filled the room, all the same. Ra moved to her left, and Athena glided toward the edge of the hall, neither mixing with the angels, nor taking a place at Elah's side.

"Would you have me strip him of his own will in the matter, as well?" Elah asked. "Perhaps I am guilty of setting him in her path, even of encouraging him to pursue her at the start, but his affection for her is his own now, grown up from the experiences they've shared. To call him away would be to rob him of much of his past, and even in her irritation, I do not think my mother would approve."

"And what of me?" he demanded. "Have you set me in her path, encouraged me as well, that you might crowd her into loving?"

Elah flushed. "Is it so wrong that I would send her the comfort you might provide? The world suffers, Thor. If I crowd her, it is with good reason, and I am well within my rights to take what measures I must to protect that which I am charged to guard."

"I cannot be any comfort to her if she does not trust that I am not some creation of yours, and why, exactly she would believe that is so, I would know, now, before any more damage is done."

The angels behind her erupted into a chorus of bells, and Elah lifted one hand to silence them, looking anything but childlike. A queen of her domain, and well aware of her power. "It is not your place to make demands upon me, Thor of the North. Nor is it your right to tell me how I must conduct myself in relationship with my mother."

"When you have used me for your own ends, you give me the grounds," Thor said, his eyes burning with power and anger he did not dare to unleash here. "I may have sworn myself to peace with you, even to your service, but I am not one of your angels to be directed without thought or consideration or reason, and I was sworn to the protection of your mother first. Make no mistake, Lady, it is an oath I will not forswear, even for you."

The chorus exploded again, a cacophony of noise capable of bringing even Athena such discomfort that she reached for a nearby trunk to steady herself, but Thor stood unmoved. The ring of bells could not match the roar of thunder through his blood, and he would not bend his knee to Elah by force, least of all in this.

"Enough!" Elah said, and the chorus died as quickly as it had begun, leaving Thor unsure if it had been her intent to call upon it at all. Her jaw tightened, and she looked away. "If it were anyone but my mother, Thor, what you have said this day would mean your exile."

"If it were anyone but your mother, Lady, I would have gone willingly long before now."

Her eyes flashed, her chin rising, and there was Eve, in the line of her jaw and the shape of her face. But Eve had never looked on him with such righteous indignation. Adam, perhaps, but never him.

"Careful, Odinson," Elah said, her voice low and controlled. "Or do you forget that it is by my favor alone that you remain? My *Grace*." The word was clipped short, rife with bitterness. "And I do not possess so unlimited a supply as my mother."

"And what would you have done had I not stayed? Who would you have sent to tempt her? Another Marcus? Another child, Elah, when she has lived life already to exhaustion?"

"Better you had never come at all," Elah snapped, the whole hall trembling with her anger. "Better she had never known you! Perhaps then she would be with my father, where she belongs."

"Then you know nothing," he said, the color draining from the trees, the angels and their rainbow wings all shifting toward shades of gray. "Nothing of love, or trust, or heartbreak!"

"Thor," Ra warned, his eyes darting anxiously between them. "You mustn't—"

"Must not what?" Thor demanded. "I did not break free of my father's noose only to become her dog, let out of the kennel when it suits her. I will not have my love for Eve twisted into ruin, to be used to bring her pain! She deserves better, and from her daughter, most of all."

"Thor," Athena said, and when she had moved to his side, he did not know, but she grasped his arm now, nails biting deep. "This is Elah's hall, and you are her guest."

"If you had any idea what she suffered," he said, his vision much too white. But he could not stop. Could not stand the thought that Elah would believe, even for a moment, that Adam deserved her. "If you had any understanding of what she went through to bring you into this world, what she risked for the love your father threw away so quickly, you would fall to your knees before her and never rise. Certainly you would never have taken her adversary into your bed!"

Elah drew herself up, the edges of her form blurred with fire and smoke, wind whipping the leaves and rattling the branches that did not already sway with sympathy. "If you ever speak to me this way again," she began, "ever call your lightning in my hall, whether it is in defense of my mother or not, I will give Michael your head."

Thor's lip curled. "He can try to take it, Lady, and knowing how he threatened Eve, I would be glad to watch him die."

"And how will you keep your oath, then, when you are cast back into the void? Do you imagine you serve my mother by threatening her daughter? Do you think even in her anger, she would ever suffer you for a moment, knowing you had done me harm?"

He clamped his jaw shut, slowly forcing his fists to uncurl, only realizing then that he had called *Mjölnir* to his palm. That Athena had her hand wrapped over his upon the haft, holding him back. He released it, sending the war hammer back to Asgard. That he had summoned it at all was reason enough for Elah's fury. An argument, even one so poisonous as this, would be forgivable. But to bring a weapon into her presence . . .

"Forgive me," he murmured, dropping his gaze. "To threaten you was never my intent or my desire."

Elah let out a breath. "I am relieved to know it. But I meant what I said, Thor."

He ground his teeth, but did not argue. It was well within her rights even to banish him. That she did not proved she was Eve's daughter more than Adam's. Or at least that she realized he was more valuable to him at her mother's side.

"You will return to my mother," she went on, "and I hope you will not give me any further reason to regret the freedom you have been granted." But her face softened then, and she ducked her head, catching his eyes. "If she will not accept you, I have little hope that she will ever recover. And the world needs her love, Thor. I need her Grace. One way or another."

There was something about the grief in her expression, the fear in her eyes when she said it that made his hackles rise, and a chill slip down his spine. But Elah had already turned away, nodding once to Raphael and flicking her fingers, and Thor had spent enough time in his father's hall to know when he was being dismissed.

"Come, Thor," Ra said, again, leading him out to the vestibule where he had entered. And when Athena joined them, Thor did not miss the look they exchanged, nor the flash of concern, quickly buried. "You *must* watch your temper, my friend. Every outburst only lends strength to Michael's arguments, and Elah favors his council too much, already."

He scrubbed his face with his hand. "If Eve would only allow me to explain—would simply trust—"

"Whatever has passed between you, making Elah your enemy will not fix it," Athena said. "Now. As for the rest, I will see to Marcus, though I do not think he will consider it a kindness before we are through."

"There is the girl, Ashley," Ra suggested. "If he could be made to see her interest . . ."

Athena shook her head. "She is too near to Eve. Whatever interest he might have in her, it will not last, and then we will have bruised two hearts instead of one."

"What I would not give for one of Eros' arrows now," Ra murmured.

"Better that be used on Eve, herself, had we the power," Athena said sourly. "If she would only *love* . . ."

"It is her choice," Thor said, before they could go on any further, but he was careful to keep his tone even, his temper in check. "To give of herself or not, it is her right to do as she wishes, and I will not hear otherwise from either of you."

"You must see reason in this, Thor," Athena said. "Even with everything Adam has already done, a full third of the world goes hungry, and the deserts are still expanding, the lands growing more barren every year. With Eve's help, all of this could be averted. At the very least, she could persuade the other nations to act with him to stem the tide—if she would only stop hiding herself away, and make use of her talents."

But it made no sense. Eve had never been a goddess of fertility or the field, and why the withholding of her power would manifest in such a way, he could not understand. Whether she could influence the politics of the world was another matter, and even if she had been wholly herself, Thor doubted she would have taken part in such a scheme.

"Elah is not so limited that she cannot simply will more food to grow, more water to fall, more crops to harvest."

"She cannot create life from dust and breath as Elohim did," Ra said. "Not in the barren lands. And Michael is convinced it is because Eve will not grant her access to God's Grace. Elah draws her power as much from her parents as she does from Creation itself, you must realize that by now."

"I cannot believe Eve does not have reason," Thor said. "If she has caused this, and I am not so certain she is capable of such a thing, perhaps it is for a greater purpose. Perhaps Elah has given her a reason for mistrust."

Ra fell silent, exchanging another glance with Athena.

"If you know what has happened between them that might cause this, I would know, Ra, before I return to her."

"Other than her exile, fully rescinded now and softened even in her last life from what it might have been, I do not know for certain, myself," Ra said. "Not of anything that might have occurred in the past. Elah was a difficult child to raise, to be sure, but Eve managed well enough, even before I arrived."

"Before her ascension, then?"

Ra shook his head. "I remained with Elohim until his death."

"What of this life?"

"Beyond tempting her with Marcus, and now you, Elah has done nothing untoward. Quite the opposite, in fact, for she has given Eve every advantage, every blessing to heal this breach," Ra said, but the angel caught him by the arm, his grip almost painful. "I cannot promise it will remain so if you cannot persuade her, Thor. For all our sakes, you must succeed."

"Perhaps if Elah had gone to her mother directly from the start, I might have succeeded already," he said, pushing Ra's hand away and gathering his own power. Lightning crawled over his skin, eager to pull him into its embrace. “You might suggest honesty to your goddess the next time she despairs of earning her mother’s faith.”

And then he left them, before he lost his temper for a second time.

CHAPTER FOURTEEN

Eve

❦

"Three days and four hours," Eve said, when she found Thor waiting at the entrance to her building. At five in the morning, on her way back from the gym. It could have been worse, she supposed. It could have been Marcus. And at least she was finally feeling herself again. Or at least no worse than usual. "I'm shocked you let those extra hours slip by you."

He held the door for her, careful, she noted, not to touch her in the process. "I didn't think you'd care for it if I went in search of you elsewhere."

"Ah," she said, keeping her gaze fixed firmly on the stairs as she climbed them. If she looked at him, she would see his concern, fluttering with butterfly wings at the edges of her awareness. Every therapeutic bit of her run evaporated in his presence, her body humming with something else at his proximity. Something she refused to consider long enough to name.

Her lack of eye contact didn't stop him from following. "Will you make me beg for your forgiveness?"

She shook her head, hitching her bag up on her shoulder. She'd changed out of her sweaty gym clothes, but that was all she could really say for herself. Not that Thor hadn't seen her elbow deep in blood and guts, once upon a time, skinning and cleaning his kills. "It wasn't your pride that offended me."

"Tell me what you would have me do to prove myself, Eve, and I will do it. Without hesitation."

She rolled that idea around for a moment, prodding at it. Asking someone to prove their love was a little bit like asking science to prove God, it never quite worked out. Certainly not neatly. The people who already believed didn't need science to know God existed, and the people who didn't believe would just keep excusing the positive data as some sort of fluke.

And besides, this particular proof was less about being convinced he loved her, and more about making him realize he didn't. That it was all just some influence or persuasion of Elah's. But making him see that would require time and energy she didn't have and didn't want to invest. Just being near him tugged at her heart.

How often had she dreamed of Thorgrim? Longed for him? And how much time did she really think she could spend in his presence now without losing herself to that same longing? It had only taken two days for her to begin to rethink things. To begin to want. Even knowing why he'd come, she didn't think she could risk it.

At the top of the stairs, she turned to face him and he hesitated, two steps down. But the words—she couldn't find the right ones. And the way he looked at her, with this mix of determination and concern, searching her face. Like he believed he could heal her, and he had no intention of giving up until she let him. And his face was swimming, then, blurred and strange, and she wanted so, so much to be wrong.

"If you're just here because Elah sent you—"

"Eve," he sighed, taking the last two steps in one bound. "Is that what you fear? Truly?"

She blinked back the moisture in her eyes and turned her face away. "You don't understand what you're asking of me, what she's asking. The world, it hurts. Everything, every ache is magnified a hundredfold until pieces of my soul rip away. It just hurts too much when it ends, and it will. It will always end. I'll grow old and die, or Elah will lose interest, or change her mind—"

He cupped her cheek, slid his fingers into her hair, and her body betrayed her, just like that, filling with warmth and love and need. "I have waited three thousand years for you, *hjartað mitt.* Your daughter did not send me to you then, nor has she influenced my love for you since. How could she, when she did not live? As Aesir, a god in my own right, I exist outside of her control."

"But you serve her. You said yourself, you serve her." *Hjartað mitt.* My heart. He'd called her that before, and she still remembered the endearment, the way he'd spoken it when they were married in his strange Northern tongue. "If that's all this is, I can't. I can't risk *my* heart. Not again. The grief of it will open up the world beneath my feet, a giant hungry maw, and I won't survive it, this time."

"None of this is about Elah," he said firmly. "Not for me. Look at me, Eve." He tipped her chin up, catching her gaze and holding her heart. She told herself to pull away, but her hand closed in the fabric of his shirt, instead. And she didn't want to let go. "If you don't want the world, we can leave it. We'll live in Asgard, together. Just you and me, where Elah cannot reach you, and you'll never grow old, never die."

Her heart stopped, and she wasn't sure she could breathe. That she would ever breathe again. "What?"

"You can be free, Eve, and still have love."

She gripped his shirt so hard her nails dug into her own palm through the fabric, and stared into his eyes, so wide and blue and earnest. "Never grow old, never die—that's what you said."

"Yes," he agreed, cautious now. "As long as you remained in Asgard, your body would not age."

Blood was roaring in her ears, though she didn't know how because her heart had definitely stopped. Everything in her had stopped. She wouldn't have to die. And Elah. Elah wouldn't be able to reach her. The world wouldn't swallow her whole with grief and sorrow and pain, if she opened her heart, because Thor wouldn't die, and neither would she.

Freedom, true, real freedom, and he'd waited this long to tell her so.

"Take me there."

§

Eve stood in the center of the quad and stared at the tree, with its golden fruit and blood red leaves. Thor had offered to take her to Bilskirnir, but she had waved him off and stepped forward instead.

The tree even smelled the same, all cinnamon and sweetness, and if she closed her eyes, she could taste it again, the fruit melting in her mouth, its texture closer to a perfectly ripened plum rather than an apple. One of the branches rustled over her head, and her eyes snapped open again. But it wasn't the serpent she'd been expecting—and where *had* Lucifer gotten off to, in all this time?—just Thor reaching up to pluck one of the golden apples, and causing a shower of leaves to float down, feather-like, around them.

"Here," he said, offering it to her. "It's perfectly safe."

She pressed her lips together. "I'd rather not."

"You've eaten it before." When she opened her mouth to protest, he laughed, touching his finger to her lips. "Not the fruit from your Garden, Eve. The apples from this tree. I brought them to you myself, when you were ill."

"I can't believe I wouldn't remember." But her fingers itched to touch it, to make the gold ripple with crimson beneath the surface of the skin. It was beautiful, dazzling in the sunlight. "I can't believe I would have ever eaten it, if I'd known."

"You were not yourself, then. Poisoned in mind and spirit by Jormungand's venom." He dropped his hand, then lifted the fruit to his mouth.

Eve's eyes widened, her hand going to her throat as he took a bite. He couldn't just—"What are you doing!"

He'd already swallowed. He'd swallowed, and was holding it out to her again, as if nothing had happened. She made a strangled noise, and stepped back. She couldn't. Not again. Not when she remembered so well how much it had hurt, that first sip of knowledge and understanding, and the world exploding with voices and minds and life. She flinched even from the memory, though it had been different then. It hadn't gnawed at her with hunger, hissing and spitting in her ear.

But Asgard was empty. Except for Thor's two goats, a few chickens, and one lonely horse who had refused to leave with his owner, there was no one to hear. That's what Thor had promised her. That this place, wherever it was, and however it had been made, was just separate enough from the world. She inhaled deeply through her nose, forcing the tension away, the fear, letting her body breathe, letting her mind open. Carefully at first, just cracking a window to let in the good clean air, testing the atmosphere. Peace washed through her, and glorious, glorious silence, but for Thor beside her, burning with love so bright it put the sun to shame.

"It won't hurt you, Eve," Thor said gently, and for a dizzying moment she thought he meant his love for her. "I give you my word. Whatever you experienced in the Garden, this fruit is not the same. It heals the spirit and nourishes the body, nothing more."

Heals and nourishes. She stared at the mark of his teeth in the pulp, pooling with liquid, her thoughts drawn back from her own mind to his words. The sweetness of the fruit made her mouth water, and she frowned. Heals and . . .

"I don't remember being sick." She lifted her gaze back to his face in time to see his expression shutter. "How is it possible that I don't remember being so sick you came to me—"

And then she did. A rush of pain and agony and blood, so much blood. Lying in pools of it on a checkered, tile floor, in a room with cinderblock walls and jaundiced light. Green where it should have been white, like staring through a poisoned fog. The sharp cut of leather through her skin, and the man who had been her husband lying unconscious beside her after she had fought back.

"Oh." Eve sucked in a sharp breath, and stumbled, reaching for the stone bench behind her. Thor moved faster, steadying her with a hand at her waist and easing her to the grass. She clutched her head, wishing she could force the memories back out again, forget it all. Except Thor. Crouching before her, speaking to her in the old tongue and telling her to call him cousin. Promising to free her, to make her safe. "You came to me."

"Too late." He smoothed back her hair, the fruit gone from his hands. "I came too late, and it has haunted me for centuries, since."

"But you came." It was a patchwork, still, but she remembered that. The way he had helped her from the floor, handling her like spun glass. She frowned, chasing the memories. The moment he had bundled her into a car, his eyes anguished. Kissed her forehead and murmured farewell. "There was another man."

"Ra," Thor said. "Your Raphael. He cared for you, after, in France, but it was too late to save your mind. I nearly killed my father for what he'd allowed to happen. You cannot realize how close we came to Ragnarok, in that moment. How near I came to raining destruction upon this world, like all the others. For your sake, for what they did to you, and the women I couldn't save. We weren't sure, then, that you'd ever heal. That even rebirth would be enough to make you whole again."

She pressed the heel of her hand against her forehead. Her head felt as though someone had plucked it from her shoulders and squeezed. Not quite the same as one of her migraines, but something similar, lurking inside her memory, hidden until now. Forgotten. This wasn't the first life to leave the tang of bile and despair in the back of her throat. Nor the first time she had wanted to escape, to crawl back into the womb of the void and never return.

"Raphael." She struggled against the pain, lurching for the surface of her thoughts, her present. "That was what he meant, when he came to help me with Elah. He said it wasn't the first time he'd cared for me, and the things I couldn't quite remember—it was this. All of this."

"He thought it would be easier for you," Thor said. "And then when Elah was born, it was more important than ever that you not dwell upon it. Not that we could keep it from her forever, and nor did we, but at least while she was an infant, to subject her to that kind of trauma, even in memory, risked far too much."

"Yes." Eve could understand that. Even the memories she'd been able to call upon easily had been far from helpful in trying to persuade Elah that the world was worth saving. "I just didn't realize."

He'd done so much for her. So, so much.

"And you let me accuse you of not loving me." She laughed, hollow and broken. "How could I have ever doubted, even for a moment?"

Thor pulled her into his arms, and she hid her face against his shoulder, breathing him in, reveling in his closeness, all the dearer now for what he'd done. For everything he'd done.

"I'm sorry," she said into the curve of his shoulder. "I'm so sorry."

"Shh," he murmured against her hair. "It doesn't matter, now. You're here, and we're together. That's enough."

And then, for the first time in a century, safe and loved even if she couldn't be whole, Eve let herself cry.

❧

It was a long time later when she woke in a dark room, filled with strange shadows, and familiar scents. Wind and rain and springtime. She was alone, utterly, blissfully alone for the first time in . . .

Never in her many, many lives, had she ever been alone so completely, without the hum of strangers' thoughts beating against her own, and all their pain and heartbreak and excitement, and pleasure leaching into her mind. Even in her last life, isolated as she'd been, it hadn't been so quiet. Or at least the quiet had not felt so comforting.

She sighed, throwing her arms up over her head and stretching out in the oversized bed—Thor's bed, she realized, when a glance to the right revealed *Mjölnir* sitting on the low table beside it. How had she not noticed the quiet when he'd brought her here the first time?

But she already knew the answer. That first time, she'd been so tightly wound, so completely cut off from everything around her. She hadn't wanted to hear or see anything that would tempt her heart, either. Not any further than it already had been.

And now?

She closed her eyes and let every muscle in her body relax. And then she started on her mind, her very heart and soul. The window in her mind had cracked wider while she'd been so upset, the tracks greased by Thor's concern, his gentleness, and the way he pressed kisses into her hair as he lifted her up into his arms, murmuring reassurances all the while. Her tears hadn't startled him, hadn't disturbed him at all, in fact, she could have sworn she'd felt some small tendril of relief slip between them.

Eve eased her mind open wider, luxuriating in the quiet sense of growing grass and blooming flowers, and then wider still. There was Thor, his presence unmistakable and steady, and a heartbeat later, she felt his recognition and pleasure, too, flooding her with warmth until her cheeks flushed. A bonfire of love and peace and joy, coming from the kitchens, below, and . . .

She frowned, tracing the emotions back. Most of it was Thor, without question, but there was something more, delicate strands of the same from another source. Eve pushed back the fur blanket and slipped out of the bed, ignoring Thor's silent question in the back of her mind. She could feel it, tugging at her now, and threw open the wooden shutters, letting purple twilight spill into the bedroom on a chill evening breeze. The room looked out over the quad, as everything in Asgard seemed to, and the flow of peace and love wound its way back to its center.

Pulsing out from the tree at its heart, and welcoming her home.

Eve closed her eyes and opened herself completely, the better to understand, to know. She soaked up the love, the peace and the silence, letting it fill her up until her heart felt too big for her chest and her whole body tingled. How had she survived on so little for so long?

"Eve?" Thor asked, from the doorway. "Are you well?"

She smiled, though he couldn't see it. He'd feel it well enough. "Better than I've been in ages."

CHAPTER FIFTEEN

Thor

❧

She was different, in Asgard. Like a rosebush, barely budding, and every trip they made back, she grew closer to blooming. Her aura, once as bruised and dark as her heart, lightened, her smile and laughter coming more easily. Most often, she did little more than lie upon his bed and read, wrapped in the fur blanket for warmth. Sometimes she asked him questions about the gods, reading aloud from the book of myths she'd acquired for her class. Other days, the warmest days, she would sit in the grass outside with his cloak to ward against the chill, her fingers plucking the blades anxiously, and her gaze trained determinedly upon his goats as they grazed beneath his mother's tree.

He did not press her. Nor did he comment upon the changes he observed, for fear of stifling her progress. When she desired his company, he sat with her, reading books of his own, or he would lie beside her in the grass, telling her the true stories of his people, or himself. He confessed his marriage to Sif, his murder of Loki, his father's fury, and what he knew of the life she had spent in the ward, which even with her memory restored she remembered only in broken pieces.

The days she spent in Asgard began to outnumber the days she didn't.

But on earth she struggled. Smiles and laughter faded into grimaces and more often than not, her mind snapped shut again, laced with pain. She attended her classes, but did not linger beyond them, preferring to spend her afternoons and evenings in Asgard and only asking to return when she would begin to doze.

Thor cleaned out one of the hundred bedrooms one day, a month later, while she listened to a lecture on the functions and mapping of the brain—a topic which kept her well distracted, he noticed, for she puzzled over what differences might be responsible for her own powers—and presented her with her own room, that afternoon. A modern bed, glassed in windows which caught the sun, and an armchair beneath, if she wished to read in their light. Eve fingered the heavy down comforter he'd folded neatly at the foot of her new bed and looked up at him, a brightness in her leaf-green eyes that he'd missed these last weeks.

"You did this for me?"

He kept himself in the doorframe with an effort of will, for seeing her gilded with sunlight, and brimming with joy, he wanted nothing more than to show her better uses for her bed beyond sleeping. But it would not do. Whenever their time together shifted toward intimacy, she asked to return home. Not because she did not want him, he knew, but because she worried the wanting was unrelated to love. A selfish thing, born of her own needs. Her own desire to be healed and whole again. She feared she was using him, for though she knew she wanted Asgard, she was not yet certain she wanted him. Thor could have told her otherwise, but it was better if she learned it for herself. He had waited millennia already, another handful of weeks, or even months, made no difference to him, now.

"If you desire to spend so much time in Asgard, it seemed only right that you should have a space of your own in Bilskirnir." He nodded to the bed. "You can sleep here, undisturbed, if you wish it."

She considered the bed again, and Thor swallowed against the absent thought that rose in her mind, of how much more easily they might share it than the bed in her dorm. And then her gaze caught on the table beside it, and Thor smiled, watching the play of emotion as it spilled into her aura. Surprise so intense it bordered upon shock, and then, as her fingers closed upon the ivory bracelet he had left there, wonder and delight. He allowed himself to enter the room, then, and stand at her side. The better to see her face.

"You kept this," she said, looking up. "All this time?"

"It was what I had of you, of our marriage and the life we shared."

"It looks exactly the same," she said, her fingers tracing the vines he had carved and filled with gold so carefully. The blisters had been worth it, to see the way her eyes had lit. A bridal gift fit for a chieftain's daughter. Fit for a goddess.

"As it should," he said. "While it was here, it did not age. And I kept it safe."

"Thor, this is . . ." She shook her head, her gaze falling back to the bracelet, and he smiled. Wordlessly, he took it from her, then slipped it over her hand and onto her wrist.

When she lifted her face, her eyes searching his, he tucked a soft curl behind her ear.

"It is still my gift to you."

She caught his hand, pressing it to her cheek. "Thank you."

He searched her eyes, drinking in this moment. She was his Tora, his Eve in a way she hadn't been in centuries, and this time, he would not make the same mistakes. "So many times, I've wondered what our lives would have been if I had trusted you in that life with my secrets, as you trusted me with yours. I wish I had told you everything. I wish I had truly stolen you away, as you asked, taken you all the way to Asgard when we left that beach. But I was too afraid you would turn from me if you knew me for a god. And I was too selfish to risk the truth, to risk losing you.

"I am so sorry, Eve. If I had known how long we would be parted, how much pain you would suffer between that life and this . . ."

She pressed a finger to his lips, stopping him. "If you had told me then, asked me to follow you to Asgard, I'm not certain that I would have agreed. We would have lost that lifetime together, completely, and I cannot see how we would be standing here, now."

He lowered his head, resting his forehead against hers. She made a soft sound, pleasure and desire mixed together, and her eyes closed. Their noses brushed, her breath against his lips, making him ache, and the scent of sunlight on her skin, of summer and cream, filling his head. He wanted to kiss her. He wanted to do more than kiss her. He wanted to remind her, body and soul, of everything they had shared together, every gift of love they had given to one another.

But he did not dare. She was still so fragile, and when she was ready, when she knew her own mind, she would come to him.

She would ask it of him.

He let his hand fall from beneath hers, rubbing the memory of her skin, rose-petal soft, from his fingertips, and stepped back.

"I should leave you to your reading."

Eve let out a breath, her cheeks flushed and her eyes half-dazed with need, naked and hungry. When she looked at him that way—he clenched his jaw against his own desire and left her, before he changed his mind.

❧

She did not spend that night in Asgard, for she had classes the following morning, but when Friday came, and he went to meet her, as had become his habit, after the finish of her last class of the day, she was filling a canvas bag with clothes enough for the weekend.

"Sorry," she said, absently, as if she had caused him some delay. "I didn't have time to pack earlier."

She had bruises beneath her eyes, betraying sleepless nights, but her mind was more open than usual. Affection and pleasure at the sight of him trickled through. Progress, to be sure, if Elah cared to notice. But it would not be enough to satisfy her. What Elah wanted, what Elah required of her mother, was not something Thor was certain she could give. On earth, Eve was much more miserly with her presence, and he had seen her wince more than once at some parade of students beyond her window. As if the pressure of so many minds and emotions against her own had become painful, salt in an open wound she had not quite managed to heal, even in all the time they had spent in Asgard.

"You mean to stay."

She flushed, tucking a strand of her hair behind her ear, and for the first time, he noticed the ivory bracelet on her wrist. "I wouldn't want you to think I didn't appreciate everything you'd done."

What he would have given to see her thoughts then, fully, but whatever they were, she had hidden them away. She was growing more practiced at keeping them from him, but he could hardly fault her for it. Privacy within one's own mind was rarely overrated, and if she felt it granted her some protection from Elah as well, all the better.

"It's just for the weekend," she admitted, after a moment. "It's easier to think there."

"You could stay longer, if you wished."

She smiled, almost sadly. "If I could come and go with a thought like you, maybe. But traveling by lightning every morning to make it to class doesn't sound all that appealing. Would an alarm clock even work in Asgard?"

He grunted, taking the bag from her shoulder even before she had settled it there. "I've always kept time by the sun."

Eve tilted her head, glancing up at him sidelong as she brushed her hand over the door release. "I shouldn't be surprised, I suppose. It isn't like you had appointments to worry about. But didn't you ever try living as a human? In the more modern world, I mean."

"I walked the earth, certainly." He followed her out of the room, ignoring the curious glances of the other women in the hall. Every day he came, they stared, but the girl, Ashley, had made no mention of Marcus when they met her in passing, and Eve had not had much time or attention for any of the others. A sign she was not well, yet, for it was not like her at all to live apart from the people around her.

But Thor hesitated, watching as one of the girls ducked into the lounge. He'd thought, for a moment, that he'd seen a flash of silver in her eyes—

"What about going to school?" Eve asked.

He shook his head, frowning. "Do you know that girl?

Eve stopped, looking back. "You mean Sophia? She's some friend of Ashley's, but I think she's seeing Marcus now. It's been a relief to come home to a message every other day, just checking in, instead of ten every day, each that much more anxious than the last."

Athena?

The dark haired girl looked up, and now he knew he had not imagined the silver in her eyes. *You're taking an awful risk, Thor. If Elah realizes where her mother keeps disappearing . . .*

Eve has earned her peace.

But in Asgard? Whatever progress you've made, if Eve will only open herself within your halls, what good is it to the world? To Elah? She will think the worst!

"Thor?" Eve's hand on his arm drew his attention back. She rarely touched him freely, most especially on earth. "What's the matter?"

"Nothing," he said, turning away. "Forgive me, I only thought I recognized her."

"From your school days together?" Eve asked, her lips twitching. Her spirits had clearly risen with the prospect of a weekend away, and surely even Athena could feel the difference in her. Elah must recognize it as well. Asgard had done more good than harm, and he would not take it from Eve, now. Not before she was wholly healed.

You can't know that day will ever come, Athena said.

I can choose to believe it will. As I have always believed in Eve.

He forced himself to smile, continuing down the hall at Eve's side. "From days gone by, to be sure."

"Everyone starts to look familiar after a while," Eve agreed. "So no job, then, either?"

He touched a hand to the small of her back, letting her feel his amusement and lowered his head to speak against her ear. "Remind me to show you the treasury, later."

"Spoiled prince," she mumbled, her cheeks flushing again.

He chuckled softly and opened the door for her. "Not so spoiled as all that, I hope."

"Maybe not," she said. "But it was obviously a near thing."

He didn't argue. It pleased him far too much to know she teased him at all, after so long. That she was comfortable enough with him, even here, to do so. It was proof that she was healing, slowly, becoming more and more herself with every passing day. And a weekend in Asgard could only help, even if it only allowed her a full night's rest, without pain, without any discomfort.

No matter what Elah's response might be when she learned of it, if Eve had been made whole, it would be worth it.

CHAPTER SIXTEEN

Adam

It only took a day and a half before he got his first report. Eve had been surprisingly easy to find, once Elah had supplied him with a glimpse of her latest face, her delicate features framed by soft chestnut curls that made him ache. What he wouldn't have given to run his fingers through her hair and pull her close, breathing her in, all sunshine and spring flowers.

He'd passed her description on to his Intelligence people, and sent them off with a warning. Any hint of affection or interest from any operative, and they were to relieve themselves immediately and leave the country. The last thing he wanted to do was create an army of rivals, if by some miracle the time ever came that she wouldn't run in the other direction if she saw him coming.

The odds weren't in his favor judging by the steady stream of information that came across his desk, at least not in this lifetime. But it was reassuring somehow, to hear about her life. So completely ordinary. Boys vying for her affection, classes, working out in the middle of the night, and studying the rest of the time, hidden away in her room. She was obviously avoiding social interactions, particularly with said boys, and the more he read of her habits, the more he began to worry.

She was short tempered and impatient when she should have been kind, asocial when she should have been engaged. Maybe he hadn't lived with her all that long as her husband, but as her brother-in-law in the life before that, they'd been close enough that he could see, even third hand, that something was very wrong.

And then she disappeared altogether. Without a trace of any kind, just up and gone between one breath and the next. She'd been seen entering her building with a man Adam had no doubt was Thor, but she'd never made it to her room, or anywhere else after that until she reappeared late that night as if by magic. Day after day after day, the pattern repeated. His agents would see her in Thor's company, and then she would be gone again, completely untraceable. But she always seemed to come home.

Until one weekend, when she didn't.

If she was with Thor, she was safe. That much, at least, Adam was certain. And probably better off, though it pained him to admit it. Thor had always been better at loving her, and if it had been Thor who'd given her a goddess for a daughter, no one would have been worried about *her* destroying the world. Unmaking the Archangels, perhaps, but no child of Thor's would ever have had the nerve to do any harm to Eve or Eve's world, and unlike Adam, Thor would have had the power to stop her when she tried.

But Elah wouldn't like it. She wanted, maybe even needed Eve to be engaged and involved with the world, and disappearing to Asgard was as close to being exactly the opposite as it got, short of wandering the void. And Asgard was the only place he could think of which would leave Elah just as perplexed about where Eve had gotten off to as it did his spies. The only way in or out for a mortal, or even a not-quite-mortal was through Thor, as far as Adam could tell, and he'd certainly wasted enough time looking, since he had come to power.

Not that he was planning anything nefarious, mind. Just that if there was some bridge into Asgard in the North Country, rainbow or otherwise, it meant access to more land. Fertile land. And Adam needed every last acre he could cultivate. He snorted, imagining the headlines. If they thought sending refugees to Greenland was some kind of trick, they'd positively crucify him over Asgard, no doubt dredging up references to Guantanamo and the like. The rest of the world should be grateful. If Adam truly wanted to make people suffer, he could do far worse than giving them a living wage, fresh food, and comfortable housing.

He had done much, much worse, before people had gotten all up in arms over human rights (Eve's influence of course). A fact which he wasn't proud of, though it had certainly made conquering nations a lot less trouble. It wasn't like the world wouldn't benefit from a good dictator, and with Eve at his side to make sure the power didn't go to his head—

Father?

Adam filed the report with a flick of his finger across the screen. Elah wasn't in the habit of co-opting his eyes, but there was no reason to tempt her. *Yes, darling?*

Are you dreaming of making yourself emperor, next?

He smiled. *Actually, I'm starting to wonder if they wouldn't be better off with someone truly awful rising to power first. Then when I swooped in, all benevolence, they'd appreciate my restraint.*

Elah snorted. *Mother would never approve.*

No, I don't suppose she would.

But it was still a tempting thought. Maybe he could talk Lucifer into commandeering the East through some kind of puppet government. Start in India and work his way outwards, making it all look like a nightmare to the outside observer—it was just the kind of stunt he'd prefer, and he had to be bored by now, sitting on his thumbs for so long on that mountain with Bhagavan. It had only taken Adam five years with Buddha and Bhagavan to realize retirement of that variety didn't suit him at all. Of course, he hadn't had a fiery sword of death hanging over his head if he left, either. Thank the Goddess.

She's hiding from me again.

"The Russian Minister of Agriculture is here, sir," Hilda said, sticking her head in through the door. And she wouldn't have done that much if the man wasn't having some kind of snit or another.

"Thank you. Hold him off for just another moment, would you?" Russia hadn't liked it at all when he'd started exporting grain in quantity, cutting deals for free trade with the North Country if other nations would drop their tariffs on food altogether. It had hurt their pocketbooks. Well, it had hurt his, too, but food prices had been astronomical, and completely unjustified. If Russia wanted to drive up the price of oil, that was one thing, but food was something else altogether. For starters, it had fewer alternatives that didn't include starvation.

"Of course, sir." Hilda withdrew, but he'd only bought himself another five minutes at most. *Thor will find a way to draw her out, Elah. He's been a part of her life for so long, she won't even realize she's been had until it's too late.*

He's furious with me. And if he's told her—

Trust him, Elah. Adam rose from his desk chair and reached for his suit jacket. A casual air wouldn't do him any favors with the Russians. *If there's one thing I know with certainty in this world, it's that Thor will always have Eve's best interests at heart. He won't tell her anything that will cause her more pain. Not if he doesn't have to.*

I'm beginning to fear that Mother's happiness, even her love, if he convinces her to share it, won't be enough.

Adam frowned, his hand hovering over the door release. There was something not quite right in his daughter's tone. A steel behind her words, tempered with anguish and pain. *What do you mean?*

She's sucking the world dry, Elah said, the words broken even in her thoughts. *And even if she opens herself to me tomorrow, lending me all her power, I'm not sure I can fix it. If I had only listened to Michael . . .*

I promise you, Elah, whatever's happened, listening to Michael is never the right choice, Adam said firmly, but the way she'd stopped herself, withdrawing before she completed the thought sent a chill down his spine. *I've got to meet with the Russian Minister, but when I'm done, I'll clear the rest of my day. And then, I'd like it very much if you would tell me everything.*

Elah sent him a whisper of affection. *One of my Host will be waiting for you, when you're through.*

Athena or Raphael, if you would. He did his best to keep his mental tone light, but if she was sending one of her angels to collect him, it was worse than he'd feared. Elah usually came to him, in the rare instances when he saw her at all. *I'd like to speak to them about cultivating Olympus.*

Then he said his farewells to his daughter, and struggled to drag his mind back to the task at hand. Either Russia had to start cooperating—he was honestly still tempted to use Lucifer to apply pressure from the south—or he would have no choice but to orchestrate its fall and subsequent absorption into the North Country. He was growing tired of playing politics while people starved.

And he didn't believe for even a moment that whatever was wrong with the world, Eve was to blame. That she might be the solution made perfect sense, but the cause?

Never.

"Secur—!" Adam strangled Hilda's cry with a thought, though her eyes went wide at the sudden loss of her voice, her hands going to her throat. He smiled at the other secretaries in his outer office, and guided Hilda the rest of the way inside the inner chamber. Athena was sitting at his desk, Raphael staring out the window behind her, his hands clasped lightly behind his back. They both looked like vagabonds, which accounted for Hilda's response, he supposed.

"Why don't you have a seat, Hilda, my love." Adam settled her in a chair and poured her a glass of water. "Nothing at all to be concerned about, I promise you. These are just—friends. Expected friends. I quite forgot to let you know they were coming."

"Surely you're not going to let her remember this fright?" Athena said, her eyes narrowing in a way Adam didn't appreciate.

"Let me handle my secretaries, thank you," he replied coolly. "And the least you could both do next time is dress a bit more decently for the time period. A nice summer dress, Athena, to show off those pale shoulders perhaps? And I can recommend an excellent tailor to our wingless friend. Tweed is not only out of fashion, but utterly ridiculous in this weather."

Athena rolled her eyes. "You asked for us, remember? Why didn't you send her off before you walked in the door?"

"I don't know," he said. "I'm only the leader of the most powerful nation on earth at the moment, I can't imagine how that particular thought slipped my mind. Hilda always comes with me back into the office to take any notes or orders after a meeting. You could have blinded her to your presence once you realized she was at the door, instead of sitting there, in my chair, bold as brass."

"Isn't that the pot calling the kettle black?" Athena asked.

Raphael sighed, rubbing his forehead. "You mentioned something about farming Olympus?"

"Farming Olympus!" Athena's eyes flashed, and she leaned forward. "You presumptuous little—"

Raphael's hand closed on her shoulder, pressing her back into her seat. "Perhaps it would be better if we simply showed him why it's a completely preposterous idea. We have a moment, yet, before Elah will expect you."

Adam searched Raphael's face, but the Archangel didn't meet his eyes. "Yes, I think that would be best."

Raphael stepped out from behind the desk, and extended his hand to Hilda, who hadn't stopped staring. "My dear, forgive me. We've been abominably rude."

The minute she took his hand, her face went blank. "No apology necessary, sir."

"The President would like you to clear his schedule for the rest of the day, if you would be so kind. He isn't to be disturbed for any reason. In fact, you didn't see us at all, but left him quite alone in his office." She nodded and Raphael smiled, squeezing her hand. "Goddess bless you, Hilda. Off you go."

"That was hardly necessary," Adam murmured, watching her leave.

"Nevertheless." Raphael nodded to Athena. "If you would?"

Athena rose, smoothing her gray robe, a perfect match to her eyes. Maybe vagabond had been too harsh, though a Roman *stola* certainly had no place in modern style. "I'd really rather not carry him."

"Then I will," Raphael said. "But you must lead the way."

She sniffed, giving him a hard look. Feathers patterned themselves across her skin, and suddenly, she was staring at him with an owl's eyes, perched on his desk. Raphael went to the window, opening it wide.

"The force field—"

Athena hooted disdainfully and spread her wings, flitting through without so much as a singed feather. Evidently she'd already dismantled it, somehow, or Raphael had. The Archangel looked back at him expectantly.

"You're not going to fly us, are you?"

He offered a withered smile. "Not this time. Though if you insist on provoking her further, I'll be tempted to let you hang from your ankles above the clouds."

Adam snorted, joining him at the window. "It's almost enough to make me miss Thor. I used to think she was the reasonable one."

"Mm." He slid the window shut again. "She took your side, before, against Thor. You can see how that might rub her, now, I'm sure."

If she weren't holding his mistakes against him, he might have been warmed by the knowledge that someone had championed him among the gods. But as it was, he could only grimace. "I can see that there are a great many people who take a personal interest in my private business, in any event."

Raphael laughed. "I think the mistake you make is believing that any of what passed between you and Eve was ever private. Now, come. We've given her time enough to reach Olympus, and she will only grow more cross if we make her wait."

The Archangel took hold of him by the elbow, and the office shimmered, and then faded away. White marble columns took its place a moment later and Adam let out a breath he hadn't realized he'd been holding, rolling his shoulders to release the tension which had taken up residence between them. It was amazing how much less stressful it was to travel when lightning wasn't crackling over his skin.

And then he took in his surroundings. It wasn't just white marble columns, but marble courtyards, and marble buildings. Everything was stone and precious metals, with the exception of a gated garden in the distance, tucked behind what looked like a temple.

"Ah," Adam said, understanding why Raphael had used the word preposterous. But he couldn't quite tear his eyes away from that garden, all the same. A hint of red leaves caught his eye, the color so perfectly beautiful . . . "I suppose it's a good thing I didn't actually mean it when I suggested we might plant here, though it would have been a relief to know it was an option, were times to become desperate."

Athena sidestepped into his line of sight, and he blinked, forcing himself to refocus on her narrowed quicksilver eyes. "Then what exactly did you want with Olympus?"

"Privacy," he said. "And we'd better not linger, or Elah is going to notice my absence here feels similar to Eve's more recent disappearances. I'm sure I don't need to tell you how she's likely to respond if she realizes Thor's swept her mother away to Asgard."

"Poorly," Raphael said, sharing a knowing glance with Athena. "And if She believes for a moment Her mother means to abandon Her—I'm sorry to say, Adam, that even Elah's love for you won't be enough to save your lives. Michael is quite determined, and his argument is distressingly compelling, particularly when he speaks from the other side of Her bed. I wanted to warn you, before you saw Elah. She can't know."

"Thor is a fool if he thinks he can keep it from her for long," Athena said, turning her face away. "And when Elah learns what he's offered, he'll be lucky to escape with his head."

"Wait a moment." Adam held up a hand to slow their exchange. For all the words they'd used, he was alarmingly short on information. A threat to his own life and Eve's from Michael was nothing new, but the rest . . . "What exactly has Thor offered her?"

"Immortality," Raphael said grimly. "With an eternity of peace, besides."

Adam sighed, pinching the bridge of his nose to relieve some of the tension. That Norse oaf was going to be the death of them all. "So much for tempting Lucifer out of hiding. If I ask him for help now, Michael is going to use it as proof that I'm conspiring, too. Didn't Thor consider the consequences of this at all? Never mind if Elah finds out. What if Eve *agrees?* And let's be honest, she'd be a fool not to."

"I can hardly imagine an Eve capable of abandoning a child of her blood, never mind the world," Athena said. "I know she's struggled, but has it really come to that?"

"Yes," Adam said, not an ounce of doubt in his body. And if he thought too hard about it, he was going to be crippled by guilt. If he'd never left Eve, Elah wouldn't have been so determined that they make up, and everything that had followed never would have come to pass. But he had. And it did. And he'd be damned before he stopped trying to fix it. "But Thor can't be so great a fool that he doesn't realize what it will mean if she accepts."

"I will not say it was a ploy, but certainly it is desperate," Ra said. "He hopes still that she will heal, and once she is more herself, she will wish to remain on earth."

"That's an awfully big risk to take," Adam said, his mind buzzing with the possibilities for chaos. "If Michael is already jumping at shadows and he gets wind of this, it's going to be all our heads. You know as well as I do how he's going to twist this. It's going to become a kidnapping at the least. Thor stealing Eve for the sole purpose of weakening Elah. A violation of the Covenant, and a rallying cry for the expulsion of the rest of us. Well. Expulsion for Athena and Bhagavan. I'm more likely to face an unmaking. It's going to be a mess."

"Worse than that, I'm afraid," Ra said. "As weakened as the world has become, if Elah chooses this war, there is no guarantee at all that She will win."

CHAPTER SEVENTEEN

Eve, Before

They were the most difficult two years of her existence, and every moment so precious, so bittersweet.

Elah was beautiful. So utterly perfect, Eve lost hours to staring. And by her second birthday, she was the size of a girl twice her age, with the understanding of a child even older still. Eve and Raphael took her for walks together, Elah between them, holding tight to both their hands. Birds followed them, flitting from branch to branch over their heads, and rabbits and squirrels came out of their burrows to watch them pass. Elah had taught them friendship with Eve's guidance, and the way she played with the wolves was so reminiscent of the lions Eve herself had once tamed, she couldn't bring herself to tell her no.

"Just like her mother," Raphael said, when a female and two cubs came barreling out of the woods, and Elah threw herself into the fray, squealing with delight as they licked and mouthed and rolled in the mulch.

"Not entirely," Eve said. "I tamed the lions out of self-defense more than the joy of their companionship. Elah just wants a friend."

"Then perhaps you ought to give her one," he said. "She needs to know humanity, too."

Eve sighed, watching her daughter growl and pretend to bite, just as the wolves did. "I can't ask it of them. How could I face a mother, after, if Elah loses her temper and breaks the girl's mind?"

"She hasn't broken the wolves, why should she hurt a child?"

"What child would be a match for her? An eight year old won't have any interest in playing with a baby, and a four year old won't be able to keep up."

"Perhaps a six year old, then," Raphael suggested, always so infernally reasonable. "But would you have her go to Michael without learning that lesson? Without teaching her real friendship? When she is Goddess, her people will reach for her, and she must know how to love them in return."

"Love is love, Archangel. The who and the what aren't nearly as important as the loving itself. That's the lesson that matters most."

He smiled, slanting her a knowing glance. "And how will you know she's learned it, unless you let her test herself against those less easily persuaded? Until she has been hurt, and forgiven it, and turned her heart to love again?"

She said nothing, thinking of Adam, and the wound he'd left that hadn't yet healed. How could she teach her daughter what she wasn't able to do herself?

"She's asked me about him, you know," Raphael said gently. "I told her it wasn't my place to speak of it, but she has the right to know, and were it me, I would set the truth before her now, before she goes to Michael. I would not want her to learn of her father from him."

"No," Eve agreed. "But I'm not sure the story I might tell her will be so different, now. I'm still angry, Raphael. With him. With all of this. It isn't how it should have been—it isn't what she deserved from us."

"But it is what she has been given, and she hardly suffers for it."

"Only because you're here, helping me."

"Because you've devoted yourself to her completely, Eve. Nothing less."

And in a way, that had been Adam's doing, she supposed. He hadn't left her without the support of material wealth, at least. Freedom from the hand-to-mouth existence she'd been living, working in that tobacco shop, safety and security in this little cottage among her Lions, where he knew she would be most comfortable, and money enough to live on for lifetimes, and Eve didn't feel any guilt about making use of it.

But she would have rather had him beside her, and been poor. She would have rather been able to show Elah how to love by example, with her father. Maybe Adam would have made mistakes, the same as she did, but he should have tried. For her sake, for Elah's sake, he should have tried!

"Hm," Raphael said, watching her. "Why don't you have dinner with your Lions tonight, my dear? Spend some time with your family. I'll take care of our little goddess."

She shook her head. "Every day now is borrowed. I don't want to lose any of the time I have left."

"Better for her if you spend an evening away, and clear some of the bitterness from your mind before you return."

He was right, of course. Raphael was always, infernally, right.

But maybe, just maybe, she could do both.

Elah almost disappeared in the pasture, the grass grown so high only the top of her dark head was visible, with flashes of rainbow-black braids flopping as she ran.

"You'll frighten the goats," Eve called, laughing. And then the trip of them lifted their heads all at once, square eyes seeming to widen at the sight of a child careening toward them. A heartbeat later, they broke, as if Elah were the cue ball, struck right into the rack, and the goats scattered like so many balls toward the corner pockets of the field.

"They weren't afraid at all until you startled them," Elah said, bouncing back toward her. "Do you suppose they'll forgive us?"

Ryam and his wife still lived at the manor with their oldest son and his family, tending the grapes. The children cared for the goats, milking them and learning to turn the milk into cheese and butter and soap under their grandmother's eye. Eve had helped, once or twice, telling the children stories while they worked.

"I'm sure they'll have forgotten by the time we're done, and we could come to visit them again, another time. But you must be on your best behavior, Elah. You remember what I taught you about using your voice, not your thoughts."

"Are they really all my family?" Elah asked, latching on to her hand.

"The whole world is filled with your family, sweetheart." Eve squeezed her small fingers. "But yes, the people you'll meet tonight are especially mine, and that makes them especially yours, too. Ryam's grandfather was my son, Alexandre, and Alexandre was your brother."

"Did Alexandre go to live with Grandfather, too?"

It had seemed the best way to explain what was coming, to tell her that her Grandfather had invited her to live with Him, and better to get her used to the idea of going away before the time came. "Not until he was much, much older."

"Then why do I have to go so soon?"

Eve swung her daughter up into her arms, and hugged her. "There are things you need to learn that only your grandfather can teach you, and He's looking forward to having you stay with Him so very much."

"But why can't he come *here* to visit *me*, instead?" Elah asked, her lower lip jutting out in the slightest of pouts.

"Because He's very old, and very tired," Eve said, kissing her nose. "Too old to come this far, and where would He sleep? There aren't any more beds in the cottage."

Elah sighed, a perfect mimicry of Eve's own. "I suppose."

"I'll only be a thought away, love."

"But what if Grandfather says to be on my best behavior, too? What if I'm not allowed to use my thoughts?"

"While you're with your grandfather, you can *always* reach for me. Best behavior or not. How does that sound?"

"Promise?"

"I promise," Eve said. "And if anyone says otherwise, you tell them I said so."

"*Madame!*" It was Ryam, come out to meet them at the gate, smiling. "And who is this?"

"Ryam, this is Elah," Eve said carefully. "My daughter."

Ryam's smile froze, his gaze searching Elah's face. Elah searched back, one hand curling into Eve's hair.

"*Déesse?*" he breathed.

Eve raised her chin, daring him to object, but Ryam only gave a quick headshake, as if in answer to himself, and offered them both a bow.

"*Madame, Mademoiselle*, we are honored."

"*Tout le plaisir est pour moi*," Elah said.

Ryam thawed at her French, so perfectly formal, and took her hand, pressing a kiss to her fingers. "It is our pleasure, as well, *mademoiselle*. If you would come with me, both of you, dinner is nearly ready and Marie will be relieved to know you've arrived in time. She was beginning to fear that the wolves had found you."

"The wolves came to play with me this morning," Elah said. "But I sent them home. Mama always reminds me to keep them from the goats."

"Indeed," Ryam said, giving her a sidelong glance as they walked down the hill from the pasture. "Then we are in your debt, *mademoiselle*! As near as they have been to the pasture, we were certain it was only a matter of time before we lost one. But you must know that your mother raised us among lions, once. In the first days after Creation."

Elah's eyes went wide. "Lions lived here?"

"A very, very long time ago," Eve said. "Before there were quite so many people."

"But it is from those lions that the House of Lions takes its name," Ryam said, warming to his audience. It was always the first story told, never forgotten. Told to every child from the moment they were old enough to listen. "When we were smaller than you, Eve used to leave us with the lionesses and their cubs while she planted and cooked, and we would all play together, never knowing it was strange . . ."

Eve allowed herself to relax into the story and the comfort of being among her family. She wasn't sure, now, why she had ever doubted them, and even if there weren't any children her age, at least Elah could make a few friends among men. And Raphael was right, she needed to be tested. She needed the opportunity to prove what she'd been taught.

Maybe Marie knew of some likely boys and girls in the village.

If Elah could be trusted to behave.

And what power did Eve have, truly, to stop her if she didn't?

CHAPTER EIGHTEEN

Adam, Later

"Daddy!" Elah smiled, the whole hall lighting with her joy. The branches had physically parted over their heads, allowing sunlight to spill into the hall. She ran to him, and for that moment, when Adam caught her up in his arms, she was just a child, the little girl he hadn't had the chance to know.

He tossed her up in the air, and she squealed in delight, clinging to him when he caught her again. "How's my girl?"

"It's so good to see you." She hugged him tightly, and when she pulled back, she was an adult again, with rainbow-black hair and perfect hazel eyes, shifting from brown, to green, to blue again, depending on the light. "Why does it always have to be so long?"

"I'm always available to you, darling. You know that."

She took his hands, pulling him toward a group of roots which hastily rearranged themselves into a wide bench, perfectly contoured to cradle them both. "Did you have any luck in Olympus?"

Adam shook his head, burying the memories of his visit there along with his responses to everything he'd learned. He was eager to return home, to set things in order before he departed again. Because he had to reach Eve, and the sooner the better.

"I'm afraid the Olympians like their marble a bit too much, and Athena assures me that what ground lies beneath is hardly fit for farming, all scrub and rubble. Asgard is something else, though, from what I remember. I'll have to speak to Thor."

"He's likely to be in a foul temper," Elah said glumly. "I'm only glad Michael wasn't here, or I would still be growing the Redwoods back together."

Adam smiled, though mention of Michael twisted his stomach. He'd been hoping for some time that Elah would have sense enough to send the Archangel from her bed, but when she spoke of him, there was still affection and warmth in her eyes. How she could have settled for Michael of all the creatures on God's green earth, he would never understand, and he'd overlooked it long enough. Michael was a danger to them all, now. Far more so than Thor had ever been. "If he's made any progress with Eve, I'm certain his temper has improved with it. He was always tied to her."

"Yes." Elah frowned. "Too closely for the ease of my mind. I cannot think what passes between them that she guards herself from me so completely. But I fear . . ." She made a soft noise in her throat and shrugged. "It hardly matters, I suppose."

He took his daughter's hand, pouring encouragement through the contact. "It matters, darling. Tell me what's happened."

She drooped, and the branches above them rustled back together into a vaulting ceiling, blocking the sun. "She's turned from me completely. From all of us. So far that she would work against me."

"You can't believe that Eve would do anything to harm the world," he said gently. "Not after she went through so much effort to save it."

"My Host can explain the barren lands no other way, and nor can I. I tried at the very beginning, you know. I let it rain on the desert for forty days, and there was nothing. No sign of life, no skittering of any creature across the sands. The water sank into the ground as quickly as it fell, and still it was bone dry. There's nothing left, and I can't revive what's dead. Not without Mother's power, and more and more, she keeps me away. These last weeks, it's only grown worse. I can't reach her at all for stretches of the day. If she would only open herself to me willingly, so much could be avoided, but I cannot wait much longer, Father. I dare not."

He pressed his lips together, his gaze flicking to the Host, floating above them. "It seems odd to me that Eve could have so much control over something and never know it of herself."

The branches of the Redwoods parted and a white-winged angel dropped through in a blaze of light. Sun and fire and Adam narrowed his eyes against them both, studying Michael as he landed lightly on the mulch before them.

"My lady." He bowed, his expression perfectly composed into regal, terrible beauty. "Had I known your father would be here, I would have come sooner. You should not be alone with any of the others. It is too great a risk after Thor's threats."

Adam laughed. "Thor blusters, nothing more."

"Any god who draws a weapon in the Redwood Hall does more than bluster," Michael said, his voice sharp.

"And what good would it do Thor to bring harm to Eve's daughter?" Adam asked.

"What indeed?" Michael's lip curled. "Perhaps you'd like to tell us, for I'm certain if there is any plot against the Goddess, you are part of it."

Adam laughed again, but he was the only one in the hall who did. "Are you insane, Archangel? Elah, you can't honestly believe this. That anyone is plotting against you. The Covenant binds the gods that are left, and even if it didn't, you're more powerful than the rest of them put together, now."

"I should be," she said quietly, not meeting his eyes. "And perhaps if Mother had not kept to herself what is mine, I would be yet. But as the lands grow more barren, my power wanes."

"Eve can't drain your power." Adam squeezed her hand, willing her to look at him, to see the truth in his eyes. "If she were at all capable of something like that, she'd have done it to me the first time I made a pest of myself. Or the second. Or the third."

"And risk her own life?" Michael scoffed. "She's too closely bound to you to dare."

"It's got to be something else. A god who dug in like a tick during the Purge, hidden too well to be found, or some parting gift from Odin for the theft of his son's loyalties." He ignored the angel, not even bothering to look at him while he spoke. Michael's rhetoric had always been malicious, and it wasn't his opinion which mattered. Not truly. "Elah, you're her daughter. If something is draining your power, it isn't her. She wouldn't do this. She would never sabotage you knowingly. Even unknowingly, I find it difficult to believe. Her power lies in love and grace. She was made to care for God's people."

"And it is through her body that humanity is renewed," Michael said. Elah looked away altogether. As if she believed every word, but couldn't bear to see Adam's disappointment. "The same renewal which has halted throughout the barren lands. If it is not her alone, it is still through her that this is done."

"This is—it's preposterous!" Adam launched himself to his feet, too frustrated to sit still any longer. Even warned by Raphael, he couldn't stand listening to it. *Elah, darling, please,* he begged. *Listen to what I'm saying.* "How would it benefit anyone to create these barren lands to begin with? The gods need living worlds. We need a living world. And if it's so bad you don't think you can stop it, what hope do any of the rest of us have?"

"As long as you and Eve live, there's hope," Michael said, and never had Adam heard the word hope used with such accusation. "Another godchild to steal Elah's throne and remake the world in your image."

"I already have the world," Adam snapped. "Sitting in the palm of my hand, with the blessing of my daughter. And when have I ever so much as hesitated when Elah had need of me? When have I done anything in the last century to risk her? I sacrificed my *wife* for this world, for Elah's sake!"

Michael only lifted his chin, a cold smile playing across his lips. "Is that not reason enough to resent her? To wish for a second chance to prove yourself?"

Adam's hands closed into fists, but if he struck at him now, if he advanced even one step, Michael would take it for an excuse to draw his sword, and none of it would matter for much longer. What he'd done in the North Country would unravel overnight after his death, food prices would soar again and half the world would starve, assuming, of course, that the world didn't burn in some unholy war between the gods first. And Eve . . . There was no telling what it would mean for her, but he didn't think she would escape for long, no matter how disconnected she was from the world.

He made himself laugh, and opened his hands, holding them up, palm out, all innocence. A misunderstanding, that was all. Because it was all a big joke. But he'd never thought he'd have to use a politician's tricks in the Redwood Hall. He never thought a day would come when Elah would listen to the ravings of her sword-arm over her own father, regardless of any carnal pleasures the former might have provided. "If Eve and I were plotting against anyone, I can promise you one thing, Michael."

The Archangel's eyes glinted. "Oh?"

Adam bared his teeth. "It wouldn't be Elah." *That isn't how love works, Elah. You know that, even if he doesn't.*

Do I? she asked. *I'm not so sure anymore, Father. I'm not certain that Mother feels anything for me, anymore.*

Don't doubt it for a moment, he said fiercely. Now wasn't the time for accusations, even if he was sorely tempted by more than a few. Elah had made this bed, and now she resented sleeping in it. But he wasn't going to stand by and let blame fall on Eve's head for the results. *She's just hurting now, that's all. You'll see.* He leaned down to kiss his daughter's cheek. *A little more time, that's all I ask of you. If you fear you can't trust Evey, at least trust me.*

Elah searched his face, but though she brushed her mind across the surface of his thoughts, she didn't dig any deeper. A show of faith, all things considered, and he was grateful to know she hadn't given up on him completely. At least not yet.

"When you're ready to talk to me, darling girl, just the two of us, you let me know," he told her, pressing his forehead to hers. "And in the meantime, I'll see what I can do to find out what's really going on, all right?"

"Father," she caught his hand as he pulled back, her hazel eyes swimming. "I don't want to lose you, too."

He forced himself to smile, to keep his expression light and ignore the itch between his shoulder blades where Michael glared at his back. If he drew that sword now, Elah would unmake him, and that would be one problem solved. But it was too much to hope for, really.

"Sweetheart, I'm not going anywhere you can't find me. Just make sure you keep your guard dog on his leash, hm?" Michael hissed behind him, and Adam winked. "He sounds like he's getting a little bit rabid in his old age."

He snapped his fingers at some golden-winged angel above him for a lift back home. The way Michael was watching him, he couldn't risk showing any coziness with Raphael or Athena. He didn't dare give the Archangel anything to go on at all.

⁂

"Hilda, my dear," Adam said into the intercom, once the angel had dropped him back in his office. Rather more literally than he'd liked, to be honest. He'd nearly turned his ankle. "Plan me a trip to the Free West, if you would. I'm leaving tomorrow."

And tonight, he was going to get nice and drunk.

Because if the world was dying, he wasn't going to have time for it later.

CHAPTER NINETEEN

Eve

The bed was much too large, and much too empty. Eve stared at the pillow beside her own, pale blue and faintly glowing in the moonlight. She should have been able to sleep. It should have been the best sleep she'd had in weeks, without the buzz of billions of minds, and the hungry ache in the pit of her stomach.

But the quiet only made the small presences in Asgard all the louder. The sleepy murmur of the goats, content in their stalls, the sound of the lonely horse, galloping beneath the stars for the joy of running, and Thor—not in his room where she'd expected him to be, but outside, with his mother's tree. The two presences so similar, so intertwined, so brightly lit in the back of her mind. And love, crashing over her in wave after wave of peace. She was suspended in its heart, in his heart.

He was open to her, as he always was. She knew it from the pulse of his affection, rising on the tide. But he wasn't beside her, either, and she was alone in her too-large, too-empty bed. She touched the extra pillow, imagining him there, and her gaze caught on the ivory bracelet, cool against her skin.

He'd saved it, all this time. Treasured it, protected it. As he'd treasured and protected her, she knew. From Moses on.

And when she was in Asgard, it was so easy. So simple to fall into the ocean of his affection, of the peace of this place, and float away.

Everything was easier in Asgard. But on earth, it was different. It was hollow gestures and awkward conversation. On earth, she felt like a stranger, even in her own mind, and all she wanted was to leave again. To leave with him, and never come back. So why was she in Asgard, and still alone?

Eve swung her legs out of the bed, and rose, taking up Thor's cloak against the chill. The stone beneath her feet had given up what heat it had absorbed long ago, and her toes froze before she'd made it out of her room.

Slippers, she promised herself. The next time she came, she would bring slippers. And a proper robe, so she wasn't dragging Thor's cloak and wearing through the bottom hem of the heavy wool.

The hallway was slightly warmer, insulated by bedrooms on both sides, with thick wood doors blocking the drafts. But when the corridor opened into the feasting hall, cavernous and unheated, with unglassed windows and shutters open wide, she almost turned back. Would have, if she hadn't heard his laughter in her thoughts, warm and teasing and goading her on.

She pulled the cloak tighter around her body, and pushed the massive oak door open, skipping quickly off the near-frozen slate path outside and into the grass, though she wasn't entirely certain it helped her poor, cold toes. At least the brisk walk warmed her core, if nothing else, and she found herself slowing as she approached the small garden surrounding Yggdrasil, then hesitating at the point where she had no choice but to cross the path.

Thor was standing, head bent, beneath the canopy of the tree, bare from the waist up, and a mug of something steaming in his hand. And even though he'd urged her on, now that she'd found him, she almost felt as though she was interrupting something . . . sacred.

He reached out, pressing his free hand to the trunk, palm flat. As if bestowing a blessing, or maybe something else. Maybe receiving one, instead. Then his hand dropped away and he lifted his head. "You never did care to sleep alone."

"What's your excuse?"

He turned, his lips curving. "I hadn't realized how difficult it would be to listen to you toss and turn, so I came out here. Like a child reminded to say his prayers before bed, I suppose. I like to think she's listening, somehow. That some part of her still lives here, if nowhere else."

In the moonlight, when he talked this way, the similarities to her own tree didn't seem so upsetting anymore. Maybe it looked the same, but it didn't feel it. Eve picked her way through the garden beds to avoid the cold stone walk, conscious of Thor's gaze, and the laughter he didn't allow to break from his lips.

When she reached him under the tree, he was grinning, and she hastily tugged the bottom hem of the cloak beneath her feet, not quite suppressing a shiver. Now that she was still, a chill was sinking through the wool to her skin. She eyed the bench which curved a quarter of the way around the thick trunk, but it was marble, and she'd only trade the cold earth beneath her feet for the cold rock against her backside.

"Here." He held out the mug, and she eyed it dubiously. Taking her hand out from beneath the cloak seemed like an imprudent choice, all things considered. And then he did laugh. "It will warm you," he urged. "And I have need of both hands for a moment."

She took the mug, holding it close against her body and letting the steam tickle her chin. It *was* warm, and smelled honey-sweet. A sip confirmed that it was mead, and not the kind that came from someone adding extra honey to white wine, either, which was so common, now. Honey was so expensive, and bees were so hard to keep alive.

"It's strong," Thor warned, nodding to the mug.

"All the better to warm me, then." She smiled over the rim.

"I can think of other ways." He bent, running his hands over the stone bench. Lightning sparked and then settled into a soft glow beneath his palms. The marble cracked quietly, like cereal meeting cold milk.

"What are you doing?"

"Turning thought into deed," he said, letting the lightning fizzle out. He took the mead from her hands and gestured to the bench. "Sit."

When he'd mentioned other ways, she'd been hoping for something a bit more hands on. He wouldn't though. Not until she asked explicitly for more. She tried not to show her disappointment, until her fingers touched the stone, and she realized how warm it was, regardless of the cool night breeze.

"Oh!" She sat, her back against the rough bark of the tree, and drew her legs up. The warm stone under her toes was divine, and she sighed, some of her tension easing with the heat. "That's wonderful."

He chuckled, passing her the mead again, and standing so near she could feel the warmth from his body against her cheek. "Lightning has its uses."

"Is that how you heat your water as well?" Another sip of the mead warmed her insides pleasantly, even as her body began to defrost from the outside.

He shrugged, bracing one long arm against the trunk beside her. "Sometimes a warm rain is enough. But to boil water, lightning is faster."

She let her shoulder brush against his naked torso, and tipped her head back against the trunk, all the better to see his face in the sprinkles of moonlight that reached them beneath the canopy. He wasn't ruddy, the way the myths would have described him, but she could well imagine that he might have been, once upon a time, on a world of ice and snow. Centuries upon centuries in a new world, under a new sun, even his fair skin had learned to take a tan. She cradled the mead to her chest and drank him in, instead.

"Does this mean you're not afraid of Yggdrasil, any longer?"

She laughed, feeling so light, so alive. "You can't blame me for being alarmed. All this time later, and I'm facing the tree that started it all. My sins come back to haunt me in a place I was hoping might offer some kind of sanctuary."

"Has it been?" he asked, voice low and earnest.

"More than I ever could have hoped for. This tree—it's like it knows me. An old friend, taking me in until I can get back on my feet again and find a place of my own." She stared up into the branches, considering the flavor of it all, so familiar, so right. "It's Elohim's voice in my ear, alive and beckoning. Telling me to breathe as He drew me forth from the void. I'm so far from everything I'm meant to love, to be part of, but I feel closer to my father here than I ever have, in all my lives."

She shifted her gaze to his face, suddenly self-conscious. She was rambling on, and she wasn't even sure she was making sense. "I'm sorry. I know this tree is everything you have of your mother. Is that strange to you? That I might feel Elohim, here, too?"

But he shook his head, his expression betraying nothing worse than bemusement. "The earth and stone beneath your feet is part of Elohim's creation. Maybe a piece of his power resides here as well, given strength by my mother's tree, fed by its fruit the way everything else in Asgard has always been."

"I'd like to believe that, I think. To believe there's a place where Elohim's spirit still exists."

He made a low sound, deep in his throat. Not quite agreement, but acceptance, or consideration. "Do you remember that day on the beach? When you told me you had no god, but you wished you could have faith. Wished you could feel the touch of something greater and know yourself safe within its power."

Eve closed her eyes, sinking into the simple pleasure of his presence, the touch of his mind where it had lingered for so long. She'd never recognized it for what it was, never realized it was him, but she remembered the reassurance of it, the swells of love and support, of promise, that whatever troubles her life brought, she would surmount them, and even if in any one life, she was not granted peace, it waited for her.

"I could not give you everything you deserved as a husband, then," Thor said. "But when I heard those words from your lips, I promised myself, if nothing else, I would give you that much."

"You're wrong." She let out a breath, opening her eyes and meeting his. "When you were my husband, you gave me everything. You spoiled me so completely with love. With joy." She bumped her shoulder against his body, his bare skin still warm enough that she could feel it through the cloak. All she wanted was to fit herself against the furnace of his body and let him warm her, head to toe. Maybe give back just a measure of the comfort he had given her, all this time.

And then she laughed at the absurdity of it all. How warm he was. How warm he had always been, and how he was standing in the cold, now, showing not even the slightest concern, or the smallest of goosebumps."When I think of all the days I spent hauling water from the stream to the hut and heating cauldrons of it for you to scrub the blood and dirt of the hunt from your body . . ."

He grinned, his eyes filled with so much affection, and his love lapping at her memories. "And how many times did I tell you I would bathe in the sea just as happily?"

"And then come out frigid, with ice in your hair," she said, leaning toward him. His hip against the right side of her body was a nice complement to the warm marble beneath her. "I wanted you to warm my bed, not refrigerate it."

"And now?" he asked, his voice low.

She turned her face away, looking out over the garden. The lonely horse slept just on the other side of the tree, head drooping and a hind leg cocked. His dappled hide was silver under the stars.

"I love you," she said into the night.

He brushed a strand of her hair behind her ear, his finger tracing the shape of her earlobe, then trailing down the column of her neck, warming her far more effectively than the mead or the heated bench, and sending another shiver down her spine. She leaned into his touch, into his body and his warmth, and closed her eyes, soaking in the surge of his love, his joy. It was everything she remembered. "When I'm here, I can't help but love you," she said. "But when I leave, when I'm on earth . . ."

"You're here, now," he said. "We're both here, now, and you need not sleep alone, Eve. Here, or there. You know I will hold you to nothing more, if sleep and warmth is all that you desire. I would rather wait until you are as certain of me as I am of you."

"You'd never fit in my bed," she said, to avoid responding to the rest. It was easier to imagine his feet dangling off the end of the mattress in her little dorm room. He barely fit in the room itself, ducking to make it through the door, as it was.

He lifted her up, just like that. One minute, she was sitting, and the next she was in his arms, clutching at his shoulders with one hand and desperately trying not to spill his mead with the other.

"Fortunate then, that there is more than enough room for you in mine."

She laughed, and wrapped her arm around his neck, mead and all, burying her face in the curve of his neck and breathing in the spice of lightning and storms and stone, and by all that was holy and right in this world, it felt so much like home.

He felt like home.

And it was just as he promised. Warmth and the comfort of his arms wrapped around her, her head upon his shoulder, and the eternal patience of a god who knew those small quiet moments of soul-deep peace with the person you loved were often far more important than fleeting pleasures of the body.

She had not slept so well in centuries.

§

Thor delivered her back to her dorm Saturday night, though how he knew where to rematerialize without causing a scene, Eve still hadn't quite figured out. She needed warmer clothes, and he needed groceries desperately, and there were a few other supplies Eve had in mind if she was going to be spending the majority of her time in the Dark Ages, technologically.

"Ugh." Eve swayed when the lightning evaporated, pressing a hand to her forehead. Her stomach had flipped unpleasantly when her feet had touched the ground. "I'm not sure I'll ever get used to that."

"I can carry you, if you'd like," he offered.

She shook her head, frowning. "No. I'm—do you smell that? Like scorched earth, almost. Or burning rubber?"

Thor sniffed, his gaze shifting into the distance, and she wondered just how much he *could* smell. If he was a god of the storm, could he taste the wind? Draw scents from around the globe on a whim? But he shook his head after a moment and refocused on her. Lines of concern fanned out from the corners of his eyes, and she could feel it, too, like a soft touch in the back of her mind.

"Perhaps you ought not to travel for a few days, to give yourself time to recover."

She wrinkled her nose. "I'd rather not."

How he didn't smell it, she wasn't sure. Maybe long association with lightning-scorch. Her stomach lurched again, and she frowned. It could have been the blue spinach he'd served her. She probably shouldn't have tried eating it at all, but he'd been so apologetic about the lack of hospitality—which he'd clearly meant in the oldest way possible. Food and drink befitting of a guest, as well as a room and a bed.

"It would be a simple thing to replace the bed in your small room with the one you scorned in Asgard," he teased, holding the door for her as they entered the building.

She stopped at the top of the stairs, and Thor opened the door to her hallway, still watching her expectantly for a light-hearted response she couldn't give. It felt so long ago. She felt so, so different now. And not all to the better.

"Something isn't right," she said as she moved down the hall.

"It could be you're simply readjusting to being back within the grip of time."

"Would that make me feel . . ." But she didn't have a word. Queasiness, to be sure, and something else. Something that reminded her oddly of cinderblocks and artificial lighting. She shook her head. It was like the moment before her migraines, when she could feel it coming, but the pain hadn't started yet. She pushed it away, shoved it back down. Nothing was tinted green. Not yet. "Maybe I'll turn the second greenhouse into a vegetable garden."

Thor grimaced. "The blue spinach?"

"I don't know." She touched her palm to the door panel, and it quirked at her. "That isn't right, either."

"Modern conveniences," Thor said drolly. "I can't imagine why they did away with key locks."

"Too easy to jimmy, I guess." She pressed her hand to the reader again. "Pretty please," she begged it. "I really just want my clothes, that's all. Maybe my books, too."

The door hissed open, and Eve let out a breath of relief. The last thing she wanted to have to do was hunt down the building manager for the override.

"Why don't you go ahead and get groceries," she said, touching her hand to the sensor to keep the door from closing before she got inside. The less time she spent here, the better she'd feel, and the way she was feeling now, she was beginning to rethink her decision about spending her nights there classes or no classes. "I don't want to linger any longer than I have to."

But Thor was staring into her room, his eyes flashing blue-white. A shiver went down her spine, and Eve turned.

Adam.

Sitting on her sofa, arms spread wide across the back, and legs stretched out in front of him, as if he hadn't a care in the world. He smiled, lifting one hand palm out and wiggling his fingers. "Twins, remember?"

"You can't just—" But he had. He had, and the damnable door had let him right in. Apparently genetic perfection read the same to the biometrics whether it came in male or female. Just looking at him was a punch in the gut. That smile. She closed her eyes and clenched her jaw. No wonder she'd felt off. He'd been sitting here, waiting for her. "What are you doing here?"

"Leaving," Thor growled. "That's what he's doing."

"Now, now," Adam said. "Is that how you welcome foreign dignitaries in Asgard? By throwing them out? A prince should know better, I'd think."

Eve's eyes narrowed. "Is that really how you want to start this conversation?"

But Adam's gaze was still on Thor. "If you can't control your temper, perhaps you'd better go do that shopping instead. You're already in enough trouble with our Goddess, and there's only so much I can hide from Elah."

"If you touch so much as a hair on her head without her explicit consent . . ."

"I couldn't if I wanted to," Adam assured him. "Eve is twice as powerful as I am on my best days. Even more than that, if Elah and Michael are to be believed."

Thor's jaw worked, another growl building, or maybe that was the roll of thunder in the distance. He dropped his gaze to Eve. "I won't go if you don't wish me to."

Adam cocked his head, listening. "You know Elah hates it when you fool with the weather patterns. Especially now when things are balanced on a knife point as it is."

"Maybe you'd better go," Eve said, though she hated to admit it. If just being in the same room with Adam put him this on edge, listening to Adam go on in his smarmy politicians' way was bound to cause an even larger problem. And she couldn't help but notice that *Mjölnir* had fitted itself into Thor's fist. "I can handle myself, and him, if I have to."

"You need only reach for me, and I'll return at once," Thor promised.

She nodded, but kept her eyes on Adam. His jaw tightened at the lightning flash of Thor's departure, his gaze skittering away. The only uneasiness he'd ever shown about anything, and it gave her a certain amount of pleasure to see it, now.

Eve stepped into her room and let the door shut behind her, determined to ignore the way Adam's expression had warmed now that they were alone.

"It's good to see you, Evey. All the rest aside."

She couldn't say the same. "I'm just here to pack some things and then I'm leaving again, so whatever you've come for, you'd better make it fast."

He sighed, his eyes following her as she tugged her suitcase out from beneath the bed. "You can't leave, Evey. With him."

She froze, just for a moment, and then flipped open her bag with renewed determination. Adam had given up any right he had to tell her what to do when he'd walked out on her after Elah's birth. Period. "I'm not sure why you think I need your permission."

"Not mine," Adam said. "But Elah's, certainly. And he most assuredly doesn't have her blessing to steal you away. Whatever he's offered you, whatever promises he's made about your freedom, they come at the expense of the world."

"And I'm just supposed to trust you." But her stomach twisted, anyway. Elah had sent Thor to seduce her. That's what he'd said, however long ago. To make her love again, even if it meant giving up on her reconciliation with Adam. Elah wouldn't have, hard as she'd fought for it, if it hadn't been necessary, somehow. Eve knew better than anyone just how far her daughter would have gone to see them reunited again. In love. She didn't like to dwell on it, and in fact, part of her wanted to believe that Thor's arrival had been some—some gesture of apology. But of course that wasn't true. If Elah had been going to apologize, she would have done it years ago.

"If you would let yourself feel anything, you'd know the truth of it for yourself. How you've ignored it this long, I don't even begin to understand." He clamped his mouth shut and leaned forward, elbows resting on his knees. "Evey, if it weren't serious, I wouldn't be here. You know that."

"No," she agreed. "You're much too busy trying to make yourself King of the Universe all over again. If you've gotten in over your head, I'm sorry, but I'm not cleaning up your mess."

He rubbed his face, digging the heels of his hands into his eyes. "This isn't about that. And if anything, it's the other way around, now. Everything I'm doing is cleaning up the mess you've made, cutting yourself off from us."

"By turning refugees into indentured servants! That's what you call cleaning up?"

He rocked back as if she'd slapped him. "For the record, I'm not shipping people off as indentured servants or slaves anywhere, or abusing anyone, least of all my constituents," he said coldly. "I don't have time to give you a tour to prove otherwise right now, but I promise you, you'll have one before we're through, if you can tolerate my presence long enough to actually see what I've done. I'm trying to *feed* people, which is more than you're doing to help anything, last time I checked."

"You have no right to judge me, Adam. Not now, not ever." She threw sweaters into her suitcase, sending it skidding across the tile. "And I won't sit here and listen to any kind of lecture on responsibility from you, of all people."

"Look," he said, the word half growled between clenched teeth. He unclenched his jaw with a visible effort. "If it were just me suffering, that would be one thing. You deserve whatever happiness you can find, at my expense or otherwise. But doing this to your daughter? She thinks you're sucking the world dry to spite her, Evey!"

"Why in Creation would I be doing anything of the sort?" she demanded. Oh, she'd been angry with Elah, that was true enough, even furious at times, but she'd recognized the futility of it a long time ago.

Adam let out a breath, his whole body drooping with a relief that was frankly insulting. "I knew it couldn't have been you, or at least certainly not maliciously." And then he grimaced. "Of course that doesn't get us any closer to the answer, really. And if we don't find one, Michael's theories will still hold sway, and we'll both be dead."

"What are you talking about?" Eve asked, looking up from her sock drawer. "Honestly, Adam. You're not making any sense. Elah is sworn to protect Creation, she'd never let Michael hurt us—we're part of it. Part of what Elohim made, and even if she and I don't agree about a lot of things, we're her parents. She's our daughter."

"Unless Michael has convinced her we're a threat." He buried his face in his hands, and then raked his fingers through his hair. "And she's half-convinced already. She thinks we're plotting to overthrow her—or at least that you are. I've benefitted a bit too much from her position to be plausible. But imagine how much more convincing that argument will become when you run off with Thor to Asgard."

Eve shook her head, struggling to follow it all, but she felt as though half of his thought process hadn't made it out of his mouth. Nothing was connecting the way it should. And why would Elah ever believe she was a threat? She didn't have anything close to the kind of power her daughter did, and absolutely no desire to wield it, even if she could.

"Thor said he was sworn to her protection."

"And then he threatened Elah in her own hall. Over you." Adam's mouth twisted ruefully. "After which, it seems, he came promptly back to your side, and offered to steal you away, along with the power Elah is convinced you're withholding from her to the detriment of us all. The power which Thor's presence in your life was meant to unlock for her use, by the way. And if Elah finds out—Eve, if you leave with him, we die. Maybe if circumstances were different, and the world weren't suffering from a swath of barren land, she'd be more reasonable, but as it is?"

Slow down. And she didn't have time to consider the implications of what he'd said about Thor at the moment, either, but it wouldn't be the first time she'd encouraged him to steal her away when he shouldn't have. "What do you mean, barren?"

"That's what they think you've done," Adam said. "By not loving, and hiding yourself away, hoarding your power. I don't see how it's possible, frankly, but—"

She cut him off with a look, funneling her exasperation into a jab directly into his thoughts. He winced, but offered a lopsided grin in apology that squeezed her heart.

"The deserts, Eve. I thought it was just that—desert. Maybe not fit to grow crops, and certainly putting a strain on the food supply as it expanded, but according to Elah and her Host, it's utterly barren. Not a whisper of life to be found, and as such, Elah can't do anything to fix it. Not without your power, anyway, and maybe not even with it."

Eve blinked, cracking open that window in her mind, slammed shut again at Adam's arrival, and flinching as the world flooded in. People and animals and plants, thoughts and dreams and emotions and instincts. Adam's unrequited desire, Thor's blinding love, Elah's shock, followed swiftly by guilt and regret, and that deep, throbbing ache of loss and need, despair and hunger. So much hunger it hurt, and she sank onto the sofa next to Adam, gripping the arm. This was why she'd closed herself away. Because there was so much pain, and she was so, so tired of it, and the only way she could breathe was to force it away, to tune them all out.

But the worst of it was—had always been—coming from the deserts. She'd assumed it was the people there, struggling ever harder to find food and water. It had only made sense that it must be. And if there was one thing she knew, it was that an absence of life couldn't produce that kind of noise. Of course, it hadn't occurred to her that no one might be living there. That nothing might be living there, and it might still be that loud.

"Those lands aren't barren, Adam."

He laughed, dry and humorless. "What do you mean they aren't barren? Elah told me so herself."

She grasped his knee, and showed him, letting everything she felt spill out into his mind, narrowing her focus slowly, until it was only the deserts, the so-called barren lands, and the hunger, and the anger, and the ache unraveling the threads of her soul. He hissed, jerking back, but she didn't let go. Because he had to realize this had been her life. Fighting this back, for so long it had become habit to keep herself apart.

"If they were barren, they wouldn't be hungry."

CHAPTER TWENTY

Eve

❧

Eve knelt in the sand, the sun pressing down on her back until her shoulders hunched against its glare. She sifted the dry grains through her fingers, squinting out at the golden wastes, and trying to ignore Adam's growing frustration, and Thor's rising alarm. There was life here, she had no doubt, but the closer she looked, the more difficult it was to see, and that was without the distractions of their minds, behind her.

"I don't understand," Adam said, kicking a spray of sand out over the dunes.

Thor had brought him only grudgingly, and Adam hadn't cared for the means of transportation, or even his presence. Eve hoped he regretted coming at all.

"If Eve isn't doing this, what is? And if there's life—if it isn't barren—why can't Elah feel it? Why can't I? Or you?"

"I'm not certain," Thor said. "Just as I wasn't certain the first three times you asked it of me."

"There aren't any insects," Eve said, climbing to her feet. She brushed the sand off her knees and hands and turned back to them, willing herself not to show the flood of lightheadedness that came with the movement. "There should be an uncountable number, and even if they were all hiding from the worst heat of the day, I should have been able to draw a few out. Sand fleas, if nothing else. But it definitely does not feel dead here."

Thor didn't answer, his head cocked, as if listening to something on the wind, and Adam stood with his arms crossed, impeccably dressed in a perfectly tailored black suit. Not a hair out of place, and how he wasn't raining sweat, she wasn't sure.

"It doesn't make any sense," Adam said again, easily for the fifth time. He raked a hand through his hair, and then smoothed it back down again. "Do you have any idea what *is* here?"

Eve shook her head. "It just . . . hums. In the back of my mind. When I try to reach for it, it's like there's this tunnel, and I can't break through to the other side. It's exhausting to try, to say nothing of the rest of the discomfort involved."

"Michael has the sword. The God-Killer. Could it do something like this? Burn everything out and transform it into wasteland?"

"No ash," Thor said. "Michael's sword is flame, and there's nothing the slightest bit scorched about the sand."

"What if he's altered it somehow? Or found some other weapon during the Purge?"

"I know of none which could accomplish this," Thor said. "And if one such existed, I would have been aware of it, and learned how to defend against it as well. To protect Asgard."

"I just don't see how it could be me," Eve said, when Adam's gaze slid back to her. "I'm sorry, I know that would make all this neat and easy but I never had this kind of power. And if I had, I never, ever would have used it like this. Even subconsciously."

"But your presence in the world nourishes it," Adam argued. "And you've got to admit, Evey, you haven't been present."

"This isn't a slow withering, caused by Eve's withdrawal," Thor said firmly. "No matter what Michael thinks, or Elah might choose to believe. Devastation of this sort, on this scale, requires far more than neglect. It needs intent. Purpose. Deliberate malice."

Adam snorted. "Michael certainly has the last in spades."

"But he's bound by Elohim," Eve said, glancing at Thor for confirmation. "To the protection of Creation. This, whatever it is, is the complete opposite."

"Famine and drought," Thor murmured, more to himself than anything. "And all the more effective against Elah, whose power is tied to the world through its making."

Eve tilted her head, shielding her eyes to look up at him. "You've seen this before?"

He grunted. "Not this exactly. But yes, on the old worlds. When a god sought to sway the followers of another to himself."

"The only god left with this kind of power is Bhagavan," Adam said. "And I can't see him doing something like this."

"No," Thor agreed. "He'd never betray Raphael, even if Elah had offended him, and he is bound by the Covenant, besides. You're certain, Eve, about what you sense?"

"This isn't new, Thor. I've been tuning it out for so long it's giving me a headache to do anything else." She shivered, looking for some patch of green to stand on, some oasis from the hunger which chewed through her now that she was on top of it. There was nothing but sand as far as she could see in any direction. "I don't know how you *can't* feel it."

He held out a hand to her, and when she took it, his presence flowed into her mind, his love and concern a balm, and better yet, a barrier. She sighed relief, and closed her eyes. If she could only get back to Asgard, and the quiet, the peace . . .

Soon, he promised.

And what about Elah?

"How long have you felt this?" he asked gently. *You cannot serve her if you are not well, in body, spirit, and mind.*

Eve frowned, searching her memories. Before Elah's birth everything had looked so bright, so possible. And then Adam had left, and she'd had to keep pieces of herself apart to protect Elah. And then she'd just been alone, perfectly isolated in misery. When had the impulse shifted? When had it stopped being about Elah and started being about self-preservation?

"Before Elah's ascension. Maybe even before she was taken, but I can't be sure. I started breaking away after her birth to keep her from any kind of negativity. Maybe it was here then, but too minimal for me to pinpoint. Maybe it wasn't. But. It's been worse in this life. I don't know if it was because I was shielded by my exile in the last, or I've just been more sensitive to everything around me after living so long alone."

Adam was studying her, regret and guilt softening his gray eyes. "I should have realized something was wrong. I should have come to you, done something to help."

Should've, could've, would've, she said. *None of it helps now.*

His gaze fell to her hand in Thor's, and he looked away. *No, I suppose not.*

"Fed by Elah's power, perhaps, growing more and more bloated after her ascension, as she focused more and more of herself upon these lands, hoping to heal them," Thor said. "How long it was here before then, I'd dearly like to know."

"You'd think in all this time, some scientist would have noticed." Adam crouched down, collecting a handful of sand. "Done a study. This is exactly the kind of thing those environmentalists harp on and on about."

"No," Eve said. "Maybe they can't sense things the same way we can, but it's still here, that ache, the hunger. No one would want to come here if they didn't have to."

"What of the dead?" Thor asked. "Did some plan expeditions and never return?"

"I can look into it easily enough," Adam said, throwing the sand away. "I'll have Hilda get our scientists on all of this, in fact. We'll need the proof, if they can find some evidence of life. Any kind."

"They won't find it."

"I have to try, Evey." He stood up, offering her a sad smile. *For the times I didn't, if nothing else.* "Elah isn't going to listen unless we can give her some other answer, and all the better if we have a solution attached. Whatever is in this sand, there's got to be some evidence of it, and maybe that's all we need to get the fingers pointing in the right direction."

"Then we will go East," Thor said. "Perhaps Bhagavan will have some sense of that which eludes the rest of us."

Adam shook his head. "If you go together to meet with another god, Michael is going to use it against us. It'll just be more proof that you're plotting against Elah."

Eve laughed to keep from weeping. "And you wonder why I would choose Asgard."

"Freedom to live as you like, escape from all this." He opened his arms, gesturing to the desert. "Real immortality, and a husband who's already proven he can love you for eternities. No. I don't wonder, Evey. I just ache for what I'm going to lose."

She swallowed, her throat thick. "You lost me a long time ago."

He half-smiled. "But not the hope of you."

Her heart hurt, and her head ached, and Adam's words cut through her so completely, she wasn't sure how she was still standing.

"I'd like to go," she said to Thor. And maybe with a bit more distance between herself and the desert, she'd feel a little more stable. "Take me home."

❧

Eve lay on her bed, counting the dots on the ceiling tiles, fighting the beginnings of a migraine she didn't have time for. Adam had excused himself the minute they'd reappeared in her dorm room, mumbling something about his security suffering from heart failure if he didn't check-in, and she'd sent Thor away, once he was gone. She'd needed the space, and he hadn't argued, only searched her face and promised to return the next day, after her classes had finished.

She couldn't go back. Eve rolled to her side and closed her eyes, the darkness behind her eyelids glowing faintly green. If Adam was right, she didn't dare. Not for any length of time. Not to stay, as she'd hoped she might. And it wasn't even just if Adam was right. It wasn't even just about Elah. She couldn't leave, if her absence would make things worse. If the world would die in exchange.

But she wasn't sure she could live here, either.

Just an hour on those sands had left her drained and aching in her joints. As if whatever was there was sucking her dry, too. And just being here, lying on her bed, she felt as though she were being pulled in two directions at once, like a game of tug of war, and her spirit stretched thinner and thinner in the middle.

She hadn't noticed it before she'd gone to Asgard and opened herself to its warmth, its welcoming peace. She hadn't noticed at all that she'd been living this half-life for so long, and she hated the way it felt to leave, the way being on earth shriveled her up again. Thor had said his tree's fruit nourished and healed, and she was starting to believe it wasn't just the fruit, but the tree itself, taking in carbon dioxide and expelling tranquility and health and *life*. Now that she'd tasted of it—

Her eyes snapped open, and she rolled out of her bed, lurching across the room to her desk. One of the books for this semester, for the class on mythology, had been the Hebrew Scriptures. Full of half-truths, to be sure, but still truth. Small pieces of it. And when had it been assembled? She wasn't sure it mattered, but tapped the query into her tablet and pulled the small, blue Tanakh from her shelf. She'd read it at least a hundred times before, hoping, in those days before Elah for some kind of understanding of what God had wanted of her, and knowing it would never have the answers she sought.

But there was one passage, about the Tree of Knowledge being placed at the heart of the Garden . . .

She found it quickly. There wasn't all that much to the Book of Genesis, really, and what she wanted was nearer to the beginning anyway. She'd always skimmed over it before, sure she already knew the truth. Sure she knew the lies.

Chapter two, verse nine. And a second tree. One she had ignored for so, so long.

A Tree of Life.

Thor? she called, and she had only to reach out to find him there, reaching back. To have him in the back of her mind, so close, felt as if she'd lost a hand and only realized it was gone when they'd sewn it back on again. But now that she knew to look for it, recognized it for what it was, she remembered it. Generation after generation, always there, always present, offering reassurance and love. So much love. *I think I'd like one of your apples, after all.*

CHAPTER TWENTY-ONE

Thor

❧

Leaving Eve on earth with whatever power lurked in the deserts, draining the world, had been a trial to his self-control, and when she had called to him for the fruit, Thor hadn't been able to resist the opportunity to reassure himself that she was well. What he had not expected was to find Athena waiting for him in the form of an owl on a tree branch outside Eve's window. He shouldn't have been surprised. Not after he'd seen her lurking about in mortal guise.

He left the apple on Eve's desk, and went out to meet her.

She fluttered down, her owl's body melting into a woman's form as she dropped from the tree. Her expression was grim, her silver eyes dark with grief and pity. It wrapped thick fingers around his heart—there was only one reason she would look upon him in such a way.

"You must have known it was only a matter of time," she said.

"I hoped for a different outcome. That Elah might see reason."

Athena shook her head. "Reason is in short supply among the redwoods while Michael whispers in her ear."

"She has only just begun to find happiness again, Athena. To find any sort of peace, for any length of time. She has only just realized her capacity for love again, and Elah would rip it from her!"

"I'm only the messenger, Thor. Elah does not ask for my counsel, and I do not impose it upon her while I live as a guest in her hall. I've come only to warn you, and even this much I should not have risked."

He rubbed his forehead, his gaze rising to Eve's window. "How did she learn of it?"

Athena spread her hands. "The world is hers. She has only to look, and she will see. When her father came here, it was natural that she would be curious as to his business."

Adam. Thor ground his teeth. Always it was Adam at the heart of Eve's pain. *If I took her now, if we fled to Asgard, what then?*

It would be the excuse Michael has been looking for to begin a war against those of us who remain. Olympus would be razed, for if I refused, it would mean my death, and the Host would descend upon Bhagavan.

Surely Ra would never stand for such measures? Thor searched her face but saw nothing but resignation looking back, and his blood ran cold with it.*Athena, this cannot be what the world would come to. What Elah would make of it! After everything Eve sacrificed for the dream of better...*

And why should Elah uphold her mother's dream, if her mother does not stay to bear witness? Athena asked. *If her mother has turned from her altogether?*

"How much time do I have?" he asked softly. "How much time do I have to explain myself?"

"A day perhaps, before you are called to face judgment."

His chest went tight. "A day."

"Use it to your advantage, Thor. If you can convince her, yet, to open herself, to give herself and her power up to the world, to her daughter, perhaps there is still some small hope, some chance that she might offer forgiveness for your sins."

"Forgiveness." He snorted, his hands balling into fists at his sides. "Forgiveness for what, Athena? For doing as she asked? For loving her mother? And now, after all I have done to earn Eve's trust, you would have me betray her to save myself some punishment?"

"To save yourself from exile," Athena said, her face moon-white with distress. "If not death, Thor. Please. Even Eve must understand. Surely she would not wish you to sacrifice yourself this way—for her misery!"

"Let her try," he growled. "Let them try to take my life, and they will regret the attempt, I promise you."

"And then what?" Athena snapped. "What do you think will happen to the rest of us if you make good upon such a threat? It will be the same, again. The Covenant broken, and Michael free to hunt us once more. War!"

But it wouldn't just be war. He shut his eyes, taking a breath to calm the burn of lightning in his veins. It would be Ragnarok. A war between Bhagavan and Elah could be nothing less, to say nothing of what havoc his own fury might bring if she tried to take his head.

Ragnarok, because he had offered Eve the peace of Asgard. Another world cursed and destroyed by the touch of the Aesir. No, Eve would not want it at all. The senseless waste. The endless suffering of the innocent. But to tell her of it, here, before she had healed fully—she would not take it well. Elah believed falsely that her mother had turned against her, but to confess such a truth to Eve, to tell her that her daughter could even conceive of such a course, would certainly make it so.

"Ra and I will do what we can," she said gently, after a moment. "But I fear it will not be enough if Eve will not serve."

He didn't bother to tell her that it had never been a question of will.

He did not bother to respond at all.

CHAPTER TWENTY-TWO

Eve

§

The fruit had appeared sometime in the night, the sight of it on her desk conjuring a half-memory of Thor pulling her blanket up over her shoulder and leaning down to press a kiss to her temple before leaving again.

She wished he'd stayed. She was glad he hadn't. If what Adam had said was true, it twisted everything, and facing it—she wasn't ready. Not here. Not now.

For two glorious days, she'd thought she could be free. She'd thought they could both be free, and happy, and fall in love all over again, together. And then Adam had come, and the delicate framework of the future she'd hoped for had been shattered.

And why was it always Adam delivering these blows? Why couldn't she live one life without heartache because of him?

She rubbed her eyes, green fireworks exploding behind her eyelids, and sighed. Now that she knew what she'd been missing, embraced all the parts of herself she'd hidden away for so long, it only made her that much more miserable to come back here. And what good would that do Elah? What good was she to the world, if she couldn't give hope and love and grace? The three things she could not hold to her heart on earth, no matter how hard she tried. Even with Thor.

Oh, it had been easier in Asgard. She'd felt like herself for the first time in ages. But every time she returned, all she had left was this emptiness, as if she'd been drained overnight of everything that Asgard and Thor had given her.

Eve showered and dressed, trying to put it all out of her mind. But of course her gaze kept returning to the apple, reminding her all over again. She swore, and grabbed her bag. Breakfast, and then she'd go to class, and at least she wouldn't be staring at the fruit, agonizing over what she hoped it might do. Terrified of what it wouldn't.

The door quirked, and Eve looked up, her eyes narrowing. The panel flashed green, and hissed open. Adam grinned at her from the other side, as if it were some delightful magic trick.

"I wonder if this means you could launch nuclear missiles from the North Country," he said. "How sensitive do you suppose these metrics are?"

"Manners still apply whether you're the president or a dictator. You can't just invite yourself into my room any time you want." She grabbed the books she needed, sliding them into the bag at her hip. And then the apple, too. "I'm on my way out, so whatever it is, you'll have to wait."

"Class, Evey? Really?" He leaned against the door frame, blocking her exit. "At a time like this?"

"Why are you still here?" she demanded. "Don't you have a country to run?"

He crossed his arms, something in his expression softening. "Sharp-tongued this morning, aren't we?"

"You just broke into my dorm room," she said. "And now you're going to try to tell me that I'm the one with the problem?"

"You are the one with the problem," he said gently, stepping inside and letting the door whoosh shut behind him. "This isn't you, Evey. Even when you were married to Garrit you weren't this . . . prickly."

She stiffened. Marcus's word from Adam's mouth. "If I am behaving that way toward you, I think I have plenty of reasons."

He held up both hands, palm out. "I'm sorry. That isn't why I'm here. And you're right, it was rude of me to walk in this way but I didn't think you'd speak to me if I announced myself, and the longer I loiter around, the more likely someone will notice I've come. You don't know how difficult it is for me to get this kind of privacy."

"Oh you poor thing," she snapped. "Made yourself a king and now you don't get any time to yourself."

He pinched the bridge of his nose. "Evey, I'm trying to save the world. I think I should get a pass on the rise to power."

"It isn't mutually exclusive, Adam. You want the world for yourself, and it isn't any good to you if it's dead. So fine. You have it, you're doing what you can to keep it. It doesn't make you noble or good, or even responsible."

"I didn't do any of this because I wanted the world to myself," he said, the words ground between his teeth. "I did it for the people who were starving. I did it to stop all the unnecessary suffering caused by greed. I did it for *you*!"

Eve flushed, looking away. What could she say to that? What did he expect her to say to that?

"I told myself for so long it had nothing to do with you." Adam barked a laugh and dropped into her sofa. "It didn't make it any truer. And now you're just," he waved a hand vaguely. "It breaks my heart, Evey. Knowing what you used to be, what you were. Thor must realize it, too. After all this time, he finally gets to have you, and you're not even . . ."

She swallowed, not sure she wanted to hear this. Any of it. "Even what?"

He looked up at her, pity in his eyes. "It's like you've forgotten what love is. You make all the right gestures with Thor, but there's nothing there. No emotion behind it, outside of some kind of relief."

"That isn't—" Eve shook her head, stepping back.

Adam of all people to say such a thing. To tell her she didn't know how to love. Didn't he understand? Didn't he realize that he'd done this? He'd made her this way. Leaving her. Abandoning her. And then the isolation that had followed. If anyone didn't know love, it was him. It was always him.

"You should go," she said.

"Evey, don't be like this." Adam was on his feet, one hand outstretched.

But she had to be. This was who she was. This was all she was. And he'd made her this way. He'd changed her. That was what Thor had said, wasn't it? Adam had changed her, and if she was going to change back, if she was going to be anything, it couldn't be here. Not near him. Not part of this world he'd built with Elah after she'd worked so hard to make it possible. To make Elah a force for good. To teach her love. She'd given everything she had to their daughter, and it wasn't enough. After all that she'd done, everything she'd given up, Elah was willing to kill them both for more.

She didn't want this. To be this person. Not anymore.

"I'm going to class, Adam," she said firmly. "And when I get back, you're going to be gone."

"Evey, please. I'm not trying to hurt you. I want your help. That's why I came. I want you to help me, in the North Country—"

"No." Eve touched the door release, not looking back. If she looked back, she'd see how much this hurt him. How much she'd hurt him, and she'd hesitate. He'd sink his claws into her, and she'd never be free. "I don't ever want to see you again."

And then she left. To prove Adam wrong.

To take back her life.

She sat down at a corner table with a view of the quad. Thor wasn't supposed to be meeting her for breakfast, but she could call him with a thought. She just wasn't sure she wanted to see him, yet. Or even to eat. She needed to sort herself out, but she couldn't do it here. There was too much noise and too much pain, and she didn't even know who she was when she was on earth. But if Adam was right, and she left, and Elah learned of it . . .

She couldn't depend on Asgard. Every moment she'd spent there, whether she'd known it or not, was borrowed time. And what happened if Elah took it away? What happened if she was trapped here, forever, lost in this strangeness, disconnected from herself, from everything. Even if Thor stayed with her, she wouldn't deserve him. As things stood, she wasn't sure she would even be able to love him. Not properly. Not the way she could in Asgard.

The fruit sat on the edge of her tray, winking at her in the sunlight. She picked it up, turning it over in her hands, the delicate skin rippling from gold to crimson beneath the pressure of her fingertips. If it was God's tree, its power wouldn't be limited to Asgard. There was no reason why it couldn't work here, too. On her.

"Anna?"

Eve let out a breath. "Marc."

"I've been trying to get a hold of you, but it was like you dropped off the face of the earth." He slid into the seat opposite, tray and all. "I'm glad you got at least one of my messages."

Oh. She glanced out the window, searching the sky for some flash of lightning, some rumble of thunder. But then, she wasn't sure that would be any better, either. At least his plate was scraped clean, just a collection of dirty dishes to show for his already-finished meal.

"Ashley said you've been keeping busy."

"I really wish you'd stop asking her to spy on me."

He shrugged. "When you don't return my calls I have to rely on gossip to know you haven't gone off the deep end, Anna. The way you've been acting, it's all the classic warning signs—"

"I'm *fine*, Marc. Really. But when I'm not, you'll be the first person I call, since you're so platonically concerned."

"You know, I don't appreciate your sarcasm. My concern for your well-being has nothing to do with—"

"Oh, Marcus! There you are." Sophia appeared beside them, her gaze flitting over the fruit in Eve's hands before she turned a blinding smile onto Marcus. "We've got to go, handsome. I've got that test remember?"

Eve arched an eyebrow. "I guess I'm not the only one staying busy, huh?"

Marcus's hands tightened around the edges of his tray. "Sometimes I wonder why I bother."

She should have been glad to hear him say it, but it bruised all the same. Another blow landing on her already beaten spirit. Marcus rose, taking his garbage with him.

"Maybe you shouldn't," she heard herself say to his back, and he stopped, just for a moment. But Sophia slipped her arm through his, and they disappeared together through the doors.

Eve dropped her gaze back to the apple, turning it over in her hands. Marcus deserved a better friend, even if she could never love him. Thor deserved a woman who was whole, in Asgard and out of it. Adam deserved . . .

Her lips twitched. Adam still deserved to suck lemons. But maybe, just maybe, with a little bit of help, she could put all that pain behind her. A selfish forgiveness, perhaps, but forgiveness all the same. For Adam, for Elah too. Because her daughter should have a mother capable of love and grace, regardless. And Eve was so tired of this despair, this ache.

She deserved better, for herself. A better life. With joy and love and peace, from the inside, out.

She deserved to be healed and whole.

So she lifted the golden fruit to her lips and bit deep.

CHAPTER TWENTY-TWO

Elah, Before

§

At first, Elah thought the winged angel outside the cottage was Raphael, and she broke into a run, smiling. "I want to fly! You never have your wings."

But then he turned, and she saw his eyes. Hard and strange, and so different. Raphael was always warm, joy in his face, and he wore no scabbard at his hip. Elah slowed to a stop, frowning at the angel. His white wings rustled at his back, and his lip curled as his gaze shifted over her head.

"Elah," Mama called, her voice strained. "Come back to me, sweetheart."

Elah didn't retreat, but she didn't move any closer. "Did Grandfather send you, too?" The angel's hard eyes flickered, and his eyes returned to her. Elah felt a pressure in her head and scowled. "It's very bad manners to try and see into someone else's mind! It's only allowed if you're in danger, and you're not."

"I suppose I shouldn't be surprised that your mother is raising you with human restrictions," he said, his eyes narrowing. "But a Goddess is above those small rules, as are her Host."

"That's enough, Michael," Mama's tone was sharp. "She's my daughter, and she'll treat others with respect as long as she lives under my roof. The world would be a better place if you'd learned to do the same."

Michael bared his teeth, like a wolf's snarl more than a smile. "How fortunate that she will not be living beneath your roof any longer, then."

"Come, my dear." Raphael held out his hand to her, standing in the doorway. "Your dinner is getting cold."

Elah glanced back at her mother. If she went to Raphael, she'd have to walk by the other angel.

"Go on," she said, but her smile didn't reach her eyes. "I'll be there in just a moment."

Elah skipped across to Raphael, taking his hand. "He doesn't seem very nice."

Raphael smiled down at her. "Michael and your mother have never agreed on much. But no one will ever harm you, so long as he stands at your side."

"Why would anyone want to hurt me?" Elah asked, glancing over her shoulder as Raphael closed the door. Michael had spread his wings, making himself look twice as big. "I can just tell them not to, can't I? That's allowed. Even Mama said so."

Raphael swept her up, depositing her in her chair at the table. "I'm sure that will serve you just fine, most of the time. But other gods are not so easy to manipulate."

"Like Mama?"

"Your mother doesn't like to be considered a god."

"But she is, isn't she? That's why she can talk inside my head, and keep me from going inside hers. Like you, too."

"Your mother and father are special," he said, tapping her nose. "That's true. But they don't grow stronger on faith, or answer prayers. They simply live, and die, and live again."

"Do you answer prayers?"

"I did once." He set her dish in front of her.

"Why don't you, anymore?"

"Because I help your mother, now, and the people pray to your Grandfather, instead. As they should." He nudged her dish closer.

"Can I trust you to eat your dinner nicely while I go back out to help your mother?"

Elah sighed. "If you insist."

Raphael laughed, mussing her hair as he left her. "I won't be but a moment."

❧

She didn't pay much attention to what they talked about as she ate, though she could have listened, if she'd wanted to. Most of the time, it wasn't anything worth listening to. So she ate, and when she finished, she sent her bowl to the sink, without using her hands at all. Mama would have frowned at her, but Elah didn't see what the point of having teleke- telkana- teleka-whatsit was if she didn't get to *use* it. And if she was a goddess, and the other angel was right, then her mother couldn't *really* be *too* angry.

Elah climbed up on the kitchen counter so she could see out the window. Mama felt sad, and her eyes were all shiny as she argued. Raphael looked just like Raphael, and she never knew what he felt like anyway. The other Archangel was snarly as a wolf, still, but even wolves didn't stay snarly for longer than it took to make friends. Maybe if she gave him a present he wouldn't snarl so much, and even if he didn't like Mama, he'd at least like her.

She frowned. What did she have for a present for an angel? Raphael liked pretty things, she knew, and bright colors, but she didn't know anything about the wolfy one. She hopped off the counter, and went to her room. The wolves liked food, and new games. She'd taught the cubs to play tag, and they'd pestered her for a week after. But she couldn't think of any good games that the angel would like. Raphael didn't play with her very often, besides swinging her around like a monkey.

Her collection of feathers hung from the ceiling over her bed, spinning idly in the breeze from the open window. Raphael's gleaming white feather was the first, but the other birds had brought her feathers now and then, when she admired them. Cardinals and ravens and once, a great golden eagle. She eyed the eagle feather now, amber in the sunlight. She'd have to reach it no-handed, in order to get it down, and Mama would know what she'd done. But if it made the angel nicer, then that would help *her* too.

Elah twisted her face up, staring at the knot that held the feather. She ducked under it, and *imagined* the knot undoing. Mama had taught her how to tie a bow, and the knot almost looked like one, but when she tugged on the ends it only tightened it more. She tried pushing instead, and the string unraveled neatly, the feather floating down. She snatched it up and ran back to the door, making it open no-handed too. And then she was outside, and both the angels, and Mama were staring at her, scowling.

She stopped just short of their small circle and put on her best I-didn't-do-anything-wrong face. Mama crossed her arms, her eyes narrowing, and Elah ignored her.

"Excuse me," she said, looking at the new angel. Michael. That was what Raphael had called him. She stuck out her hand, carefully holding the feather by the stem. "I thought you might like this. It's the only one I have like it and its bright and pretty and it seems like angels like bright pretty things, but if you don't like it I don't mind. I'll put it back up over my bed. Or Mama will. It just seemed like you weren't happy to be here, and Mama said the best way to make friends is to help, so I thought this would help you be happier."

Michael's hard eyes glinted, but his lips didn't curl back, even if his eyebrows dropped low. "You might have just as easily commanded it of me."

"That isn't very nice. Angels are people too, and it isn't fair to *make* people do things if they don't want to."

"So says your mother?" he asked.

"Would you have liked it if I'd made you be happy, just like that?"

He glanced at Raphael, and Elah did too. There was laughter in his eyes, even if Michael was still all gloomy in the face. "Did you put her up to this?"

"Not at all," Raphael said. "I left her to eat her dinner, nothing more. But you must admit she has a point, Michael. Had she commanded anything of you, you'd have been even more resentful."

Elah frowned, dropping her hand. "Maybe I should have picked the red one, instead." Mama squeezed her shoulder, hugging her against her side, and washing her with pride, but her face still felt too warm, and she kicked at the dirt. "I'm sorry you didn't like my present."

"I never said I didn't like it."

She peeked up at the Archangel. He'd crouched down, his wings spread to keep the ends from dragging in the mulched earth. His eyes were still hard, but the rest of his face had softened, somehow, and his lips twitched. He held out his hand, waiting.

"Don't you dare make light of this, Michael," Mama said lowly.

"Only a fool rejects the gift of his Goddess," he said, ignoring her mother. "And whatever else I am, Lady, I am no fool. It is generous of you to think of me at all in such a way."

Elah gave him the feather, but she frowned slightly at his words. "How should I think of you?"

"As a servant, to be commanded. A tool of your will."

"But why can't you be my friend?"

He ran the feather through his fingers, and bowed his head. "Why should you want me at all, when you have the power to make creatures of your own? A world of your own, if you will it."

"If we were friends, I would want you. Just like I want Mama, and Raphael, and the wolves and the goats and the birds and the Lions."

Michael grunted, and rose, his wings rustling before he folded them neatly to his back. "Do you know why I've come, Lady?"

"Grandfather must have sent you," Elah said, shrugging. "Mama said he wants me to visit. I don't mind, so much, because Raphael said he would come, too. I can bring my feathers, can't I?" She glanced up at her mother. "Are there birds where Grandfather lives?"

"You'll have to tell me when you get there," Mama said. "But I don't see why you couldn't invite some of the birds who sing at your window to visit you there, if you like, and I don't see why you couldn't bring whatever else of yours that you wanted to have with you."

"You'll be given everything you want or need," Michael said. "If that means birds to sing at your bedside, they will come."

"Only if they *wanted* to," Elah said, frowning up at him.

Michael's lips curved then, and even if it wasn't a real smile, she knew one day it could be. They *could* be friends. She'd just have to keep trying.

"If they want to," he agreed. "But if they are your friends, as you say, I hardly think they'll refuse."

&

Mama tucked her into bed later that night. Her last night before she went to Grandfather's house, where Mama had never been before. It was strange to think she hadn't. Mama had been so many places . . .

"Raphael said you asked about your father some time ago," Mama said softly, sitting down on the edge of the mattress and smoothing the blanket under her chin.

Elah squirmed deeper into her bed. "He said you would tell me when you were ready."

Mama sighed, a crease forming between her eyebrows. Not quite a frown, just that look she got when she didn't want to answer. "Do you still want to know?"

She picked at a loose thread on her quilt. She didn't like when Mama was uncomfortable, and she didn't want her to be sad. Not when she was leaving the next day. "You could just tell Raphael to tell me, if you wanted. You don't have to say."

"He probably knows the story better than I do," Mama said, looking away.

"Did you love him?" The question burst from her lips, and she bit down on them after, folding them into her mouth to keep from saying anything else.

Mama closed her eyes, longer than a blink, and Elah felt her pull away. Not from the bed, because she was still right there, next to her, but in the other way, when she didn't want her to know something, and hid it away inside her heart. "Very much."

"Did he love you?"

She let out another breath, and then smiled determinedly. "If I hadn't thought so, I wouldn't have let him give me you." Her voice was light, but it didn't match the way she *felt*, or the crease between her eyebrows. If she'd really been happy, there wouldn't have been a crease. "The thing you need to know, sweetheart, the most important thing you need to know, is that he loved *you*. And he would never have left if he hadn't wanted you to have the very best life and the very best future. Don't let anyone ever tell you otherwise, all right? And if they do—if they do, they don't know what they're talking about, or they're only trying to hurt you for reasons of their own."

"Mama, I don't understand," she said, frowning. "Why would anyone want to hurt me? Raphael said it too. About no one hurting me if Michael was here. But he didn't say why."

"Oh, honey. It isn't that they would want to hurt you, exactly. Just that they're afraid. You're so strong, and so special, and they're worried that *you'll* hurt *them*. Like when Michael asked you what you would want with him, when you could make your own everything—he's been scared of you for a long time."

"Then why won't he hurt me?"

"He isn't allowed, sweetie. Grandfather wouldn't let him. When you're older, you'll understand. But you're safe, honey. Even with Michael, you're safe."

But the way she said it made her wonder. He wasn't allowed to hurt her. But it sure seemed like Mama thought he wanted to.

CHAPTER TWENTY-THREE

Eve, Later

❦

It tasted like sunshine and rainstorms, honey and champagne. She caught the juice that ran down her chin, licking it from her finger even as her mouth watered for more. Another bite, another taste of sweetness on her tongue. The texture was just as she remembered, an overripe plum rather than a proper apple, and melting in her mouth like spun sugar. She let herself take a second, slurping bite, and then a third.

She'd never had more than one mouthful of the other, but this was different. There was no swell of pain, no explosion of life into her consciousness. It warmed her, instead. Like hot soup on a cold day, and her body hummed in response, craving more.

And then the warmth turned into something else, a phantom tingling just shy of a shiver, slipping down her spine, her hips, her thighs. Eve closed her eyes, wishing she'd thought to do this somewhere else. In her dorm room, or at least the quad. Her skin felt too sensitive, the soft cotton of her shirt too scratchy and rough.

She stumbled out of the dining hall, her head swimming, the fruit still clutched in her hand. Through the irising doors, out into the quad, and then she dropped to her knees in the grass, and just breathed.

Good, clean earth, and fresh cut grass, and the familiar sounds of laughter in the open air, suddenly far less abrasive to her senses. She wanted to laugh with them, to cry, to throw her arms out and spin until she couldn't see straight anymore. She contented herself with falling back into the grass, smiling at the way it tickled her neck, her arms, her ankles where her pant legs had risen up and her socks had fallen down.

The sky had never been so blue, the leaves never so alive. She lifted her empty hand up, as if to touch them, and when she couldn't reach, she stretched out with her thoughts instead, feeling the shape of the tree with her mind instead, listening to its history of rain and drought and sun and snow.

"Eve?" Thor appeared above her, upside down. "Are you well?"

She laughed, her hand meeting his face instead of the leaves when he crouched beside her, and then she held out the fruit, too. His eyebrows rose, and he pried what was left of it from her fingers. She shivered, her eyes sliding shut again, basking in the glow of his presence, so much brighter, so much stronger than the tree. So much more—more—

"Told you I shouldn't eat it."

His amusement washed over her, a soft caress of silent laughter. "The euphoria won't last, and had you been yourself, you'd have felt nothing at all."

"Myself!" He helped her to sit up, one strong arm supporting her back, and she wrapped her arms around his neck, pulling herself closer. "I've missed myself."

He sighed, swinging her up into his arms. "You might have called to me, hm?"

She giggled, nuzzling his neck. He was incredibly tall. And perfectly proportioned, for all he was immensely large. And he smelled so—so—

"Take me to bed?"

"Directly," he said, his voice rippling with mirth. "Where you will likely fall straight to sleep, much as I might wish otherwise."

She hummed, low in her throat. Because the rest of her was humming, too, all the more so because of him. The way he cradled her so carefully. He'd always been careful of his strength, gentle and tender and loving, and deliberate, when something more was called for. Controlled, even in passion.

"I don't know why I've waited so long."

He chuckled softly, carrying her toward her dorm. "You'll remember soon enough."

"There's so much I've forgotten," she sighed. "So much, and not enough."

"Hush now," he said, pressing a kiss to her forehead that lit a fire in her heart. "Just rest, now, *hjartað mitt.* Rest, and heal. We have time, yet. Time enough for this much."

He was wrong, Eve thought. So rarely wrong, but wrong again. She was going to fall asleep long before he put her to bed.

§

She woke to the glow of sun through her curtains, and the warmth of a body beside her own. She burrowed deeper into Thor's arms, and he stroked her hair, then her back, dropping a kiss to her temple.

"Welcome back," he said.

But she didn't want to wake up, yet. She didn't want to leave this place, nestled so perfectly against his chest. "Shh."

He sighed, his breath tickling her ear. "If I could stay here for an eternity, I would, Eve, I promise you. But I fear time runs short."

He'd said something else about having time, earlier, and all it took was a brush against his mind to bring her fully awake. There was a reserve that shouldn't have been there, a grief she liked even less when she realized he'd kept it half-concealed. He had always been open to her before, utterly and completely honest in his emotions. She leaned back slightly, searching his face.

"I thought time wasn't an issue for you," she said slowly. "That it never had to be a problem for either of us."

"I had no reason, then, to believe otherwise. And I hoped . . ." He caressed her cheek. "There is nothing I have ever wanted more than this, Eve. To be with you."

"Then why?" she asked, half-sitting up. "Why can't we have it? Even if I can't go to Asgard, why can't you stay?"

"Elah believes I am subverting her."

"Because you offered me Asgard?"

"It will likely mean my exile." His mouth made a grim line. "For stealing you away when she needs you most."

"But you aren't!" Eve flopped back down onto the bed, and slid her fingers through her hair until they knotted in the curls. It had always been a risk—Elah changing her mind for whatever reason, for any reason—but now she regretted fighting him for so long, for not enjoying as much of him as she could while she was able. But this didn't have to be like before. Thor was strong enough to protect himself, for starters, and Elah . . . "What is wrong with that girl? I never raised her to be paranoid, and she was always so good natured as a child."

Thor's hand slid across her stomach, somewhere between soothing and teasing. "As you have always been, as well, until recently."

She let out a breath, closing her eyes. If she had been affected, how much more so might Elah be? Eve was only connected to one facet of the world, really, but Elah, for all practical purposes, *was* the world.

"She must be terrified," she murmured. "Going out of her mind. And Michael—it must drive him demented, not knowing how to fight this thing, so he keeps pointing his sword at the old problems. Me, and Adam, and you. All of you."

When she opened her eyes again, Thor was grinning, pride and joy mingling with bittersweet longing and regret.

She dropped her arms, feeling suddenly self-conscious. "What?"

"Welcome back," he said again, smoothing her hair from her face. His fingertip lingered over the shape of her mouth, and her lips tingled beneath his touch.

"I didn't go anywhere." Her voice was suddenly hoarse, and she swallowed. "I was always right here. Waiting for you."

"But you were lost, all the same." His hand slipped down, along the line of her jaw, the column of her neck, the length of her collarbone. Goosebumps rose on her arms, and her breath caught. The way he was looking at her, his eyes hazed with desire, made something inside her tremble with the same need. "I only wish we had more time, now."

"We have time enough," she said.

His gaze locked on hers, his whole body going still. "You know what it will mean."

She lifted her hand to his face, brushing the pad of her thumb across his lips. "It will mean love, Thor. Just as it always has between us. And what does the rest really matter, beyond that? Beyond us, in this moment."

He let out a breath. "I am not certain I will have the strength to stop myself, if we start."

She smiled. "Why should you need to?"

"If you were to change your mind—"

"Thor." She pressed her index finger to his lips. "I'm not Elah. I'm not going to change my mind. Not about this. Never about you."

His eyes flashed white. "I would have married you. Treasured you for eternities and still wanted more. I would have given myself up to you, made myself yours in every way possible."

"I know," she said. "I always knew how much you loved me. I always felt your love. But no matter what Elah believes, it doesn't mean we can't still have this moment. It doesn't mean we can't swear ourselves to one another, for this day, this night."

For forever. She pressed her lips together to stop the words before they escaped, but the way his eyes softened and his love for her swelled, crashing over her, she knew he'd heard them anyway.

"I never stopped being your husband, Eve."

"If I'd known you lived . . ."

He kissed her, then, and the rest of the sentence didn't matter anymore. Nothing mattered, except for the slant of his mouth over hers, the taste of mead and thunder on his lips, and the heat of his palm at the curve of her waist. She wrapped her arm around his neck and kissed him back, but it only made her ache for more.

His hand slid up along her side, his fingers pressing hard against her ribs, drawing her nearer, and then she was beneath him, his body settled perfectly over hers, just heavy enough, but not near enough, not close enough at all.

She tugged at his shirt until her hands found warm skin, pushing the fabric up, and up as she trailed fingers along the planes of his stomach, the muscles of his chest, the strength of his shoulders. He groaned softly into her mouth, the rumbling sound starting a frisson in her stomach. She pulled his shirt off, throwing it away, and he lowered his head to trail kisses along her jaw, until his teeth grazed her earlobe and she shivered in response.

He chuckled, low and rich and caressing, all on its own.

"Shall we see what else still makes you shudder?"

He kissed her pulse, just beneath her jaw, and she tipped her head back, baring her throat to him, wishing she were bare all over.

Soon enough, he promised, and his need filled her mind, feeding her own until she gasped, desire coiling tight in her belly, flooding her senses. *If this is all we might share, I mean to make it last.*

She opened her eyes, staring into the clear, sky blue of his own. Her fingers curled into his hair, holding him, twining through the strands as if it could somehow keep him in her bed, for days and nights and eternities. She wished she could stop time, and make love to him in this moment forever.

"Make me your wife," she said softly. "Marry me, with your own name, with mine, and make me yours."

Much later, sated in body and spirit, Eve studied his sleeping face, smooth and clear and hers. Forever and always hers, no matter how they might be parted.

She brushed a kiss to his chest, over his heart, and fit herself against his side, one thought, half-formed, repeating over and over in her mind.

What God has joined. What God has joined. What God has joined.

CHAPTER TWENTY-FOUR

Adam

Gabriel was waiting for him in his hotel room when he returned that afternoon, white wings folded neatly to his back. The guards playing cards at the coffee table didn't seem to notice him at all, for which Adam could only be marginally grateful. He hated being surprised by Archangels of any kind, though if he had to choose one, Raphael was probably the least disturbing to stumble across. He still hadn't quite forgiven Gabriel for the part he'd played at Elah's birth.

"If you would give me the room, please, gentlemen," he said to the guards.

Hilda hesitated in the doorway behind him, stopping herself at his request. "Sir, we really do need to discuss your schedule for the rest of the week—"

He held up a restraining hand, not taking his eyes from the angel. "I have a feeling my week is about to be hijacked even further, actually, so it might as well wait until morning."

"Yes, sir," Hilda said, though her tone was one of clear disapproval. He flashed her a smile, one of his most charming, and shut the door on her anyway. She didn't like that he hadn't explained his agenda for this trip. Didn't like at all the fact that he kept slipping away. Jealousy, he knew, but there was little he could do about it, short of reprogramming her altogether, and that wouldn't inspire anyone's confidence. Least of all Eve's.

"Something I can do for you?" he asked Gabriel, once the room had cleared.

The Archangel inclined his head. "I'm to collect you, on behalf of your daughter."

Adam loosened his tie, the room suddenly just a hair too warm for comfort. When that didn't help the odd feeling of suffocation, he pulled the silk free from his collar altogether. "Funny that she didn't mention it."

"As you've kept your own secrets these last weeks, you can hardly be surprised."

"Ah." He poured himself a glass of whiskey, running through a quick catalog of his most recent sins. Not that he didn't know what would offend her most. Eve's absences, the escapes to Asgard he'd kept to himself. Not that he had known for certain, truly. Not until he'd spoken to her himself. "Should I finalize my will before we leave, then?"

Gabriel offered a crooked smile, almost pitying in its kindness. "It is not your fate which troubles Her, as yet, but I would keep it current, were I you. What the future holds, it is difficult to say."

"More opinions, Gabriel?" He sipped the whiskey and checked the time. "If I'm gone for more than an hour, it's going to be a problem."

The angel arched an eyebrow. "Surely not anything you cannot overcome."

"I prefer not to readjust the memories of my guards if I don't have to. It makes them rather less effective in the field." He set the glass down. "They ought to have noticed some disturbance from your presence, whatever mojo you worked, not sat here, placidly playing cards."

"Raphael had said you would prefer it if we did not show ourselves."

He searched the angel's features, but Gabriel had always been opaque. Sympathetically opaque, to be sure, but impossible to read all the same. "I don't suppose you'll tell me whose fate is currently being debated among the redwoods?"

"As long as it isn't your own, I should think that would be reassurance enough."

Adam grimaced. "So that's how it is."

Gabriel spread his hands, palms up. "Did you truly expect something more favorable?"

"No," he said, frowning at what was left of the whiskey in his glass. But it didn't make it any less painful to hear. And if Elah believed it of him, there was no hope of ever convincing Eve. Not in this lifetime.

He finished the drink and nodded to Gabriel. "I'm ready when you are."

❧

Gabriel left him in the antechamber, and Adam did his best to ignore Athena's jittering, beside him. He'd never realized she was capable of it, and seeing her chew on her perfect silver nails was distinctly unnerving.

"What exactly are we waiting for?"

Athena blinked, and it was only when her gaze refocused that he realized she'd been elsewhere. She gave a dismissive flick of her fingers. "Raphael's gone to fetch Thor, but there were . . . complications."

"That accounts for Gabriel's presence in my hotel, I suppose. Though I wouldn't have thought Raphael would provoke Thor, no matter what message he brought."

"Oh." Athena's eyes had gone distant again. "It's not that."

He wasn't even certain she was answering him. Worse than useless, the lot of them. Adam edged toward the doorway, but all he could see through the branches was a flittering of angels hovering above the throne. No matter how he leaned, the living trees shifted with him, keeping him from glimpsing anything of the throne itself, or Elah.

"At last," Athena murmured, just a moment before Raphael entered the anteroom, Thor upon his heels. She smiled, reaching a hand out to Raphael.

The wingless Archangel kissed her knuckles, a sparkle in his eyes. But Thor looked grim enough for all three of them, his jaw tightening at even such a slight display of affection. Odd, that. Raphael, Athena, and Thor had been thick as thieves for as long as Adam had been aware of them. Practically family, from what he'd seen.

Athena broke away from Raphael, but when she would have greeted Thor, he only shook his head, his lips pressed thin. "Let us have done with this, the sooner the better."

Even odder, Eve wasn't with him. But surely Raphael wouldn't appear half so pleased with himself if they were here to debate Eve's continued presence in the world.

"Tell me Elah didn't send Michael for Eve," Adam said.

Thor's eyes flashed white. "Over my dead body."

"But she isn't here," he said carefully, too conscious of the fact that he was poking a dragon. "Whatever this is, I can't imagine it doesn't affect her, too."

"She's sleeping," Thor said, shooting a narrow look in Raphael's direction. "And if Elah wishes to keep her mother's Grace, it is in her best interests to leave her so."

"Yes, yes," Raphael said, waving away his friend's ill-temper. "But the most important thing is that you've succeeded, and we can all be assured of leaving here with our heads attached."

Adam's jaw locked. "Succeeded at what, precisely?"

But the leaves rustled a warning, and the trees groaned as the main entrance into the throne room unraveled open.

Raphael nodded to Thor and Adam both. "After you."

Athena and Raphael followed them inside, though Raphael left them to stand with his brothers, at Elah's left, and Athena, too, went to stand apart, beside one of the redwood pillars. Adam took the opportunity to reach for Eve, and nearly tripped in shock. She was asleep, as Thor had said, but she was burning bright, her presence only barely muffled, and love spilling out from her in waves of contentedness and peace.

Thor caught his elbow, steadying him, and Adam jerked himself free. "Success, huh? As if she's just another notch on your bedpost, Thunder God?"

Thor's hands closed into fists. "At least I've said a proper goodbye."

Adam stared, but no matter how he turned the jibe over in his mind, it made no sense. For Thor to leave her—Thor would never leave her. Not after all this time. "What?"

But the god didn't answer, his gaze on Elah, seated primly upon her throne. Adam redirected his own attention with an effort, but he couldn't stop his thoughts from spinning around Thor's response.

"Father." It was the barest of acknowledgments, and enough to jerk him from his contemplations. Elah had never greeted him so coolly. "Have you a defense?"

"For?" he asked, forcing a lightness he didn't feel.

"For your deliberate deception," Michael answered, his hand closed around the hilt of his sword. "For lying to your Goddess, and concealment of this traitor's actions."

Adam lifted his eyebrows. So it was Thor's head on the chopping block, then. "How could I lie about anything I didn't know? Or conceal the actions I had no information about?"

"Your spies observed Mother's disappearances."

"Of course," he agreed.

Elah's eyes narrowed at the easiness of his reply. "You said nothing to us of your suspicions."

"Should I have?" he asked. "When I didn't know for certain anything more than that my spies were having a difficult time keeping track of Eve's whereabouts? Thor could have been taking her to Australia, for all I knew, and Eve is more than capable of keeping me from finding her on the far side of the world."

"Liar!" Michael snarled. "He is no better than Lucifer, the great deceiver!"

Elah frowned, ignoring the Archangel and studying Adam's face instead. "You knew my concerns."

"I knew your concerns were born of Michael's paranoia, and nothing more," Adam said firmly, looking into his daughter's eyes. "And I knew, too, that as long as your mother remained in Thor's company, she would be safe, and far happier than you or I could make her. Those were the only certainties I possessed from the information my spies had gathered, Elah, I promise you."

Her gaze shifted to Thor, her expression unreadable. "And what is your defense, Thor of the North? Or do you deny that you meant to take my mother from this world, when I made clear to you my need of her and her power here? A flagrant act of betrayal."

"Eve needed the time and the space to heal," Thor said, his nostrils flaring. "Asgard provided it. Or do you object also to my results?"

"What good does she do us, healthy or otherwise, if she gave up all her power to you?" Michael sneered. "You would have taken it all, and had the power of her womb as well! What would stop you then, from taking this world? From stealing Elah's very throne and summoning your Aesir back from the void?"

Thor growled. "If my loyalties remained with the Aesir, I would have left this world long ago. I stayed for love of Eve, and everything I have done was done for her sake, as I have sworn from the start."

"And what has Eve sworn?" Michael demanded, turning to Elah. "What oaths have your parents made to you, Lady? They are not bound by the Covenant, nor even their own honor." His gaze flicked to Adam. "Weak as it might be."

Adam rolled his eyes with false confidence, tucking his hands in his pockets to hide his own fists. "What promises does any parent make to their child? We're both bound to Elah by love. But I shouldn't expect you to understand something outside of your limited experiences, I suppose. That you would point your sword at either one of us is illustration enough of your ignorance."

"And yet, my mother yearns for Asgard. Happily retreated there, time and again."

"If you knew what she felt here, Elah—the pain she's suffered—you would only wonder how she's lived for so long as meanly as she has. There's something wrong with the world. Something Eve can sense that the rest of us can't. She says there's something living in the barren lands."

"More lies!" Michael said, stabbing his finger at Adam. "He would say anything to save himself. To serve his own purposes! As he always has, in everything he's ever done. That's why he abandoned you, Lady. Because he realized he could not use you for his own ends!"

"You heartless snake!" Adam surged toward him, tasting bile. Thor caught him by the shoulder, and wrenched him back. "How dare you! You know why I left! You *know!*"

Not now, Adam. Thor said, twisting his arm up until his shoulder spasmed in protest. *It's what he wants. An excuse to draw his sword and lay waste to all of us.*

"Name me snake?" Michael curled his lip. "With your own forked-tongue spilling lies at the feet of your Goddess? I know more than why you left, Adam. I know everything you've forgotten. All your cruelty. You were a deceiver from your first breath, abusing God's love for your pleasure, demanding more, and more, until He was nothing but wasted, rotten flesh. Why should you not do it again, now? All of this just some game, some trick to lure your daughter into ruin!"

Adam lurched against Thor's grasp, and his shoulder popped, flaming hot with pain. And then it was there, in his head. Michael's words branding memories against his mind. A broken woman, bruised and beaten and whimpering as he tore apart her will, just to see what would become of her. The face of God, gray and lined, sunken eyes and hollow-cheeked, as He shaped the dust into another form, and breathed His last into Eve's mouth.

Adam fell to his knees, grasping his head, digging his nails into his scalp to rip it out. Every memory. Every last piece of the man he was. The man who had sentenced Eve to slow starvation with gleeful abandon. Who had twisted men and women into slaves—and Eve had still forgiven him, after everything he'd done? After everything she'd witnessed?

Thor cursed lowly, and then Athena was before him, her hands on his cheeks, lifting his head. Adam wept, choking on his sobs, blood mixing with his tears and stinging his eyes. Athena grabbed his hands, forcing them from his face.

"Shh," she said, gathering him into her arms. "Hush, now. It's done and gone, and long over, long finished."

He had killed God. He had killed God, just as Michael had said. Asking for more and more, demanding another companion, another lover, disgusted and dissatisfied by everything God had offered. And Lilith, poor, innocent Lilith, whose mind and life he'd destroyed only because he could . . .

He was a monster, and Michael was right. They had all been right, all this time.

He couldn't be trusted.

He shouldn't even be allowed to live.

CHAPTER TWENTY-FIVE

Thor

§

"You see what he is," Michael called out. "You accuse me of paranoia, of fear-mongering, but every evil in this world was spawned from his rule! I do not forget what he was, though my brothers would have it kept from you. I do not forget what he might yet be again."

Elah had risen at Adam's fall, her eyes wide, though Thor was not certain if it was fear or grief which filled them. Perhaps it did not matter either way. He crouched beside Adam's stricken form, meeting Athena's gaze over his head. *Did you know?*

She shook her head, holding him to her breast as she would a fretful child, rocking him gently. But Raphael had known, almost certainly. Must have known, and still, he had helped them to restore Adam, so long ago. Trusted him, now.

"You can see for yourself what those memories do to him," Raphael said. "Would the man he was weep for the pain he's caused? Revel in it, perhaps, celebrate it, laugh at all he had accomplished. But weep? Claw at his own flesh to tear the knowledge from his body? No, Lady. Whatever your father was once, he is not that any longer. He will never be that again."

Thor climbed back to his feet, for his presence would hardly offer Adam comfort, and the man's torment was palpable. "It was my understanding that Adam's loyalty was not in question, this day. If it is his role in my actions that you must know, I can answer for it just as easily, and he is, it seems, no longer in any condition to speak in his own defense. Send him home, Elah. Allow Athena to see to him until Raphael can be released for the purpose. He should not be left alone, now."

"You presume to tell the Goddess how to treat Her father?"

Thor ignored Michael's sneer, keeping his eyes on Elah. "*Your father* deserved better than this, Lady."

She flushed, but gave Athena a sharp nod. Thor helped her to steady Adam as she rose, and Athena took his hand, betraying no surprise at the spark of lightning and surge of power he offered with the contact. Having wielded her father's lightning, Athena was no stranger to the power of the storm. Though she could not summon lightning on her own, she could control it, when some portion of that power was gifted into her keeping.

If I fail. He squeezed her hand, and let her go.

The Host jangled above him, murmuring amongst themselves, and Thor struggled against his temper. It was more important than ever now that he keep his head. Leaving Eve with Adam's support had been one thing, now that she had healed, she might one day find some peace in her relationship with her brother, but Adam was in no position to aid her with those horrors in his head. And Eve, for all her strengths, did not have her brother's discernment, nor his particular skills in debate. There were times, after all, when a small measure of deceit went a long way toward the greater good.

Elah retook her seat, looking far more troubled than when she had left it. Her fingers curled into the living wood of her throne, and her gaze remained unfocused, as if she watched her father, still, though Athena had taken him from the hall.

"Without my father, my disadvantage is all the greater," she said at last. "Whatever role he has played, he has always granted Us his full support, never hesitating to offer himself to Our cause. But you, Thor, you are a different matter. Your motives have ever been strange, your methods more so."

When he took a breath to respond, she held up a hand to stop him, her eyes hard. "I do not deny your love for my mother, but I was a fool to blind myself to the dangers of your presence in her life. Were my mother's loyalties to shift, her love for you set above that which binds her to me and mine, it is clear to me now, that it would be the beginning of the end."

"Lady." Thor stepped forward. She had made up her mind. He had known it from the moment Athena had warned him, but he could not stop himself from trying. "I beg of you to listen to your father's words, if you will not hear mine. There is a threat upon this world, growing ever stronger at your expense, at Eve's. Allow me to stay, as your champion. Allow me to search out this threat and destroy it. Allow me the peace of knowing I have left Eve safe, at the least, if I cannot be sure of her happiness."

"It is the same tired lie, Lady," Michael said. "A flimsy excuse for his presence, that he might continue on, as he always has, with no respect for any laws but his own. He will promise you his loyalty and all the while, work against you through your mother!"

"And if it is true?" Raphael asked. "Would you face this threat without the power Thor offers freely? If it steals your own strength, Elah, you will need the help of the other gods."

Michael sniffed. "She needs nothing more than what She has, already. The sword will strike it dead, should this mysterious power rise."

Elah let out a breath, a glance enough to silence them both. "If there is a threat to Us, my Archangels will find it," she said. "But I cannot trust you, Thor. Not as my champion, and certainly not as my mother's consort."

"Husband," he corrected her, lifting his chin. "And no matter how far you send me, there is little you might do to break that bond."

The angels exploded into Chorus, and Elah slumped against her great throne, the import of his words not lost upon her. As long as they were married, he would be able to reach her, exiled or not. She would be able to reach him, no matter what barriers Elah raised against his return. Perhaps he could not be with her in body, but in spirit—in spirit, they could not be parted.

Michael bared his teeth, drawing the sword at his hip. "Then you have sentenced yourself, Odinson."

Lightning burned in his veins, but he did not allow himself to call *Mjölnir* to his palm. Not yet. He would not sentence Athena to death for his own foolishness. Would not bring war upon Bhagavan. And he would not abandon Eve so easily, by courting his own death.

Elah's hand closed on her angel's sword arm, stopping him. "If my mother has married him, bound herself to him in love, she will not forgive his death at Our hands. I have not risked this much to have her back only to lose her so soon after she has returned to me."

Thor forced his hands to unclench, and rolled his shoulders against the tension which had settled there. "My thanks, Lady, for your understanding."

"It isn't understanding which gives me pause." She released Michael, and folded her hands neatly in her lap. Then she leaned forward, her eyes narrowing. "I promise you, Thor, if we meet again, even my mother's love will not save you from my fury. I cannot exile you from your Asgard, but I will not tolerate your presence on earth itself beyond sunset, this night, and if you are wise, you will not test the patience of my angels. Say your goodbyes to my mother, and go."

Thor bowed. One last strained gesture of respect for her authority, if not her decision. And then he left before she changed her mind.

It was not failure exactly, but it was near enough.

He only hoped Eve would survive it.

CHAPTER TWENTY-SIX

Eve

"Adam?" She stepped away from Raphael once the floor was firmly beneath her feet again, and squinted into the darkness. There was a rustle from the bed, a shifting of blankets, but nothing more.

Of course he would be staying in the penthouse suite, but darkening all the windows seemed like an awful waste of good sunlight. She lightened the opacity, leaving the privacy settings intact. It wouldn't help the situation if the press started taking snapshots of his wallowing.

"You can't hide away in here forever. Your poor secretary is on the verge of a breakdown, and if you don't give her a raise after the job she's doing covering up your fit of depression, you'll deserve every word the press has uttered related to slave-driving."

Nothing. Not even a rustle. She glanced back at Raphael behind her, but he only shook his head. This was normal, then. And from what the Archangel had told her, he'd been this way since Thor's exile.

Eve sighed, repressing the pang of heartache that came with the thought. If anyone had a right to be wallowing, it ought to have been her. Adam should have been consoling her in the wake of Thor's departure, banging on her door and making a nuisance of himself—not that she would have let him carry on for long. Not that she had the patience for her own misery. Or rather, she didn't dare give it her attention for long.

Already, she could feel herself slipping toward darkness. Not because of Thor's absence. He was still with her, a balm in the back of her mind, where he'd always been. But there was a leak, somewhere. A constant, hungry drain on her entire being, just waiting for her to feed it.

She sat down on the edge of his bed, resting her hand on the curve of his shoulder, humped beneath the linens. "Whatever memories Michael gave back to you—none of that matters, now. What matters are the people depending on you for their lives. Not because you've hurt them, but because you're helping them, because you're working toward peace on their behalf. And the moment Russia catches even the faintest whiff of weakness from the North Country, everything is going to unravel quickly. You've got to come back to work."

It's my fault.

"It's God's fault for spoiling you rotten," she said, tugging gently at the blanket to see his face. When she caught sight of him, she pressed her lips together. The long red welts on his forehead and cheeks weren't the worst of it. Clumps of his hair were missing, and the rest was matted with dried blood and scabs. "Oh, Adam. What have you done to yourself?"

He rolled over, covering his head with a pillow. *Just go.*

"And miss my opportunity to give back all the pestering you've done to me over the years?" She pulled the pillow out of his hands and ran her fingers through his filthy hair. "Not even Thor would leave you like this. It's far too pathetic."

How? He took a shuddering breath. *How could you ever forgive me—ever trust me, or love me, even for a moment?*

"Because you aren't him, Adam. You haven't been him since they took your memory."

The things I did. If you knew what I was. The things I did before you were made.

"Reu told me enough," she said, her fingers still moving through his hair, checking his wounds. "And even if he hadn't, I saw it firsthand. I knew what you were. Just as I know now what you aren't. Just as I know that your North Country needs you as you are. The world needs you."

Crusted blood flaked off between her fingers, gritty as sand and staining her skin. His scalp had healed beneath it, she thought, but the hair would still take time to grow back. Better if she didn't have to resort to the apples Thor had left her. There was no telling what affect they would have on Adam, and she wasn't sure she wouldn't need them herself. She'd already wasted one. Thor had shown her how to twist the stems off, to keep them from ripening into solid gold, and she'd saved one, just as it was. It had hardened into a perfect rose gold, leaf and stem and all, and when she looked at it, touched it, she felt closer to Thor. As if, even ripened, it wanted to heal the breach between them, bring them together again.

I should never have done this. Any of it. I should have listened to you. I should have kept myself from it. They would be better off without me.

"Without you, there would be a great many more starving people, and that is the truth of it. You've done more good than harm since you've remembered yourself, and even before, it wasn't all awful."

"I had my own son murdered, as Suleiman the Magnificent," he grumbled. "Invited him to come to my tent with the promise of absolution, and had my eunuchs kill him before my eyes."

Eve almost smiled, but for the gruesomeness of the confession. At least he was talking, and not just thinking. A glance over her shoulder told her Raphael had slipped away, probably to be sure he wouldn't have anything to tell Elah. "You always did like honorifics."

"It was after they returned my memory," he said, not looking at her. His knuckles were white, he grasped the sheets so tightly. "Even then, I was a monster, and that part of me—it's still here, bemoaning the difficulties in staging some Russian coup, when it would be so much easier just to kill Volkov and be done with it, or better, take control of his mind."

"Because you're so eager for Russia to fall into your hands? To expand your reach, your influence, your power? For the fun of watching them dance?"

"Because he's holding at least a third of the world's food supply hostage!"

"There," Eve said. "That, exactly, is the difference. Before, you'd have wanted to take control of his mind just for the pleasure of it. Now, it's to save lives. But it's not what some small part of us thinks would be easier that counts, Adam. It's what we actually do with the power we have. You're doing good work. Saving lives. And now, you and I, we have to do what we can to save the world, too."

She wouldn't have known, if it hadn't been for me. If I hadn't come to speak to you. If we hadn't gone to the barren lands, all three of us. She exiled him because of me.

She closed her eyes, breathing deeply to steady herself. If she gave in to the pain, it would swallow her whole, and then they'd both be useless. *She exiled him because of Michael. All of this has been because of Michael. And if we're going to survive his paranoia—I'm going to need your help, and your resources. Scientists sent to the barren lands to begin research, and Elah looking in the other direction. I need you well, Adam.*

I—

"Please, Adam." She squeezed his arm. "If not for me, for your daughter. She needs you, too."

He laughed humorlessly. "Why should she listen to me at all, knowing what I was?"

"Because she loves who you are now, that's why. She loves her father."*And I did, too.*

Did.

"Do," she said. "Now that I have something left inside me beyond that pit of despair. Thank Thor for that. And—" she hesitated. But if she believed what she was telling him, that he had changed, there was no reason to keep it from him. *I found the second tree, Adam. The Tree of Life.*

There was no second tree, he said miserably, shrugging out from beneath her hand and pulling the blankets back up. *Just the one I burned to ash along with the Garden.*

It wasn't in the Garden.

He stilled, even the rise and fall of his chest stopping for a moment. *Where?*

"Asgard," she said. "Thor says it was a gift from his mother."

Adam rolled to his back, searching her face. "His mother?"

She nodded, resisting the urge to touch the healing scrapes on his face. He'd even clawed at his neck, as if he might be able to tear his head from his body, altogether. Calendula tea, or maybe some white vinegar and water to help him heal—if he scarred, people would ask questions.

"What are you thinking, Evey?"

"I think there was a reason Thor found me. A reason he watched over us both. And I think it has to do with that tree."

"How?"

Eve shook her head. "That's why I need you. And everything you remember, now. Everything God told you, before I was made."

"Ah." His eyes flickered with pain, so easy for her to recognize when she'd suffered it herself for so long. "And here I thought this was an errand of mercy."

"You've rubbed off on me." She leaned forward, pressing a kiss to his forehead. Because no matter what else had passed between them, he was still her brother. He was still the only man on earth who could understand.

And seeing him this way . . . She could only imagine how difficult it must have been for him to watch her descend into the same madness, every action he took only making it worse. Maybe they could never be lovers again, certainly she couldn't continue on as his wife. But they had to stand together, now, if they wanted to survive. And that meant letting go of the past. For both of them.

"Let's get you out of this bed, all right?"

§

She helped him wash the blood from his hair, careful of the healing skin beneath, and when Adam called to Hilda through the door, asking for some sort of calendula based cream, the woman almost wept in relief.

"She loves you, you know," Eve said, checking each of his scrapes for any sign of infection. Adam sat on the edge of the tub, naked from the waist up, and she'd settled across his lap for convenience. She knew herself well enough to realize she needed his closeness just as much as he needed hers, and if she wanted him to forgive himself, she didn't dare hesitate.

His lips twisted. "I can't give her what she deserves."

Eve picked up the soft tube of cream, and started with his poor, ruined scalp. "You sell yourself short when you say things like that. Maybe love isn't exactly your gift, but you're not incapable of it by any means. You proved that with Mia, and with me."

He tried to turn his face away, but she caught him by the chin with a firm hand, dabbing at his hairline. "I left you. I didn't even try."

"You thought your presence in our lives would destroy the world, Adam. I'm not saying it was right, or that I understood, then. But it was love that drove you to it." His hair. Maybe she would part with an apple. It was bound to heal him faster. "I wish you'd just told me."

He opened his eyes, looking up into hers. "Not as much as I do."

She smiled. "I don't know. I only had Elah for two years, but I don't think I can count the number of times I cursed you for leaving me alone to cope with her. She was the most outrageous handful."

He caught her hand when she moved to apply the cream to his cheek. "Evey, I'm so sorry. For the Garden. For leaving you. For everything in between. I'm not sure I ever said it, but I want you to know. I keep trying to do right by you, to make it all right, and it never seems to work the way I hope it will. But I never want to hurt you again, Evey. Never again."

"I know," she said.

It was the best she could do.

CHAPTER TWENTY-SEVEN

Eve

Eve left him that evening, unseen, thanks to Raphael's help, and returned to her dorm. The lonely apple on her desk winked in the darkness, and she stood there for a long moment, watching it flash, reflecting the dim notification light from her desk. It had been a very long day, but the worst part was that she still had to face the night.

"Play messages, voice only," she said, and the flashing light turned solid, the fruit illuminated in a crescent of red light.

"Three messages," a smooth voice responded, the perfect balance between masculine and feminine. "Message one:

"Anna, I'm sorry about the other day." Marcus, of course. "Things have been so strained between us, and I just—can we hit a reset button? Erase and correct these last couple of days and just go back to the way things were? Call me when you have a moment. I want to catch up."

She snorted. How much of Marcus's desire to catch up just at this exact moment was his own, and how much of it was Elah's prodding, she wasn't sure. She would never be sure. But Elah's instincts weren't wrong. Eve needed friendship, needed laughter and pleasure in her life, generating and inspiring love to restore the constant measure that was draining away and leaking out. It wasn't enough that she be open to the world—she had to be part of it, continually. That was the role she had to play if she wanted to keep herself whole.

"Message two," the computer announced.

"Hi Anna, it's Ashley. You weren't home when I stopped by, but I thought it was only fair to warn you—Sophia's dropped off the face of the earth, and Marcus is pestering me about your schedule again. I told him if he wanted to know what you were doing, he'd have to talk to you himself, but I think one of the other girls told him your boyfriend hasn't been around this last week. Good luck! And when you're done breaking his heart, send him back in my direction, would you?"

Eve picked up the apple and lay back on her bed. So Sophia had left Marcus, and Marcus was looking for a rebound. Or hoping to cash in on some sympathy. Mutual support and shoulders to cry on. Well, she'd have to thank Ashley for the warning. Maybe set her up with someone else who wasn't so fixated. It shouldn't be too hard to arrange.

"Message three:

"Anna, you're making me sick with worry over here. Please, just call."

Obviously, that had come after he'd learned that Thor had begun to absent himself from her life.

"Reply?"

She closed her eyes, bringing the fruit to her lips, cold, smooth, and honey-sweet beneath her nose. *I miss you.*

There was a pulse of warmth, but that was all. She wasn't even certain he heard her, because it was the same any time she thought of him, brushing against his presence in her mind. She ought to have been able to reach him, to speak with him, but it was like shining a flashlight into thick fog. Everything bounced back, and she was afraid that if she kept shouting, everyone would hear it. She grimaced. The idea of Elah and Michael eavesdropping on her silent love letters, cataloging every exchange and dissecting it for proof of some conspiracy didn't appeal at all. In fact, it was downright inhibiting.

But she *did* miss him. More at night than any other time, with nothing to distract her. She was afraid to sleep, afraid to let her mind wander and fall into that hungry, gaping green maw of depression and pain. She couldn't risk it. She couldn't risk getting lost in it again, and she didn't want to live in that darkness. Not anymore. Not ever again.

"Reply?" the computer prompted again.

Eve sighed, and reached for her earpiece, tucking it into place. "Call Marcus."

§

"You're glowing," Marcus said, touching her cheek.

Eve stepped back from the door to let him in. She hadn't been fooled by his claim that he was on his way back from another friend's place and might as well stop in, but she hadn't called him to start an argument, and she wasn't going to create one now. The good thing about Marcus was that it was practically one distraction after another to keep his hands off her.

"I'm happy," she said.

"Because of Thor?"

She lifted her eyebrows. "Ashley called me, you know. I know you were grilling the girls on my floor again."

He half-smiled. "You're avoiding the question."

"And what about Sophia?"

"Seems like the Ashley grapevine grows both ways."

"I'm sorry it didn't work out." And she meant it. Marcus would have been a lot easier to handle in a relationship with someone else. "What happened?"

He shrugged. "What happened with Thor?"

She pushed him toward the sofa, and slid open the chiller. "I'm trying to stay happy, Marcus, not descend into madness. What would you like to drink? I have cider and water—though the cider might be on its way to vinegar."

"I'll risk it," he said.

She took out two bottles and sat with him. "I wanted to apologize for my behavior, lately. Not that it excuses yours in the slightest, but I just—I haven't been myself for a very long time, and I want you to know I appreciate the fact that you were here for me, even when I kept pushing you away."

Marcus popped open his bottle with far too much deliberation, and stared at it. "So what does that mean?"

"It means I'm sorry for being a jerk."

He shook his head, just slightly. "That isn't what I meant, and I think you know it."

She leaned forward, elbows on her knees. "I can't give you what you deserve." The words were bitter on her tongue, and she grimaced. Hadn't she just had this argument with Adam, and now here she was, using his excuse for herself. "I love Thor. I'm always going to love him, and you're always going to be hoping for more from me, but it isn't ever going to compare."

"You don't know that, Anna."

But she did. She knew it, because she'd already lived it, lifetime after lifetime. And it had been one thing when she'd believed he was dead. But now?

"It wouldn't be kind of me to encourage you."

"But you still called."

"I needed a distraction."

He laughed. "Is that all?"

"It was you or Ashley, and if it had been Ashley, I would have been spending my evening talking about you, anyway."

"I always knew you couldn't stop thinking about me, but I didn't realize you couldn't stop talking about me, either." He spread his arm out along the back of the sofa, smirking.

"You know that isn't—"

"Just wait," he said, his smirk shifting into something softer. He set his bottle aside and took hers, too, leaning closer in a way that told her he wasn't at all dissuaded. "Let me make you an offer you can't refuse."

She crossed her arms, and eyed him. "Go on."

The last thing she wanted was this night to end by having to walk him out of her room against his will. Not that she wasn't above it, in self-defense. Anymore. But if she didn't let him say his part, knowing Marcus, she could be sure he wouldn't forget, and she'd be treated to it at their next meeting, all the same.

He grinned, an acknowledgment of his own foibles as much as it was his confidence. "If you need a distraction, I can give it to you. I can keep your mind tied up in knots of pleasure, if that's what you want. And as a *friend*," he emphasized the word with a comical leer, "I'm more than happy to provide you with that service. There's no reason this has to be all or nothing, Anna. We're not living in the dark ages, no matter how many paper books you buy."

She shook her head. "That isn't the kind of woman I am."

"Then it's going to be a long lonely life waiting for Thor to show up again," he said, leaning back. "I don't think you're that kind of woman either. And don't cite the last however many years to me. I've had a lot of time to think about all this, and when we were younger, you had no problem snuggling up with me. You were a lot more friendly across the board when you weren't denying yourself every kind of affection. Case in point, tonight."

Eve snorted. "Unbelievable."

He wasn't wrong, and that was what made it all that much more ridiculous. He really wasn't going to give up. No matter how many times she told him she couldn't love him the way he deserved to be, it wouldn't make a lick of difference. He'd just change his attack plan and try again. Though she had to admit, this "it's okay if it's completely meaningless" approach was the last thing she'd expected.

"And yet, it's all true," he said. "You can't lie to me, Anna. I know all your secrets."

She reached over him for her bottle of cider, trying to ignore the chill that slipped down her spine with his assurance. "I didn't know I was keeping secrets."

"Deny it all you want, sweetheart, but I'll tell you right now, I'm not the only one who's taken an interest. Someone's trying to get a peek behind your firewall, and they're going a lot further than just asking Ashley if your boyfriend is still making regular appearances."

She sat up, rocking back to her side of the small sofa. "What?"

"Whatever it is you've been hiding, with Thor or anyone else—and don't think the girls on your floor missed your second visitor, and all the fighting that was going on behind your closed-but-not-well-sound-proofed door—it's going to come out, Anna. Someone is tailing you."

"That's ridiculous! Why would anyone be . . ." Michael, maybe? But that seemed awfully mortal of him, and he wouldn't be seen if he didn't want to be. Not by anyone. If someone had identified Adam though, realized the President of the North Country had been paying her visits—that would not end well.

"The fact that you're sitting there cataloging a list of either things you've done recently, or people who would actually be interested in you might hold the answers," Marcus said, looking even smugger. "So are you going to confess, or are you just going to keep pretending that you have nothing to hide?"

"You've known me my whole life, Marcus, what could I possibly have to hide?"

"Sophia had some interesting theories."

"You were talking about me with your girlfriend?" Eve arched an eyebrow. "No wonder she left you."

He shrugged. "I never said she was my girlfriend."

"Spill, Marcus."

"You know, I think I'd rather savor the experience of having some small piece of something you want for a little bit longer." He stretched out his legs, crossing them at the ankles, and took a drink of his cider. "Yugh!" His nose wrinkled. "How long has this been in your chiller?"

Eve narrowed her eyes. It wouldn't be so hard to find out what he knew. He'd never even notice she was in his head, really—

"Don't even think about it," he said, still examining the bottle.

"What are you—?"

"Please," he said, looking up. "I've been friends with you all my life, remember? Whatever you're thinking right now, it's trouble."

"If you weren't being so impossible, I wouldn't have to think it."

He laughed. "Says the president of impossible-land. I'll tell you what, I'll give you two options. You can tell me why someone might be tailing you, or you can let me take you out for something a lot less offensive to drink, and I'll tell you what I know. The latter comes with a three drink minimum, which should be just enough to get you nice and cuddly, and I'm giving you fair warning in advance that's the entire point."

"There's a third option you haven't taken into consideration," she grumbled.

He smiled slowly. "Haven't I?"

He was worse than Adam, she decided, and he knew exactly which of her buttons to push. But Thor had thought there was something about Sophia that was odd, too, and if someone was watching her—Eve had no desire to ever be a scientific experiment again, not after the ward. Human or god, she wasn't going to be under anyone's microscope.

"Drinks," she said. "And you start talking right now."

CHAPTER TWENTY-EIGHT

Elah, Before

Grandfather wasn't always old. It was the first thing she noticed, when he welcomed her to the Redwood Hall, after she finished staring at the trees, tipping her head back so far she would have fallen over if it hadn't been for Raphael standing close behind her. At first, when he bent his tired body down to greet her, he seemed to creak and crack at the joints, exhaustion in every line of his face. But when she took his hand, he changed. His wrinkles smoothed and his back and shoulders straightened, and when he stood back up again, he was grinning with bright old eyes in a face as young as her Archangel's.

"Your Archangel, is it?" Grandfather asked, laughing.

That was how she'd always thought of Raphael. As hers. He'd always been with her, after all, and he'd said they were the most important things. Her and Mama. But she'd never *said* it. Not out loud.

"Mama says it isn't polite to read anyone's mind, *especially* not family."

"And she's quite right," Grandfather said, his voice warm as a wolf's howl. "But you and I are not just anyone, Little Goddess. You and I are two parts of the same whole. Not the only parts, mind you, but the most important in this moment, to this world. Through us, all of creation will live or die, and as such, it is crucial that I know your mind. Do you understand me?"

"Is Mama a piece?"

"My first born, as well. Your father—"

"Mama says he left because he loved me, and he was afraid if he stayed he'd hurt us."

Grandfather's eyes crinkled. "That is one reason, yes."

"Why else?" she asked.

"You'll learn the answer to that question soon enough, Little Goddess. When you're old enough to understand it. But there are reasons, and there are *reasons*, and that which is known is usually only a part of the whole. Your birth was necessary. What comes after . . . it is merely an old god's hope that his house be left in order. Or at least that it might hold the potential to be ordered, if those he leaves behind desire it. I tire of my daughter's struggles, of my son's imprisonment by those who have no right to interfere. Now that my family is returned to me, I would see them free. All of you, free, upon my death, to forge your own fates, together or apart."

Elah dug at the mulch with her toe. "Does that mean Mama and Father could be together, too?"

Grandfather smiled kindly. "I expect she will forgive him one day, but to the rest, I cannot say. It will be her choice, who to love, how to live. It is the least she deserves after everything I have not done."

She wrinkled her nose, not sure what any of it meant. "Will I ever get to meet Father?"

"When you're a bit older, you may go to him if you wish. It would delight him, I'm certain, if you chose to."

"Then I will," Elah said, nodding to herself. "And maybe if he sees how happy I am, and how good I've been, then he'll come home to Mama." She frowned over her shoulder at Raphael, still standing with them, though he hadn't spoken. It wasn't like him to be so quiet. "Do you think?"

Raphael's eyes were sad. A long time ago, she'd decided he had eyes like an eagle, but when he looked like that, they weren't at all. "Not in this life, dearest. But perhaps, if he is very careful, in the next."

She didn't know what that meant either. But she didn't like it.

"Mama shouldn't be alone."

Grandfather squeezed her hand. "You needn't worry, Elah. As long as my son lives, she never will be. Not in spirit. Now. Raphael and I must speak, but Michael will show you to your rooms, and later, I'll teach you all the ways you might come and go between them, and how to make them grow the way you wish, if anything displeases you."

She hadn't noticed Michael until he dropped to the mulch beside them. But when she smiled at him, he bowed, and his eyes weren't *so* hard anymore. She took his hand, rough and cool around hers, and skipped to catch up to his longer steps. Grandfather was old and brittle again, when she glanced back, lowering himself slowly into a chair made of roots and branches and leaves. Raphael kneeled beside him, his shoulders bowed and bent and sad.

"Come, Lady," Michael said, stiff and formal. "This way."

§

Days turned into weeks, and weeks turned into months and months and months, and she began to understand. Why Michael had feared her, why her birth had been so necessary, why Grandfather had insisted that she come, and taken her from her mother. Why, when she left a room, the strength drained out of him, and he aged a thousand-thousand years in just a heartbeat.

Grandfather was dying.

She did her best. Stayed with him, as much as she could. The trees would shape her a seat beside him, and they would sit, her hand tight around his, and she would give him enough to be young, to be strong, to laugh with her, and teach her what he knew, and then she would try to give him more, but he'd only smile and pat her hand, and refuse.

"Save your strength, my girl, I've already lived long enough. It's your turn, now."

But not *now*, now. Not yet. She was growing, she knew that. Every night, just like at home, Raphael measured her against one of the redwoods, straight and tall and smooth as a column. But it wasn't just height, she gained, as the months passed. Her mind grew sharper, her thoughts clearer, every day. And being with Grandfather—the things he saw, and showed her. The cry of so many voices, calling out, calling for him.

"It's the only the reason I'm still here," he told her the first time he shared it all. "If it hadn't been for Michael. For the churches he built and the faiths that sprung from them, I wouldn't have lasted this long. For a time, I didn't think I would live long enough to see you born—your father and mother were so stubborn. And I was asleep for far too long. Had I realized sooner what kept them apart . . ." He gave a little flick of his fingers, just like Raphael did, when he didn't think his own words mattered. "What's done is done, and you're here, now. You're here, and you're learning what you need to know. Enough to see you through, until you've experience enough to learn your own tricks, hm? But you won't be alone, my girl. You'll have Michael and Gabriel, and *your* Archangel, Raphael." He smiled at his own teasing, pinching her cheek with affection. "And you'll have your parents, of course, if you have need of their advice. They've lived a long time, the both of them, and they know this world. They know the *people* of this world, so well."

The older she got, the more she realized he rambled on. The sharper her mind grew, the more misted his thoughts. The taller she stood, the more bent and bowed and wasted his old body became.

"It's happening so fast," she said to Raphael, one night, after he'd marked her height against the tree. She'd grown at least two handspans in the last half-year.

"Two parts of the same whole, my dear," he told her gently. "You're growing quickly, and so he fades, as well."

"And how do we know she isn't sucking Him dry?" Michael asked from the doorway. He always stood outside her door, his arms crossed, his sword—an empty scabbard, she'd come to realize, for Grandfather had taken his blade long ago—at his hip. Her guardian, though he rarely spoke to her, rarely so much as looked at her, if he could help it. "If she hadn't been born, He'd still be as He was."

Raphael sighed, straightening. "As He was. Just a pale version of Himself, a shadow lingering on, and on. Until His people turned away again. And they would have Michael, they would have gone back to Odin, to the gods who still remained—"

"You think I don't know they took this world with your help?" Michael snarled. "That you aren't still trying to talk Elohim into making an exception for that Greek of yours? If it hadn't been for you, I might have driven them off, or set them to killing one another at the very least. We'd have thrown off their yoke long ago!"

"Not Odin's," Raphael said. "He'd have come all the same, and if he'd found this world at war, he would have won it. That was the risk. That was always the risk, and I did what I could to limit it."

"And what do you think will happen once he realizes Elohim is gone? When One-Eye sees a slip of a girl standing in His place?"

"Odin has wanted to leave for centuries. It's only pride that keeps him here. Elohim's death changes nothing, and Elah's birth, everything. His son will stay, and the father will go."

But Elah didn't care about that. The other gods meant nothing to her. It was Michael's words that stung, that burned in her heart. All this time, and she still couldn't say he was her friend, though Gabriel had been warm and pleasant and kind, telling her bedtime stories about her parents' lives, and Raphael loved her, always. She hated it. She hated that no matter how kind she was, no matter how hard she tried, Michael still looked on her with those same hard eyes. And it had only gotten worse. That glimmer of hope she'd had, when he'd accepted her feather, he'd stomped upon it. And it wasn't that she didn't understand. She did. His loyalty was to Grandfather, and he was watching her grow, watching Grandfather weaken. It broke her heart too, but there was nothing she could do. It was what he wanted! What he'd meant to happen, whether Michael liked it or not.

"Mama was right about you," she told him, lifting her chin the way she'd seen her mother do. "You're so afraid. And you've been so afraid for so long, it's like you don't remember there's another way. When you say these things, about me and Grandfather, you insult us both, and Him most of all!"

Michael's teeth flashed, the snarling wolf still there beneath his quiet, brooding body. "Your mother knows nothing. Haven't you learned that much, yet?"

"Enough, Michael," Raphael said, soft and sharp at the same time. "You'll speak of Eve with the respect she deserves or not at all. If I have to go to Elohim, ask Him to command it of you, I will."

Michael hissed.

"It doesn't matter what he says, Raphael," Elah said. "If he knew anything about my mother he'd know he didn't have to be afraid of me. He'd know how much I love this world, and everything in it. Even if everything in it doesn't love me."

She turned her back on both of them, then, and asked to be left alone. Raphael bowed himself out, and Michael—she could feel his eyes, hard and angry on her back. She didn't even have to twitch to shut her door in his face. The branches wove together with nothing more than a thought, and no matter how he stared, he'd never see through them.

But that was the problem, wasn't it?

He didn't see *her*.

And until he did, she'd never have his faith.

❧

If she could win Michael, she could do anything. And she had to win him. She had to have his loyalty, freely given, because she couldn't stand to rule the way Grandfather did. She didn't want to command him, demand his obedience. She didn't want his resentment, simmering beneath every exchange. Maybe her mother didn't know everything, and maybe she'd tried to give Elah rules to live by that wouldn't matter much longer, but her mother had taught her love. The power in it. The necessity. Grandfather had been their Creator, and they had been bound to him by that, but Michael, all the Host, looked on her as their destruction. Their death. Pieces of the whole to be reabsorbed and reforged into something new, something else.

But that wasn't how she had been taught to see the angels. And it certainly wasn't how she looked on Raphael or any of his brothers. Not after he had helped to raise her for so long, not when he stood by her and her mother so loyally, for reasons far beyond any command he'd been given. And if she could just convince Michael, the rest of the Host would trust her too.

She never considered what she would do if she failed.

Failure just wouldn't do.

CHAPTER TWENTY-NINE

Eve, Later

Marcus didn't talk until they'd reached the bar, and, at his further insistence, Eve had taken her first sip of her drink. A monstrous concoction made with at least three shots of alcohol, which also hadn't been her first choice.

"I'm about ten seconds from utilizing my third option, Marcus, if you don't start spilling your guts."

He grinned, sliding into the booth next to her in spite of the perfectly comfortable seat wide open across the table. "I can't remember the last time I had this much power in our relationship, but I could get used to it."

"You're going to get used to my hand colliding with your face pretty shortly, and I'm not sure that was the cuddly you had in mind."

"That's my Anna, all spice, and never anything nice. Makes me wonder what in Creation you could possibly have done to attract the attention of a world leader—and not just any world leader, but Mr. President for Life himself."

Eve took another drink from her glass with a new appreciation for the three shots of liquor involved. "That's a pretty outrageous fabrication, even for you."

"I bumped into the guy on his way out of your room at nine in the morning, Anna. And shortly thereafter, Thor wasn't seen or heard from again on your floor. Though, now that I think about it, it would make a whole lot of sense if Thor himself were some North Country buffoon."

Eve winced. "I really wish you'd stop talking about him. And I wouldn't use the word buffoon. Ever again."

Marcus gave a dismissive wave of his hand, brushing the word off the table. "All right, he-who-shall-not-be-named, then. So what, are you going to tell me you met President Simonsen over the summer, too?"

"That would be a lie."

"Ah." He stretched his arm out behind her. "So you're sticking with outright denial, altogether. A shame. Especially since Sophia already told me the truth."

She choked on her drink. "What?"

"That's a terrible poker-face, Anna."

Eve adjusted her expression, pulling up what she hoped was polite disinterest, instead. "Oh?"

He smirked. "Better late than never doesn't exactly apply in this scenario. You already showed your hand, so spill."

"If you already know the truth, why do you need to hear it from me?"

"Because it's bound to be far more entertaining that way."

"That wasn't the deal." Eve lifted her glass staring into the bottom—she'd barely drained a quarter of it. "Unless of course answering questions means I get to stop drinking myself into oblivion?"

"No, no," Marcus said. "Carry on."

She smirked and took another sip, pointedly.

Marcus rolled his eyes. "Sophia told me he was trying to recruit you because your family is some distant relation. Typical, really. Trying to stack his government to secure his shining dynasty."

Eve coughed, fighting laughter. "Oh, that."

"*Oh, that* nothing," he said. "And I can tell by the way your eyes are dancing that there's something else. Really, Anna. You'd never make it a week in politics making faces like that. Is that what happened when Simonsen met you? He realized how utterly useless you'd be because you can't keep a straight face?"

She shook her head, hiding her smile behind her glass and taking another, much larger drink. Distant relation. Who was this Sophia, anyway? She wished she'd asked Thor when he'd brought it up, but she'd been anxious to get to Asgard for the weekend. For the last weekend, as it turned out.

Her smiled faded, and she downed the rest of the glass.

"Uh oh." Marcus reached around her to code in the order for another drink. "Don't start getting mopey on me, now. I've got plans for tonight, and none of them include weeping. Tell me Simonsen wanted to marry you so you could have little incestuous Simonsens together, and rule the world. Or something. Anything, but it has to be outrageous."

She hiccupped a laugh. "I thought you just wanted me to get cuddly."

"Cuddling you while you cry isn't what I had in mind, sweetheart." He tugged at one of her braids. "Our goal is to keep you happy, remember? Happy and distracted, and if I have to switch it up from intellectual distraction to physical, I'll do it."

"You say it like it would be the worst thing in the world."

"Having my future plans derailed by tears? Totally the worst. Showing off my not inconsiderable skills in your bed—you just try me, Anna. You'll be flying so high, they'll hear you call my name on the moon."

She snorted. "Speaking of outrageous."

"Not as outrageous as little Simonsen babies." Her drink arrived, and he slid it toward her. "Drink up."

She did as she was told. And thanked all that was holy that was all he thought it was. Dynasty building. If he only knew. But he didn't. And that much, at least, was a relief. Maybe she could actually just . . .

enjoy herself. A novel idea. "How many other people think they saw me with Simonsen, anyway?"

He shrugged. "None of the other girls on your floor mentioned it—and for the record, that was the only reason I was asking about you. Between those guys following you all over campus and the Simonsen business, it seemed like a good idea to test the waters, just in case reporters started sniffing around, or something. For all I know, your spies *are* the press."

"Let's hope not." If the press found Adam now, he'd have a heck of a time explaining himself. He hadn't even wanted to show his face to Hilda.

Marcus slipped his arm around her. "Because . . . ?"

She elbowed him in the ribs. "I'm drinking, not satisfying your curiosity."

"Oof. Well, maybe you should drink faster." But he didn't give her any space, he just leaned in closer. "Drinking is only half of your side of the bargain, remember?"

§

She was buzzing before she finished the second drink, and Marcus was making her laugh so hard her stomach ached. By her third drink, he was drinking too, saluting her with each shot he took.

"Next time, maybe you won't make me blackmail you into coming out," Marcus teased.

"Next time, shmext time." She lifted her glass and scowled. "The ice is all melty."

"More ice for the future first lady of the North Country," he said, tapping the order into the table. "Goddess above, you smell amazing."

She laughed, pushing him back when he nuzzled her neck. "No tickling."

"Tickling is part of cuddling, North Country. And I like it when you get all squirmy."

"Shh!" she said, slithering out from under his arm to collect her cup of ice. She was so warm, and he wasn't helping her to cool off at all. "You're not supposed to talk about that."

"Doesn't matter if it isn't true, North Country," he said, grinning.

"Shh!" She slapped a hand over his face, and tipped an ice cube into her mouth. Marcus licked her palm and she jerked her hand back. "Yeck! No licking, either!"

"Biting?" he asked, his eyes dark. He captured her hand again, and her breath caught as his teeth grazed her wrist. "Really? I never would have guessed."

She swallowed, cold ice offsetting the heat inside her. "There're a lot of things you wouldn't guess."

"I'd love to find out, Anna." His voice was husky, his lips tickling against her wrist, even more sensitive now, and making her shiver. "We're good together, you and me. If Thor hadn't come, it would have been easy. The easiest thing in the world."

She let out a shaky breath and drew her hand back, suddenly feeling like she needed another drink. "Two hundred years ago, maybe."

He laughed. "Why two hundred years ago?"

"That was the last time my heart wasn't broken."

"Oh, no," Marcus said. "No wallowing, and absolutely no figurative language that isn't related to my sexual prowess."

She smiled faintly. If only, if only, if only. But he was just a man, another man who would die. At least Thor would live. She'd always have that place in the back of her mind, even if she couldn't have him.

"Anna," he warned. "I'm not kidding. If you go all sad, I'm going to have to take you to bed. So you either have another drink, and get happy, or we're going back to your dorm, and I am taking all your clothes off and tickling you until you can't breathe. I think you know which I'd prefer."

She knew. She knew what he wanted, and right then, she wasn't sure she wanted to argue. Simple, easy, uncomplicated pleasure, flooding through her body and washing the darkness away. "Should've stuck to two drinks."

"Next time we'll remember that."

"And this time?"

He kissed the corner of her mouth. "I think it's time for Plan B."

"Tickling?"

"Sex." He pulled back, his lips curving. "Before you say yes to Simonsen and I never see you again."

She laughed at that, and caught a fistful of his collar. "I'm not marrying Simonsen."

"I don't know. Money, power, he's got everything a girl could ever want."

"I'm not that kind of girl."

"Then what kind of girl are you?"

"The kind that wants love. Forever and ever and ever, with no goodbyes, no death, no grief, ever again."

"Is that all?" he asked, laughing. "Sorry, North Country, but that isn't how the world works."

She sighed, leaning back. "You can't even begin to know how well I know that truth."

"Enlighten me."

"Not uh," she said, pressing a finger to his lips. "I already had my drinks. You don't get to ask questions."

"I didn't hear a question mark." He nipped at her fingertip, and she smiled. "If you had any idea what you're doing to me right now . . ."

She tilted her head, closing her eyes to listen, just for a moment. He really was wound up, all tension and lust and eagerness. *Don't blow it,* he was thinking, over and over. *Now or never.*

"Now or never," she murmured, opening her eyes.

And his lips were on hers, his hand cupping her cheek, his thumb brushing along her cheekbone. He wasn't asking a question, or waiting for her to answer, and she knotted her fingers in his shirt and pulled him closer. Because he was right, he was right and it was easy, and even if she didn't love him, couldn't love him, his kiss still made her flush, head to toe.

He groaned, tearing his mouth from hers, and grabbed her hand instead, drawing her, stumbling after him, out of the booth. She laughed, her head swimming and the ground tipping back and forth beneath her feet, and somehow, she managed to vault herself up onto his back, and he was laughing too, fingers digging into her thighs, keeping her from sliding off.

He carried her out of the restaurant and into the night, and she bit his ear, which nearly made him trip before they got to the carport.

"In you go," he said, and then climbed in on top of her. "Back to campus, my gentle steed, before the future Mrs. Simonsen changes her mind."

The car started moving, and Marcus wasted no time, his lips leaving trails of rainbows behind, along her jaw and her neck and her shoulder, and her breast. And she knew she should stop him, stop this, but it felt like golden apples and she'd much rather drown in his kisses and his touch than in darkness.

They half-fell out of the car when the doors opened abruptly—it had only taken three tries for Marcus to match his thumb to the reader to accept the charge—and she squealed when he tossed her over his shoulder to carry her inside.

At her door, he swung her down, and she fumbled for the reader. But when she made to pull him inside, he hesitated, catching her hand and searching her face. "You sure?"

"Not at all," she said, taking his face in her hands. Stubble on his jaw scratched her palms, and she slid her fingers through his short hair, her eyes on his mouth. Eve stepped into him, wanting his lips on hers, on all of her. "But I promise you it won't be the thing I regret most."

He didn't hold back, after that.

Neither did she.

CHAPTER THIRTY

Eve

❧

She met Raphael again, after her classes the next day, one of the precious apples in her bag. Marcus had been reluctant to leave her bed and eager to seduce her into staying in his arms, but she'd slithered free, and thrown his things into the hall, earpiece and all. Of course he'd gone after it, laughing at her methods, and she had only shaken her head as she watched him strut past the lounge in nothing but what the Goddess had given him. He'd even saluted the other girls, when they stared, wide-eyed.

And so, another dozen hearts were stolen, and he, completely oblivious to the riches he'd acquired. Well, maybe not completely. He certainly knew his own worth. Not unlike Adam, really.

"How is he?" she asked the Archangel, forcing further contemplation of Marcus's dubious virtues from her mind.

"He rose from his bed of his own accord," Raphael said, inclining his head in greeting. "But he insists, yet, on sitting in the dark, and he's forbidden his people to enter his room."

"Of course he has," she sighed. "Can I prevail upon your power again? I don't think they'd let me in if I knocked."

Raphael smiled, thin and brittle. He seemed more worn than she had seen him before, his youthful face aged by stress. "By Elah's command, I am meant to see to your brother's needs while he recovers, my dear, and there is no doubt in my mind that one of his needs is most certainly your presence. As it has always been."

"No pressure, then." She took the hand he offered, and closed her eyes against the lurch of her body's relocation. At least the lightning gave some kind of transition, with Raphael, there was no warning. One moment, she was standing in the shadow of a tree, and the next she was in the cave of Adam's penthouse, her balance all skewed.

She took another moment, getting her feet under her again, and then felt for the window controls. It was so dark, she couldn't even see the furniture.

"You need only reach for me, and I will return," Raphael said, not that she could tell he'd gone at all until she found the controls and let the afternoon sun spill in.

And there was Adam, sitting in an armchair. He turned his face away from the light, grimacing. The expression was all the more gruesome with the welts on his cheeks. "Do you mind?"

"Yes, I do," she said. "There's already enough darkness in my life, thank you very much. I'm not going to let you add to it."

He squinted at her. "You're back."

"Of course I'm back." She sat down on the arm of his chair, and dug out the fruit. "And I brought you some help, since you clearly don't have the temperament or the time to heal up the old fashioned way."

He stared at it, a muscle twitching along his jaw. "I'm not sure—"

"I know," she said, offering it. "I wasn't either. But it will help, I promise. At least to get your head back in the game, if nothing else."

"What if it makes me . . . different? Like I was."

"Then I will personally knock some sense right back into that skull of yours," she promised, stroking the back of his head. The worst of the damage he'd done had been at the front, to the crown, but the back of his neck was still soft, his hair short enough to be fuzzy. "Trust me. I won't ever let you be that man again."

He took the fruit from her hand, his fingers playing over the delicate golden skin. "There's got to be something else."

"Nothing that will do the job as quickly or as easily," Eve said. "Modern medicine doesn't work miracles, contrary to popular belief."

"I never thought it did." But he didn't make any move to eat it, all the same. "I've always taken the paths of least resistance, manipulating my way to the top, instead of earning it. If I do it again, now, instead of facing my past . . ."

"It isn't about you, Adam. That's the difference, the thing that matters. You took the easy ways for your own gain, for your own ends, but this? You need to heal to keep the North Country from faltering, to keep Russia in line and the wheels of the food supply greased so that people don't starve. So that the world doesn't tip in the wrong direction."

"Is it really that simple?"

"Sometimes it is. This time, it is. You can't hide in here forever, and you can't show your face until you're healed, or bewigged, or made up. We might be identical according to my blasted door lock, but I can't order Hilda to send research teams to the desert, and I certainly can't wrangle your country for you. They'd notice if you became a woman overnight."

He smiled at that. "You can't tell me you wouldn't be able to convince them."

"I'm not really interested in exhausting myself trying," she said. "I'm already pushing it to keep my equilibrium as it is."

His head came up, his attention shifting completely, just like that. A caress of his thoughts, the wave of his support and love. It reminded her of Thor. He'd always been a wellspring of affection and love and peace, and she hadn't even realized how much she'd relied on it until he was gone.

"And here you are, wasting what little you have on me. I didn't even think—but of course, I can't imagine." Then his eyes narrowed, searching her face. "Are you hungover?"

"Never mind that." She got up, busying herself by pulling the blankets up on his bed. "You might feel drunk, after the first bite. Some mild euphoria. And then you'll need plenty of sleep. That's how it was for me, anyway."

"Evey?" She could feel his amusement, which was almost worse than anything else. Jealousy, she at least could have scoffed at, discounting altogether, or played at offense. "What in Creation have you been up to while my back was turned?"

"None of your business, that's what." She spun, pointing at the fruit in his hand. "Eat."

"Bouncing back nicely, are we?" He was smirking. "Or should I say rebounding?"

She flushed. "I can't just cut myself off from the world, again, much as I might like to. Not if we want to keep our heads. And Marcus saw you, you know. He has some friend named Sophia who told him we were distantly related, and apparently I'm being followed! By whom, I don't know, but it's all a mess."

"Ah," he said, suddenly interested in the fruit in his hands.

"Ah, what?" she demanded. He wasn't smiling anymore, and he should have been. Unless . . . "You've been *spying* on me! For how long?"

"Only since Thor arrived, really." He cleared his throat. "Elah was worried, and frankly, so was I. There was no knowing what she might do, and I needed—well, it wasn't as if you would have answered my questions, if I'd asked."

"I can't believe you." She snatched a pillow from the bed, then threw it back down again against the headboard. "Do you have any idea what I was going through? The idea that I had no space, no privacy, no freedom at all, and there you were just piling more surveillance on top of me! What's the matter with you? The minute I find someone else I can love, you have to show up and destroy everything!"

"Evey, I didn't know," his voice was low, thick with guilt.

"You didn't think!"

"I thought," he said, standing. "I thought about how the world was suffering, and you were hiding yourself away, head in the sand, when together, we might have snuffed out starvation, abuse, war—"

"Don't you *dare* put the blame for all that on me."

"You say what matters is why we do what we do. You say what's important, the reason I shouldn't hesitate to eat this fruit, to act as a leader of the North Country, is because for once, I'm not doing it just for me. For once, I was being the selfless one, and all you cared about was yourself."

"And why do you think that was, Adam?" She asked, stabbing a finger at his chest. "What betrayal set me on that path?"

"I'm not saying I'm blameless, Evey. You know I don't believe for a minute that it wasn't my fault, all of it. But I needed you. We needed you. And I wasn't trying to do anything worse than you are now, putting this fruit in my hand and telling me to eat it. I wanted to help you, and I was trying, very hard, to respect the fact that you didn't want to see me."

"Next time, maybe you should consider the fact that if I don't want to see *you*, I have even less of an interest in seeing your spies." *Raphael!*

"Evey, wait," Adam said, reaching for her. "Don't go. Not like this."

She twisted her arm free from his grasp. "You want to know the one thing that hasn't changed? From that madman in the Garden to today, you've *never* respected me or my boundaries."

Evey, love—

Get out of my head, and stay out of my life.

Raphael appeared, his expression perfectly neutral, though his eyes flicked between them, questioning.

"I'm done here," Eve said, extending her hand to him. "If you don't mind."

He took her hand, and the room disappeared, replaced by grass and shade and trees. She made for the nearest, supporting herself against the trunk. She'd thought she could put it all behind her, everything he'd done, everything that had happened in that last life, but then Adam went and did something else, bringing it all back. She took a deep breath and straightened. She couldn't dwell on it. Just as she couldn't dwell on Thor's exile. She had to keep her mind on the present, and the good in the world, and every stupid outburst like that drained off just a little bit more of her strength which she couldn't afford to lose. She had to keep it together, because more and more it seemed like she'd be figuring all this out alone.

"You aren't alone, my dear," Raphael said, beside her. "You've never been alone."

She laughed hollowly, lifting her head. "That isn't exactly a comfort either."

"Perhaps not." He smiled faintly. "But rest assured, you do not face your future without support. Your daughter, for one."

But she shook her head. "If she was going to listen, she would have listened to Adam, and look what happened to him instead?"

"Her affection for Adam runs deep, there is no question of it, and what happened to Adam—She regrets, perhaps even more deeply—but you are still Her mother."

"She's made it clear how much that means to her, Raphael. If I'm not the wife of her father, I'm nothing but a tool to be used. What she wants from me, all she wants from me now, is my power." Eve laughed again, leaning back against the tree. Her heart ached so much, just thinking about all this, and if she didn't laugh she was going to cry. "She's her father's daughter, through and through, isn't she?"

"It isn't Her father's influence you're thinking of," Raphael said, his eyes sharpening, searching her face as if willing her to understand—how he could believe for a minute she didn't, she'd never know. "For all his faults, all his mistakes, Adam is not so cruel as that. Not anymore."

"And if I go to the Redwood Hall cursing Michael's name, telling her to abandon him, what do you really think that's going to accomplish, Raphael? I'm not so great a fool as to make the same mistake twice, in that regard. And if what Michael did to Adam isn't enough to wake her up, she certainly isn't going to be convinced by my anecdotal accusations of his past cruelties."

Raphael grunted. "You might at least make it clear you have some small love for Her. That She has some hope of forgiveness, one day."

"It's never going to be enough, is it?" Eve laughed. If she didn't, she was going to weep. "Nothing I do is ever going to be enough. I can't live my life by her terms. Don't you understand that? All this pressure to forgive Adam, to forgive her—it isn't worth anything if it isn't real, Raphael! And it never will be if I'm never made *free*."

She sighed, rubbing her forehead to fight the spike of what was definitely going to become a migraine she couldn't afford. Marcus had filled her up, and between Elah and Adam, she was running dangerously close to empty again.

"I'm sorry. I thought I could do this, now that I was well. Doctor Adam, work with him, but I can't. I can't be near him without losing my head, and I can't keep it up without shutting down again. It's still there, that—that vortex, and until it's gone, I can't face all the rest of this. I can't keep myself whole and hold everyone else together, too. I need to just be Anna, for a while. Let go of Eve, and just live this single life as one small person."

Raphael bowed his head, whatever opinions he might have had hidden beneath a mask of peace. "If that is so, it may be the last."

"And if I don't, Elah might make it my last anyway."

His lips thinned, but he said nothing. It was as good as an agreement.

"I'm not saying it's going to be forever," she said, after a moment. "But I need a little bit of time. A little bit more time. Maybe if Thor were still here, it would be different, if I had the option of Asgard, too, to recharge, to get away from whatever it is that's sucking me dry. But losing him, and everything else on top if it . . ."

"God has always asked much of you," he said gently. "But never more than you were capable of overcoming. Just remember that, while you take what time you need to steady yourself. And remember, too, that you need only reach for me, and I will come."

It was something. She just wasn't sure what.

CHAPTER THIRTY-ONE

Adam

And that was it. His second (third?) chance with Eve, gone before he'd even realized it had arrived. Adam dropped into the armchair, only then remembering the fruit in his hand, the skin bruised crimson beneath his fingers. Likely, it was Eve's last gift to him. Her last kindness. That she'd had any to spare at all was a miracle, in and of itself—one which seemed to have sprung from her own experience of the same fruit.

From the Tree of Life.

She was right, he thought, turning it over in his hands. It was virtually identical to the fruit from the Garden. How it had gotten to Asgard was a mystery they'd probably never solve, now that Thor had been exiled. And if Elah had known, or Michael, surely they wouldn't have let him keep it all this time? But why hadn't Thor used it in trade? As leverage? The Tree of Life in exchange for Eve's freedom, or his right to remain at her side, at the least.

He set the fruit aside, resisting the urge to scratch at the scabs on his face, in his hair, and tipped his head back against the back of the chair. Thor was a fool. Why he hadn't taken Eve and run, Adam really couldn't understand. Especially if he had a tree of God in his hands to barter with. Instead, he'd left her behind to take up with some mortal idiot who believed anything he was told . . .

Adam frowned. Who *had* told him that they were distantly related, anyway? Just close enough to the truth to be the perfect lie. Anyone looking for a resemblance between them would find it without any trouble, but who would think to look at all?

"It was Athena," Raphael said. "To quiet him before he created a problem for both of you."

Adam lifted his head, eyes narrowing. "It really isn't polite to sneak up on a person."

"A lesson Eve taught you, I'm sure." The Archangel stepped forward, his gaze caught on the fruit beside him. "She brought you this?"

"Not that I deserved it." Adam picked it up, tossing it to the angel. "She isn't coming back, is she?"

Raphael caught it easily, but he didn't seem nearly as interested as he should have been, just set it down again on the table without a second glance. "I think it will be some time before she's able to do more than live, even with the help of the fruit."

Adam leaned forward. "You know something."

The angel smiled wryly. "I know a great many things, Adam."

"About that fruit. About the tree, in Asgard."

"Having lived, briefly, in Bilskirnir, I must admit, it was impossible to miss. The World Tree is the heart of Asgard. We were all shocked to learn that Odin had left it behind."

"Since it never belonged to him to begin with, is it really that surprising?"

Raphael arched an eyebrow. "A gift is a gift, I should think."

"Unless that gift was designed as something more. A Trojan Horse."

"I always did find Eve's solution to be fascinating. The cultivation of one family, to whom she might send tokens of her pasts, collecting her own history. Her House of Lions must have a fortune in heirlooms. But then, I always found both of you to be fascinating. The way you were molded from infancy to fit among the people who surrounded you, even the expectations of those to whom you were born influencing the genes which might be expressed in any given lifetime, from the color of your skin to the shape of your face . . ."

"It's not so different from Elah, I suppose," Adam said slowly, searching for the connection. Raphael was wily. All those years living among the gods as one of them, hiding his true nature, and now, living with Athena as his wife, he had reason to be cautious.

"Oh yes," Raphael agreed, his eyes warming. "One need only expect Her in a certain form, and She will appear. Elohim was much the same. Tall or short, slender or plump, young or old, male or female."

Male or female. And Thor claimed the tree had been a gift from his mother. Adam had seen it himself in his daughter, Elah's form blurring from male to female as she passed through a crowd, but never considered it in such a context. If Odin had looked for a goddess to give him an heir, and Elohim had allowed himself to be shaped by that desire, perhaps to avoid a confrontation. Knowing Thor, Adam had no trouble believing that Elohim saw discretion as the better part of valor. Odin may have been a god of order, but that did not always mean he preferred peace, and if he had thought Elohim was a threat to his people—better to live as his lover, for a time, and learn what could be learned that way.

"Even the greatest of gods are travelers. The power to change one's shape serves them well in defense. I can only imagine that Elohim believed it would preserve you both, allowing you to do the work you were meant to do without quite so many interruptions."

"It didn't hide us from the gods," Adam said, chewing on his words. If he could only speak to Eve, now! If he'd only known to ask Raphael the question before she'd come to him. But how could he have known, without the fruit in his hand?

"Like has always called to like, and blood to blood. He knew, too, it would not hide you forever. And perhaps He did not mean you to remain hidden from some. Perhaps He wanted other gods to know His presence, through you, through Eve."

Adam let out a breath, staring at the angel. "Then Thor was meant to find her."

Raphael shrugged. "Who can say what was God's will?"

"Thor was meant to find *us*."

"Thor was *meant* to return home," Raphael said. "To guard that which was His."

It was subtle, that capital H, like the royal we, but Adam didn't miss it.

Thor, as Elohim's son, had been meant to find them, to find this world, drawn here perhaps by the Tree which God had left him, so long ago. A gift to his child, more than to Odin. And Thor had been meant to stay, whether he'd known it or not—and clearly, he hadn't. Clearly, he'd had no idea the wealth he possessed with that tree, or he never would have failed to use it in order to remain with Eve.

"She should know," Adam said.

"And what good would it do her, now?"

For that, Adam had no answer. And until he did . . .

After today, he didn't dare to disturb her without good reason.

❧

If nothing else, Eve's arrival and subsequent departure had shaken him out of his wallow. Adam showered and dressed and let the sunlight stream through the windows, even if he couldn't yet risk stepping out on the balcony. He'd been here too long, and his overstay was likely to have drawn comment, if not photographers camped upon nearby roofs. If he appeared now, scarred and misshapen, it would destroy the confidence of his nation, and weaken everything he'd worked so hard to build.

But Eve was right. She was always right. He needed to throw himself back into the ring and keep working. Even more so if he'd lost his chance at having Eve at his side to help. He stood in the sun, closing his eyes. The comforting warmth turned to flame and soot and the sizzle of lightning. He stumbled back, gasping for air that wasn't scorched and groping for the window controls.

The light dimmed, the heat filtered out with the darkened opacity, and Adam dropped the temperature on the climate settings as well, just to be safe. But even then, he could still see it. The flames licking at the trees, the heat on his skin, the laughter burbling up from his throat.

He could still feel it. That pleasure, that thrill of utter blasphemy and absolute destruction. Eve was so sure of who he was now, so sure he was different, but he still took joy in the wrong things. The slow, deliberate failure of an empire, the knowledge that he had been the architect of its fall, doing just enough to cripple it politically without raining chaos down on its people. He could still become that man he'd left behind, if there were no checks upon his power, upon his ego.

He should have told her that was why he needed her. He should have begged her to stay at his side, to stop his hand when he reached too far. To remind him of the man he wanted to be. The man she had helped him to become.

Adam leaned his forehead against the wall, cool against his skin. He wasn't ready to go back to work if a little bit of heat sent him reeling back into the past. And that was why Eve had given him the fruit he hadn't asked for and didn't want. Especially now that she wasn't there to keep him in check.

Euphoria. He didn't even want to know what that might mean for him. What darkness that might nurture. And without Eve to police him, how could he be certain of what he would become? What if this part of him, this conscience he'd developed, was part of what was broken, and not the other way around?

"Hilda!" he called.

A clatter of movement outside his door answered before she did. "Yes, Mr. President?"

"I need to speak to our Spymaster, if a secure line can be arranged."

"Of course, sir," she said.

Better if he settled what he could now, at least in regard to Eve. She wouldn't thank him if he left her under surveillance. Though part of him wondered if it wouldn't lure her back just long enough to shout at him again. Not that he needed to give her any more reasons to find him repulsive. Quite the opposite really, if they were going to get through this, together or apart.

And then, before nightfall, he'd do as she said. There was no point in letting her last kindness go to waste. And who knew? Maybe it would do just what she hoped it would. Maybe it would give him the edge he needed to annex Russia, and sort out the mess of the barren lands. And maybe, possibly, some day, he could repay her for everything he'd done wrong.

But he had to be well in order to accomplish it.

CHAPTER THIRTY-TWO

Eve

Eve's days ran together into her nights, until she couldn't remember one from the next. She lost count of how many had passed since Thor had gone and she'd given up on Adam. But it was all the same blur. Classes during the day, and then she'd meet Marcus in the evening, and let him talk her into drinking, and then talk himself into her bed.

It was laughter and carelessness, and an irresponsibility she'd never experienced before, and more importantly, she slept like a baby through the night. No bad dreams—or at least she was far too tired at that point in the evening to care if they came. And Marcus had been right about his talent for distraction. She didn't think about anything when she was in his company. At least not beyond what she might eat that night, or if she'd had enough to drink.

They didn't only go out alone, either. More than once, Sophia joined them, with her strange silver eyes, and a boy Eve didn't know. Tam? Tom? She didn't care enough to remember, except that Sophia smiled at him with obvious affection, and Eve wondered how she'd ever mistaken her friendship with Marcus for anything more.

But it was Sophia who followed Eve into the bathroom that night at the bar, and Sophia who held her hair back, while Eve heaved up her dinner, along with the single drink she'd managed to swallow down, and Sophia who looked at her knowingly, one perfect eyebrow rising.

"You know, I thought you were glowing a little bit more than even Marcus's notoriety could account for," she said, while Eve cupped water into her mouth to rinse the taste of vomit away. "It wouldn't surprise me in the least if Marcus's sperm found a work around."

Eve shook her head. She couldn't be pregnant. She had her implant, and Marcus had assured her he was sterilized—reversible, of course, but neither one of them should have been fertile. Birth control had always worked for her, except for the once, with Adam, and that had been something altogether different. Fated.

"Must have just been something I ate."

"Except we all ate the same thing, and none of the rest of us are tossing our cookies." Sophia was searching her face. "Maybe it was that other guy. He wasn't Free West. Do you even know if he was sterilized at all?"

"No," she said, her heart constricting. Thor. "I had my implant, even if he wasn't."

But Thor was a god. An exception. Another exception, but God couldn't have predicted . . . Or had it been the fruit, itself? Would the fruit have seen the implant as an illness, and nullified its effects on her body? And she'd eaten it before. Before they. And he'd left.

"All you'd have to do to know for sure is ask Marcus to get himself tested. If his fertility is dead in the water, you know it couldn't have been him."

Eve closed her eyes, leaning against the sink. If it wasn't Marcus. If the baby was Thor's. The only reason he hadn't given her a godchild before had been his father's interference—wasn't that what he'd said? Odin had stripped him of his immortality. But this time?

"Honestly, I wouldn't be surprised if Marcus had never been sterilized to begin with," Sophia was saying. "He's so ridiculously smug about himself, I can just imagine him thinking his sperm was too precious to handicap."

"Don't say anything," Eve said, her hands tightening on the rim of the sink. A godchild in her womb, and Elah already mistrusting her, exiling Thor to prevent something like this from happening to begin with. "To him. To anyone. Don't even—can you just forget this happened?"

Sophia laughed. "Forgetting about it isn't going to make it go away, Anna. I mean, sure, I'll keep it to myself, but how long are you going to be able to hide it? You've got to be at least a month in, maybe two."

Had it been that long? She should have realized before now. Would have, if she'd been paying attention. But she hadn't wanted to pay attention to anything. She hadn't wanted to worry about anything at all, and it had been beyond foolish to rely on her implant, on Marcus's sterility. It wasn't as if she was normal. Half of her study of medicine these last years had been an excuse to see how her own physiology might have been different, now that diagnostics were advanced enough to test it. What did perfect mean?

She touched a hand to her stomach. Well, fertile, for one. And she should have considered that long before now.

"Marcus doesn't need to know yet."

And if it was Thor's baby, he didn't need to know ever. She'd need to hide it as long as possible. All it would take was one stray thought of one student on campus when Elah was looking in the right direction. Michael would have his sword through her stomach before she even knew he was there.

"Whatever you say," Sophia said, looking unconvinced. "But I think he's going to notice that you're not carousing it up all night every night anymore—unless you're not going to have it?"

She forced a laugh. "We don't even know if I'm having a baby at all."

"But if you are—"

"I thought we agreed we'd just forget about this. For tonight, at least, please." She pushed off from the sink and smiled. "I'm feeling better, and you know how Marcus gets when he's left alone in a room full of women."

But one thing was absolutely certain in her mind. No power on earth or off of it was going to take this baby from her. Not this time. Godchild or otherwise.

"What are you two doing in there?" Marcus called through the door. "Sophia, you'd better be keeping your hands off my girl, unless you're going to invite me in."

"Not your girl!" Eve called back.

Sophia rolled her eyes. "Men."

"Marcus is some kind of throwback, that's for sure." She rinsed her mouth one last time, and went out to meet him, tossing a wink over her shoulder to Sophia. Pretending everything was just fine was getting to be one of her greatest talents, these days. Adam would've been so proud.

"There you are, North Country." Marcus grinned, slinging an arm around her shoulders. "What do you say we head back to your room and I can show you just how much my girl you really are."

"Boys like you are the reason fathers don't sleep at night, you know that?"

"Boys like me are the reason their *daughters* don't sleep at night," Marcus corrected her. "And they could do a lot worse. Besides, you've got nothing to worry about. Your dad has been rooting for me since we hit puberty."

Someone had been, anyway. She spun free of his arm, and then leaned in to kiss his cheek. "I'm going back to my room, alone. And you're going to find some other girl to impress tonight."

"Come on, Anna," he made a grab for her, but she laughed, sidestepping. "Tease!"

"It's good for your ego," she said, walking backwards. "And there's no fun in a sure thing."

"I'm going to go with her," Sophia said. "Big exam tomorrow, and if I stay out with you boys, I'm going to get sloshed."

"You trying to make a point, North Country?" Marcus asked, ignoring Sophia altogether. "Because if you're just looking for an excuse to break things off, I'm not playing that game."

"I'm not looking for anything but a good night's sleep, playboy." She hoped her smile didn't falter. Soon enough, there'd be more than enough excuse to go around, and Marcus wasn't the type to get himself tied down. Not even for her. And she wasn't about to let him tie himself down to someone else's baby, regardless. "Go. Have fun. And you can brag about your conquests at lunch."

"You're still a terrible liar, sweetheart."

"Yeah, but which part was the lie?"

Sophia looped arms with her, and Eve threw one last grin over her shoulder before leaving Marcus behind.

That night, for the first time since before Thor had left, Eve took one of the unripened apples from the chiller. She'd hidden them in the back, wrapped in a scarf to keep them from winking every time she opened the door. All the drinking she'd been doing, all the late nights and early mornings. It wasn't for herself that she sliced a wedge from the golden fruit, but if she was pregnant, and the child was Thor's, she couldn't bear the thought of a having done it harm.

So she ate, slowly and carefully, a quarter of the apple, and sealed the rest in a container before the first wave of giddiness crashed over her. Eve curled up on her bed, closing her eyes. Thor had said the euphoria was only a result of her own illness, and to be sure, it wasn't nearly so severe this second time. But she still felt herself reaching, stretching toward something more, something bright and beautiful and pulsing with love.

Thor.

In that moment, riding the crest of the wave, she could almost see him. His lips shaping her name, and his eyes flashing open, even as his hand searched the bed beside him, seeking her warmth, her body, so far away.

And then it was gone. He was gone. Just a gentle wash of love in the back of her mind, tinged with longing and loneliness. He was so alone, and here she was, surrounding herself with noise and people and laughter, as if it would fill the empty spaces. How much of it, she wondered, was her own desire for distraction, and how much of it his wish that she not share his fate, needlessly.

She blinked back tears at the thought. He would. Knowing what was required of her, what she needed. He would put her happiness above his own heartache, and never hold a breath of it against her if they met again. And he would know, too, that she wished for him, dreamed of lying in his arms, of being his.

I love you, she said into the silence that stretched between them, deep and dark and aching. *Always, you.*

CHAPTER THIRTY-THREE

Eve

❧

The door was chirping, over and over and over. Eve groaned. It had been a long week, and she'd been lucky to be able to keep down the single wedge of the fruit she made herself eat once a day. Between the nightmares that were haunting her—Michael's sword burning through her body, his face shifting in the firelight, twisting and darkening as he grew larger and larger, feeding on the life that drained from her body— and fighting with Marcus on top of it, her carefree days had taken a decisive and less pleasant turn. And of course Marcus didn't understand. He just kept pressing her, wondering why she'd suddenly switched back to early nights and a sober lifestyle, and she'd kept dodging him. Though at least Sophia had helped, all the while giving her narrow-eyed looks. It was easy for Sophia to say she ought to tell Marcus the truth, but she wouldn't have to face the consequences of the admission.

The room was still black, not even a patch of moonlight crowding through the window. She rolled over, pulling the blanket up over her head.

"Anna." His voice was slightly slurred, dragging out the ns and almost forgetting the final a, but it was Marcus. And now he was beating on her door, in addition to making it chirp, obnoxiously loud. "If you don't let me in, I'll serenade you through this door, I swear."

She smiled in spite of herself. Count on Marcus to come up with the strangest threats. She slipped from her bed, and crossed the room. But she hesitated, leaning against the door frame. Her stomach was still iffy.

"An-na, An-na, An-na-bana-na," he began, completely out of tune. "She swings from the vines and blows up with land mines, my An-na, An-na, An-na-bana-na."

Eve laughed, letting the door slide open. Marcus swept her up, spinning her around the room. "An-na, An-na, An-na-bana-na. Oh what can you do when she springs monkeys from the zoo, my An-na, An-na, An-na-bana-na."

"You're ridiculous!"

"An-na, An-na—"

"And a terrible songwriter," she said, covering his mouth.

He grinned against her palm, and pulled her hand away. "But you let me in."

"I let you in."

"Because you're my An-na, An-na, An-na-bana-na." He picked her up off her feet, spinning her again.

"Stop!" She swallowed hard, closing her eyes against the motion as her stomach got left behind. "Stop, please, let me down."

He eased her to her feet, and pulled back. "What's the matter?"

Eve pushed away, slithering down the side of her bed to the floor. It wasn't normal, morning sickness. But then Elah had been meant to happen, what she'd been made for. Thor's child? If it was his child. She gulped air, and closed her eyes.

"Anna?" Marcus crouched beside her, his hand on her forehead. "Are you all right?"

She shook her head. "Fine. Just. Food poisoning."

"She of the iron-stomach, suffering from food poisoning?"

"Air," she said.

He moved away, and a cool night breeze flooded the room a moment later. She rested her head against the side of her mattress, tipping her face up toward the window.

"Come on, banana-girl." Marcus draped her arm around his shoulders and lifted her up, settling her on the bed instead. She curled up on her side, hugging her stomach, and he slid a pillow under her head. "Why didn't you say you were feeling sick? I would have taken care of you."

She sighed into the pillow. At least her stomach had stopped fighting her. For the moment. "Not part of the deal."

"Anna, whatever else we are, I'm still your friend. First and forever. Tell me what you need."

More fruit? She wasn't sure, but it couldn't hurt. Could it? She wished she knew. Thor would have. But she'd gone through an entire apple this week, and if she went through them all while she was suffering from mundane morning sickness, she wouldn't have any if she needed them later for something worse. "Some water."

Marcus pulled a bottle from the chiller, then helped her to sit up. "You look better. For a minute there, I thought you were going to hurl on me."

Eve glared at him over the bottle, even the word hurl making her slightly queasy.

"Maybe I should have left you on the floor, after all," he teased, leaning back against her headboard. "What did you even eat? Just that pizza at lunch with the rest of us, right? Was Sophia sick, too?"

"Marcus, I appreciate your solicitude, but I really just want to go back to bed."

He opened his arms. "Body pillow, reporting for duty."

It made her laugh—he was good at making her laugh—and she curled up against him, pillowing her head on his shoulder. "You're still ridiculous."

"You mean that isn't why you're keeping me around?" He kissed the top of her head. "Go back to sleep, North Country. I'll be here if you need help throwing yourself at the sink."

It was a very strange bit of comfort, but it was comfort, all the same.

§

Sophia had been right, though. Marcus wouldn't be shaken loose after that. One night and a day of supposed food poisoning might have been overlooked, regardless of whether he'd entirely believed her or not, but when it stretched into weeks of the same dodges and the same excuses, with growing circles under her eyes and the beginnings of a twitch at any sudden movements—a result of her nightmares—his disbelief blossomed into full-out suspicion.

"What's really going on, Anna?" he asked her one night, when she'd begged off dinner for the fourth time in a week.

He'd come to her room to drag her out, and found her throwing up in her sink. Not, she was sorry to say, for anything close to the first time. Instead of dinner, he'd helped her back to bed and set her up with a glass of water and a bucket.

"And no more of this food poisoning nonsense. It was thin to begin with, and I'm not buying it anymore." He pulled the blanket up to her chin and sat down on the side of her bed with that look on his face that told her he wasn't leaving until she gave him an answer.

"It's nothing you need to worry about," she said anyway. One last ditch attempt. "It's personal, and I'm handling it."

"Spending most of your afternoon puking your guts out does not, in any way, meet the definition of 'handling it.'"

"I'm fine, Marc. Really."

He raised both eyebrows. "Just because I like to have a good time doesn't mean I'm that big of an idiot."

She dropped her gaze, staring at his chin instead of meeting his eyes. She had to admit, even when she was irritated by him, he had a very fine chin.

"So why are you lying to me?" he asked, when she didn't respond. "If you won't tell me what it is you're keeping, at least tell me why you're keeping it."

She let out a breath. "If I tell you the truth, you have to swear you aren't going to go all noble on me. You've got a lot of youth left and you shouldn't be throwing it away taking care of me. You should be out having fun with Sophia, or Ashley."

He snorted. "Sure thing, Grandma."

"I'm serious, Marcus. I'm not going to do this with you. I'm not going to do this with anyone. I've had enough of the grief that goes with it."

"Anna, you've never had to go it alone a day in your life, and your life has barely been a blip on the map. Stop talking like you're an octogenarian, and spill."

She bit her tongue on a protest and ground her teeth. The problem with being Anna and not Eve at this age was the utter discount of her experiences. Marcus was the worst of all, because she couldn't bluff on what her life had been like before they'd met. Well, fine. She'd given him an out, and she'd give him plenty more, and if that didn't work, she'd find some other way.

"I'm pregnant."

His jaw tightened, and he rocked back. "Whose is it?"

She shook her head.

"So it could be mine."

"It doesn't matter either way. You're not ready to be a father, and I'm not interested in entering into any contracts."

"Anna, for the last month and a half, it's been you and me. No contracts, just us being us. You're my girl, and no matter who the father is, I'm not going to leave you high and dry."

"I'm not your girl, Marcus," she said, even the thought of the old argument making her tired. "We have fun together, and you're a great distraction, but that's it. That's all that this is ever going to be, and I made that clear to you from day one."

"Now who's being ridiculous?"

"You are! You're supposed to be sterile. Why should you take any responsibility for a child that isn't even yours?"

He shrugged. "I always knew my boys could take care of business, if they really wanted it. I mean, it isn't unheard of. Sometimes implants fail, and you certainly didn't impregnate yourself, but mine or not, even if you insist that we're never going to be more than this, *this* still means we're friends. And friends don't ditch one another when things get rough. I'd never be able to look your parents in the eye again, if I did."

"This isn't about my parents."

"No, it's about you. And denial. And lie after lie after lie. I'm not even sure you tell yourself the truth anymore, Anna, because you can keep saying this is just about fun and you're eternally in love with someone else, fine, but he left you, and it doesn't seem like he's planning on coming back."

She rolled over, turning her back to him, and focusing on the wall. On the touch of Thor's love in the back of her mind, promising eternity, if she could only reach him. It wasn't his fault he wasn't coming back. It wasn't his fault they couldn't be together. "You don't know what you're talking about."

"I know there's no way you'd have let me in your bed if you thought this was only some vacation. If you really believed there was any chance you'd be together again, you'd have kicked me right back out of your room, no matter what secrets I knew."

She didn't answer. She didn't want to think about anything that he was saying.

"Maybe what you feel for me won't compare to what you shared with him," Marcus said, much more gently. "But it doesn't mean there isn't something here. It doesn't mean there isn't love, Anna. And fun. And happiness. Tell me I don't make you happy, and I'll leave right now."

But that had been the whole point. The distraction. The pleasure. She wouldn't have been with him at all if he hadn't given her that much. And he knew it. He'd known it from the start. She pulled the pillow over her head and shut her eyes.

"Just tell me one thing," Marcus said, lifting up a corner of the pillow so she would hear. "Is this Simonsen's super secret baby, raised in a far away land to become the next president of the North Country?"

She moaned into the mattress, then rolled to her back and swatted him with her pillow.

But Marcus? He just laughed.

CHAPTER THIRTY-FOUR

Elah, Before

❧

She should have gone to see her mother first, she supposed, when Grandfather gave her permission to leave the Redwood Hall, at last. And perhaps she would have, if it hadn't been for Michael, who'd been commanded to guard her on her journey. She didn't like it anymore than he did, but she didn't show it. Instead, she smiled and said, "I think I'd like to see my father."

Michael's expression told her everything she needed to know about what he thought of that, but she couldn't have guessed he'd be so disgusted by the idea, and he would have been just as disgusted and irritable if she'd said she wanted to see her mother, anyway. Worse, he would have been rude to her, and Elah didn't want to bring her mother a guest she didn't want. Her younger self hadn't quite put it together, but it was clear to her now, looking back. It wasn't just that her mother never agreed with Michael, as Raphael had said. Elah was almost certain they hated one another, completely.

Or at least Michael hated her. Unsurprisingly.

"Don't you like anyone?" she asked him, once they'd left Grandfather's throne room. He rarely left it, too weak even to stand, most days. Her power helped less and less, though she wasn't sure if it was because he didn't let it, or because he didn't remember how to use it the way he once had.

"It isn't my place to like. It's my place to serve."

"Well I'm sure you'd be a lot less miserable if you *did* like *something*."

Michael grunted, and said nothing. That was only marginally better than a snide rage, she supposed, but not by much.

She touched one of the saplings in the outer hall, then another, feeling for the one she wanted. Each had its roots in a different place. China. Mongolia. Siberia. Hm. She stepped back the other way. India. She thought of her father, and the branches parted, creating a portal. "I thought you'd prefer it if I went to see Father over Mother. I'm sorry I was wrong, but I'm curious about him. Gabriel tells so many stories—"

"Gabriel only tells you the stories you'll like," Michael said. "He glosses over all the rest. All the murders, all the ruthlessness, all the death."

"But that was before he was given back his memory."

"And after."

She bit back an accusation and took a breath. "You know, you could have told me the other stories yourself, instead of simmering in the corner, listening."

Michael snorted. "Raphael would have put a stop to it before I'd started."

"Raphael wouldn't have had to know."

She moved to go through it, but Michael caught her by the elbow, his fingers hard. "Those are Bhagavan's lands."

"The world belongs to Elohim first, and through him, me." Elah fought the instinct to jerk her arm free. It wasn't like Raphael, who always gave her a reassuring pat on the shoulder, or mussed her hair. When Michael touched her, it was strange. A possessive, jealous shock, from her elbow to her heart.

"The interlopers feel differently. And if you'd like to survive long enough to ascend, you'll enter claimed lands with a bit more caution, or not at all."

She hesitated, then nodded. If he wanted to go first, it was a small concession she could grant him, and every small concession, she hoped, would mean a little bit less resentment later. Michael let go of her arm and passed through the portal, his form wavering slightly as he did, like looking through water. It wasn't distorted enough that she didn't clearly see his hand resting on the hilt of the short, wicked blade he carried opposite the empty scabbard, and she didn't miss the jerk of his head that told her she could follow, either. She told the two saplings to obscure the portal from any who passed, and marked the place in her mind. It had been years since she'd left the Redwood Hall, and breathing in the scent of the jungle, thicker and more floral than the redwoods, made something inside her calm.

Then she turned around. An immense stone form of a seated man stared at her with expressionless eyes. The pedestal of the statue was covered in food and offerings, and vines looked as though they'd only recently been torn away. Like the statue itself had torn them from its body, but all four of his hands rested neatly in his lap now.

Four hands, and four arms, a crescent moon in his hair and a cobra coiled around his neck. He was beautiful, too. Large eyes, a strong nose, perfectly arched eyebrows, and wide lips. A rumbled scraping brought Michael's hand to her elbow again, dragging her back as one stone hand lifted up, thumb and forefinger joined, palm out and the rest of the fingers open, but slightly curled.

Michael sneered. "Shiva."

"The gesture means peace," a voice called from behind them. "Bhagavan has no quarrel with Elohim, and the daughter of Eve will always have safe passage within the lands of his people."

"The lands of his people," Elah said, turning to look at him. He looked—jolly. Like a man who always saw beauty and goodness before him, no matter how dark the storm. His eyes were bright as they met hers, and merry. "Not *his* lands."

"You listen closely, Goddess." The man bowed.

"Isn't that the duty of a god? To listen, first and foremost, to the needs of the world?"

"And is that Elohim's teaching, or your mother's?"

"It's something I can imagine my mother saying, easily." She smiled. "But in this case, Grandfather said it first."

"You are fortunate to be guided by such wisdom."

"Fortune has little to do with it," Michael said coldly. "And we aren't here to pay respect to Bhagavan or you. We come in search of Adam."

"Might I offer my own courtesies?" the man said, his voice so mild, Elah could hear no rebuke—but it was one, all the same. He offered another bow, not waiting for Michael's response. "I am Siddhartha Gautama, the Enlightened One, and it is my greatest honor to meet the daughter of Adam and Eve. Bhagavan also greets you, as you have seen."

"As the destroyer!" Michael said.

"Shiva is also the transformer," Siddhartha said. "And there is no question that transformation is upon us, as Elohim wanes and Elah rises. As Shiva, Bhagavan acknowledges this change, preparing himself and his people for what comes."

"If Bhagavan greets me with peace, my peace is also with him," Elah said. "And all his people."

"A generous answer, Lady."

"Too generous," Michael grumbled, at her shoulder. "If you've finished making friends?"

Elah gave him a sharp look, catching the edge of a mocking smile on the Archangel's lips. She flushed. "When the hand of friendship is extended, refusing such a gift is hardly forgivable."

He lifted his eyebrows, his fingers tightening on her elbow. Her skin prickled beneath his touch. "I never said I refused."

"You've never said a great many things, Archangel." And she did pull her arm free then, to offer an apologetic smile to Siddhartha. "Would you be so kind as to show me to my father? Though Michael's manners are poor, it is true that my grandfather has need of me, and I should not overspend my time."

The Enlightened One offered her his arm, and she accepted, ignoring Michael's low growl. Nothing she did ever pleased him anyway, but she almost liked that she could irritate him so easily. There was something to be said for having his attention, either way. And it felt like progress of some sort.

And the way he touched her.

She wasn't sure what that meant at all.

§

"Did I hear—" her father stopped at the sight of her, his eyes widening, flickering with a series of emotions, but too fast for her to recognize any of them. He cleared his throat and straightened. "You're so much bigger than when I saw you last. And I wasn't expecting—I didn't think you'd be allowed to see me."

"Why wouldn't I be?" she asked, dropping Siddhartha's arm.

His gray eyes shifted just slightly, taking in Michael behind her, probably. Buddha had brought them to a temple, all old stone held together with vine and Bhagavan's will, more than anything else. But that wasn't so much different than the Redwood hall, really.

"I'm generally considered to be the worst kind of influence on impressionable young minds like yours." He inclined his head, just slightly to her guardian. "I can only imagine the stories you must have been told about me."

"Gabriel and Raphael had nothing but good things to say about you," Elah said. She wanted to run toward him, throw herself into his arms, but she wasn't sure. She wasn't sure of anything, looking at him. Her father. She was in the same room as her father. "And Michael has nothing good to say about anything at all."

He smiled. It was full of self-deprecation and self-awareness for his own faults, and then he had bounded across the space between them, the movements as easy and graceful as her mother's. She hadn't expected him to remind her of Mama, but he did. Something in his face, in his very essence.

"You're even more beautiful than your mother," he said, and she felt he was drinking her in, feasting on her features for any glimpse of Mama, too. She could feel his heartache, even in his joy, in his smile.

"You love her still."

He took both her hands, squeezing them tightly. "I'll love her always, darling. I never stopped loving either of you, even if I had to go, and believe me, it wasn't my idea. If my staying wouldn't have meant losing you, I never would have left."

Michael gave a soft snort of derision behind her, but she ignored it. Her father wasn't lying, and she didn't have to read his mind to know it. Sincerity was written in every line of his face, in the warmth of his eyes, in the grip of his hands.

"We should go see her," she said, already imagining the reunion. The way her mother would cry, so happy to have them both home. "If it was only because of me, there's no reason you can't be with her now. Why we can't be with her together, when I'm able to come visit. Just because we couldn't be a family before, it doesn't mean we can't be one now."

He shook his head, his hand cupping her cheek, stroking her hair. "I want that as much as you do, Elah, I do, but it just—it isn't time yet. Evey's gone through enough without me barging back into her life. Losing you would have undone her."

She laughed. "After all the trouble I gave her, I doubt it. She was probably relieved to see me go. No more worrying that the wolves would steal the goats, or guarding her every thought from mine. She didn't put up a fight anyway, when Michael came."

Her father's lips twitched. "If it was Michael who came for you, you're dead wrong. Even if you didn't see it, I'm sure Evey had any number of things to say, all of them cutting, and I'm just as sure she didn't hold anything back."

"Well none of that matters now. And I don't see why she wouldn't want to see us both. Why have you been hiding here, all this time?"

"Any closer, and I would have come up with reasons to drive past the cottage every day." He half-smiled, his hand falling away. "I don't have any right to even put a toe into DeLeon lands, anymore, and I'm sure more than one person would escort me from the property if I tried."

"I wouldn't allow it," she said firmly. "And it's my home too."

"Do you think you can take on a thunder god and win, then?" he asked, laughing. "You're barely a teenager, by the look of it, and I *know* you were born less than five years ago. How on earth have you gotten so big, so fast? You shouldn't even be waist high on me, and here you are, up to my shoulder, already."

He was subtle, her father. But insistent. No matter how many times she tried to draw the subject back to her mother, to going to see her, together, he turned it back around on her, coaxing stories of her time in the Redwood hall, of her experiences with Grandfather and the Archangels. Stories of her time with Mama, in the cottage. His eyes glowed with warmth for those stories, more than any others, so why wouldn't he see that they'd both be better off together? Especially if he loved her so much.

Do you spend much time with Michael? her father said at one point, hiding the question beneath some story of his past, before he'd gotten his memory back.

He's always guarded me. She frowned slightly. *But nothing I do is ever right. He doesn't like me at all, and I'm sure he resents it. Mama said he was afraid of me, once, but I'm not so sure now . . .*

Maybe it was in the beginning, but it hasn't been fear that's motivated him for a long time, now. Before you were born, he commanded. Elohim trusted him to rule, and power is a strong drug, Elah. No one knows that better than me.

He thinks I'm going to unmake him.

Her father's gaze was as steady as his tone. *Maybe you should.*

That's murder!

That's your mother's influence—and I'm not saying she's wrong, so don't bristle, but as your father, I'd rather see him dead than you. That's all.

He isn't allowed to do me any harm, she reassured him. *Grandfather would never let him.*

Your grandfather won't live forever, sweetheart. And you're going to need to start thinking about what you're going to do with that Host of his after he's gone. The lesser angels wouldn't know what to do with themselves if you set them free. They're hardly more than drones. But the Archangels—they could be gods, all on their own. Raphael already was.

Raphael is loyal to me, above all. And Mama, too.

But Michael isn't, he said, his voice firm. *Just think about it, love. While you still have time.* He smiled and leaned forward, pressing a kiss to her forehead. "I'm glad you came. This was more than I ever hoped for, so soon. Ever, really."

"You're my father, of course I'd come."

"If you hadn't, I wouldn't have blamed you in the slightest."

She had a feeling she'd be thinking about that, too.

❧

"What did he mean?" she asked Michael, as they walked back to the portal. "Why did my father think I wouldn't be allowed to see him? Or that I wouldn't wish to?"

"He is arrogant and he believes himself better, even than Elohim. To say nothing of his cruelty."

"But that was before," she said. "Before his memory was returned, and before my mother."

Michael snorted, his hand cupping her elbow again as they neared the statue of Shiva. "So they say."

"It isn't true?"

"He consorts now with your enemies, Lady. Is that not proof enough of his intentions?"

"Bhagavan is not my enemy. Nor is Buddha. All they want from me is peace, and to know their people will be looked after and cared for."

"That is what they say."

"That is what they mean," Elah said, her voice sharp. "Bhagavan has been here for so long, he might have taken the whole world when he came, but he settled here in this place and bothered no one. When people came to him, asking to be taught, to learn and find peace, he provided them with the ways. But he never pursued them. Never looked for converts, or sent his people to bring others back to him. Is this not true?"

Michael's eyes flashed, and his jaw clenched. "It is not false."

"Then why should he change, now? Why should his intentions be anything but peaceful toward me, in Grandfather's place?"

"His loyalty is to the others. The rest of the interlopers who still loiter upon the earth, sucking it dry."

"I think you're wrong."

"Then you are as blind as your mother."

She pulled away from him, offering a nod to Shiva's statue, as they passed, and opened the portal. "I don't think we're the ones who are blinded, Michael. An offer of friendship is the opposite of a threat, but you stiffen at the very idea."

"Friendship is a risk," he said. "Every offer you make is another enemy you won't see coming. Another manner in which you might be attacked, betrayed, hurt."

Elah turned, staring. There had been something in his voice. A roughness that didn't come from frustration so much as—"You're afraid *for* me."

His lips thinned, his eyes not meeting hers. "Elohim made your safety my concern, and your carelessness helps nothing."

But she knew, now. It was so painfully obvious in all his bluster, all his crossness. It wasn't fear *of* her, like her mother had thought. Maybe it never had been.

Elah hid her smile, and passed through the trees, back to the Redwood Hall, Michael close upon her heels.

For her safety, of course.

CHAPTER THIRTY-FIVE

Eve, Later

❦

The baby was crying. Marcus stirred beside her, but Eve nudged his mind back into sleep, and sat up, rubbing the sand from her eyes. Even exhausted as she was, she hated to let Marcus get up in the night. Lars was so much more likely to do something outrageous, waking from bad dreams, and the less Marcus noticed of her son's odd behaviors, the better. Friend or not, Marcus was Elah's. Her eyes, her ears, her spy, even if he'd never know it. And their time together was running out.

Eve touched Lars's thoughts as she rose, pulling on a robe against the night's chill, and by the time she found him in his crib, she'd soothed the worst of his tears away. He stared at her, wide-eyed, a thumb in his mouth. Eve gently tugged it free and lifted him up, humming to him. The same song she'd sung to Elah, to her Lions before that. The same song Reu had taught her in the Garden, and she and Thor had sung together to their son.

Lars quieted, his head resting against her shoulder, his mind all trust and innocence. And strong. He was so strong. How Marcus hadn't noticed it yet, Eve wasn't certain, but more than once, Lars had called to them with his thoughts rather than his words. She'd seen Marcus respond to it, his head jerking up, turning toward Lars's nursery.

She hadn't been five months pregnant before she'd known without any doubt she carried a godchild. She'd tried to shake off Marcus then, manufactured fight after fight, even going so far as to push against his mind, his feelings. Nothing stuck. By the next morning he'd be back at her door, teasing her about her hormones, and his own sympathetic responses. He'd moved off campus into an apartment, and together with Sophia, began a campaign to convince her to move in. They'd worn her down over the course of a month, and Eve suspected they'd bribed her neighbors into the most obnoxious behaviors to accomplish it. Wall-shaking music blasted in the middle of the night, screaming matches she couldn't escape even with ear-plugs. And there had been the baby to consider, too. She would have had to move once Lars was born, anyway.

But she hadn't wanted Marcus to witness the way Lars grew, or the speed with which he developed. At six months old, he was well on his way to toddler-sized, all blond hair and blue eyes, and Eve was beginning to fear that it might start raining when he cried, or thundering with his tantrums. Elah hadn't been particularly fixated on anything elemental, but Elah's father hadn't been a thunder god, and Eve had had Raphael's help in raising her.

She didn't dare call on the Archangel now. Once Elah learned of Lars's existence, it would be his death, and probably her own. If not that, at the very least he would be taken from her, and Eve refused to give Thor's son to Michael. Not after everything that had happened with Elah.

Not after seeing what Elah had become.

Eve settled Lars back into his crib, stroking his hair until his eyes drooped closed again. Just a bad dream, it seemed, though she didn't remember Elah suffering from nightmares. Lars's dreams were haunted by darkness and hunger and green, sickly light. The same darkness she'd fought since before Thor had gone. The darkness Elah hadn't managed to stop, even with Eve's power in her hands.

And she was drawing more of it every day, stretching Eve thinner and thinner. If it hadn't been for Lars, and the small joys he brought her, the extra furnace of his love, Eve wasn't certain she could have kept up. Her reserves were limited, and she had only one withered apple left. Not enough. Not alone.

She let out a breath. Much as she didn't want to admit it, she needed Adam. His resources, his help, his influence. Whatever Elah and her Archangels were doing, it wasn't going to fix anything, Eve could feel that, clearly. But she would have to hide Lars. What Marcus, Sophia, and her boyfriend Tam had seen of him was already risk enough, and every good thing in her life only required Adam's knowledge of it to turn to ash. Lars wasn't going to be another casualty of her brother's discernment.

It might be time to leave Marcus and his friends behind. Before Lars started showing signs of his godhead beyond accelerated development. Adam could provide her with the means to do so, and she need never tell him why she'd had her change of heart. Or at least she could tell him what he wanted to hear.

She could tell him she was ready to save the world.

§

Two months later, Adam sent men in black suits and dark glasses—no longer just sunglasses, but a full interface and display allowing the network to track the faces and movements of everything around them for tactical advantage. Eve had sent Marcus out shopping with Lars, though she hadn't liked to let him leave her supervision, and packed everything he would need in two suitcases before the government agents had arrived. They did the rest of the packing for her in less than half an hour, and swept back out of the apartment again. She'd refused to allow an escort. What one of these men knew, Adam would know, and that meant taking herself and Lars to her new home without their assistance.

You're sure about this, Evey? Adam asked, just before his men left with all her belongings. No doubt he'd had a steady stream of updates regarding their progress.

I'm sure. It's time. And Marcus would never let me pick up and go, otherwise. Not alone.

You could still bring him with you. It isn't as if I haven't danced around one of your mortal husbands before.

She shook her head, even if he couldn't see it. *He isn't my husband, and what I need now, more than anything, is privacy. Marcus is too observant to fool for long.*

We'll keep your appointment nice and quiet, Adam promised. *Everything is in order, and I don't even feel the slightest bit guilty about putting a PhD and an MD at the end of your new name. You probably know more about medicine than most of your professors have forgotten, and certainly more about life on this world.*

Eve grimaced. It hadn't been what she wanted, but she understood the necessity. Her degree program had always been a formality, anyway. *I appreciate this.*

I'm just relieved you've changed your mind. I have all this data and not the least idea of how to put it together into something meaningful on our own level. To them, it's just dead desert, mostly likely caused by acid rain and chemical runoff, but I'm hoping you'll see what they can't.

Me too. For Lars's sake as much as her own.

She wrote Marcus a letter, all the better to weave the lies he'd never believe if she looked him in the eye. Lars needed special care which she couldn't find locally. It wasn't entirely untrue, but what Lars really needed was his father, and barring his father, a safe place to grow up where Elah's eyes and ears wouldn't see what he was capable of. None of it was anything she could explain honestly. Marcus believed in the Goddess, of course, but why should he think her anything but crazy if she admitted the rest? Every mother thinks her child is special, after all.

Marcus and Lars came home not long after, Lars with a balloon tied to his wrist, and squealing with laughter as Marcus lifted him over his head, making jet noises and teaching him to stretch his arms out like an old-fashioned airplane.

"Mayday, mayday!" Marcus shouted, swerving around Eve. "Mom-zilla sighted!"

She forced herself to laugh, snatching Lars out of Marcus's hands and attacking her son with kisses. "Mom-zilla wins again!"

Lars laughed with her until he saw her eyes, and she felt his small hand press against her cheek, a soft question behind his touch. *Sad, Mama?*

She kissed his hand and settled him against her hip. *We'll both be happy again, soon.*

"You should have seen him at the store," Marcus said, kissing her cheek in passing. "I'd read off what we needed from your list, and he'd point it right out, just like that. I'd swear he's a breath from talking, and only eight months-old. I wouldn't be surprised if he burst out with sentences, the way he's going."

"He's amazing," she agreed, tousling Lars's hair. She gave Marcus a smile. "I'm glad you're back. I completely forgot that Lars has an appointment with a specialist today. That man who's supposed to check his developmental progress, you remember?"

"Just let me get these groceries inside, and I'll come with you."

"I'd rather take him myself, if that's okay. I don't want him to get anxious. This way it's just another errand."

"You're sure?" Marcus asked, searching her face.

She kissed him quickly. "Thank you for offering."

And then she left before she lost her nerve.

Because the truth was, she was going to miss Marcus. All those nights, after Lars went to bed, when she had been on the edge of madness and he'd drawn her back with laughter, with his love. He had been so good to Lars, to both of them, and if Lars hadn't been Thor's son. If he hadn't been a godchild, but just a boy—

But he was. And she didn't dare stay.

She just hadn't realized how hard it would be to go.

§

Adam had prepared a cottage for her, just outside of Ottawa. Two bedrooms, a cozy fireplace with a real wood fire, and a large, eat-in kitchen that opened into a living room, all furnished with a tasteful selection of essentials.

She carried Lars inside, half-asleep still. The trip had taken them most of the day by airship, which had cost Eve what was left of her gold, not counting the apple she'd let harden. That, she had no intention of ever spending, especially now. With the ivory bracelet, it might have earned her a small fortune, but it was all she had left of Thor.

All she had left but Lars, anyway. She tucked him into her own bed, nudging him back to sleep with a kiss and a caress. Adam would want to know she'd made it, and she had half a mind to begin going through the data he'd promised would be waiting. The sooner some progress was made, the safer Lars would be. The safer they would all be.

The front door chirped, followed by the brush of Adam's mind against her own, anxiety mixed with his eagerness, and beneath all of it, a certain satisfaction. There wouldn't be any getting rid of him until he'd seen she was comfortable, she supposed.

Eve touched her hand to the door closure for her bedroom, waiting until it whooshed shut behind her, and prayed that Lars would sleep soundly.

"Open," she said.

The door slipped into the wall and Adam smiled. "I wasn't sure I'd get another chance to see you without an entourage."

"Is that what I should expect in the future?" she asked, leaning against the doorframe. "I hope you're not planning to keep me under some sort of surveillance."

"It certainly isn't my intention, but if you mean to leave me standing on your doorstep, I can't make any promises regarding the press." He held up his hand, wiggling his fingers. "I hope you noticed I didn't invite myself in, though I did code the door to us."

She stepped back, jerking her chin toward the kitchen. "I appreciate everything you've set up for me, Adam, but I really did mean it when I said I needed privacy, more than anything."

He lifted his eyebrows. "Even from me?"

"From the entourages and the press that come with you, certainly." She put a kettle of water on to boil, and reached for two mugs. When she closed the cabinet, she frowned. Opened the next. And the next. And the next . . .

"I lifted the plan from your DeLeon cottage," Adam said, his lips curving. "I thought it would make things easier."

That he'd thought to give her a stove at all was more consideration than she'd hoped for. Printed food wasn't quite the same—something about the consistency, and a lack of subtlety in the flavors. Of course being able to afford to cook was a luxury she didn't have, stove or not. In the North Country, food prices were considerably lower, subsidized for citizens, but the demand for real, fresh produce had fallen off, and supply even further. People just didn't cook the same way anymore, and they had no idea what they were missing.

"Check the chiller," he said, nodding to it.

She opened it, giving him a suspicious glance, and then her eyes widened. It was full. Stocked with everything she loved. Parsnips and carrots, red and yellow peppers, parsley by the bunch, and fresh basil—oh the basil! A hint of spice and memories of roasted garden tomatoes.

"There's a vegetable garden out back," he added. "I thought about finding you some goats and chickens, but I wasn't sure you'd want the trouble, even for the milk and eggs."

"You did all this?" It was a stupid question. Of course he had. But how had he found the time?

"I gave Hilda very explicit instructions."

"But you remembered all this?"

"Evey, I never stopped thinking about those days with you."

The kettle whistled, and she snatched it off the burner before it could wake Lars. Where he'd found a whistling kettle, she wasn't certain, and she hadn't even considered how odd it was until then. He'd gone to a lot of trouble. Or he'd made Hilda go to a lot of trouble, anyway.

"She must have thought you were crazy, asking for all this."

He laughed, passing her two tea bags. "Hilda's overlooked crazier things. That week I spent in bed, feeling sorry for myself, for example."

Eve poured the water, giving him the briefest of glances as she did so. There wasn't a scar to be found on his face, no raggedness to his hairline. "You ate the fruit."

"I did," he said, all humor leaving his expression. "It healed me, body and mind, as you said it would. But it didn't change who I am. What I am. I'll admit, I'm selfishly glad to have you back. Everything with Russia is coming to a head, and I could use you, to be sure I don't overreach."

"At this point, I'm not sure I could stop you, either way." She slid one of the mugs to him, with a spoon and honey, not meeting his eyes. She'd only been half-listening to the world news, too afraid of what she might hear. But even under her rock with Marcus, she'd been aware of the riots in Moscow and St. Petersburg. Rising food prices and unemployment tended to provoke that sort of thing, especially when the people at the top were living in luxury.

Like she was, with her chiller full of fresh produce and her little plot of land.

"You're walking a tightrope, Adam. The Russians might just as easily inspire your own people to the same kind of demonstrations."

He leaned back against the counter, his gaze unfocused. "I thought of that, too, but even if they call for an election, I can swing the vote again. Even more easily, if I have your help. But my people aren't going hungry, or freezing to death in the winters. The only lands I've kept out of private hands have been in Greenland, and I'm employing enough of my own citizens there, too, to do all the training and supervisory work—the only people who object to that project are the foreign powers who insist on painting me as the next Napoleon. I have strong support in the Indian subcontinent, but in the west, it's only going to get worse when I've annexed Russia."

"Isn't that where Napoleon failed? And Hitler, after him? Maybe you've already overreached." Come to think of it, she wasn't entirely certain Adam hadn't been Napoleon himself—surely he would have mentioned it, if he had been? She couldn't actually imagine Adam ever being so short, even if he absolutely had the ego.

"But I'm not invading," Adam said, his lips twisting. "If all goes as planned, they'll be voting themselves into the North Country. All I need to win is their hearts. I'm leaving tomorrow, in fact, to tour and make pretty speeches and plant suggestions—Evey, is it wrong of me? Is all of this wrong? You'd never have used your power this way, but it isn't as though we have decades to waste with gerrymandering. The sooner we have the northern lands united, the sooner I can get the food supply in order, and get everyone fed properly."

She stirred her tea, watching him, and listening to the currents beneath his words. Frustration and distress, worry, fear and self-doubt. The old Adam never would have even questioned it. He would have believed, under it all, that this was what he had been meant for, that the Russians should have bent their knee to him long ago.

"The North Country still has its freedoms," she said. "Your people aren't being subjugated or oppressed and the Russians will be freer than they've ever been. Is it so different from what the gods did, before? Was it wrong of them to act, when they could see the larger threats?"

Adam choked on his tea. "Did you just—I never in my wildest dreams thought I'd live to see the day that you compared either one of us to a god!"

She flushed. "Well we never were exactly mortal, were we?"

"All those years, I tried to tell you the same thing, and you just lifted your chin and looked down your nose!"

"That was different," she said. "You didn't have anyone's best interests at heart but your own, and I'm not saying we're *better* than them, or that they're beneath us. I'm only saying we can see things they can't, know things they don't. If we don't use that information to guide them, to help the world, what's the good in having it at all?"

He hid a smile behind his mug.

"What?" she demanded.

Adam shook his head. "Nothing."

I know it's something.

He laughed, light and familiar, and touched her cheek. Just the barest of caresses. "I was just thinking that I understand, finally, why the gods didn't want you to know them."

"Why?"

"You'd have shamed them, argued them right back out into the void. I can just imagine the kinds of riders you would have added to the Covenant, if you'd been one of the founders."

"Too bad it doesn't work on Elah, hm?" she smiled sadly.

"I don't know that it doesn't, really." Adam set his mug in her sink. "She's apologized to me quite profusely, you know, and Michael was disciplined for what he did to me."

"Not severely enough if he's still alive," Eve said fiercely. "She should have unmade him completely a long time ago. Turned her power on him, instead of innocent minds."

"It's a nice thought." He smiled faintly. "But for now, at least, he's no longer finding a warm welcome in her bed, thank all that's holy for that much. Maybe one day, if he takes the next step and attacks us without her permission . . ."

She swallowed, looking away. Then, it would be too late. And Lars, poor Lars. "I hate him. I'll never forgive him, and I hate him."

Adam sighed, giving her arm a brief, light squeeze. "I am glad you're back, Evey. And when I get back from Russia, we'll sit down and figure all of this mess out, you and me. Then we'll both go to Elah and see just how far your parental powers of persuasion still go, all right?"

She nodded, though she couldn't say she was looking forward to either part of that plan. Not while she had Lars to hide.

Adam brushed a kiss to her cheek and stepped back. "If you need anything at all while I'm gone, just call Hilda. She'll take care of everything."

Eve walked him to the door, and locked it behind him, leaning her forehead against the panel. *Thor, give me strength.*

She was going to need it.

CHAPTER THIRTY-SIX

Thor

Asgard was empty. He had his goats, and the lonely horse, Grani, and the chickens, and he had days which turned into nights, and nights which turned into days, and all of it he spent drunk, half-dreaming of Eve.

When she reached for him, he could feel her, catch a glimpse of her days, a confused, fleeting idea of her nights. He could taste the bitterness of darkness, the empty joy of pleasure and life without love. Together, apart, they drank away their sorrows, their loneliness, their grief, and he could not blame her when he caught the flash of a man's body, naked beneath hers. He'd made her promise, after all, in that last goodbye, when he'd pressed the fruit into her hands. He'd made her promise not to give up again, not to turn away from the world, and shut herself from it. For him, if not for Elah. For him, if not for her own sake.

He could not blame her, but it shattered his heart, all the same, made him ache to have her in his arms again, to roll her beneath him and show her how she was meant to be loved. He would have filled her to bursting with it, until the love they made spilled out over the whole world in crashing waves.

There was ale in the treasury, a cask which never ran dry, and he drank it in quantity enough to wake in a puddle of his own drool upon the table, just to drown out the pulse of her pleasure in another man's arms. Before, it had been different. When she had not realized he lived, it had barely pricked his consciousness when she married or took a lover. His grief was only in her pain, if her husband treated her poorly, or she lived a life without love.

Now, it was something else. Not that she had betrayed her vows to him, for they had been careful to make no promises they could not keep, and what Elah demanded of her mother could not be accomplished through her celibacy, but to know that she settled, that she yearned for more, and he had taught her that desire, only to enter into this exile—

He had made her life, her lives, that much harder by revealing himself, after he had promised her freedom and peace.

It ate at him, gnawing at every shred of contentment he might have found alone, and even while he drank himself into stupors, he could not put the thought of Eve's suffering from his mind. Days turned into weeks, weeks into months, and the hours he spent conscious were fewer than those he spent otherwise, his days growing shorter and shorter, until he woke only long enough to fill his mug or from the prodding of Eve's own thoughts, reaching toward him, the feather-light caress startling as a branding iron, searing his heart.

At first, she reached for him with frequency. Her thoughts turning to his a handful of times during the course of the day. But as the days wore on, the months turning into a year, and then some, she became more distant, the clear pulse of her love shifting into something else, just as powerful.

Prayer.

Thor, give me strength.

When she prayed, he did not simply feel her, or catch a glimpse of her life. When she prayed, he heard every word clearly. Heard *her* clearly. Did she realize?

Thor set aside his ale, sending her his love, his adoration, and what fortitude he had to give. She had appealed to him directly, and as such, he felt the flow of her will, some small share of her own power, in return, binding them all the more closely. Her frustration with Adam came with it, and her need for safety and privacy and peace, though he could not quite see the why, for she guarded something so closely to her heart—

I'm going to need it.

And then she was gone again. The brief communion broken as she turned her attention away from him to the mundane.

He let out a breath, half-broken with a sob, and then swallowed his grief again, lest she feel it. If she had found any peace, he would not ruin it with his own heartbreak. He would not do her any further harm than he had already.

So Thor reached for his cup again, and drank, drowning himself along with his sorrows.

Just to be safe.

CHAPTER THIRTY-SEVEN

Adam

Russia fell. Without so much as a shot fired or a dictator disposed of, Russia toppled into the collective of the North Country, falling into line exactly where Adam wanted them. Food prices dropped almost overnight, and Adam had succeeded where every other conqueror had failed. Succeeded, because he had not invaded their country with soldiers, he had invaded their minds.

The thought made him uneasy, though he smiled as broadly as he was supposed to, posing with Russian officials and betraying no signs of his discomfort to the Russian minister who would join his cabinet, to ensure that the Russian voice was heard.

But what did that really mean? The minister would be no more difficult to sway than the population, which he'd won through suggestion more than any of his pretty speeches. There were no checks upon his power, not really, and any nation that chose to stand in his way could be absorbed as easily as Russia. It was simply that he had no use for the South—Africa was mostly desert, and that the DeLeon homestead hadn't become more of the same was something he could only attribute to the protections Thor had placed upon those lands. Southern Europe was far from prosperous anymore, between what humanity had wrought upon itself with greenhouse gasses, and the menace of the barren lands, edging further north. Central America, that foolish attempt at a Republic of Texas, even the swamplands of

Florida had shriveled and shrunk into dust and sands. Water use heavily restricted and barely more than subsistence level farming possible.

Lucifer and Bhagavan would see that India never troubled him, but eventually the Free West and the United East would be a problem. Eventually, South America might unite against him, prejudiced as they were against any dictatorship, after those nations had fought so hard for their freedom. But he expected trouble from China long before any of that. And what then? Lucifer had made it clear the last time they'd talked that he had no interest in making himself a target by entering politics openly, even as an ally to the North Country.

Did he mean, truly, to conquer the world? One nation at a time? Elah wouldn't stand in his way, he knew. Whatever Michael's whisperings, Elah knew his affection for her, his love. He'd never hidden it from her, and even when he expressed his disappointment, he was certain, always, to let her know it did not change his feelings. She was his daughter, the only child he could ever have with Eve, and treasured all the more because of it. Eve could leave him, but she could never take Elah from him. She could never take back those moments they'd shared which had led to her birth. Elah would always be a symbol of that love, the ultimate expression of everything they'd shared with one another.

Elah was his reminder that he was more than a conqueror, an oppressor, a tyrant. He was capable of good, too. And it was good which he was trying to accomplish, now. For the world. For his people. For Eve. Always, always for Eve.

Elah?

Daddy. Her voice was so much more vibrant now, though there were still hints of frustration and sorrow beneath. Eve's return to the fold had helped, he knew, but not enough. The barren lands were still barren, and if Elah'd had power enough, they wouldn't be. And what would he do then, when the world wasn't starving anymore?

Am I helping them, truly?

Elah laughed. *How can you doubt it when so many people can afford to eat again, on their own? You don't only take away their hunger, you give them back their pride!*

But could he give it up again? When the time came, and the world was whole, could he give up his influence and walk away? *At what cost?*

It isn't as though you treat them badly, Daddy. And if you did, Mother would never stand for it. No matter how many times she forswears you, if you were doing them harm, she would act. You would know her fury even before you felt mine.

He snorted. *She's come back to me, you know. Accepted an appointment, even, on my staff. I thought at first it was because she was unhappy with what I'd been doing but now—I'm not sure what it is that changed her mind, Elah, but knowing she'll be waiting when I get back to Ottawa . . .*

She married Thor, Father, Elah said gently. *She chose him. She would have abandoned us both if I hadn't exiled him.*

She was ill.

She's been well for more than a year now, and still kept her distance from us, still she yearns for him. Elah's sorrow washed through him. *I'm sorry, Daddy. So sorry, for everything that's happened. It isn't what I wanted for you, but it will only hurt you that much more to hold these dreams so near to your heart.*

He let out a breath. *I've always been guilty of wishful thinking, darling. I hardly think I'll ever be cured of it when it comes to your mother.*

She had loved him, once, after all, and with Thor gone . . .

If she could take up with Marcus, there was no reason she couldn't find some comfort in him, too, one day. And it would be motivation enough to keep him from reaching too far, perhaps. Earning Eve's love again was the best incentive he could ever hope to have.

§

He didn't have a chance to see her right away. Government slogwork came first, much as he hated to admit it, and she wouldn't be impressed if he neglected his country in his pursuit of her, besides.

"I'll meet with the full cabinet tomorrow morning," he told Hilda when she met him outside his office the evening of his arrival. "I want the Russian minister to be welcomed warmly. Have the minister of agriculture take him out for drinks, after, and encourage him to talk—gently—about Russian potentials. We need that land producing. And I want to speak to research and development about the aeroponics system they've been fiddling with for the last six months. They've got to have something up and running by now with some kind of reliability, and I want costs bottomed out and units in production to get things rolling on the borderlands with our relief teams."

Hydroponics was all well and good, but along the edges of the desert they didn't have the water to spare, and the soil quality was so poor, growing anything in backyard gardens was out of the question. Food printers were a start, but there were essential nutrients lost in the transition that could only be found in real produce. Anyone who had land or windows enough for gardening did so, to supplement their food supply and take some of the pressure off, but not everyone had access to good soil, or even water and seeds. In response, Adam had been sending his newly trained and transitioned refugees back home in relief teams, offering food and water and teaching basic subsistence off what little they could grow. Everywhere but the Republic of Texas, anyway. They didn't let anyone back in without proof that they'd had government approval to leave in the first place, regarding anyone who fled the country as a traitor to their great nation.

Yes, he was going to have to do something about Texas. Maybe even before China, which had grown more and more democratic and progressive in response to the North Country's continued expansion.

"There's a backlog of messages on your tablet, Mr. President, and you're in back to back meetings for the rest of the week," Hilda said, passing him the pad in question. "I did do my best to weed out the worst of them, but I'm afraid the rest of these all require your personal attention."

Adam grimaced at the number blinking in the top corner of the screen. He hadn't been gone that long, surely. "Any news from our latest arrival?"

Hilda pressed her lips together. "Nothing as yet. I did check in on her as you asked, and she assured me she had everything she needed."

"I'm sure she did," Adam murmured, scrolling through his messages for subject and sender. Nothing from Eve. "Well, I suppose I'll just have to believe her for the time being. It certainly doesn't seem as though I'm going to have even half a moment to myself for the next two weeks, regardless."

"The next two months, at least, sir," Hilda corrected him. "Though once we've reorganized the Russians, things should quiet down."

"We won't have the Russians reorganized for another six to nine months, Hilda." She met his eyes, the soft blue filled with sympathy, and said nothing. He sighed. "Very well. Book me. But I want at least one Sunday every month left open for my own sanity."

"Of course, Mr. President."

He sent her off and collapsed in his desk chair, leaning back and raking his fingers through his hair. It had been a lot more fun to rise to power when he hadn't cared quite so much about the actual governing of the nation. If he could trust any of his ministers—but he knew firsthand how easily the kind of power he wielded would corrupt even the best of men, and not all of his ministers were anywhere near the best. Evey, on the other hand, would have made a very fine second in command. Not that she would be willing. And not that he necessarily wanted her saddled with his responsibilities, even unofficially. It certainly wouldn't help them steal any time together, and he couldn't hope to win her if neither one of them had any time to spend in the same room. Still. It might be worth making her official, somewhere near the top of the food chain. He'd have Hilda look into it tomorrow.

I'm home, Evey, he sent silently. *But I won't be able to see you for a few weeks, yet.*

I'll survive on my own just fine, Adam, I promise.

He grunted. *You might. I'm not so sure about myself.*

The longer it takes for you to get away, the more likely I'll have something to report on that data you sent me. And I really do work better undisturbed.

His eyes narrowed at her tone, light and teasing, and utterly false. She didn't want him there. For what reason, he hadn't the foggiest notion, but it had nothing to do with the data, and everything to do with his physical presence in her home.

If you're worried I'll impose myself . . .

No, she said softly, sincerely. *It isn't that, I promise you. I just need some peace and quiet, that's all, and I'll never get it with you popping in and out.*

Well. He couldn't argue with that. Not really. Every trip he made out there was a risk, and if she was distracted just by his presence, generally—maybe that wasn't such a bad thing. But. *You can't hermit yourself away, Evey. It isn't healthy. Especially not for you.*

It won't be forever, she promised. *Just give me a little more time, all right?*

I'm not sure I have much of a choice, if Hilda has any say in the matter. He tried to keep his voice light, but there was something not quite right about the whole situation that he couldn't put his finger on. She'd come to him. Asked him for help. If she hadn't wanted him in her life, why would she have agreed to move to Ottawa? To work with him at all? He could have moved her anywhere, and he would have, if she'd wanted it. Australia, the North Pole, the heart of the barren lands, if she'd asked it of him. *I'll have Hilda set something up for next month. A meeting, here, with the science team, once you've had time to settle in, and acquaint yourself with their findings.*

Thank you, she said softly.

But he wasn't sure at all what she was thanking him for.

CHAPTER THIRTY-EIGHT

Eve

There was nothing in the data that would help them. Just more evidence of lifeless lands, completely barren even of the smallest sand fleas. The only thing she'd found that was even remotely worth looking at more closely was a chemical residue of some kind, and that was outside her purview as a biologist. Eve pushed the tablet away, leaning back in her chair. She had another meeting with the science team tomorrow—the third since she'd accepted Adam's appointment—but what was the use? They wouldn't be able to tell her anything she didn't already know, and the only person who could tell them more, who might have some hope of uncovering what was happening had been sent into exile.

"Mama?" Lars looked up from his toys, frowning. At fourteen months, he was the size of a four year old, and even smarter than one. His development had sped up since they'd left Marcus, and Eve was beginning to think he'd eclipsed Elah, though that might have been due to his temperament, at least in part. Lars was obedient in ways Elah had never been, cautious and attentive, and keenly aware of her own emotional state.

Like his father, she supposed. Incredibly powerful, but incredibly sensitive to the world around him, always trying to heal, to help, to soothe. Since Lars had been born, she hadn't suffered from a single migraine. At the first sign of the yawning pit behind her eyes, he was crawling into her lap, snuggling against her neck and murmuring about bad dreams and spoiling dinners.

"I'm fine, love," she said, forcing herself to smile. "Don't worry."

Lars tilted his head, expressive blue eyes shining with the reflection of her own frustrations, and the tears she didn't dare shed. "What's exile, Mama?"

She left the tablet on the table, and sat with him on the floor. "It's complicated, honey. But remember what I said about not peeking into anyone's head without permission?"

"Yes, Mama," he said, all contrition and guilt.

She stroked his soft, blonde hair, and kissed the top of his head. "If we don't behave, if we don't live by the rules of the Goddess, exile is one of the punishments she might choose. To send us away from the world, forbid us from ever coming back again."

"Never?"

"Never," Eve agreed. "She could take you away from me, Lars. Send you into exile alone. That's why we stay here by ourselves. Why it's so important that you do as I say."

Lars crawled into her lap, small arms wrapping around her neck. "I won't go!"

"You might not have a choice, honey. We might not have a choice." She hugged him tightly. "But I promise I'll do everything I can to keep you with me. And no one will ever hurt you, not as long as I live."

She felt a surge of his love, his adoration and confidence in her power to protect him. The complete faith of a child in his mother. Elah had believed in her this way once, too. Eve sighed into his hair, rocking him in her arms. No matter how many promises she made, she could only pray that she lived up to it. The stronger Lars grew, the more she worried, and the harder it was to keep him a secret from Adam.

Even if Adam hadn't seen him, or felt him, he'd noticed her distraction, to say nothing of her stress level. And she couldn't keep him at a distance forever, besides. Not after she'd approached him, come here to work with him. And when she was honest with herself, she knew she didn't want to. Not that she wanted anything romantic with him—not that she could ever pick back up with him where they'd left off, so long ago—just that she missed having a friend, a relationship with someone who understood her.

Lars was wonderful, and she loved him, but he was so young. He wanted to comfort her, wanted to sooth all her sorrows, but he couldn't understand them, couldn't realize how dangerous this all was, and she had no intention of burdening him any further than she already had. She didn't want him to be inhibited by her fears. To have to live his life in hiding from everyone . . .

But what other choice did they have? When Elah's eyes were everywhere. When the wrong attention would mean death for both of them.

"I wish you weren't so sad, Mama," Lars murmured against her neck.

"Me too, honey." She kissed the top of his head again. "Me too."

§

"Surprise!"

Eve suppressed her irritation, hitting the door closure with more force than necessary. It whooshed shut behind her, brushing her heels. Adam at her front door wasn't exactly the kind of surprise she preferred. Especially not when Lars had been playing in the living room, behind her.

"You're early."

"And here I thought you'd be pleased to see me. Outside of those committee meetings, we haven't had any time together since I left for Russia."

"Adam—"

"I know," he said, grimacing. "I ought to have warned you. I'm sorry. I wasn't expecting to have the time, really, and then the meeting with R&D was cancelled, so I just thought, since you were coming in shortly anyway . . . Aren't you going to invite me in?"

She shook her head. "Let's just—go."

"You can't be serious?" He lifted both eyebrows. "I've a full hour for the first time in half a year, entourage free, and you're going to throw it away that easily? If we go, we won't have a minute uninterrupted. Hilda will have me scheduled for four different meetings the minute I set foot in my office. And! We made some small progress with that chemical compound. The pharmaceutical company is fighting our access, but if the lawyers don't convince them, I'm sure we can find a way, between us."

"While I appreciate the news, I told you before, you can't just drop in on me this way," she said.

"Evey, I know. I know. And this isn't about any lack of respect, I promise you, it's only the longer I stand here, the more likely someone is going to notice." He reached around her, pressing his palm to the door lock. It chirped, whirred, and slid open. "In, please. Unless you want the press swarming you."

Lars! The bedroom! Eve closed her eyes, swallowing a whimper of dismay as Adam pushed past her into the cottage, then caught her by the arm and pulled her with him.

"Really, I'm not sure what you're so—" He tripped, and the sound of plastic crunching under his shoe made Eve wince. Don't let it be the Bird of Prey. It was Lars's favorite, and he'd never forgive her. "What on earth, Evey?"

She slid the toys beneath the sofa with her foot. Lars had hidden himself, at least, but the proof of a child was impossible to miss. "What?"

Adam crouched down, picking up the broken pieces of—thank goodness, it was only one of the generic pilots. Lars must have had ten of them.

"Evey. Since when do you collect spaceships?"

"They're fascinating," she said, moving briskly to the kitchen. "Tea?"

Adam caught her arm as she passed, stopping her. "What's going on, Evey? You've been on edge since you came, and I didn't press you, but this?" His gaze swept over the toys littering the carpet, the sofa. The whole house was a staging area for a space battle. Lars was fascinated by the stars. "This is why you didn't want me here. Why you kept pushing me away, isn't it?"

"It's private," she said, jerking her arm free. "And absolutely none of your business."

But he shook his head, his jaw tight, and then his eyes locked on hers. "This is why you asked for my help. Why you left Marcus?"

"Adam," she breathed. "Please. Just let me have this. I'm begging you, leave it alone."

He laughed, bitter and wild. "Leave it alone? You've been hiding a *child*, Evey! For how long? Were you pregnant before—no. No, that was why you wouldn't come with my people. Of course. You'd already had him, and if he were Marcus' you'd never have left him." He stumbled back, steadying himself against the sofa. "It's Thor's, isn't it? It has to be! And you thought you could just hide yourself away and no one would ever find out?"

"What else could I do?" she said, clutching at the collar of her shirt. "What other choice did I have?"

"You could have told me, Evey!"

She shook her head, backing away. "If Elah found out, she'd kill him. Kill us both!"

"Do you really think I'd tell her?" His face had paled. "After what happened before, do you really think I would have done anything to endanger either one of you?"

The whole room blurred, her eyes swimming with tears. "Elah, and then Thor, and Asgard, and I just—I couldn't risk it, Adam. I couldn't risk Lars, too."

He barked another laugh. "Lars? Of all the most obvious—you might as well have hung a sign around his neck and called him Thorson."

"It was all I could give him!" It was half sob and half shout. "If he'd never know his father, at least he could know one of his names. Share that much!"

"Mama?"

She gulped a breath and swiped at her tears before she turned, forcing her lips into a smile. Lars stood in the bedroom doorway, his arms wrapped around a plush wolf half his size. His eyes were brimming with the same tears she was trying to hide.

"It's okay, honey." Eve crossed the room, sweeping him up into her arms, and squeezing him. "I'm okay, I promise."

Behind her, Adam was silent. Not even breathing. And she could feel his sympathy, his frustration, his concern, a bruise of pain and emotion in the back of her mind.

"You're crying," Lars said, his soft voice strained.

"It's okay," she said again. "Sometimes even adults need to cry, sometimes we get upset, and shout, and it doesn't mean anything's wrong."

But Lars was craning his neck to look at Adam, to stare at him, and Eve closed her eyes, hiding her face, for a moment, in his small shoulder. Even just holding him helped. Stopping the slow drain into green darkness that always followed her anger. And if she hadn't had Lars all this time, she didn't even begin to know how she would have survived, open as she'd been forced to be.

"Who's that?"

"Oh, honey. He's—"

"Your uncle," Adam interrupted. "I'm your uncle, Adam. And I'm going to help your mother keep you safe and sound, all right?"

"Are you going to make her sad?"

Adam made a strangled sound, but she couldn't bring herself to look at him. Couldn't even bring herself to open her eyes. "Never again, Lars. Not if I can help it."

She couldn't stop the sobs, then. Couldn't stop her tears from escaping.

Because for the first time since Thor left, she wasn't alone. She wasn't facing any of this alone.

Thank you.

Adam let out a ragged breath, pulling them both into his arms. "It's all right. I swear to you, this time everything is going to be all right."

She wanted so much to believe him.

So much.

CHAPTER THIRTY-NINE

Adam

❧

It was amazing, the transformation, then. He hadn't realized how much of herself she'd been keeping back until she opened to him, welcoming him into her life, into her son's. And the first time Lars reached for him, all on his own—Adam had been in the middle of a meeting with the Chinese minister of trade, and even if it had been a meeting with Elah herself, he wouldn't have given up that moment. But as much as he rejoiced in knowing that Lars wanted him, that Lars had learned to love him, too, it only emphasized how much of a danger he was to himself, to his mother.

And it was only a matter of time until Elah learned of him, if he didn't slow down. So that night, when he slipped Hilda's leash to join Eve and Lars for dinner, he waited until after they'd eaten, after Eve had put Lars to bed with a song and a kiss, and she had come back out again, stars in her eyes and joy in her heart for the son she'd born.

Adam couldn't help but smile, lifting his arm in invitation. "I meant to tell you, we finally broke through the lawyer stalemate on that chemical problem."

She laughed, pausing on her way back across the living room to toss a few of Lars's toys into his bin. "You know just what to say to a girl."

Not that he'd done more than hold her, or that she'd have welcomed it if he tried, but he treasured these moments, when she all but danced through the house, half-dreaming and drunk on motherhood. It was just reflected glory, what she shared with him, but for those heartbeats, it was as if he'd never left her. As if nothing had ever gone wrong between them, and it wasn't Lars asleep in his bed, but Elah.

Which was why he wanted so much for it to last. This easiness between them.

"Not the sweetest of nothings, I know, but I thought you'd be interested, even if it isn't exactly your bailiwick. It seems it was a briefly used drug to treat schizophrenia, way back when. Some doctor had the only viable sample dug up from only the gods knew where, and they were never able to duplicate it after what he had ran out. They had it buried because of his questionable ethics in regard to human experimentation. Seems he was something of a Freud, with a focus on women in asylums."

She dropped onto the sofa next to him, and leaned against his side. "Terrible P.R., I suppose. But what in God's not-so-green earth is it doing in the barren lands?"

Adam shook his head. "Maybe the source was some kind of desert plant, and it was released in decomposition over time. That's all I can think of."

"No," she said, her forehead furrowing. "It wasn't botanical. I'd have known of any desert plant with medical properties, and this was completely foreign. Like some dysfunctional take on a helicase."

"Should I know what a helicase is?"

She rolled her eyes. "Helicases are the enzymes that unzip the double helix. But I can't believe that in all these years you never thought to investigate the process of DNA replication. I would have thought you'd be dying to have our genetic code unlocked."

"I think I was more concerned with preserving our natural advantages. Can you imagine the havoc it would cause if someone tried to clone us? Let's not forget there were entire lifetimes when you were convinced that just one of me wandering the earth was one way too many."

She snorted. "Both prudent and true."

"So where does that leave us with this dysfunctional protein-enzyme-compound business?"

"If it isn't identifiable beyond some doctor three ages ago testing the only sample on some poor uninformed woman, who hadn't the slightest notion what was happening to her?" Eve asked, not bothering to hide her disgust. When he nodded, she shrugged. "It's another dead end."

It was exactly what he'd feared she'd say. What he'd tried to deny, and why he'd put off bringing it up at all.

He cleared his throat, forcing himself to finish what he'd started. "Then there's something else we need to talk about, Evey."

She sighed. *It can't ever last, can it?*

I wish it could. More than anything. And I swear to you, Evey, one day, I won't be this man anymore, the one who brings nothing but ruin to every good thing. But without some kind of proof for Elah, and with Lars's life in the balance . . . I guess I'd rather ruin this small happiness, than hold on to you, to whatever this might become, and be the reason you lose your son.

You're the reason my son is still safe, Adam.

For now. But I don't dare press my luck. Or yours. Or his.

"I know," she said softly, turning her face into his shoulder. "Every day is stolen and every moment is a gift. But I don't know how else to protect him, beyond hiding him away."

"Call to Thor. Send him to Asgard. Elah won't be able to touch him there. Michael won't be able to reach him."

"He's so young. And after Elah, I can't bear to give him up. I can't."

Adam smoothed her hair, tucking her head beneath his cheek. "But you'll be giving him to his father, not to the angels, not to God."

"If Thor could even reach him," she said. "Without coming back, I don't see how, and the moment he returns, Michael will have his head."

"It would take less than a breath. Thor wouldn't even have to manifest, entirely. Just enough to grab hold of Lars, and whisk him away in the lightning."

"You say that as if it's easy. As if even telling him his son exists won't warn Michael that he's coming. I can't reach him, Adam. Not without calling out so loudly the whole world hears me, Elah and Michael included."

"As long as he's here, Eve, he isn't safe. He'll never be safe."

"But if I can protect him for another couple of years, keep him hidden, let him grow, it won't be long before he's powerful enough to protect himself. You've seen him. How fast he grows, how strong he's become, even in the weeks you've known him."

"Lars isn't a fighter, Evey. An engineer, maybe, a builder, a healer, even an explorer, but not at all a fighter. He likes to make things whole again, not tear them apart. And would you want that for him? A struggle for his own life? Against his own sister?"

She fell silent, slouching down, snuggling deeper against him, and he felt the stubbornness of her thoughts, the determination in the words she didn't say. Hollow emotions, born out of the realization that he was right—she never liked admitting to it. Truthfully, he didn't like being right about this anymore than she wanted to agree.

"You should take him to India," Adam said. "If you won't risk calling to Thor, at least go to Bhagavan. He'll be able to hide Lars more easily among the rest of his aspects. You could stay with him, take care of him, raise him, and you wouldn't be alone."

"Why should Bhagavan help me?" Eve asked. "Why should he risk himself or his people for me? For Lars? We're nothing to him."

"But Thor was. And there is no question, looking at him, that Lars is Thor's son. If you go to him, beg for sanctuary, he'll grant it. I'd stake my life on it."

"What about you?"

He smiled. "What about me?"

"Lars is so fond of you," she said, not quite meeting his eyes. "And you'll never get away long enough to see him there. And even if you could, Elah would notice. She'd wonder."

"It wouldn't be the first time I gave you up, Evey," he said gently. "For your own sake, for his. I won't make you go, and I won't walk away as long as you want me in your life, as a brother or otherwise, but India is his best shot. Maybe his only shot."

Eve hid her face against his chest. "I'm going to miss you."

He lifted her chin, looking into her eyes. Those emerald pools, misted with everything she wouldn't say. *Evey, love . . .* Her face was so close to his, her breath tickling his skin. All he had to do was lean down, and she would melt into him. Because there was love there. Just the first small spark of something more than friendship, and he'd been waiting for it for so long. If he only fed it, only gave himself up to it now, up to her . . .

But he couldn't do it. Not to her, not to himself.

Because she had to go to India. She had to take Lars to India.

And if he kissed her, he'd never let her go.

"I'll make the arrangements tonight," he said, letting his hand fall away. "You'll be in India before the week is out."

He would go with her, he decided. Disguise the whole thing as some diplomatic visit, and see her to safety. Eve had had so little experience with the gods, and he didn't think asking Lucifer to meet her when she arrived would help. But that was his only contact, and he didn't dare try to reach Bhagavan directly, himself.

Adam scrubbed his face, lying awake in his bed and staring at the ceiling. He'd been half-tempted to spend the night with Eve, just to keep her company, to be in her presence just a little bit longer before she disappeared again. He'd miss her, he knew, but there wasn't anything more she could do in the North Country, and even if they could discern the trouble in the barren lands, it would only risk Lars for her to be part of it.

Maybe they were fooling themselves, anyway. With all of this. Maybe the barren lands were just the result of God's death, the world dying in His absence, too. Maybe His plan hadn't been as perfect as He'd hoped it would be, and something had been lost in spite of how careful He'd been to preserve it. Just some awful kind of divine decay.

Either way, if they could preserve Lars, if they could give him time enough to grow, to come into his own, there was a chance, small and fragile, but a chance, that together with Elah, he might be able to do what the rest of them couldn't. After all, if Thor was God's son, too, His first born, and he'd been meant to come home, to protect the world Elohim had made, maybe his son had a role to play, too. Maybe the missing piece in all of this was Lars, himself.

Adam grunted. Convincing Elah of it was going to be a battle. One he wasn't sure he could win. And in spite of what Raphael had said, he was beginning to think that Eve deserved the truth, too, about Thor. About Lars.

Just like Thor deserved to know Lars had been born.

But how? There had to be a way to reach him that wouldn't alert Elah in the process. Raphael and Athena must have some way to contact him. Adam couldn't imagine that Athena didn't have the power to travel to Asgard, herself, if she willed it, and passing along a message wouldn't be nearly as difficult as that.

If she could afford to risk it. If doing so wouldn't mark her as a traitor, somehow, in Michael and Elah's eyes. That was the greatest difficulty, he was sure. Athena, of all of them, would be under the severest surveillance, her loyalties the most suspect, and even more so when it came to Thor.

And Raphael?

Well, he knew he could trust the Archangel not to tell Elah, either way. And if there was a way—maybe it wasn't his place. More than likely, Eve would be furious. But if it had been him. If Lars had been Elah, and he'd never even known she was born . . .

Raphael?

He rolled out of bed, reaching for a stylus and a notepad. As much as he might have teased Eve in their last life for her love of paper, he'd found it to be invaluable still, to keep private notes private, all the more so when everything floated in the ether. He scribbled a brief line on one of the small sheets and tore it free.

Raphael!

The Archangel formed out of moonlight, dark hair mussed and looking far from pleased at his summons. "You might very well rule the world before this life is over, but I would remind you, Adam, Elah's father or not, you do not rule me."

Adam grimaced. "Sorry. It wasn't a command so much as a need." He folded the sheet of paper in half and held it out. *Can you get this to Thor?*

Raphael arched an eyebrow. "This is your need?"

"Desperate, really. For Eve's sake."

The angel plucked the note from his fingers. *She won't thank you.*

Adam's eyes narrowed. *How do you know?*

"I'm not certain you've ever done anything for Eve's sake that she's been pleased about."

She'll be more upset if I don't, and things go south. Can you get it to him, or not?

Once, and only once, do I dare risk this. Whatever your message, you're certain it's complete?

"Yes."

"You're sure you want to brave Eve's displeasure?"

"More than sure."

He'll have it before dawn. For all the good it will do anyone.

Raphael disappeared, and Adam lay back down again, hands behind his head. The day after tomorrow they'd leave for India, and maybe then he'd be able to sleep at night, knowing he'd done everything he could to help her, to help them both.

It didn't hurt, either, that if Thor ever found his way back, the thunder god would owe him a debt.

CHAPTER FORTY

Eve

She would have been lying if she'd said it wasn't reassuring to have Adam at her side for this.

Thor had been one thing—she'd known him for so long, even if she hadn't realized the significance—but to go before Bhagavan and beg sanctuary for herself and her son was something else altogether. If only she'd been able to go with Thor to see him, when he'd suggested it the first time. As it was, she had no idea what to expect, no concept of the protocols involved. Thor had spoken of a Covenant and a Council, but she hadn't been part of either.

"Relax, Evey," Adam said, squeezing her hand. "This isn't my first rodeo."

His other arm was wrapped around Lars, who clung to his neck like a monkey, alternating between excitement and fear. Eve couldn't blame her son for either, but she'd been subtly nudging him toward the former whenever the opportunity presented itself. Even if it did make her a hypocrite.

Traveling with the President of the North Country did have its perks. Customs agents met them in a private room, swiping their passes and bypassing most of the bother of traveling into a foreign country. Not that she couldn't have nudged them, too, if need be, and she was prepared for it, since her documents weren't exactly authentic to begin with.

"President Simonsen, welcome to India." The North Country ambassador met them with a broad smile and a firm handshake. "Ms. DeLeon, I hope that you and your son enjoy your stay with us. If there is anything we can do to assist you, please don't hesitate to call."

"Thank you," she said, carefully extracting her hand from his grasp. "But I sincerely hope that won't be necessary. I doubt you'll have any reason at all to see much of me once we're through here."

"Her wish is your command, Ambassador Jensen. No matter what she says. Is that understood?"

"Absolutely, sir," Jensen agreed. "Now, I'm afraid there's just a small hiccup, today. The press got wind of your plans, and half of India has turned out to goggle at the Caesar of the North."

"Caesar, now?" Adam demanded.

Jensen spread his hands, helpless. "After Russia, you can hardly expect anything else."

He sighed, and shifted Lars to his other hip. "Is there a way we might allow Ms. DeLeon and her son to slip past the crowds? I wouldn't like any attention to be drawn to them, unnecessarily."

"By now, customs has already sold her name and description to the press, sir."

Adam swore, and Eve bit her tongue on a similar urge. She'd kept Lars out of sight for so long, and now that they'd reached what was supposed to be her sanctuary, half the world was going to be analyzing every angle of his face for some stupid resemblance to Adam that didn't exist—aside from what she'd contributed, anyway. From the feel of it, they were about to face a mob.

I know you don't like to abuse your power, Evey, but under the circumstances . . .

She shook her head. *Under the circumstances, even if I erased our passing from their memories, I can't do anything about the photography or the videos.*

"I'll do my best to keep his face hidden," Adam said. "And we power through the masses, as quickly as possible, to the car. Which will have opaque windows," he said, pointedly, his gaze falling on Jensen with the weight of command.

"Of course, Mr. President!"

"And any surveillance tapes in the building will also be taken care of, I hope."

"We'll certainly do our best, Mr. President," he said. But Eve had a feeling his best was likely to involve some positive cash flow in his own direction for allowing the leak. Judging by Adam's expression, he was thinking the same thing.

"If Ms. DeLeon's son's face makes it to the media, Jensen, I'll be appointing a new ambassador before the month is out."

The man grimaced. "I understand, Mr. President. Had I realized the importance—"

"As a resident of the North Country, I would have thought you recognized the value of privacy. That's why we have laws protecting it, for all our citizens. Ms. DeLeon and her son, included. Myself, even, included. Perhaps you've been away for too long."

Jensen's face had gone blotchy, and Eve wasn't entirely sure that Adam was helping the situation. "I'm sure Ambassador Jensen has done his utmost to protect your privacy and mine," she said. "And I, for one, won't be holding him responsible, Mr. President. I hope you'll find the same generosity in your own heart."

Adam let out a breath. "I suppose my own generosity will be dependent upon tomorrow's headlines."

"That is more than fair, Mr. President," Jensen said. "Now, if you'll both just follow me."

Keep your head down, Lars, Eve said, and wide-eyed, he did as she asked. Adam lifted a hand to shield his features from the security cams, scattered throughout the facility. All her gratitude for his presence was rapidly turning into irritation. Not that it was his fault, really. Just that they'd been so close, and not even Bhagavan's power was going to save them if Elah and Michael got a clear view of Lars's face. He was Thor's son, through and through.

They made it out of the airport, but even the side entrance which had been cordoned off for them was a mob scene. At least a hundred people were waiting outside, pressing up against the static barriers until they threw sparks. The familiar sight of black glasses told Eve more than half of them were recording images of her face, running it through their own networks, looking for a name and a match. Not that they wouldn't be able to get the information from the customs officer when that failed, but at least with her false identity, they wouldn't trace any of it back to Marcus.

Mama?

She stroked his hair, helping Adam to hide his face as he ducked into the car, waiting for them with windows at full opacity. *It's all right, honey. They're just fans of your uncle.*

They want to see me, too, Lars said. *There are so many!*

It doesn't matter what they want, she assured him. And then they were all in the car, the door closed, and the vehicle moving away from the crowd. Lars reached for her, and she pulled him across Adam, into her lap. "It's all right, honey. They can't see you anymore."

"I'm sorry, Evey," Adam said. "I didn't expect anything like this. They shouldn't have even known I was coming. Hilda made all the usual arrangements, and this kind of thing is terrible for security."

"What about the Indian Prime Minister?"

Adam raked his fingers through his hair, falling back against his seat. "I don't know. I don't know why she'd want to throw me to the wolves, unless it was just on the off chance that it might set me off balance."

"Has it?"

He bared his teeth. "Not off balance enough to let her get away with whatever she's trying to pull. But the press back home are going to have a field day with this. They've been hoping to catch me in some affair since I took office, and the international community—Evey, they aren't going to let this go. Maybe they didn't get any good shots of Lars today, but it won't be long before someone does."

"Then I guess it's a good thing we're about to disappear, isn't it?"

"Not quickly enough," he said, his expression grim. "The hotel is going to be just as bad, and we're going to have to get through them again to get out when my contact arrives. If he can risk coming at all with this mess. He isn't all that eager to be seen by Michael, either."

She held Lars tighter and ignored the chill settling into her veins. "But Bhagavan will help. Once we reach him, he'll help us."

"It might be too little too late by then, Evey."

Eve closed her eyes and counted to ten. Then back to zero again. If they'd just stayed in Ottawa . . .

"We've come this far," she said, keeping her voice even, calm. She didn't want to upset Lars any further than he already was. "We'll see it through. I've got to try."

But she was already regretting not turning around and getting back on the jet, and when they arrived at the hotel, packed with just as many people, all clamoring for a glimpse of her, of Adam, of Lars, she wanted to weep.

The car door opened, but when Adam moved to get out, a green-skinned hand stopped him, pushing him back inside. Eve reached for the man's mind, but it was slippery and blank, and then he'd climbed in with them, grinning.

"Now, now, love. I'm hardly sssusceptible to that sort of trick, even if I weren't here to guide you on." He licked his lips, and Eve blinked, sure she was imagining a forked tongue, until she looked again at his face. His skin was patterned with subtle, green and brown diamonds, like scales, and his eyes. Slitted like a snake's. "Though as it happensss, I'm afraid I've had to make some executive decisionsss regarding your plans. The bit including Bhagavan, for instance."

She stiffened, sliding as far from him as she could get, and reaching for the other door handle. If she had to brave the press, she would. She'd brave anything, but she had to get out. She had to get Lars out—

"It's all right, Evey," Adam said, though his eyes had narrowed with irritation. "He's a friend."

"But he's—"

"Lucifer," the man said, his tongue flashing again over his lips. "How kind of you to remember."

CHAPTER FORTY-ONE

Elah, Before

Elah crouched beside her grandfather's throne, pressing his hand to her cheek. But even the power she offered him wasn't enough on days like this one, and his smile, as he looked down on her was feeble, his eyes cloudy with age.

"Sweet girl," he murmured. "You need not waste yourself seeing to me."

"Hush," she said, kissing the back of his hand. "I am not so disloyal as to leave you, now."

His skin was so paper thin, and she didn't need the grim faces of his Archangels to know that he was dying. Before long, he would have no skin at all, no strength to keep to any form, and then even his spirit would fade, his power flowing back into the world. Michael hadn't been wrong, so long ago, when he'd said she was draining him dry. Every day, she grew stronger, heard more of the world, felt more. Creation became more hers and less his, and even the people had begun to pray differently, though she wasn't sure how they could know. The Host, perhaps, spreading word of her coming, even if she would not fully ascend until Elohim was gone.

The angels already obeyed her as if she spoke with his voice. The Archangels, less so. Her father was right that they were powerful in their own way, but it was a power she could draw upon at will. Perhaps she would never be able to read their minds, to command them as she would the others, as effortlessly as a limb, just another part of her body, but they were tied to her, all the same. Grandfather had made it so.

"Lady," Raphael said gently, touching her shoulder. "The Council has been called. We cannnot keep them waiting."

Elah sighed, resting her forehead against their clasped hands for another moment. "I've left it too late, haven't I?"

Raphael's fingers tightened, then his hand fell away. "Any sooner and they would not have believed you capable, my dear. But the time is upon us, now, regardless."

"You must stay, Grandfather," she said, squeezing his hand. "You must wait for me to return. So I can tell you what's happened. Promise me, please."

"As you will it," he said, the corners of his eyes crinkling at the corners.

The show of humor did more to reassure her than anything else, and she rose, pressing a kiss to his wrinkled cheek in farewell. But his hand tightened around hers when she sought to step away. "What more, Grandfather?"

He let out a rattling breath, his eyes closing. "The Aesir."

"They've answered the call to Council, with the others. Bhagavan warns me that their king is wily, but his first son serves us."

Elohim smiled, and his cloudy eyes met hers, though she was not certain what emotion he meant to convey. Caution, or indulgence. "Blood calls to blood."

"I'll remember," she promised. A warning, then. A reminder to place her trust in her own. Her father had promised to come, to stand at her side. But she had not wanted to shock her mother. She'd lived so long in ignorance of the other gods, there seemed little purpose in exposing her to them now. Elah could only imagine she'd be hurt and angry, and she was still so raw. Every time they spoke, she could feel the current of pain, an undertow pulling at her own emotions.

If she could only see how much Father suffered without her, how much he regretted what had happened . . .

The Council first, she reminded herself. And when the world was settled, she'd see to her parents.

Elah hadn't dared bring Michael into the Council room, a crumbling temple of Bhagavan's, deep in the jungle. She had Bhagavan's promise of safe conduct, the protection of his aspects, not so different from her own Host, and she had Raphael and her father, both, besides.

She had believed it would be more than enough protection until the moment she stepped to the rostrum, every god left in the world focused upon her. And in that moment, she understood completely Michael's concerns, his fears. Were they to unite, to stand all together behind Bhagavan, perhaps even had they stood without him, she was not completely certain she could stop them.

But they won't, her father said, and how he'd wormed his way into her thoughts, she wasn't sure. She'd been open to his, but hadn't realized she'd given up her own. *Too much ego, too much pride. They could barely agree to inaction, never mind anything more, and that was when one or two of them were agitated enough to call a Council at all.*

It was enough to calm her nerves, and she fixed the mask of her own confidence in place. The same confidence her father wore so casually, lounging behind her with a complete lack of concern. As if these gods had never threatened him at all. As if he had always been their equal, their superior.

But if the stories Gabriel had told her were true, the stories Michael told her, as well, now that she insisted on hearing them, he had always believed himself a god. Had always seen himself as one of them.

And she, doubly so.

Elah lifted her chin, searching the faces of the gods who stood before her. Gods who had so little power they sought to siphon her own, incapable of shaping a world from nothing but their will, or breathing life into dust. That power belonged to Elah alone, upon her grandfather's death, whether she chose to wield it or not.

"I have no desire for a war," she said, her gaze stopping on the one-eyed bear of a man, dressed in leather and furs. Odin. But for Bhagavan, the Aesir were the most plentiful of the gods left. There were some Egyptians, still, though they stayed out of loyalty to Raphael, lending their services to him and to Elohim as a result, and a goodly portion of other Africans, South Americans, and Islanders. The more remote the people, the more faith they placed in the gods of their ancestors.

Of the Olympians, only a handful remained. Raphael had always spoken of Athena with warmth and respect, and Elah had no trouble recognizing her. Gray-eyed and white-armed, with a thick braid of silky black hair spilling over her shoulder, she had the look of an Amazon. Her eyes did not leave Raphael, even when another god leaned down to murmur something in her ear. Thor, she thought, judging by his red-gold hair and the breadth of his shoulders. Curious that he did not stand with his father.

But Odin looked ill, his jaw locked and his single eye narrowed in a gray, pinched face. As if he stared at an enemy, come back from the dead to haunt him again. As if he knew himself defeated before a challenge had been issued at all.

"I have no desire for conflict with those of you who have nurtured this world and those within it, offering it your protections when my grandfather was too weak to defend His own Creation," she went on. "But I cannot turn a blind eye to your continued presence. To your attempts to grasp at my power, your desires to undermine my authority among His people. The people who will become mine, in time. I will not suffer wars fought over faith through your champions, nor inspire my own to rise, for I see no reason for innocent blood to be spilled for the sake of your pride or mine. This has been your way, I know. The only way, perhaps, for the greater peace to endure. But it is not my way."

Odin's face had grown grimmer still, but Thor, his son, the god who Raphael had assured her would stand as her ally, had crossed his arms, his gaze trained upon her with no sign of compromise.

"Those of you tied to this world by true bonds of love may petition Us for the right to remain," she said, and from the corner of her eye, she saw the bunched muscles of Thor's shoulders relax, the lines of tension in Athena's face ease. But Odin looked away, flinching from her words. "A new Covenant will be forged between us, and those of you who stay will be sworn to it, bound to Our service above all. This is my offer, and you will have a year to decide how you will answer. If, after that year has ended, you remain within the bounds of Elohim's Creation and have not sworn yourself to Our Covenant, you will be banished. By force, if necessary." She swallowed, searching each of their faces, looking for some sign of understanding, of gratitude. There was little of it, beyond what she had been told to expect. "I hope very much to avoid such an outcome. I hope, very much, for peace."

Bhagavan stirred. He had taken the form of Vishnu, perhaps in the hopes that it might reassure the others. Now he stood. "The Covenant has been made."

A grumble ran through the council room, the gods all shifting, casting glances at one another. Elah offered Bhagavan the barest of nods, respect and gratitude both.

Breathe, darling, her father said behind her, his mental tone rippling with pride and humor. *You've won already, even if they won't admit it yet.*

Thor lifted his chin, catching her eyes. He still stood with his arms crossed, his shoulders broad as mountains in the small space. "It shall not be broken," Thor said, raising his voice to be heard above the others.

"It shall not be broken," Athena echoed, beside him, her silver eyes flashing with hope.

"It shall not be broken," another god agreed, one of Odin's pack of sons, though he was far more beautiful than most, and almost glowing with his own strange light.

Elah let out a breath of relief as the grumble faded, replaced by the ripple of the ritual phrase. Odin's wife, and then the rest of his sons. The Africans, the Islanders, the Americans. The Egyptians and the Olympians, and each and every one of Bhagavan's aspects, one after another, after another.

All of them, but for Odin, she realized, who stared at her once more, as if the sight of her brought a foul taste to his mouth. She met his gaze, lifting her chin, and stared him down.

"Allfather?" she prompted, keeping her tone carefully cool, stiffly respectful.

The god bared his teeth in so wolfish an expression, she wondered if he had not had some role in the breeding of the creatures in all the time he had lived within her world. "You of all people to ask it of me. As if it is my choice. As if it ever were!"

Elah kept her confusion from her face, but she felt her father step forward, saw Thor tense, his eyes narrowing at his father's words. But when Raphael would have shifted nearer, she lifted her hand, stopping him.

"I assure you, Allfather, the choice is yours. Go peacefully, or remain, to be hunted by my angels and driven into the void. Just as it was your choice to come here. To let your Trickster dog attack my mother and drive her to the brink of madness. You are fortunate she had any Grace left with which to succor me, any mercy or love left to give, or this meeting might have gone much differently. For you. For all of your kind."

"And what of the betrayals we have suffered?" Odin snarled. "You ask me to leave, now? Had I known what world we had found, I would have never come, never brought my people to these lands. Never risked my son!"

"Enough, Father!" Thor growled, thunder rumbling beneath his words. "My decision was made long before the Goddess's birth. She plays no part in it, now."

Odin sneered. "You always were more your mother's son than mine. Too soft-hearted, too trusting, too great a fool. No son of mine would give himself up into the service of some godchild."

"As you say," Thor said coldly. "And if that is so, you can have no further reason to remain here. Nor, if I am not your son, do I owe you my allegiance."

Odin's face had gone from gray to red to purple. "My son or not, I am still your king."

"Then behave as one!"

Odin lunged, but the shining one caught him, held him back, and whatever he murmured in his father's ear, Elah did not hear it. Reason, she hoped, for the god had disgraced himself beyond measure by behaving so wildly in Council. To her benefit, she supposed, though even faced with his clear refusal of her terms, she hesitated.

If I cast him out now, what of the rest? I risk inciting a war.

You risk a war if you don't, her father said. *More of one, for Odin will want to prove himself after this, to salve his pride.*

Elah pressed her lips together, and lowered her head. If she must dispense justice, she would not do so coldly. And there was no reason, truly, why they should not see her regret.

"Odin, son of Bor, King of the Aesir, you are no longer welcome here. Return to your Asgard, and from there, depart. I will give you three days to make arrangements for the governance of your people, and if you have not gone before those days are ended, my angels will fall upon Asgard. Your halls will be razed and all your people banished. If they fight, they will be killed." She lifted her gaze then, surveying the others, all gone still and silent at her words. Odin's face had drained of all color, his eyes darting about the chamber, searching for some support, but the gods gave him none. "Make no mistake, though my desire is for peace, this world is mine and I will fight for it."

And then she left them.

There was nothing else to do, but that.

❦

"Lady," a voice called, and Elah turned, despite herself. Michael waited for her on the other side of the portal, the relief in his eyes calling her home. Her father had remained with Bhagavan in the chamber, and Raphael had done the same. To answer any questions the gods might have, and note those who would challenge her, later.

"Forgive me, Lady," Thor said, stopping a respectful distance from her. "But I would speak with you, please."

She nodded, stepping back from the portal. As eager as she was to return, she could not refuse him. Not after he had defended her. "Thor of the North. Raphael speaks nothing but your praises."

"He is generous, as ever."

"He says you are Our ally."

"I am sworn to your mother's protection, Lady. I would not see harm befall her, or those she loves."

"With the exception, perhaps, of my father?"

Thor's smile was thin. "Only before she loved him, Lady. When he hunted her, and she feared him, I stood in his way. If force was required, I used it."

"For all of that, my father still speaks well of you."

"Your father has learned from his mistakes, though much too late to save your mother from heartbreak."

"You mean because he left her."

Thor said nothing, but his silence did not lack judgment. If she had not heard Michael's stories, and even her father's own, she might have bristled. Part of her still wanted to, but it would not have been just. Her father had not always been the man he was now. At least Thor did not sneer at him openly.

"What do you ask of me, Thor of the North? For your service to my mother, to me this day, I can hardly refuse you."

"Let me go to Eve."

She blinked, the earnestness of his expression, the pain in his eyes—"My mother knows nothing of the gods."

His jaw tightened. "She knows me."

"How?"

"Let me go to her, Lady. I beg of you."

"Why should she want your companionship at all, after everything your people have done to her?"

"Of course she would not tell you." It was half-mumbled, his face turned away. His hands closed into fists at his sides, and he lifted his head, squared his shoulders, and met her eyes. "She was my wife, Lady. And I would make her mine again, if she desires it. Or at least grant her what comfort I might. Let her know that I live, still, and love her, always."

Elah's stomach twisted, her heart clenching. "No."

Thor's eyes narrowed, his voice low and hard. "You would deny her this?"

She swallowed. She hadn't meant to say it, but once the word had escaped, she couldn't take it back. Wouldn't. To let Thor go to her, to give him even the chance—she knew her mother. She knew. The love of a god. The love of a husband, lost for so long. The way she treasured her House of Lions, her connections to those men from her past. It would destroy any hope for her father.

"My mother has a husband," she said roughly. "If she desires comfort, she can find it in his arms. Where she belongs."

She didn't wait to hear his response before she fled. Into Michael's waiting arms, his hard embrace. Elah blinked back her tears, cleared her throat, and forced herself to smile at his poorly-hidden fears, letting herself be absorbed by his worries, his paranoia, so she did not have to dwell on what she'd done.

Perhaps—perhaps it was true. Perhaps she was her father's daughter, after all.

CHAPTER FORTY-TWO

Eve, Later

Lucifer. Eve slid Lars half-behind her, ignoring his squirming. Even if Lucifer hadn't done her any harm in the Garden, it didn't mean she trusted him. Not with her son. Not with Thor's son.

"Sorry about this circusss," the snake-man said, grinning. "Well, perhaps not entirely sorry in the most honest sense. I'm rather proud of it. Ssso much accomplished on such short notice."

"You were the leak." She didn't need Adam's discernment to figure that out. "Of course! Just another Trickster, playing your games at everyone else's expense."

"I'm hardly another Loki, thank you very much, though I shouldn't expect you to realize the difference. What I've done, then and now, ssserves Elohim and His master plan, nothing more, nothing less. Someone has to keep things running smoothly, after all. Have you seen the barren lands? Yes, I can tell by that adorable little wrinkle between your eyebrows. When you sssee your husband again—ah-ah!" He held up his hand, stopping her from interrupting with a hard, golden look. "Listen carefully, Eve, and tell him thisss: Jormungand won't sleep for much longer and Surt is growing impatient for his revenge."

"Surt!" Thor had mentioned him. Something about a sword, and his mother's involvement.

"Were I you, I'd be more concerned with the ssserpent of this equation. Surt is Elah's problem, and Michael's even more than that, but another round of Jormungand's venom, and you'll be lucky to be reborn at all."

She sucked in a breath, everything tripping into place. The compound they'd found—the perverted helicase they knew so little about. The doctor who had experimented on women, using it to treat schizophrenia. The needle of green liquid pressed against her throat, and his awful laughter, ringing in her ears. But of course, Adam couldn't have known. She'd never told him. Never remembered to tell him. So why should he have mentioned where the doctor had worked, or the name of the woman, if he'd known it at all.

"The Midgard Serpent," Adam muttered, his gaze unfocused. "A perfect circle of dead earth. Only how did he get here?"

"There are Tricksters and there are Tricksters. Odin was a fool to turn his blind eye to Loki's return—he didn't crawl back out of Hel empty-handed. It appears he traded his ssslippery services for the fang and its venom, which in turn, he used to poison our lovely Eve." Lucifer leaned forward, smiling gently. "You needn't hide, boy. Of all of Elohim's monstersss, I'm the last you should fear."

"Mama?"

She swallowed, but she couldn't reassure him. Couldn't comfort him when all she saw on the horizon was his death. When she was trapped in the memory of begging for her own.

"Exactly when were you planning on telling me this?" Adam asked.

Lucifer shrugged. "When were you going to tell me Thor left behind a son?"

"I assumed you'd find out through the usual channels. I've been busy running half the world, with no help at all from you, I might add."

"In my defense," Lucifer hissed, "I hadn't quite put the all the piecesss together until recently. It wasn't until Elah kicked Michael from her bed that I realized the full extent of the trouble we faced, and even that . . . Well, word doesn't reach me as quickly as I might wish, and Michael has been watching my brothers too closely for them to send much more than the barest of reportsss."

"You were waiting, weren't you?" Adam asked, his tone going hard. "For the right moment. For everything to align, so when the dominoes started to fall it would produce the desired outcome. Elohim's desired outcome."

Adam's words snapped her back, outrage grounding her in the present. Playing with them, with their very lives. Eve laughed, more out of hysteria than anything else. She was so tired of all of this, and they'd never be free. She would never be free. There would always be some divine hand, reaching in to rearrange the pieces. "You're telling me that God's plan was for us to die? For Lars to never have been born?"

Lucifer's eyes widened, his gaze flicking between her and Adam. "Is that what you think? That I've done what I've done to ensure your deaths? Why should Elohim sssentence His own grandson to death? Why would He want to harm His most prodigal of sons?"

"His own—" Eve rocked back. Prodigal of sons. Of sons, plural. Like the twin trees? "I don't understand."

"Thor is Elohim's son, Evey," Adam said, and he picked up Lars, murmuring reassurances she couldn't, too stunned even to speak. Elohim's son. It made such blinding, perfect sense, but she'd never even considered . . . "And that means that Lars belongs here, just like Elah. Just like you and me, and just like Thor. And unless I miss my guess, Lucifer arranged all this in order to bring him home."

"Without Thor, Jormungand will continue to sssuck this world dry, weakening the Goddess, weakening all of you. He must return, and he must have reason."

"You're putting an awful lot of faith in his timing," Adam said.

"My faith in the children of God has never been missplaced," Lucifer said, holding Eve's gaze. It was like staring at the serpent in the tree, so long ago, his eyes boring into her, reading every memory, every moment of her short life. "Remember that I showed you the way then, as I do now."

"Michael won't allow it," she said. Even if it was Elohim's plan, Michael wouldn't care. It gave her a bitter satisfaction to realize it. Michael did nothing that didn't serve his own ends, whatever they were. "You know he won't."

Lucifer's eyes slitted again, going hard and amber. "Perhapsss we'll be so fortunate as to witness his death, then. For this is not Michael's world, Eve. Much as he would desire it, otherwise. It is Elah's word which is law, but for what of Elohim's will ssstill prevails."

Eve snorted, looking away. Elohim's will could suck lemons for all she cared. But at least she understood now, where Elah had gotten it. And Adam before her. This burning desire to control everyone, to fit them tidily into neat little plans without any consideration for free will. It wouldn't have mattered how well she'd raised Elah to respect her people and their choices if Elohim himself had taught her the opposite.

"If Elah doesn't know, she isn't likely to allow it, Elohim's will or not," Adam said.

"What risssk is it to allow Thor back, now?" Lucifer countered. "The child she feared is already born. To refuse him is to create an enemy where she might as easily have fostered friendship. Another ssseven or eight years, and Lars will reach his majority, brimming with the power Elah requires to keep her world whole. If she does not grant Thor forgiveness, allow Lars to know his father at all, why should the boy help her, then?"

"Because she's his sister," Eve spat, glaring at him. "And I'll have had the raising of him, without any interference this time."

"Not without Thor's help, you won't. You cannot ssstand against Michael alone any more than I can, or Adam. He'll cut through us all to reach Lars."

"He wouldn't know about Lars if you hadn't told the press," Eve said. "We'd be safe, under Bhagavan's protection!"

"And when Elah learned of the betrayal, what then?" Lucifer demanded. "Have you any idea what would come, after? What you would have ssstarted? Oh, Bhagavan would have helped you, in all honor, he'd have had no choice, but in repayment, Elah would wage a war against him, against all the gods who remain. And when Lars ssstood in her way, they'd tear the world apart! Presuming Jormungand didn't beat them to it, of course."

"How long until he wakes?" Adam asked, pinching the bridge of his nose. "And what can we do, if none of this works?"

"Flee," Lucifer said. "To Asgard, to Olympus. Preserve yourselves and the power which resides inssside you. Without Thor, you've no hope of stopping the beast, and he'll tear a hole straight back to Niflheim, large enough for any number of monsters to escape to this lush world. You'll be overrun unless he's stopped, and the longer Thor waitsss, the more difficult it will be. The more likely Surt will have his revenge."

"Why should Surt want anything to do with us?" Eve asked, shaking her head. "Thor told me he drove the Aesir from Niflheim—that must have been eternities ago!"

"And who defeated Surt, before the end?" Lucifer asked, his forked tongue flicking between his lips. "Who ssstole his flaming sword and reforged it for his own use? His own gain?"

Eve pressed her lips together. Because if Thor was Elohim's son, that meant Elohim had been Thor's mother. The very same mother who had saved the Aesir and disarmed Surt.

"The sword," she said softly. "The flaming sword. It's the God-Killer, isn't it? Michael's sword."

"It's more than that, Eve. Ssso much more. Elohim reforged it, but the blade was tainted still. Or did you never wonder why Michael was so malicious? So violent? The more Elah's power wanes, the stronger Surt's influence, the more dangerousss Michael has become."

"And you're using us to bait him," Eve said, her blood running cold. "On the thin hope that Thor will realize the danger we're in, will even recognize the threat at all. He doesn't even know he has a son!"

Lucifer grinned, leaning back, and his gaze cut to Adam. "Doesn't he?"

Her brother cleared his throat, and even Lars was staring at him, wide-eyed, though how much of the conversation he'd understood, Eve wasn't certain.

"If it had been me, I would have wanted to know," Adam mumbled, then shrugged. "So I told him."

Eve clenched her jaw. "Just like that."

"He deserved to know he'd left a son behind, Evey. You said yourself you would have told him, if you'd known how to do it without alerting Elah."

Her eyes narrowed, betrayal snaking through her heart. The same old story, over and over again. In some ways, Adam had never changed at all. And no wonder, after all the rest of this. *You could have told me you knew how to reach him!*

You wouldn't have let me try.

The breath she let out was half-hiss, and Lucifer sissed his strange laughter. "Now that everything's sssorted out, shall I show you to your penthouse suite, Mr. President? Ms. DeLeon? And if you wouldn't mind making sure the photographers get a good look at your ssson's face, this time?"

"My son is not your bait, Trickster. And just because you're working according to some master plan doesn't mean I have to play along."

"Whether it's the sight of Lars or the sight of my own green ssskin which draws him, Michael is coming, Eve. And whether you like it or not, Lars isn't going to be a sssecret for much longer. If you won't give in gracefully, you'd at least better be ready to scream."

And then Lucifer pushed open the door and stood, letting in the roar of the mob outside and the subdued flashes of photographers with higher-quality equipment than just the plain black sunglasses favored by so many.

"I'll do my best to hide his face," Adam said, and how he could take all this in stride, Eve couldn't understand. As much as he had always wanted control—did he not realize how much had been taken from them? How much they'd never had? "You go first, and see if you can't draw their attention. If they're all looking at you, maybe we can keep their cameras pointed in that direction, too."

It wasn't as if Lucifer had left them much of a choice.

"Keep your head down, Lars-love, and your eyes closed," she said, stroking his hair. "Uncle Adam and I will take care of the rest, all right?"

He nodded, squeezing his eyes shut and hiding his face against Adam's neck.

She took a deep breath, steadying her nerves, then stepped out of the car beside Lucifer and smiled broadly. A wave and a grin, a wink and a toss of her hair, with a rush of sensuality and love, and every eye was on her. It wasn't a power she cared to make use of, generally speaking, but she was, supposedly, perfection, after all.

The perfect woman, wife, mother, lover.

Lucifer growled, his hand closing possessively on her elbow, bringing a surge of lust with the touch. "That's a dirty trick, Eve."

"When it comes to dirty tricks, I'm not sure you have any legs to stand on, serpent." She jerked her arm free, keeping her smile firmly in place as she did so. "Better watch out. I'd hate for Thor to mistake you for an enemy when he makes his triumphant return."

He dropped his hand to his side, his fingers rubbing together still, but his yellow eyes were still too warm on her skin. "And all this time, I thought Elah got her ruthlessness from Michael. Our little Eve, all grown up, as fierce as any wild thing in the defense of her young."

"I hope you won't forget it."

And then she lifted her chin, and made love to the crowd, one handshake, one glance, one slow smile at a time, and she prayed with all her heart that it would be distraction enough.

❧

Adam's security men kept Lucifer from following her into the suite, and she'd never been more grateful for their presence. It didn't give her any pleasure to wrap people around her finger that way, and her stomach had twisted into knots with the strain of keeping them so closely tied to her person.

Lars threw himself into her arms when the penthouse doors closed behind her, and she lifted him up, hugging him close. "I don't like it here, Mama. I want to go home."

She sighed, kissing his forehead. "I don't like it either, honey. But we can't go home. Not yet." They'd come here for nothing. Gone through all of this for nothing. And poor Lars didn't understand the half of it. "I'm sorry, sweetie."

Adam offered her a glass, half-filled with an amber liquid that she hoped was heavily alcoholic. "I'm the one who should be apologizing. I should have known better. It just never occurred to me that Lucifer would have his own plans. Or that he'd try to lure Michael out this way, into some showdown with Thor."

Thor. Eve closed her eyes, her fingers tightening around the glass, and her arms tightening around Lars. *Thor, protect us.*

Part of her couldn't help but hope. For all she didn't care for his methods, if Lucifer brought Thor back, if he was right that Elah would have to allow him to stay. She missed him so much, and to have him back, to know he would be with them both, again. That he might know his son!

"This is all a lot bigger than us," Adam said. "A lot bigger than just keeping Lars safe. If Lucifer is right about the Midgard Serpent, and Surt . . ."

Eve knocked back the tumbler, barely tasting what was, without question, whiskey. "If Surt is influencing Michael, that's why Elah doesn't know about Jormungand." She had to admit, even if she didn't want to, that without concrete proof, none of the Archangels would have had any hope of convincing Elah of anything Michael disagreed with—Lucifer included. "And if it is Jormungand, burrowing through the heart of the world, that's why I could feel him when no one else could. Why his presence affects me so much more than it does anyone else."

Adam shook his head. "You never mentioned that life. Not to me."

"I'd forgotten," she said, setting Lars down. "Go find your toys, Lars. I'm sure one of Uncle Adam's people unpacked them somewhere. It'll be like a treasure hunt."

He waited until Lars had gone, but Eve didn't miss Adam's concern, lapping at her consciousness. "How do you forget something like that? A run in with Jormungand doesn't seem like something a person just overlooks, no matter how convinced they are that the gods don't exist."

Eve held her glass out for a refill and he took it from her. Thinking too hard about that life always left her feeling like a stiff drink was more than called for. "It wasn't Jormungand I ran into. Just Loki, with a noxious potion of his venom that was being passed off as medication. I was in a mental ward in Connecticut for a number of years, going crazy. Of course I didn't know what was happening or who was behind it until Thor told me. At the time, I just . . . lost my mind."

Adam passed her another glass, more full than the last. "When?"

"The life before you found me." She smiled, but it was weak, and dropped into an armchair.

The main room was spacious, she had to admit that, and she was glad, because it was likely they'd be spending some time there, now that they didn't dare appeal to Bhagavan.

"I thought I was losing it again when I was married to Garrit, between you and Thor and everything. That was when Raphael buried the memories, so I could find a little bit of peace until I'd healed a bit more completely. I still can't remember everything about that life. But I remember the doctor." She swallowed against the memory, the needle sliding into her throat. She let Adam see it, as she spoke. Let him feel her fear, her pain. "I remember he made it so I couldn't speak. Couldn't make a noise at all. And my husband. He was a piece of work, that man. Frank Newcastle. I put him in a coma. He—" she licked her lips, her mouth suddenly dry. "He was beating me, whipping me, determined to make me talk, but when the belt-buckle came down on my back, it cut me open to the spine. Without my voice, I screamed with everything else I had in me, straight into his head, and he dropped like a rock."

Adam's face had turned gray, his fingertips pressed white against the glass in his hand. "Evey . . ."

She shook her head. "It doesn't matter. It was a long time ago, and I'm better now. Stronger, maybe, in some ways. Jormungand's venom was really the least of the horrors, but I wouldn't want anyone else to suffer anything I did in that life."

He buried his fingers in his hair. "And then I came. Before you'd even had time to properly heal. And Michael breathing down your neck, besides. I don't know how you kept it together at all."

"I had a little bit of help." She twisted a shoulder. "But after that, you can see how unimpressive your own brand of awful might have seemed. Even in the Garden, Frank Newcastle would have put you to shame. You were selfish and arrogant and thought you were a god, thought we should all be begging and scraping before you, but it wasn't . . . you weren't . . . unredeemable, once you'd lived a little."

He snorted. "I'm not sure if I should be flattered or insulted by the comparison."

She shrugged, staring into her glass. The liquid winked back in the sunlight streaming through the wide windows overlooking the balcony. Loki and Frank Newcastle had been one thing. But something inside her thought Michael was capable of so much worse. Even more, if he was really tainted by Surt. She could still see the image from her mythology book. The monster, towering above an army of the dead, laying waste to everything before him. And it had taken everything Odin had, and the help of Elohim as well to stop him the first time. A fully empowered Elohim, unweakened by Creation. Elah was incredibly strong, but not that strong, and even Thor was just one god. How could it be enough?

"Evey, we're going to be okay." His hand covered her wrist, warm and familiar. "And if nothing else, you're going to have Thor back. Lars is going to have Thor back."

"Maybe so," she agreed. "But what about Elah?"

CHAPTER FORTY-THREE

Eve

❧

Neither one of them slept that night. The guards were doing constant sweeps for Michael's face, but she couldn't bring herself to so much as lie down after she put Lars to bed. She couldn't even stand to close his door. Maybe she couldn't protect her daughter, but she wasn't going to take her eyes off her son. Without a word, Adam helped her drag a couple of armchairs near to the bedroom, giving her line of sight to the bed, and sat down across from her with a pack of cards.

"What's the fun if you don't even get to shuffle them?" she murmured, when he hit the randomizer on the exterior of the package, and then dumped them out into his palm.

His lips quirked. "They don't miss what they never knew. You wouldn't believe what I went through even to get these. Most people just play virtually."

They played poker at first, betting with peanuts that Adam had ordered from the minibar—more of a dispenser really, and Eve would have objected to printed peanuts for any other use but poker chips. Then they played pitch, giving up on anything but keeping score by points.

"How much longer, do you suppose?"

Adam tapped a query on his tablet, calling up the headlines, then shook his head. "Morning, I'd guess. No point in wasting a good story this late at night."

So they kept playing, and Eve kept half an eye on Lars's bedroom as they did. "Should have gone to the House of Lions."

Adam rocked back. "What?"

"It isn't desert, anyway, and it would have been private. A safe private place for Lars to grow up." And then hope lit through her. Elah might still be able to reach them there, but Michael couldn't. She'd seen with her own eyes what would happen to him if he tried to raise a hand against her there. "We could still go. We could pack up everything and just go. You could stay, do whatever you need to do, and I could fly out tonight, with Lars."

"I don't like you going anywhere alone right now," he said, shaking his head. "And I can cite this media circus as the reason I've left so precipitously, anyway. Security concerns. It wouldn't even be a lie, all things considered."

"Now?"

"Now!" And he was already reaching for his earpiece, arranging things with his people and scrambling his pilot. Eve left him to it, rushing to pack the essentials they'd need. Maybe she couldn't rely on her family's welcome anymore, but she could count on the land. And if need be, with a little morally ambiguous trespassing, the manor could provide them with changes of clothing, food, even gold—which she refused to consider theft when it was from her own vault of her own belongings, whether the DeLeons in residence realized it or not. She did make sure to pack Lars's favorite spaceship, and she was careful to pry his stuffed wolf from his arms, so it wouldn't be lost when she carried him out, but the rest . . . Well, if they didn't make it, they weren't likely to need it anymore anyway.

They abandoned the penthouse, meeting almost no one on the way down, and only a handful of people on their way from the front of the building to the car. Lars slept through the entire operation, with the barest nudge of assistance along the way, and she buckled him carefully onto the small couch in the back of the jet, tucking his wolf back into his arms again.

Eve took the nearest seat, and Adam sat down beside her, scrolling through headlines while he murmured something into his earpiece at the same time. Hilda, probably, and Eve didn't envy the woman her job.

"Even with the time zones, I'm not sure we'll make it to the DeLeon lands before the news hits," he said, once he'd finished.

"We don't have to," she said. "As long as we make it there before Michael and Elah catch up. I doubt either one of them monitors any kind of feed. It's Lars and I rising to the surface of too many minds that's going to tip things, and that won't happen until people start waking up."

"Until they start waking up in India, Evey."

"And when Michael flits to India first, we'll be long gone. He'll have to figure out where we went before he can follow us."

Adam grimaced. "Then I suppose we'd both better disappear, hm?"

"Not quite yet," Eve said. "Too soon, and Elah might just send him looking for us without waiting for the news."

Adam rested his head against the back of his seat and closed his eyes. "I'm sorry, Evey. I should have thought of your Lions first. I should have known that would be the safest course."

"By all rights, Bhagavan should have been. Would have been, if it hadn't been for Lucifer, no matter what he says otherwise."

"I'll go to Elah once you've crossed the border. Maybe I can reason with her, while Michael is out hunting you. If I explain things—it's the only chance we have of winning her grace, Evey."

"If Thor doesn't come. Or worse, if he does."

"Exactly."

"You'd better leave the minute we land, Adam. I'll get myself and Lars across the border alone. The minute this all hits, if she's been listening to half of Michael's vitriol, she's going to think the worst."

He raked his fingers through his hair, half-pulling at it. "Let's just hope she believes me."

Eve didn't think it was likely. But then, her relationship with Elah had been difficult for far longer than it had been easy. She reached over and took Adam's hand.

Thor, protect us all.

❧

It was raining when they landed, but Eve didn't dare open her mind enough to look for Thor's presence, just pulled her jacket up over Lars's limp body, and slipped through the airport as quickly as possible while making herself invisible to the authorities. As far as the French were concerned, the President of the North Country had touched down to refuel, all passengers still accounted for, on board.

Unfortunately, the closest airport that could accept such a jet was at Marseilles. Nice, the much closer port to the DeLeon lands, had stopped permitting the landing of anything but airships. Its field had been no more than grass even before she'd been reborn, and Toulon had been abandoned completely with the encroaching desert. Southern France was filled with such ghost towns, but somehow the DeLeons, in the mountains, had escaped the worst of it, and it meant a longer drive than she liked.

Eve cursed when she found the carport empty. So late, or early, perhaps, the usual morning business hadn't replenished their numbers from the last flight's arrival. In another century, she might have taken a bus instead, or called a taxi—a private driver! A quick query produced the name of a nearby company, but when she called, there was no answer. She swore again, and carried herself and Lars to the most private corner she could find that still had a view of the carports.

She only needed to wait until someone arrived. And at this hour, there was hardly any traffic through the airport. No one would care that she was there, or pay any particular attention to her, anyway, now that she was on the departures end of things. But she couldn't keep her gaze from traveling back to the overlarge monitors, streaming the latest news reports, ticker-style at the bottom of the screen.

India would wake up before long, and if they'd gotten a proper image of Lars . . .

She watched the screens until her eyes ached, and it took all her will not to start pacing. Pacing was something that would draw attention, and even her jittering leg was attracting looks from the man behind the ticket counter.

Evey? It was Adam, and she half-jumped out of her seat at the sound of his voice. *Are you safe, yet?*

The carport was empty. I'm still waiting for someone to arrive so I can leave.

Adam's curses were far more inventive than her own. And more modern. *The first reports surfaced. Nothing with Lars's face yet, but yours is everywhere. A shot from our experiment at the hotel.*

Her gaze snapped back to the screens. *I hadn't considered . . .*

You need to get to the manor, Evey. As soon as you can. Michael won't be able to follow you there, but any man or woman can, and you look—you look more than inviting.

And there it was. Her name, and then her face. The image side by side with one of Adam and headlined: The Caesar's Secret Girlfriend. She rose immediately, walking to the counter. The man there smiled absently, staring at her image on the screen.

"Excuse me," Eve began in perfect French, sifting through his mind to find the right strand of desire. "Is it possible that I might borrow your car? I promise I'll have it returned to you before this evening."

He glanced at her, then looked again, recognition dawning across his features. "*Madame!* But you cannot be—the Caesar is in India, still."

She blinked. "I'm sorry?" The man gestured to the screen behind her, and she turned, pretending surprise, even while she gave a twist to his thoughts. She might have forced him completely, bent him to her will, but she hated to set that kind of example for Lars, even now. "Oh no! No, that isn't me! It's my sister, you see, and I really am desperate to get home before our parents hear. I was supposed to be keeping her out of trouble, and then this! Please, sir, I really must get home, and the carport has been empty for hours . . ."

The man looked her up and down, smiling. "For you, beauty. But you must promise to introduce me to your sister when she comes home again, yes? And perhaps you'll have dinner with me, later, when you bring my car back?"

"I will!" She flashed a brilliant smile when he touched his earpiece, sending the command to his car. "Thank you so much. You don't know how much this means to me."

"You can show me later, hm?"

"Absolutely!" But she was already turning away, sweeping Lars into her arms again, and fumbling with their small bag and his toy wolf. The car had pulled up to the door. Even the most basic models had homing beacons, programmed to find their owners when summoned, just like a rented car finding its way to the nearest carport. "Thank you!"

And then she was in the car, a verbal command directing it home. To her mountains. To the safety of her family's manor.

Evey? Adam prompted.

I'm on my way. I borrowed the ticket clerk's car.

Override the governor.

Adam, I don't have the man's thumbprint. I can't futz with his settings.

You don't need it. Just pull the fuse.

While we're driving? I don't think that's safe—

Pull the fuse and override the governor, Evey.

That was when she saw him. Michael. Standing in the middle of the freeway, his wings spread wide, and his sword drawn.

"No." She yanked open the panel, but her eyes were blurred, and the car was racing toward him already, much too fast. "No, no, no. How did he find us so quickly?"

Michael lifted the sword, and she reached for the emergency brake, too late for the fuses now. *Thor! Thor, you have to protect Lars! It's Michael. With his sword. With the God-Killer!* And then she pulled the brake, sending the car skidding and squealing. Her head slammed into the side-window and she prayed, she prayed, she prayed that she hadn't imagined the flash of white before everything went dark.

CHAPTER FORTY-FOUR
Thor

He'd been staring at the strange note for half a day, his mind thick with too much drink, and his whole being muzzy.

Your son won't stay hidden for much longer.

Thor didn't know when it appeared or where it had come from, he didn't know who had written it, or how it had reached him, but the words struck him like lightning. Magni and Modi were long gone, having followed Odin to the next world. Ullr, his stepson, too. So who? And then Eve's anxiety, growing ever more constant in the back of his mind. And her prayers. Protect us, she'd said. Us. And it wasn't Adam in her head, but he hadn't quite been able to see. Hadn't understood. Hadn't believed it possible, that he could give her a child and never know it, never feel it.

And then.

He'd seen Michael clearly through her eyes. Seen the sword in his hands and the car racing toward him. He'd felt Eve's terror, and it had burned through him, taking his hangover with it, taking all reason with it.

A surge of lightning, and the car had slammed to a stop. Thor stepped out of the liquid light in time to catch Michael's wrists on the down stroke of the blade. He caught them, and he squeezed, listening to the bird bones crack beneath his fingers. But Michael only laughed, flame leaping from the sword to the car, dancing over the frame, searching for a way inside.

Thor growled, thunder answering his fury, and lightning crackling over his skin, through his palms. The Archangel's flesh burned under his hands. Rain, buckets of rain, poured over the car, and then a shield of electricity, carefully built over the melting metals and plastics, slipping beneath the flames.

"I've been waiting a long time to kill you, Odinson," Michael snarled.

"You'll wait longer, still."

Lightning cracked through the sky, and Thor pulled it down, funneled it through the sword itself, into the angel. Hands to arms to chest, and even Michael's stone heart stuttered.

The angel's body convulsed with the shock, his hands frozen around the sword's hilt, incapable of releasing what Thor had made into a lightning rod. Thor shoved him back, throwing him into the asphalt so hard the road cracked. Then he spun, tearing the door off the car in his haste, reaching for Eve.

His hand shook as he felt for her pulse, still steady, and then his gaze fell on the boy. Blonde hair and wide, frightened eyes the same color as his own, the same shape, the same everything.

His eyes, in his son's face, and he grasped for the name—the name Eve had called, praying for his protection. She'd called him something, he knew, though her terror had all but eclipsed her words, and he could only hear one, now, repeating over and over in his mind.

"Son," he breathed.

The boy. His boy. Shrank back, his haunted eyes shifting back and forth between Thor and his mother. "Mama?"

"Come," he said gently. "Quickly now, and I'll take you both to safety."

He shook his head, shrinking further. "Mama said I shouldn't."

Thunder rumbled overhead, expressing the frustration he didn't dare show. A quick glance over his shoulder told him Michael had woken, badly burned, but not dead, and one hand still clutching the sword.

Thor had no time. Not for this. Not now.

"Close your eyes, boy."

That much, at least, the child did, and Thor grasped the car itself, calling the lightning to him, letting it wrap around him, and the twisted vehicle too. The asphalt and the mountains faded, replaced by gray stone and the bright crimson leaves of his mother's tree.

He tore the seat in its entirety from the wreck of the car, afraid to jostle Eve by pulling her free any other way. A dark bruise was already forming on her forehead, but she was whole. She was whole, and unbroken, and he hadn't been too late.

Thor lifted her limp hand, pressing it to his face. "My heart."

"Don't touch her!"

The small voice wavered, but pride surged through him, all the same. He lifted his head, meeting the boy's gaze. His brave boy, standing in front of the car with all the ferocity of a lion cub, but so determined to protect his mother.

"She's all right," Thor said. "She's going to be just fine."

"What happened to the other one? With the sword and the fire?"

"He can't reach you here," Thor assured him. "You're safe. Both of you. As long as you're in Asgard, nothing of Elah's can harm you."

"Mama says the Goddess is my sister. I'm supposed to help her, when I'm big."

"Then it must be true." He smoothed Eve's hair from her face, willing her to wake. "Did your Mama tell you about your father, boy?"

His face crumpled. "The Goddess sent him away."

"Do you know where the Goddess sent him?"

He scrunched his nose, as if trying to remember. Then, "Asgard!"

"Asgard," Thor said, smiling. Even if he hadn't known his son, at least his son had known something of him. "And look around you now, little man. Didn't your mother ever tell you about Yggdrasil, the

World Tree? About Bilskirnir and Valaskjalf? Look and see where you are, now."

The boy looked, his eyes growing wider and wider as he craned his head, back and back, taking it all in. Every gray stone, every building, every leaf and apple of the tree at his back. And then his eyes narrowed, suddenly suspicious. "Mama always told me there were goats in Asgard. Magic goats!"

Thor laughed, squeezing Eve's hand, and wishing desperately that she were awake and healed enough to squeeze it back.

"And so there are," he said gently. "But I've your mother to see to first, before I can take you to meet them. Would you help me?"

"I'm not s'posed to," the boy said, but he'd been drawn nearer, all the same, frowning at Eve. "Mama says not where anyone can see."

"Even if the only one seeing is your father? Even in Asgard?"

"That might be okay, I guess," he agreed after another moment lost to scowling. "Mama said I'm good at helping."

Thor extended his hand to him, already crouched down low and doing his best to appear as nonthreatening as possible, after he'd ripped apart their car and called lightning down in front of the poor boy. "Show me how."

He hesitated, but already he was inching closer, one small hand on Eve's leg, and frowning again. So serious, this son of his, and more than anything, Thor wanted to lighten his burden, his fears.

"She's sleeping funny," he said after a moment, "'cause everything moved too fast, up here." The boy darted forward, touching her forehead. "But I can make it better."

"Is that your magic?"

He shrugged, his whole face scrunching up as he touched her forehead again, more carefully. "Please wake up, Mama. Please?"

Eve's eyelids fluttered, then blinked open. Once. Twice. And her gaze slipped from the boy up to Thor, her eyes widening even more than her son's.

"You're here," she rasped.

He smiled, stroking her cheek. Some of the tension in his body unraveled at just the sound of her voice, no matter how weak, how hoarse. It had been so long since he'd heard her. Really heard her, and felt her warmth, the softness of her skin. "Not quite."

The boy lifted himself up on his tiptoes to look into her face from the other side. "Can we go see the goats now, Mama?"

❧

"We have to go back," Eve said, while the boy—Lars, she'd told him—was distracted by the goats. Tanngrisnir was letting himself be chased, and Grani was edging nearer to them at the commotion. Laughter hadn't been heard in Asgard since Eve left.

Thor shook his head, his jaw tightening even at the thought. "It isn't safe. Not for Lars. Bad enough you kept him from me all this time, but to take him back for Michael's execution? I think not, Eve."

Eve sighed, rubbing her face. A dark bruise had blossomed above her right eye, and from the way she moved, he knew she'd suffered others, but she'd refused any further fussing, insisting that she was fine. The way her eyes had slid to Lars as she said it would have been proof enough of the lie, even if he hadn't seen the physical evidence.

"We can't stay here," she said tiredly. "I can't stay, and the longer Lars stays, the more likely Elah will believe this is another plot. But it isn't just that, either. *You* have to go back, too. Lucifer said it's Jormungand, Thor. In the barren lands. And Michael—he's been controlled, maybe even possessed at this point, by that sword, by Surt."

He tore his gaze from Lars, who was taking his turn at being chased by Tanngrisnir and squealing with delighted laughter every time the goat butted him, and stared at Eve. His head was still more muzzy than he'd like, because her arguments sounded like a mish-mash of gibberish. Jormungand's presence might have been reasonable, and leave it to a snake to recognize the stink of another serpent, but the rest. The rest made no sense.

"How has Michael anything to do with Surt's sword?"

"Because it's Surt's sword he's been wielding, all this time. Reforged by Elohim."

"My mother took Surt's sword with her," he said, lightning burning through his veins. "If Michael has it now, it means she was here, once—that he stole it from her own hand. If Elohim had my mother killed . . ."

"No." Eve was shaking her head, cautiously, to be sure, and her hand rested on his forearm, her fingers curling into the muscle, nails sharp against his skin. "Thor, just listen. Don't you see? The tree here, in Asgard. The one in the Garden. They're both Elohim's. That was why you were drawn here, why you stayed for me. Elohim didn't murder your mother, Elohim *was* your mother."

His lungs stopped, his chest too tight for air any longer. Elohim. But that would make Eve . . . All this time, he'd lived here and never known, and she had been—*he* had been—and Odin! Had his father known? Guessed? That last Council meeting. The things he'd said. Thor had thought she seemed familiar because of Eve, but Odin must have taken one look at Elah, her black hair throwing rainbows, and seen an image of the goddess who had left them behind. No wonder he'd been so furious.

"You have to come back," Eve said again. "You and me and Lars. We have to go back home. To stop Jormungand and Michael. To stop Surt and help Elah to heal the world."

Home. He let out a ragged breath, watching Lars tumble through the grass, and then leap up again, and charge his goats. Grani stretched his neck out, leaning against the berry bushes to see them. As if the old, lonely horse wanted to join in the game.

"I am exiled, Eve."

"It didn't stop you from saving us. And returning us is the only honorable thing to do. The only right thing. Once you're there, with Lars—Lucifer said it gives you reason. A right to remain."

Lucifer. He wasn't sure what to make of him. Of any of this. "Another Trickster, whispering lies we desperately wish to hear."

"Thor, we have to try. And you're the only one who knows how to fight Jormungand. The only one who has the power to stop him from tearing a hole in the world back to Niflheim."

"Then you and Lars stay here," he said. "If the danger is so great as that, I will not risk my son, I will not risk your life, again, on the off-chance that Elah has leashed her dog."

Eve made a soft sound, somewhere between frustration and long-suffering patience. "You know I can't. Elah is my daughter, still, and I need to do what I can to help, to save her from this. Even more so, if Michael is the threat. She needs the strength I can offer, the support. And she's going to need Lars, too, when he's grown."

"When Lars is grown, he can make his own choice in the matter. But for now, for this moment, he's just a boy. What kind of father would I be if I did not do everything in my power to keep him safe?"

"And what kind of mother would I be, if I abandoned him? What kind of mother would I be if I abandoned my daughter in her darkest hour?"

"Lars stays here," Thor said, thunder rumbling in an echo of his words. "Until Michael is dead, and Jormungand driven back to Niflheim."

"You can't leave him here alone!"

Thor shrugged. "The goats will keep him out of mischief, and Grani too."

"The horse that won't let anyone near it?" she demanded.

He nodded to the field, and Eve turned to look. Grani had lowered his forequarters, folding his front legs beneath him, and craning his neck as Lars scrambled onto his back, small fists twisted in his mane.

"Up!" Lars urged. "Up, up!"

Grani rose again, careful not to dislodge his burden, and cantered after the goats. Thor couldn't help but smile as the game began again,

Grani nipping and biting, and the goats butting and charging. Lars was grinning, stuck to the horse's back like a cocklebur.

"With Grani, he'll be safer here than anywhere else, and they'll both have fits if we part them now."

"But if something happens to you, I'll never be able to reach him. He'll never be able to leave."

It wasn't something he'd considered. But he rarely considered his own injury when wading into any sort of conflict. There was no purpose in dwelling on what might become of him, so long as his family was safe, and while he had lived in his father's court, there had been no shortage of people to care for his sons and daughter in his absence.

Asgard had not been empty, then.

"What about the House of Lions?" Eve asked. "Everyone is so convinced those lands are protected. The safest place on earth. Would that protection extend to Lars?"

The magic he'd wrought still protected the land, to be sure, but it was hardly perfect. Jormungand could swallow it whole, if he desired it, and Sif had proved long ago that an immortal need not cross the border to do harm to those inside. Lars would be safer there than anywhere else, but he would not be *safe* by any means.

"You can't ask me to trap him here, alone with nothing but a horse and two goats. It isn't reasonable."

He ground his teeth. "I *asked* that you stay with him."

"You *asked* that I betray everything I've ever worked toward. That I abandon my own daughter and the world itself."

"For our son!"

"It's for our son that I have to act, Thor. So he has a world, so he has a sister!"

"He has a sister. And two brothers. And a grandfather who lives, yet, on another world, where he is not threatened. Had I known he lived at all, I would have taken him there long ago!"

Eve whirled, her eyes narrowed. "You'd give him over to Odin? To Sif, after what they did to me?"

"Better to have him safe in the bosom of his family than here, with the Midgard Serpent standing ready to devour him," Thor growled. "At least they would have the power to keep him safe from such a threat. Your daughter would be happy to see him dead!"

Eve slapped him. Hard enough to make his head turn, his cheek stinging.

"Witch!" Lightning burned through him, and he caught her by the wrist before she could strike him again. "You have no right—"

"He's my son, Thor." She lifted her chin, her eyes flashing with emerald fire, refusing to be cowed. And then she twisted her arm, jerking it free. "As much as he is yours. The only way I'll let you take him from me is over my cold, dead body. And even then, I'll haunt you every second, every heartbeat, and make every breath a misery if you ever give my son to those people, after what I suffered at their hands. Do you understand me?"

His teeth were clenched so hard his jaw ached, but he looked away. That she had a right to her anger, he couldn't escape, but it did not change his own. More than two years, she'd known about Lars. For more than two years, she'd hidden his son from him. More than two years, and barely a word. She hadn't even tried to reach him, hadn't even tried to speak to him, but for her desperate prayers. And now she told him he was needed. That he must return to earth to save her daughter's world, her daughter's life, and nothing else, when all he'd yearned for was her love. Her presence in his life, once more.

"Is that all then?" he asked. "After all this time, it is my power and my sword arm that you've missed, and nothing more? Not a moment of regret for what we've lost. For what we might have shared."

Her eyes softened, all the anger draining from her features. "No, Thor."

He shook his head, stepping back, his heart a splintered, stabbing ache in his chest. "I see."

CHAPTER FORTY-FIVE

Eve

❧

"No!" She reached out, catching hold of his shirt. The stupid oaf. The stupid, stubborn, fool of a god. "No, you don't see! How could you even think that, even for a moment? That all I want from you now—" she couldn't even finish the thought, it broke her heart so completely. She wanted to shake him. To beat her hands against his chest. To throw herself into his arms and forget everything else, just to prove to him how wrong he was. "You idiot!"

He stiffened, his hand closing on hers, fingers prying hers from his shirt. "Am I? So great a fool as to believe we might overcome my exile, somehow, yes. Perhaps I am."

"Thor, I have loved you with all my heart, and from the second you left, all I have ever wanted was to have you back, to be your wife! For Lars to know his father, of course, yes, and all the rest, but more than that, I just wanted you. For me. For us. For the eternity you promised me, with nothing to stand between us, ever again." He'd barely managed to free himself when she found a new grip on the fabric, her other hand going to his face, to his cheek. Tears blurred her eyes, but she searched his face, opened her mind to his, her heart, letting everything she'd felt, all her sorrow, all her love spill out. "How could you believe anything else?"

He shuddered, his hand finding her cheek, his fingers curling into her hair. And then his forehead touched hers, gently, so gently, and she lifted her face, drawing him closer, holding him tighter. "Eve," he breathed. "My heart. My love."

His lips brushed hers, and she rose up on her toes to meet him, answering his kiss with one of her own, needing so much more. He caught her up, his arm wrapping around her, just tight enough, and she drank him in, tasted the honey-sweetness of his mouth, the spice of his lips, every part of her straining against him, needing to be closer, to be part of him, again. To be his, in body as well as heart.

Forgive me, he whispered against her thoughts, his palm finding bare skin beneath the hem of her shirt. Sparks prickled up her spine, her whole body responding. *Forgive me, for ever doubting.*

But then his fingers were pressing into her hip, and even his kiss couldn't drown out the shock of pain down her leg. She arched back with a whimper, stumbling from his arms.

"Eve?" he steadied her, his concern washing over her, his eyes searching.

"Just—just a bruise."

He shook his head, his lips curving with that same confidence she'd missed for so long. "It isn't any use to lie, *hjartað mitt.*"

She laughed. She'd spent so much time hiding her pain from Lars, her worries, it was half-habit, by now. "No, I don't suppose it is. I think—I think I cracked my hip. If you could just. Maybe. An apple?"

"Stubborn woman," he murmured, pressing a kiss into her hair. "And in this condition, you would have me take you back to fight a war?"

She looked up sharply, but his eyes were bright, teasing. "If it's only two villains, is it really a war?"

Some of the light died, and overhead, clouds drifted to block the sun. "When those villains are gods, it only takes one, and Surt brought Ragnarok upon my people already, once before."

He left her to pick the fruit she would need, and Eve watched him go, wishing there was another way. Wishing the world and all its troubles long behind them. For an eternity they still couldn't have. But maybe, just maybe, if they could win this battle, there might be a chance for more. For peace, and hope, and love.

"Mama, look at me!" Lars called, and she turned back to her son. To Thor's son, in Asgard, atop a horse much too large, and much, much too fast.

"Two hands, Lars," she called back, for he'd lifted one to wave as Grani gathered himself to leap over the bushes to escape the goats. "Hold tight!"

And she would do the same.

❦

In the end, Thor agreed to bring Lars with them. And in the end, they didn't leave him anywhere. Raphael and a woman Eve didn't know were waiting for them, when they arrived at the heart of the DeLeon lands. The Archangel's eyes were pinched, and both their faces were lined with stress.

"My dear, allow me to introduce my wife," Raphael said, stepping forward to meet them once the lightning had dissipated. "You would remember her, I think, as Minerva. And at times, Sophia, but she is known best as Athena, goddess of wisdom."

Eve blinked, searching the woman's face and finding Sophia's familiar silver eyes. Athena smiled wryly. "I do hope you'll forgive the deception."

"And Tam?" Eve asked. "That was you, too?"

"It seemed prudent," Raphael admitted.

Eve's jaw tightened. "Then you knew, all this time."

Raphael's eyes widened, all innocence. "How could I possibly have known anything? Marcus treated the boy as his son, after all. We had no reason to doubt his claims."

She let out a breath of relief, glancing at Thor, whose mouth had formed a grim line. Lars was watching from Thor's arms, his expression a miniature version of his father's. No one looking at the two of them could believe for a moment they weren't father and son.

Thor clasped hands with Raphael. "You have my thanks, old friend."

The Archangel inclined his head. "I only wish we met now under better circumstances. Elah has asked us to collect you. All of you. And She was not pleased to realize that Michael was unable to cross into these lands."

"Had he abandoned his malicious intentions, he would have had no trouble," Thor said coolly. "Perhaps she should ask herself instead why, in being sent only to collect us, he meant to do harm?"

"So her father suggested as well," Athena said, some of the color returning to her face. Eve wasn't certain she'd ever seen a woman so naturally pale. "His obvious pleasure at Michael's expense didn't help his argument."

"Amazing how he rose so quickly as a politician when he can't keep a straight face in front of his enemies," Eve grumbled.

Athena's lips quirked. "I believe he does it to goad Michael, more than anything else. To prove he has no fear. As a liar, I'm not certain even Odysseus could match him."

"Odysseus didn't need to match him," she said. "But he was certainly sly when it served his interests."

Raphael cleared his throat. "Elah's patience has already been more than tested. The longer we delay, now . . ."

"Yes," Eve agreed. "I'm rather familiar with her temperament, and I can only imagine it's grown worse since our last encounter. But you can't expect me to bring my son anywhere near Michael after this morning."

"My dear, I fear my expectations have very little to do with it." Raphael extended a hand, vaguely directional. The Redwood Hall wasn't exactly mapped. "If we arrive without Lars, it will make a difficult thing much worse. But perhaps, all things considered, it might be wiser if you carried him yourself."

She wasn't certain if it was because Elah would be more likely to hesitate in striking at her own mother, or to free Thor's hands, but either way. "You'll need to be on your best behavior, Lars," she said, when Thor settled him in her arms.

And how many times had she told Elah the same thing? She only hoped it would have a more lasting effect on Lars when he grew up. She tried not to think *if*, but it floated around them all. *If* Elah allowed Thor to stay. *If* Lars was allowed to grow up, to live. *If* Jormungand and Surt could both be defeated.

If Elah would even believe them that they were the greater threat. That they were a threat at all!

Thor's hand closed around hers. "Are you ready?"

Eve nodded, not trusting herself to speak. The truth was, she would never be ready. Not for this. But Thor was calm, his steadiness leaching through his touch, soothing her mind and her nerves.

And then the lightning swallowed them whole.

&

"Evey!" Adam searched her face, holding her—and Lars—only far enough away to look at them. "I blacked out, and when I woke up and didn't hear from you, I wasn't sure whether to fear the worst or hope for the best. You can't imagine how relieved I am to see you whole. And Lars." He gave her a private wink, and took him from her arms. "No bumps or bruises, little man?"

"I rode a horse!" Lars said, evidently having forgotten his scare completely in the excitement of livestock. "And we played tag with goats! Grani and me won when he jumped over the bushes and made it to igg-drissal."

"Yggdrasil," Thor corrected absently, his gaze trained on Michael, who paced like a lion behind Elah's throne. A crisped lion, anyway, even his feathers scorched. Elah had leaned forward, her eyes narrowed, but she made no move to interrupt.

"Is that so?" Adam said, smiling. "I've never had the pleasure of seeing the World Tree, myself. What did it look like?"

"It's big! And red leaves as big as Mama's hand. With shiny yellow apples. Da made Mama eat one, to make her better. I coulda fixed her, but I didn't know it was more than the funny sleeping."

"I'm sure you could have," Adam agreed. "You're very good at fixing things, aren't you?"

"Only sometimes," Lars said. "When I stepped on my spaceship, I couldn't get it to fix. Mama says it only works on live things, and I shouldn't do it unless they ask. But then she glued it for me, so *that's* okay."

Adam laughed. "I'm glad."

Eve stroked his hair. "He took to horseback riding like fleas to a dog. No jump was too daring, and Thor promised me that Grani will never throw him."

"Not on *purpose*," Lars said. "Grani and me are best friends now, but it isn't his fault if I don't hang on like I'm s'posed to."

"Enough," Elah said, rising. "I've heard enough, Father. Innocent or not, it changes nothing."

Lars's eyes went round, his head swiveling toward her voice.

"Lars, this is your big sister, Elah," Adam said. "The Goddess. Sometimes she forgets her manners, but I'm sure it's only because she's so busy taking care of everyone. Isn't that right, darling?"

"Insolence!" Michael hissed.

"Silence!" Elah snapped, fire and smoke blurring her shape. "After what you did today, you'll make no comment on the sins of others. Have I made myself clear?"

Adam's lips twitched, and Eve thought he was trying not to smile.

"Lady," Thor stepped forward, dropping to one knee. "I beg your forgiveness, but I could not refuse the call of my wife, nor turn my back upon my son."

"Could you not?" she asked coolly. "I don't recall allowing any such exception when I sentenced you to exile, Thor of the North. Not only did you return today, against Our Will, but you abducted Our mother as well!"

"Would you have preferred them dead?" Adam demanded. "Honestly, Elah. What do you think would have become of them, if he hadn't acted? That you turn your back on Michael now, allow him to remain armed with that sword at all, while at the same time contemplating the execution of an innocent child—surely you must see how utterly unreasonable this is?"

"And hiding Thor's son, lying to me all this time, is anything less?"

"He's distracting you from the real threat," Adam said. "The true danger!"

"Your supposed serpent," Michael snarled. "And so you believe the word of a snake over mine!"

"I believe nothing," Elah answered, half-turning her head. "Nothing I cannot see with my own eyes, realize with my own senses."

"Then you sentence your world and your people to death, Lady," Thor said, rising. "And you can have no further need for Eve's presence here, no further objection to our departure, nor to Lars. What is mine, I will take with me, and any who wish to seek sanctuary may find it in Asgard."

"Do not test me, Thor of the North."

"I assure you it is no test, Lady. But I will not leave my wife and child here to die for your pride. Family or not." He extended his hand to Eve, and then nodded to Adam. "You are welcome to come with us, if you wish it. Your North Country will have little need of you before long, if it is indeed Jormungand sleeping beneath the earth. I have fought him before, defeated him, but at great cost. Ragnarok followed in his wake, all the same."

Adam shook his head, passing Lars back to Eve. "Everything I have left to live for is here. But Thor's right, Evey. You three should go."

She hadn't taken Thor's hand, her eyes on Elah. The idea of leaving her, just like that. Giving up on her, on the world. They'd had their difficulties, been divided for so long, but there had always been some small hope that things might change. That they might forgive one another, one day, with the right gestures, the right circumstances.

It had to be now. Now or never.

"Elah, please," Eve began. "If you would just listen to us—when have Adam or I ever led you astray? What betrayal have you ever truly suffered at our hands?"

"You chose them." She lifted her chin, indicating Thor and Lars. "You denied me your power. You would have left me to die, left all of us, if I had not stopped it. And you ask me what betrayal I've suffered?"

"I gave you what you wanted, once I was able, once I knew what you needed and had it in me to provide. Has my power helped you to stop any of this?" Eve asked, keeping her tone gentle. "Has it helped you at all, truly?"

"Perhaps if you had not siphoned off a portion to your son, it would have," Elah said, her gaze hot. "If you had shown me half the love you give him so freely now."

"I loved you with everything I had, Elah," Eve said. "Everything and more, and it isn't my fault you gave it up, threw it away like so much trash. How did you think things would be between us after you betrayed everything I'd given you? Did you think I'd just forget how you hurt me?"

"You're my mother!" Elah shouted, tears streaming down her cheeks. "You were supposed to forgive me!"

"With what? What did I have left to draw from, to find the strength, when you stole every support from beneath me? When I was sick with grief and Jormungand tore pieces from my soul? Don't you see? I had to go. Leaving here, those small escapes to Asgard with Thor, it was the only way forward. The only way I could ever be what you needed. And then you took that from me, too, but I still gave you everything I had left. Between you and the Serpent, I'd have been drained dry, if not for Lars."

"A godchild," Elah accused. "A rival, powerful enough to remove me from my throne, and you expect me to be pleased? To be grateful?"

"Why should he want your throne?" Eve asked, her heart heavy with pity. Elah was so changed, so bitter and lost, but even so. Even so, there were some things her daughter should have known. "You're his sister. Why should he ever feel compelled to take anything from you?" *What happened to the little girl who only wanted to make friends? Who fought so hard to win over those who feared her?* "Perhaps, if you treated him like a brother, you wouldn't have to be afraid. You wouldn't be feeding the Midgard Serpent with all your fear, your paranoia, your anger."

"Your Serpent," Elah spat, her tone almost identical to Michael's. "Always, back to this. Maybe Michael is right. Maybe it's just another distraction. Another excuse to refuse me, to turn from me again. At least he's stood by me. Helped me, no matter what."

Adam snorted, and Eve had never been so glad to hear the sound. She could feel that too familiar pressure behind her eyes, her vision rimmed green with soul-deep exhaustion. Lars squirmed in her arms, looking up at her with that solemn, wrinkled brow. Eve wished she could put him down, could pass him off to Thor, just for a moment, but she couldn't risk it, volatile as Elah was.

"Say what you will about your mother," Adam said, "About her absence, whatever the cause, but don't you dare tell me I haven't stood at your side, supported and loved you through every moment, every mistake, every triumph. And I'm telling you right now, Michael isn't trying to help you, Elah, he's trying to drain you. You and your mother. And I can only imagine that's why he wants Lars dead, too. Maybe even why he tried to break me."

"Lies!" When Michael had drawn his sword, Eve wasn't sure, but he had it in hand now, and was whirling to face them. "Lies upon lies upon lies! When I have been your only friend. Your true protector from the moment you came to the Redwood Hall."

"Sheath your sword, brother," Raphael said, stepping forward. "There is no threat here, no need for its flame."

"No threat?" Michael flourished the blade, his movements almost too fast for Eve's eye to follow. Particularly when the flame was starting to look green around the edges. "Your words are threat enough, your lies. If only my blade cut through them as easily as flesh."

"Were the God-Killer so well forged as that, you might see your own blindness," Thor said.

"My blindness? I have been the only one to see the truth, all this time. The voice of reason in the face of such fool sentiment. What the Goddess has not seen, I have! You come here speaking of destruction, of ancient evils returned, but you carry in your arms the true threat."

"Lars threatens no one," Eve said. "And if I had been trusted with the raising of my own daughter—" She stopped herself, turning her face away. If God had let her raise Elah to adulthood. If God had not meant to take her, Adam would have never had reason to leave. They would be a family still, the three of them. Living among her Lions.

And Lars never would have been born.

"You see?" Michael said, before she'd recovered. "You see what she thinks of you? How she longs for the power to mold you, to shape you into her tool! As she does, now, with that boy in her arms. A tool to be used to strike you down, in your weakness."

"No!" Eve said, half-choking on the word. She couldn't do this for much longer. "But think, Elah. Think what might have been, if God hadn't chosen to take you from us. But He did. He took you, knowing. Elohim always knew. Isn't that what the Archangels tell us? And if He knew, somehow, that Adam would leave, that Thor would come—He meant for this, Elah. He meant for Lars to be born."

She could see the path so clearly then, as she spoke. The world that might have been, if she had kept her daughter. Adam and herself, seated beside Elah on her throne, a holy family, undivided. But Thor—Thor would have had nothing. No place in the world. No place in her life.

What mother would want that for her child? If Elohim had been his mother, if She had even half the heart Eve had, half the love for Her son that Eve had for Lars, for Elah, that wouldn't be enough. To call him back, only to keep him apart, alone, abandoned, and forgotten . . .

Elah's hesitation swept through the hall, no more than a rustle of the leaves and the ring of her silence, but it was enough. Even without understanding who Elohim had been to Thor, she must see it, too. The vision of her family, whole. It was all Elah had ever wanted. Every fight, every fissure between them because of it. And from the moment Eve had loved Thor, chosen Thor over Adam, the rift between them had only grown larger. But if it had been God's plan—if He had meant for all of it, maybe, just maybe Elah could forgive it.

"Daddy?" Elah's voice was small, a little girl, appealing to the infallibility of the parent she trusted, and it cut through Eve to know that person would never be her. No matter what she decided, today.

"I, for one, am glad the fractures we suffered were for a reason," Adam said gently. "That my actions, ruinous as they were, served some greater purpose. And if it means, in some small way, I'm responsible for giving you a brother in Lars, I see nothing to regret."

The Goddess slumped back in her throne, all the righteous anger draining out of her. "Elohim meant for me to have a brother."

Adam smiled. "And an Uncle, too. A protector, bound to you by blood, by love, through Eve."

When Elah's gaze fell on Thor, no doubt in answer to some small, silent exchange with her father, he inclined his head. "If you would grant me your forgiveness, Lady. And a reprieve, that I might serve."

"No," Michael growled, even as Elah rose, her hand outstretched. "No!"

And then the Archangel swept his burning sword through root and branch and leaf. Elah spun, her eyes wide, and Thor lurched forward, with Adam, and Raphael, and Gabriel, all, too slow. Eve screamed, covering Lars's eyes, turning him away.

The blade caught flesh, flared. Smoke and stink and before Thor could reach him, before any of them could reach him, Michael had disappeared.

And Elah fell.

Elah fell.

CHAPTER FORTY-SIX

Elah, Before

Elohim did not last long after her Council, and Elah did not dare to leave his side while he faded. With the angels, she held vigil, watching helplessly as her grandfather turned from god, to spirit, to nothing at all, but for the surge of power and strength she felt as he went. It was something, she supposed, to know he still lived through that which he had wrought. Creation, his Host, even herself. But he would only ever know the world through her eyes, now. A silent presence in her heart. And if she unmade it—

But Elah had made her choice, long ago. Elohim's world would remain whole in her stewardship. There was no point in dwelling upon anything else. Elohim would always live through her, and through his Creation, for as long as she had the power to protect it.

For eternity.

"Goddess," Raphael said, dropping to one knee beside her, after Elohim was gone. "Accept my vow. Elohim has commanded us to your service, but know, also, that I freely give myself into your hands."

She nodded, her throat too thick to speak, and her heart tight with sorrow. Raphael had always been her friend.

"If you ask it of Gabriel, he will give you the same vow."

She closed her eyes. "But not freely, if I must ask."

"Freely enough," he said gently. "And were I you, I would collect such oaths. The sooner the better."

Elah shook her head. "If you have already been bound to me, I will ask for nothing further. If your brothers desire to make promises of their own, they will do so of their own accord. I will not force them, even so gently as that."

"You take a risk, Lady," he said.

"No more of one than I have taken with the others. And do you and your brothers not deserve the same respect?"

Raphael sighed. "Gabriel is no threat to you, that is true, but Michael . . ."

"Michael is my friend," she said firmly, meeting his eyes. "My protector."

"Perhaps that is so," Raphael murmured. "I hope it is so, no matter what choices you make, but I fear his friendship, indeed his temperament has always been conditional. So long as he approves of the manner in which you act, there is no question you will have his allegiance, but beyond that?" The Archangel shook his head. "Beyond that, I cannot guarantee your safety. Not if you insist upon this course."

She squeezed his shoulder and rose. "Then it is fortunate that you are my ambassador, more than my bodyguard. Go to the gods, Raphael, and collect their oaths. I can promise you that Michael will not grant them any grace if they have not gone in time. He is already too eager to wield his sword again, now that he holds it in his hands once more."

"As you wish, Lady."

And while he was gone, she would see to her mother.

§

Michael accompanied her everywhere. Since she had banished Odin, and made her offer to the remaining gods, he would not hear of anything else, too afraid for her safety to be left behind, even when she went to the small cottage where her mother still lived, safe in the heart of the House of Lions.

"Mama?" she called, pushing the door open. The old-fashioned kind, with a knob and a key-lock, instead of biometrics. Not that biometrics stopped a goddess who could take any form, be anyone. She'd been back once, shortly after she'd gone to meet her father, but that felt like an eternity ago, now, with everything that had happened. With Elohim gone.

The cottage was empty, Elah realized, before the door had even shut again behind her. She supposed she ought to have reached for her first, rather than just showing up this way. But she'd wanted to surprise her.

"Are you sure she was expecting us?" her father asked, having followed her inside. His fingers trailed along the countertop, his gaze searching the small, open rooms. As if he was looking for something more than just her mother.

Her first impulse had been to show it off, to tell him about everything. The cupboard door that never stayed closed in the summer time. The way the table in the kitchen was always set just too close to the drawers, so when a person sat down no one could get to the silverware. It was strange to think he'd lived here, once, too. That this had been their home together, before she'd been born.

And it was even odder to walk into the kitchen and not find Raphael at the stove. But of course he wouldn't be there when he'd gone with her to the Redwood Hall five years ago, and stayed at her side. She would have felt guilty, maybe, but the House of Lions was so near, Mama would never be alone if she didn't want to be. Even without her Lions, all she'd ever have had to do was call out to Father, and he would have come to her. Groveled at her feet, if she'd just given him the chance.

"She must have gone for a walk," Elah said, searching for her mother's presence in the wooded grounds nearby. "I didn't tell her when exactly we'd be by."

Or that they were coming at all. Because if she'd known Elah's intentions—and she would have known, Elah was sure—she would never have agreed to see him.

"Or maybe she was having second thoughts," her father said, his voice carefully neutral. The same neutral it always was, when she pushed him about Mother, hiding resignation and sorrow and guilt he thought she wouldn't see in his eyes.

If she'd felt them coming, she might have hidden. Or if Father had reached for her, broadcasting his intent. Elah dragged her teeth over her bottom lip, considering. But then her mother's surprise caught at her mind, mixing with cautious pleasure. Elah smiled.

"She's tending the goats," she said, catching her father by the hand, and pulling him toward the door.

He tipped his head, as if listening to something in the distance. To Mother, probably. "Maybe I ought to wait here."

"Don't be silly, Daddy. She needs you. She needs both of us." Elah only had to brush her hand along the doorframe and the threshold shimmered, the air rippling, with a view of the goat pasture on the other side. It was easier for others when she used a doorway, though alone she'd never need a portal. Not anymore. "She'd never admit it, of course, not to me, but from what Thor said she must be miserable."

Her father stopped dead, pulling her with him. "Thor spoke to you about your mother?"

Elah twitched a shoulder. "After the Council meeting."

"He's been to see her?"

"No," Elah said. "And why should he? I won't subject Mother to that kind of shock. Not after all this time, and the gods are leaving anyway."

"Elah," there was a warning note in her father's voice, and she looked back at him, startled by the subtle threat. He'd never spoken to her with anything worse than wry self-deprecation, and certainly nothing like the edge of anger she heard, now. "What did he say, exactly?"

"He wanted to see her. To go to her." Elah lifted her chin in response to the rebuke. "He said they were married once. But Mama already has a husband, and I don't care what Thor's done for her, if she's so miserable, she's bound to turn to you, eventually, to forgive you. She has to."

But her father was shaking his head, his lips pressed thin. "She doesn't know I'm coming. Does she?"

"Maybe she's just been waiting for you to come, did you ever think of that? Maybe all this time she's been hoping you'd come back, and you haven't, because you've been too afraid."

"Elah, sweetheart, after what I did . . . You have to understand that I knew what it meant. What I was doing to her. Being with her, having you—that was already my second chance, and if she never forgives me, that's her right. If she wants to be happy with someone else, with Thor, she deserves that, honey. She deserves the chance."

"So do you!"

He let out a ragged breath, his face turning away. "She's going to be angry, Elah. With you and me, both. And if she ever finds out . . . If Thor were anyone else . . ."

"Thor has nothing to do with any of this. He's just a god. An interloper, like the rest of them. He has no right to her."

"That's her decision to make, Elah. Who she loves, if she loves him still. You can't control that."

"Can't I?" If she didn't have her Lions, if she was truly alone, long enough . . .

"No," he said, his voice hard and sharp. "Goddess or not, you can't. And if you try, you risk more than her anger."

But they were her parents. Obviously they were meant to be together, to have her, so she could protect the world. Her father just couldn't see the big picture, the truth. Elohim's plan was larger than he could possibly understand. How could he, when he wasn't a god? Not the way she was. The way Elohim had been.

"Fine," she told her father, turning her back on him. "If that's how you feel, if you're so sure, then fine."

But she wasn't finished. And she certainly didn't agree about her limitations. Michael had been right, so long ago. Her mother had raised her with rules that didn't apply.

Not anymore.

§

"It's been so long," Mama said, framing her face in her hands. Elah had gone on to the goat pasture, leaving her father to find his own way home. Or maybe hoping he'd stay. Elah wasn't really sure which. "And look at you. You're so much brighter, somehow."

"She is Goddess," Michael said, barely concealing his sneer. "Though I suppose I shouldn't be surprised that you live on in ignorance of His passing."

Her mother's eyes widened, searching her face. "I'm so sorry, Elah. If I'd known—"

"You couldn't have," she assured her. "He didn't want anyone to know, not really. He wanted the transition to be seamless. And it has been, I think, for the most part. I've done my best to make it so."

"Oh, sweetheart." Mama stroked her hair. "I thought you'd have more time. Hoped you'd have more of a childhood. And now this."

She smiled. "It isn't like I'm alone. Raphael is the wisest counselor I could ever ask for, and Father, of course. He's been so much of a help. Michael, too." She stepped back from her mother's arms, shifting nearer to her Archangel, and turning her smile to him. His eyes, when his gaze met hers, weren't hard anymore, or cruel. They warmed her, more than anything, and she needed that warmth. Needed his presence. Not just to keep her safe, but knowing she had his support, too. That she had *won* his support by her own actions. "Now that we understand one another, anyway."

Her mother made a soft noise, half-strangled with a buried flash of dismay. "You're so young, Elah. And Michael swept you away before—before you were old enough."

"Grandfather commanded it of him, Mama." And there was that dismay again, and something else. Like disappointment. Elah stiffened. "You're just afraid."

You grew up so fast. I never wanted you to go, not with him. And there's so much you haven't experienced, that you can't know, yet. Michael isn't the kind of example I wanted you to have, not at all, but you look at him like he's a god.

He's more of one than you or father. More like me than you'll ever be.

Her mother twitched, her face reddening. *You think all that power makes you something better, something greater? That no one else can ever be your equal, because you stand so much higher above them? What happened to the girl who treated wolves as her friends? Who wasn't too good to roll in the dirt and the mulch, to take part in their lives?*

"I grew up, Mother," Elah snapped. "And I'm not going to live an eternity alone, as some virgin goddess, some old maid, like you. All that talk about being one of them, so why are you still here? Hiding away in your cottage, instead of out in the world? Instead of living your precious mortal life with your precious humans?"

"And if I had, Elah, how do you think this conversation would have gone? If I had some new husband, with a new family? I wasn't going to leave you behind that way. Not when you had so much else to cope with, already. You deserved my full support."

"Then why haven't you so much as spoken to Father?"

Her jaw worked, her green eyes flashing, but whether it was hurt or anger, Elah couldn't tell. She never had been able to read her parents the way she could everyone else. Her parents, and the Archangels. They weren't hers. Even now, they still weren't fully hers, to work and mold. They were little pieces of Elohim, broken off, made flesh, and she wasn't Elohim.

"Your father chose to leave, Elah. He chose to give up on us, to betray everything we'd built. I've learned my lessons the hard way, time after time, and he's spent all my grace." *All the lives I've lived, Elah, I think I've earned the right to live the rest of this one alone.*

Then you will be, Mother. If that's what you want, consider it my gift to you. No one will bother you again. Not your husband, not your daughter, and not your Lions.

"Elah!" But there was fear in her mother's thoughts. Fear of her own daughter. Of what that power could do.

Maybe if she hadn't been afraid, she would have stopped.

But as it was . . .

As it was, what was the point? And her mother had to learn. She had to understand, that Elah wasn't a child anymore. She was Goddess.

She was Goddess, and it was time she made choices of her own.

CHAPTER FORTY-SEVEN

Thor, Later

"Elah!" Eve cried falling to her knees beside her daughter's body, her cheeks streaked with tears. "Oh, Elah! My Elah."

She still held Lars, her hand over his eyes. Thor sank to one knee beside her, reaching for Lars, to take him from her arms and give her the freedom she needed to see to her daughter. Eve resisted, clinging to him, holding him so tightly that Lars squirmed, struggling against her.

Let him go, Eve. He is as safe in my arms as yours, I promise you.

But Elah!

Your daughter needs you. Far more than Lars, now.

Carefully, he pried the boy from his mother's arms, but Lars struggled against Thor's grasp, too, craning his neck, twisting to see his sister's body, reaching for her.

"Enough, Lars," Thor said firmly.

"Mama's hurt, and the Goddess too."

"Your mother needs to be with her, now. To say goodbye."

"I can make her better!"

Thor shook his head. "Not this time, I think."

"I can, too," Lars insisted, worming himself down, slippery as an eel, the way all children were when they had no interest in being held. "I can, I can, Mama!"

And then Lars was free, somehow, and running back across the mulch.

"Lars!"

Eve clutched Elah's hand, stroking her daughter's hair, and Adam was at her side, leaning over them both. Lars had moved so quickly, Thor had no chance of checking him before he reached them.

"It's okay, Mama," Lars said, touching Elah's side where the sword had cut across her ribs and opened her stomach. "Things got all popped inside but I can fix it. I can make 'em grow right."

And where his hand touched, the tissue began to mend. Slow, at first, with his face scrunched up and his mouth pressed thin, one small corner of his tongue sticking out. Elah twitched, and Adam tensed. Thor rested his hand on Eve's shoulder, unable to tear his eyes from Lars, from Elah's body. She was so still. And Thor had never known a god to escape death after being struck by Michael's sword.

"Raphael?" Eve's voice was strained, and Thor realized the Archangel stood with them, watching, Athena's fingers laced through his.

Ra gave his head the slightest shake. "If he believes he can, I will not say otherwise."

"Help him, for God's sake!" Adam said. "It can't make it worse, can it?"

The Archangel lowered himself, his gaze fixed on Lars's hand, hovering over the tear in her abdomen. "How might I help you, dear boy? Can you use my power, if I offer it?"

"Just gotta tell it to be right again," Lars said, scowling. "That pink floppy thing's supposed to be full of air, and this other pink stuff shouldn't be all bleedy. I think."

Ra's lips twitched. "Shall I show you what it should look like? Would that help?"

Lars's gaze flicked to his mother, questioning, and she nodded. "Raphael's a friend. You can trust him, even in your mind."

"I just need to *see*," Lars said.

"And so you shall." Ra placed a hand on Lars's small shoulder and closed his eyes. "The color is important. And the shape."

His eyes widened, and Lars leaned forward, his hand moving with more confidence, now. Elah's innards began to shift, ripped edges stitching themselves together again. Thor didn't dare even to breathe as he watched, afraid of distracting his son. To bring a god so close to death back to life—to invest himself so completely in the health of another. He was so young to be so selfless.

"I can feel a pulse." Adam was triumphant. "Her heart is beating. Just a flutter, but it's there. Feel it, Evey."

Eve touched her fingers to her daughter's throat and let out a shaky breath. "Good boy, Lars."

A swell of pride and relief flooded through him, watching some of Eve's tension drain out of her. The eagerness now, of her body, as she waited for another sign. And Lars! His son. As generous as his mother. Thor felt some of his own fear untangle from the space around his heart. After this, Elah could hardly exile them. With Michael on the loose—

Michael, on the loose.

Thor stepped back. The danger was past for Elah, even for Lars, but what of the rest of the world?

"Where might he have gone?" he asked.

Eve's forehead furrowed. "What?"

"Michael. To strike at Elah and leave this way—I do not imagine he waits in the dark to be found, passive as a lamb."

Adam shook his head. "I don't know. If what Lucifer said is true, he isn't exactly himself, anyway . . ."

"But?" Thor prompted, for Adam's gaze had grown unfocused with thought.

He pressed his lips together. "He was furious when he realized he still couldn't get to the DeLeons. That those lands were still protected by your power. If I had to guess, I'd say he would start there."

"What can he hope to accomplish?" Eve asked. "If they're protected, he can't hurt them."

But he could, Thor knew. Which was exactly why he had not wanted to leave Lars there, when Eve had suggested it. "I'll go. At once. If I can disarm him—"

"It won't be enough," Adam said. "Even when he was swordless before, he was still a malicious bastard. Whatever power Surt has over him, I think he found his grip because Michael was already inclined to vengeance and cruelty. Certainly he never showed me anything else of his character, after God . . . After the Garden."

"Lucifer might help you," Gabriel said, joining the conversation for the first time. He had stood apart, since Elah fell, and grief still lined his face, his wings drooping. Whether it was grief for his goddess or his brother, Thor could not be certain. "Michael's hunted him for so long."

"Do you know how to reach him?" Thor asked. Gabriel nodded with all the energy of a wilted flower. "Go, then. Bring him to meet me in France."

"Thor." Eve's hand closed around his arm, looking up at him with wide eyes. "Lucifer said Surt was Elah's problem to face. The Midgard Serpent—"

"Will be driven back, I promise you. But I will not leave Michael free to raze this world for Surt's satisfaction. Or worse, rend it in two to release the dead."

"He could kill you," she said, the words so soft he had to strain to hear them. "Jormungand is one thing. But that sword . . ."

He cupped her cheek, crouching down beside her. "He cannot know what Lars is capable of, and I need only return to him if I am cut. But I have weapons of my own, my love, and eternity upon eternity of warring behind me. He cannot know what I am capable of, either."

She searched his face, and he was careful to keep it blank. Surt, after all, was limited by Michael's own powers, yet. But Jormungand. Jormungand had all but killed him once before, and if Eve believed that beast to be the lesser threat, he would not tell her otherwise, even if he feared the opposite. Once, his death had been tied to Jormungand's by prophecy. He had thought he'd escaped but now . . .

In his experience, Ragnarok always meant death. Perhaps this was meant to be his.

"Just be careful," Eve said at last. "I only just got you back."

He pressed his forehead to hers. "I would not give Michael the satisfaction of separating us again."

And then he kissed her, tasting her sweetness, filling himself with her love, her warmth, her softness. She burned so bright, so hot, so beautiful, and her hunger fed his own. Gods above, how he wanted her. Wanted just a moment to show her his love, shower her with it. But they had not time.

He let her go, pulling back and rising to his feet before her eyes had even opened. If he looked into them now, saw them dusky with her desire, he'd never leave.

"Athena, take them to Asgard as soon as Elah is well enough for it. You have my permission and my explicit invitation to bring any there who may require sanctuary."

"Olympus—" she began, but Thor shook his head.

"Olympus has no food, and more importantly, it does not have Yggdrasil or her fruit. Elah will need it, I think. And Lars as well, to replenish himself. Take them there. Promise me."

"Of course, Thor," she said. "But I can help you, too."

"And I will have need of it, I assure you. But not yet."

Her silver eyes flicked from him to Eve, and they had been friends long enough that she knew better than to ask for more. "You need only call."

Thor nodded, and left them.

He had to find Michael. Before he managed to wake Jormungand and bring Surt whole and hail into the world.

Before Jormungand grew glutted on fear.

❧

Mjölnir answered his call from anywhere, but Thor went first to Asgard to collect another weapon. The knife Loki had carved from Jormungand's fang, locked in its iron box in the treasury. Even Surt would not survive its bite, if it came to that. Thor hoped and prayed it would not, for he did not have his mother's strength, and it had taken his mother and father both to defeat Surt the first time.

The knife sheathed at his waist, and *Mjölnir* hanging from his belt, Thor returned to earth, to France, and the DeLeon mountains. Lucifer was waiting, diamond-printed skin glistening in the firelight, as he looked on the smoking wreckage of the stables.

"Fireball from that damned sword," the snake-man spat. "Gabriel, fool that he is, went after him. He drew him off before the manor caught—and thank the Goddess what flames he sent only struck stone—but he'll be back to finish the job before long. Gabriel might be silver-tongued, but Michael has never cared overmuch for talk that didn't serve his own ends."

"And you stayed," Thor said, his eyes narrowing. Lucifer was sparely built, sinuous rather than muscled, and though he wore a sword at his hip, Thor doubted his skill.

"No wings," Lucifer said, twitching a shoulder in dismissal. "Can't very well do more than slow Gabe down without 'em."

Thor grunted, though the creature's yellow eyes still unnerved him. "Which way did they go, then?"

"South, of course. Into the Sahara. Surt will want his freedom, and he can't make himself completely at home in Michael's husk until that stinking snake burrows through to Niflheim. Which it won't do so long as it's sucking the teat of the world in its sleep. I told Adam and Eve already, that's where you should be spending your strength. Destroy Jormungand and Surt is trapped, half in Michael, half in your old world, and weak as a kitten while he's divided. Comparatively, anyway. All it takes, then, is a thought. Michael is unmade by Elah's will, and Surt retreats back into the God-Killer. Powerless."

"Had Michael not struck Elah down, perhaps it would have been as simple as you say."

"She'll heal," Lucifer said. "But the world won't, if Jormungand wakes."

"And how am I to fight him while he slumbers?" Thor demanded. "I cannot even reach him, he's burrowed himself so deep."

Lucifer flashed him a smile. "But Eve can. Another taste of that venom and she'll be all the lure you need. Better than an Ox's head, eh?"

Thunder rumbled over his head, his eyes burning with fury for his own impotence. "You'd have me risk my wife?"

"You think she'd want to survive, knowing there was something she might have done to stop the world from dying?"

Thor growled, grabbing Lucifer by the throat. "If you're lying, serpent . . ."

He clutched at Thor's wrist, but his lips were still curved up in a smile, forked tongue tasting the air. "I don't tell lies, Thunder God. Just the truths no one wants to hear. You've the knife. Even in his sleep, Jormungand will smell her out. She's a much more tender morsel, I'm sure. But if you think you can't defend her . . ."

He threw him down, into the dirt. "I'd give my life for hers a thousand times over."

"Perhaps we should begin with just the once, then," Lucifer said, not bothering to rise. "If you dare."

CHAPTER FORTY-EIGHT

Eve

❧

A flash of lightning at the corner of her eye tore Eve's gaze from Elah, settled and sleeping. She'd given Elah the bedroom Thor had arranged for her. More than a hundred rooms and barely three of them fit for guests. Whether for sanctuary or a last line of defense, Athena had brought all of Bhagavan's host, and Eve had no idea where to put them.

But the lightning had come from across the hall, she was certain. Thor's room.

Watch Lars, Eve said to Adam, leaning down to kiss Elah's forehead before she slipped into the hall.

She pushed Thor's door open, and stopped. *Mjölnir* hummed at his hip, and his face was streaked with soot, but the tension in his shoulders spoke of failure, not triumph.

"What happened?"

Thor shook his head, kicking open the chest at the foot of his bed and staring at its contents. "The stables burned, and half the vineyard, but the manor stands. I put out the fires, but Michael was gone. Gabriel had chased him off, and they went south. To the heart of the barren lands."

"To Jormungand."

Thor grunted, his back to her still. "You're the only one who can sense him, save Surt. With the venom in your blood, the scent of you will draw him out. So Lucifer says, and much as I might wish otherwise, his argument is sound."

Eve swallowed, a chill settling in her core. "You want to use me as bait."

"Want?" He turned then, meeting her eyes, hazed more white than blue. "No, Eve. I do not *want* you even upon the earth while Jormungand surfaces. But to find him, to draw him out without waking him. I fear I am in need of your help."

"Not hers."

Adam. Eve's heart seemed to stall. If he'd heard—"I told you to stay with Lars."

"Mine," Adam said, ignoring her. "If we're identical enough to confuse the biometrics, we're identical enough for this too. Lucifer made it clear that another dose of that venom could kill her permanently, to say nothing of the physical risk."

The lightning faded from Thor's eyes, his gaze hard and fast on Adam. "You would be no safer."

Adam shrugged. "It's only fair. And in a fight, I'm the better choice. Imagine if Michael grabbed her, held his sword to her throat—you'd be hamstrung, Thor. But I can fight. And if something were to happen to me, if Michael grabbed me, it wouldn't matter."

"It would matter to me," Eve said, before Thor could respond. "And to Elah. If she lost you, now . . ."

"If she lost me, now, it would matter a lot less than if Lars lost both of you." Adam kept his eyes on Thor. "You know that I'm right. Put a weapon in my hand, and I can help. Eve might hesitate to deliver a fatal strike, but I won't."

"That isn't fair, Adam." If it were Michael—for everything he'd done to her, to Adam, to Elah, now, there wouldn't be room for hesitation. "Maybe I haven't led as many armies into war as you have, but I'm not useless. I'm just as capable as you are."

"And if Thor falls, what will you do first, Eve? Make the killing blow, or run to his side to defend him instead?"

She hated him, in that moment. Hated that he made her sound soft and weak because of love. Hated even more that he was right.

"It isn't a fault, Evey," he said gently. "It's never been a fault."

"Elah needs you, Adam."

"After a century of Michael whispering in her ear, she's better off listening to your advice over mine. She needs love, Evey, and grace. And you're far more qualified to give it."

When she looked at Thor, hoping for some support, some argument, all she saw was his resolution. His determination.

Did you hope from the start he'd volunteer? she asked, her eyes stinging.

He shook his head, slowly, stepping toward her. *I didn't even think of it. Didn't imagine it could be possible. But he's right, Eve. He's right that having you there will make all this harder and I—I can't bear it. The thought of losing you because I turned my back at the wrong moment. And if I survived it . . . If Adam is willing, I will not refuse him.*

But you'll refuse me.

He brushed the tears from her cheeks, the hair from her face. *My heart, for over three thousand years, I've protected you. Watched over you. Kept you safe. To poison you, and worse, bring you nose to nose with Jormungand, after. It goes against every oath I've sworn. And there is Lars, too, to think of. Elah, who will want her mother while she heals. You can do more alive and whole, here, than you can at my side in this fight.*

She turned away. Turned from both of them. The men she loved. The stubborn fools.

"Then go."

"Evey—"

Adam might not come back. She knew it, knew she should turn, should throw herself into his arms, and then Thor's. Tell them both she loved them one last time. But she couldn't.

They weren't supposed to leave her this way. And Thor had promised. He'd promised! No more death, no more grief. And now they were asking her to face it all over again.

She couldn't.
"Just go."

CHAPTER FORTY-NINE

Adam

He didn't particularly care for the look of the ivory knife Thor gave him, but he had no complaints about the sword. Really, the thing that bothered him most was that Eve had left them so abruptly, all bitterness and tears. Part of him wanted to be angry. Here he was, trying to be noble. Trying to be worthy of her, and she just held it against him as another failing. Because he wanted to keep her safe, for her son, for their daughter. He'd even consulted with her first, explained himself, and she still resented him for it.

This was exactly why he had left her without a word after Elah had been born. Either way, she wouldn't have forgiven him. If he'd told her why. If he'd waited to explain. It didn't matter.

At least that was what he'd told himself to sleep at night. It probably wasn't fair of him. When he'd left her the first time, after he'd found her in the shop and she'd asked it of him, she'd loved him for it. He'd hoped, in some small desperate part of his heart, that she'd love him for this too.

That was probably why it had made her so angry, he thought. Because it made it so much harder for her to believe she didn't love him, now. Now that Thor was back. Now that she'd forgiven him, whether she'd realized that much yet, or not.

"It's carved from Jormungand's fang," Thor said, nodding to the knife. "And plunged into Michael's breast or gut, I cannot imagine he will survive the bite."

"That's something, at least," Adam said, pushing his thoughts away. "And I take it I should avoid the drip of venom from the tip?"

"If you can wield Gram with one dose of it in your blood, you will prove yourself a god. Two doses, undiluted as this is, and it is unlikely you'll be able to see straight enough to swing a blade without striking yourself."

"And you were going to give this to Eve?"

Thor's mouth firmed, thinning. "She's suffered its effects before and still stood. The experience would have served her well enough for what I asked of her."

"Until it killed her."

"More likely it would have driven her mad first," Thor said softly. "What it will do to you, I cannot guess."

"How long was she in that ward, Thor?"

Thor dragged the ivory blade across his arm, swift and sharp, then clapped his hand over the wound to stop the blood. "Too long."

"And she was being dosed with the venom the whole time?"

"Diluted, but yes."

Adam tried to ignore the burning sensation, flexing his hand to keep the blood moving. The burning spread through his veins, up his arm, into his shoulder. Too quickly. "But it was more than just that. More than just the venom which drove her into madness."

Thor glowered at him, eyes flashing white. "If you hope to irritate me enough to let you die, I warn you, your presence has often been more than enough aggravation without adding this questioning as well."

He laughed, looking down at his arm when Thor released it. His skin was sickly green around the edges of the cut, but Thor had kept it shallow enough that it shouldn't handicap him. It was odd, to find himself here. They'd been enemies for so long. And it wasn't all that long ago that he'd wanted nothing more than to drive Thor out, to destroy him, along with the rest of the gods.

"I was only asking to try to judge its affect."

"Another moment, and we need not guess at all," Thor said, stepping back. "I hope you can fight one-handed."

The room was misting with green, Adam realized, and he squinted at Thor. "Odd, that. It isn't carried just by the blood is it? It's got its own momentum, somehow."

"Or your heart has picked up speed," Thor said, sounding strangely distant. "A combination of both, most probably. Stand up, Adam. And draw your sword."

His stomach cramped, and he forced himself, unsteadily, to his feet. Suddenly, he was starving, hunger gnawing at his ribs. Hunger and green-tinged darkness, which seemed to slosh around his feet.

"One-handed is going to be the least of my problems," he heard himself say. "Is this what Eve felt, all that time? She showed me once, but it wasn't so—so—"

"Jormungand will eat his own tail to quiet his hunger," Thor said, a supportive hand under his elbow. "I believe Eve didn't notice that particular element while she was in the ward, too distracted by her thirst. And it wasn't as though they fed her much, regardless. By the time I found her, she'd no doubt grown used to it."

"You're rambling, Thunderer."

"Do you know what they did to her?" Thor went on, and Adam's stomach twisted again at the coldness in his voice. "Her husband heard her speak another man's name in her sleep and believed he'd been cuckolded, so he locked her away in the ward under the guise of illness. But he still wanted his heir. Once he was sure any child she bore would be his, he began to visit her. Planted her until she grew pregnant, and then punished her when she lost the babe."

Adam's bile rose at the telling, his heart sick with it. "Stop," he begged. But Thor only grasped him by the collar to keep him on his feet, and pushed him toward the door, while he kept talking, as if Adam hadn't spoken at all.

"That was Loki's doing. Miscarriage after miscarriage after miscarriage, until she opened her own veins to try to end it. Newcastle blamed her, beat her for her failure to carry any child of his to term. And in the meantime, Loki tortured her. The madness must have been a blessing by then, though I did not realize it, at first, when I found her."

"Why are you telling me this?" Adam's throat was thick with even the thought of it all. He could only imagine Eve's pain. And to be reminded of it after—to live with those memories for so long.

"Jormungand feeds on despair, Adam. On heartache and pain. And Eve's hopelessness, her experiences then, tainted with his own venom, will whet his appetite like nothing else. Divine suffering is all the sweeter for its duration. A god's despair, languishing for centuries upon centuries, becomes a feast."

"And if I had been Eve?" he asked, stumbling over his own feet.

"The venom in her blood would have brought it all back again."

Adam half-sobbed, nearly falling, but for Thor's grip on him. Forcing him on. The hunger was rising, pulling at him, sucking at him like marrow from a bone. "Oh, Evey. Poor, sweet Evey."

"That's it," Thor said.

And somehow, they weren't in Asgard any longer. The green mist had turned to sand, tripping him, dragging at his feet. He wouldn't have called on Eve then for anything, too afraid it would draw upon her memories, remind her of everything she'd suffered.

The sand shifted beneath him, and Thor growled. "He's coming."

Adam fell, unable to keep upright any longer. Wishing he could disappear into the sands and never rise. For what he'd done to Eve. For everything that had been done to her. It hung upon him, chained him, anchored him to the deeps.

"Listen to me, Adam." Thor had caught him by the shoulders, shook him hard enough that he saw black. "You have to eat it," he said, and Adam felt the cool, smooth skin of the fruit pressed against his lips, realizing dimly that it wasn't the first time Thor had tried to feed it to him. "Quickly, now. Or it will be too late. Eat!"

He took a bite, unable even to lift his hands to grasp the fruit for himself. Thor helped him, feeding him like he would a child. Adam chewed, slow and awkward and blood mixed with the sweet, honeyed pulp in his mouth.

"More, Adam," Thor urged. "For Eve's sake, if not your own. Think how much more it will hurt her if you don't return."

Adam ate, again. His head already beginning to clear. His arm throbbed, his blood still burning, but the mist was dissipating, replaced with churning sand.

A snake's head burst free from the ground beneath, as immense as an airship, tongue flickering in and out, in and out. Adam shoved the rest of the apple in his mouth, and scrambled back.

Jormungand reared, head swaying, tasting the air. And then he struck, too fast to see.

Thor grabbed Adam by the arm, throwing him out of reach. "Run!"

Adam landed hard, jarring his shoulder in spite of his attempted roll. Or perhaps because of it. The sand offered nothing in the way of traction, and he slipped and slid up a dune, then rolled again down the other side, grit stinging his eyes, choking his lungs.

Lightning struck behind him, thunder following, so loud it was beyond his hearing. Fingers of glass spread out, chasing him as he ran, molten and hissing with steam.

"Go, Adam!" Thor roared.

Venom fell around him, a sizzling shower of poison so noxious it pitted the sand. All his talk of fighting, and what was he worth? When he glanced over his shoulder, Jormungand was towering over Thor, so large he blocked the sun. Adam couldn't outrun him. Couldn't even escape the monster's shadow, lengthening with every surge of thick muscle against sand.

"Here!" Adam shouted, drawing his sword. "I'm the one you want!"

He could hear Thor's curse, echoed in the thunder. Jormungand hissed, spraying venom, so thick it blotted the clouds. Adam dove into the sand, but the poison still reached him, pocking his clothes, his skin. Lightning crackled across the sky, coiling around the snake. A living chain of fire and light, and Thor grasping the other end, digging his feet into the sand, using *Mjölnir* as an anchor with his other hand.

The serpent shrieked, and Adam thought he saw sparks around its blunt nose. But it could have been stars of pain, the way his skin was blistering. Thor could hold Jormungand or he could strike at him, but it was clear he couldn't do both. Adam picked himself up, sword fused to his palm, now, more than gripped, and charged.

The sword was true. The armored scales of Jormungand's belly split open beneath the blade, spewing steaming green blood.

"Get back!" Thor cried. "Get away from the blood!"

Adam's shoe had melted on contact, and then the blood began to eat his toes. He gritted his teeth and plunged his sword deeper, dragging it down the length of the serpent, following it in its throes. Jormungand jerked, struggling madly against Thor's control. If he could just keep ahead of the wound. But his foot was on fire, the flesh burning with a terrible, putrid stink.

"Get clear!"

He slipped on his own melted skin and bone, and then something tore through his back, hooking into his shoulders, sharp and deep. Lifted him up before he fell into the spreading puddle of the monster's blood. And he was flying, banking away from Jormungand's towering bulk.

Fool of a man, Athena's voice rippled across his thoughts, along with a grudging admiration. Talons, he realized. It was an owl, carrying him up, pulling him away. Athena. She dropped him in the sand, clear of Jormungand, though from what he could see, the monster was straining toward them, fighting to turn.

"Thor needs help," he said. "He can't fight it alone."

She was Athena again, silver-eyed and pale-armed. Her silver breast plate glared at him, a woman with tangled snakes for hair. "He won't have to."

And then she was running, fleet as a gazelle. He didn't see her release the spear in her hand, but it was soaring, arcing through the sky. Joined by a cloud of arrows, from a thousand others. Aspects of Bhagavan. Angels. Even Lucifer. Jormungand screamed, and Adam lay back against the warm sand, closing his eyes against the sun. He couldn't feel his foot, and his calf was burning. His cheek, too, he realized, now that he had stilled. The sword was gone, but not the knife, still tucked in its sheath. He tried to open his hand, but his fingers didn't answer. If Jormungand broke free of Thor's hold now, he wouldn't be able to do more than roll in the sand. But maybe, just maybe, he'd live through all this. If Thor won.

Thunder cracked and lightning flashed, so bright he could see it even behind his eyelids, and he thought of Eve. Of Eve's strength, to have survived. The burn of the venom in her blood, the green mist, clouding her eyes. The hiss, and the hunger, and the torture, and the loss.

"Better if she had died there," Michael said, and Adam turned his head to see the angel's sandaled feet. "Better if she had died, and you had never loved her. Better if Elah had never been born, than this."

Adam rolled to his side, reaching for the knife. But his fingers didn't close around the hilt. Only knocked it from his belt. He blinked the sand from his eyes and stared at his hand. A hand that wasn't there. Just a blackened stump where his wrist had been, and the flesh still dropping away.

He clamped down on the panic, and caught the knife up with his left hand instead. One working arm. That was all he needed. One working arm to finish this. To finish Michael. And Eve would never have to fear the angel coming for her again, never dream of his sword in her stomach, never imagine Lars's death at his hands, or worry over their daughter.

Elah. His stubborn, beautiful girl. She had sworn to protect the world, to guard creation, and he understood now, her reluctance to unmake any small part. Even if that part was Michael. She wouldn't have to break her vow. He could give her that. One last gift, to make up for everything he hadn't done.

Michael laughed, the sword spitting flame, the tip level with the angel's ankles. "You really think you'll strike me down so easily? You can barely lift your head, you fool."

Adam used his stump to lever himself up, ignoring the pain of sand ground against tender flesh. It wouldn't matter, soon enough. His lungs burned, his chest tighter and tighter. That wouldn't matter, either, if he could just finish this.

Michael swept his blade sideways, and Adam screamed. His elbow flamed, burning hotter than the venom in his blood, but he caught himself on what was left of his arm. His eyes blurred with tears, misted green.

"You see?" Michael said. "How weak you are. How worthless."

That was when he stabbed the knife into Michael's thigh. Not the gut. Not the breast. But there was flesh enough, and blood. So much blood. He hung on the hilt, using it to pull himself up, even as Michael spread his wings and the Chorus roared in Adam's ears. The knife tore through the angel's flesh, leaving streaks of green and black venom, and then Michael brought the sword down on his shoulder, and he fell back into the sand.

There were no good arms left, but Michael had crumpled when he tried to land. And that was enough. More than enough. Jormungand's venom was powerful. Undiluted, as it was. So strong, it could cripple a god. Cripple an Archangel, too. Crippled him.

But Athena would come back for him. To bring him back to Asgard, to Eve. Athena and Thor. They'd come back, and find him thrashing about, no-armed, before long. He only had to wait. To hang on. Lars would fix him right up, and he'd live the rest of his days without limbs. Adam closed his eyes and thought of Eve. He hoped that it still worked. Thor's trick of hauling him to Asgard for a beating, to keep her from feeling every hit, every bruise.

He hoped it still worked, because if not, then he had killed more than Michael.

He had killed her, too.

CHAPTER FIFTY

Thor

❧

It went quickly then, Athena's spear piercing the monster's eye, straight into his brain, and a thousand arrows followed to bleed him. Jormungand shuddered, writhed, and Thor tugged him down, and down. It wasn't enough to kill him. The spear was hardly more than a toothpick to Jormungand's bulk, but between it, the pricks of so many arrows, and the blows Adam had dealt, the serpent tired, and Thor tightened the lightning noose with every gasp, every hiss, every shriek.

Another spear pierced beside the first, and another after that with a second wave from the bowmen. Jormungand trembled, and then fell, sending a cloud of sand and dust into the sky. Thor tore *Mjölnir* from the ground, and rushed forward, raising the war hammer high.

One massive blow crushed the serpent's skull, caving it beyond repair.

Jormungand twitched, and lay still.

The Midgard Serpent was dead, and with it, Surt's only hope for true freedom from Niflheim. Thor stood panting, staring at the massive head, the sand melting with each drop of blood from its eye. His lungs burned, and as the lightning dissipated, the fire in his veins remained. He'd inhaled too much of the creature's poison before he'd had the wit to muzzle it. And Adam. Adam had waded through its blood.

Thor turned, searching for some sign of him. A darker form on the farthest dune, apart from Bhagavan's army, and Elah's Host. With the glint of silver that was Athena, helmed and armored. And white. White wings. Had Raphael come, to see to Adam's wounds? He dropped *Mjölnir*, the hammer dragging too heavily on his shoulder, and moved toward them, each step feeling an eternity. Four, then five.

Eight, then nine.

Thor fell to his knees in the sand, his chest too tight, his lungs incapable of holding air. What all that blood and venom would do to the earth, Thor did not know, could not think.

But Jormungand was dead.

"Thor!"

He couldn't see them anymore, his gaze only level with the sand, sticking and scratching at his cheek. But Athena's voice roused him enough to roll over. And there was the sky. Blue and beautiful.

"Not you, as well," Athena moaned, sending another spray of sand against his cheek as she landed beside him. "Not you, Thor. Not you."

Something hot and wet splashed against his face, making him twitch, and she dropped her head to his, hugging him, holding him hard.

"Just hold on a little longer," she begged. "Just hold on."

He heard nothing else.

CHAPTER FIFTY-ONE

Adam, Before

Adam was well on his way down the mountain when the light changed, a weird orange ripple out of the corner of his eye, that made him stop, head-cocked for some kind of following thunder. Thor, probably, following on his heels to give him hell for upsetting Eve. Again.

But the thunder didn't come, and when he turned, looking back up the road to the manor, sitting on its height, he had the sinking feeling he might have preferred the lightning. It would have been more natural than the way the light was churning around the house, bubbling outward and distorting everything behind it, like a fishbowl turned upside down over the grounds.

He started back up the road, walking briskly toward the cottage. Michael had been with Elah, and she'd given him back that damn sword. No one meaning harm could cross into DeLeon lands, but did that apply to the Goddess who owned the entirety of the world? And what if they hadn't meant harm until after they'd arrived inside Thor's circle of protection? He'd never tested it personally, and it seemed awfully unlikely Thor would have ignored that loophole, when he'd been trying to protect the House of Lions from the likes of Sif and Loki. But even so.

Even so.

Evey? Everything all right? She didn't want to talk to him, he knew, and he couldn't blame her in the slightest, but that didn't mean he didn't still care about her well-being. That he was going to stand here like a fool, gaping while the light expanded ever closer to the cottage.

Not when he couldn't make sense of what he was seeing.

Evey?

Her thoughts touched his, desperate with—before he could even identify the emotion, she was gone again, disappearing completely as the goat pasture was swallowed in orange, too.

Adam broke into a run. Elah had been in rare form, but he couldn't believe she'd hurt her mother. Then again, he couldn't imagine who else might be responsible for whatever it was he was witnessing, either. Not Thor, unless it was the protections he'd wrought collapsing as Elah reclaimed the lands that were rightfully hers.

Elah! he called, not bothering with an audible shout when a mental one was far more effective. *What's happened?*

Lightning did strike, then, and the orange bubble popped, rainbow light rippling outward along a plane, like the rings of Saturn. Michael soared upward, hovering high in the air for a moment, blazing sword in hand, and then lightning exploded again, sending him tumbling backward. Adam grinned. Well, that answered that question, but he had a feeling Thor was likely to regret his strength.

Elah? he called again. *Are you all right?*

Father?

He hadn't expected to hear the tremor in her mental tone. *I'm here, sweetheart. Can you make me a doorway? I'll come to you.*

But a moment later, she was in front of him, her face white. She looked so young. Her spirit might be older than the world, tied to Elohim's, but in that moment, she was still a child. A little girl, lost and confused.

He gathered her into his arms, tucking her head beneath his chin, and hushing her before he even realized she was crying. "It's all right, Elah. I'm here."

She had to understand. I had to make her understand!

A chill slid down his spine and he felt himself stiffen. "Your mother?"

She said she wanted to be alone. That she had earned it.

His blood ran cold. "What was the orange light, Elah?"

She shook her head, breaking from his arms, tears still streaming down her cheeks, a teenager now, her long black hair short and choppy. "She wouldn't listen!"

"She's your mother, darling," he said, struggling to keep his tone light. "Mothers aren't supposed to listen to their daughters. At least that's my understanding of these things, having never been either one."

"But I'm her Goddess," Elah said, lifting her chin. "I'm her Goddess, and she had no right to refuse me. Just as she had no right to refuse you! Not truly. Not when you were made for one another so completely. My Archangels say you were cruel, but I understand. She deserved her exile then, just as she does now."

Exile. For Lucifer, it meant little. Just a change of his loyalties and a travel restriction. For Ra, it had meant a new life, a new name and place as a god of Egypt. But for Eve? He wasn't sure there was a crueler punishment. To remove her from communion with the world she had spent an eternity nurturing. And unlike Lucifer, she didn't realize there were other gods to whom she could turn. Eve didn't know she didn't have to be alone.

"And the light at the manor?" he asked again.

I gave her what she wanted. Elah turned away, hugging herself. "She said she'd rather be alone, and now she will be. Alone and apart, without even her Lions. I almost unmade them. It would have been fitting."

"But?" He didn't trust himself to say more, even to think it.

"I understand now, why she raised me here. Why she wouldn't leave. All this time, she was afraid. Terrified of what I might become."

He said nothing, just waiting. Her tone was too sharp, too sneering, and if he gave her an excuse to lash out at him, too, it wouldn't help anything. Certainly, it wouldn't help Eve.

"Elohim warded these lands, didn't He? I felt His power, His spirit standing in my way. Keeping me from doing my Will."

"If He did, I wouldn't know," Adam said, careful not to lie. After all, she would know her grandfather's touch better than anyone else. "But I saw the light, the orange and the white."

"It struck me down when I tried to break them, but it doesn't matter. They don't need to be dead. I just made them forget her. When she goes to them, looking for the help and support of the family she so loves, she'll be a stranger."

He let out a breath. It could have been so much worse. Would have been, if not for Thor. And thank all that was holy she didn't realize whose power had thwarted her. "You can take it back, Elah. Undo what you've done. Let it stand as a warning, and prove how benevolent you can be, how forgiving."

She whirled. "And should I take back Odin's exile, too? Show him forgiveness, though he treated me with nothing but contempt?"

He pressed his lips together. "Odin is different. He was a danger to you, but Eve . . . Eve is practically helpless."

"Yes," she agreed, meeting his eyes. "I've made her so."

"Her Lions were innocent, Elah," he said quietly, changing tacks. *Oh, Eve. Evey, I'm so sorry.* "They've done nothing but shelter you, they treated you with kindness and warmth. They're your family, too."

Her face flushed, and she looked away. "It's too late, now. When the lightning struck, it tore their memories from my hands. Even if I wanted to undo it, I can't. But maybe it's for the best. If they don't remember Eve, they won't remember me. They won't remember the child I was, only the Goddess I am."

He snorted. "You're still a child, Elah. Ascended or not. What you've done here, today, is proof of that much. Fortunate for you that your mother has a forgiving heart."

"She won't forgive you," Elah said, her eyes flashing.

"Not in this lifetime, no. And she shouldn't be made to." He shook his head, turning his gaze to the manor. The family Eve had spent so long building, that Thor had spent millennia protecting from exactly this. All of it undone in the blink of an eye. It made him sick. "To think that the reason I left her was because I feared my influence would corrupt you."

"Father—"

"Just listen." It wrenched him to see the betrayal in her eyes, but if there was any small chance she might hear him, he had to try. For Eve's sake. For the world's. "You're my daughter, Elah, and I love you. And when you aren't perfect, I'll love you still, because I know better than most how easy it is, when you have so much power, to make mistakes. But you're smarter than me, Elah, you aren't doomed to forget all the lessons you might learn, a hundred years at a time. Do yourself a favor and don't repeat my errors. Don't compound your own with pride. Don't look at the things I did as an example; be *better* than me. As a leader, as a Goddess, as a lover. Be better than me in every way, but especially, *especially*, I beg of you, be better to your mother."

She swallowed, her eyes damp, but she wouldn't look at him. Not really. "I—I'd better find Michael. He was struck down, and he'll be worried. I can hear him calling me."

He closed his eyes, rubbed his forehead. "And your mother?"

She hesitated, her back to him already, but then she straightened. "It's only for one lifetime. And it will show the others I'm not afraid to act. That the world is mine, and I'll defend my rights to it, even from my family, if necessary."

And then she disappeared in another flash of orange, just like that, and Adam stood alone.

All that heartbreak, all that sacrifice and suffering, all the pain he'd brought Eve, thinking it was for the best. That for once he was doing the right thing, the selfless thing.

It had all been his mistake.

And it had all been for nothing.

§

"Evey?" Adam pushed open the door to her bedroom. The bedroom they'd shared, however briefly in the cottage. She hadn't responded to his knocking, to any of his calls, and he couldn't reach her mind. But he had to come. He had to try. Especially now. "Evey, are you all right?"

She had her knees pulled to her chest, sitting on the window seat and staring out, her gaze unfocused, her face streaked with tears, long dried.

"Go away," she said, her voice hoarse.

"Evey, I'm here to help." When he tried to step through the doorway, he met resistance. A pressure, pushing him back. But it hadn't been the first time Eve had turned her power on him. "You don't have to be alone."

"I went to the manor," Eve said, expressionless.

He swallowed. "Elah told me what happened. I know I'm the last person you want to see right now, but . . ."

"But I have no one else." Eve kept her gaze upon the window. "She made sure of that, didn't she? It's so quiet. So empty. She didn't just take my Lions, she took it all. Shifted the whole world right out from under my feet."

"Evey, I'm sorry. I'm so sorry."

"Go away," she said again.

"You shouldn't be alone, Evey."

"She threw a tantrum to get what she wanted, Adam." She looked at him then, finally, her eyes as empty as her voice. There was nothing there. Nothing but hollowness in her features. As if all the life had drained from her body. "Do you really think I'll give it to her, now?"

He dropped his gaze. It hurt too much to look at her. To see all that pain.

"Go away," Eve said. "And don't come back."

Maybe leaving her was cowardly. Maybe it was weak. But he couldn't see how she was wrong.

Turning him away was the only control she had left.

After everything else she'd lost, Adam had no intention of taking that from her, too.

CHAPTER FIFTY-TWO

Eve, Later

Adam was dead. She'd felt it, even in Asgard. A rip through her heart, a strange spasm in her soul. And then Athena had returned with Thor's body, and only Lars's small frown and squirming insistence to reach him on the bed convinced her that he wasn't dead, too.

"He needs apples," Athena said, her face streaked with tears. "He'll live. He has to live."

His skin was tinged green where it wasn't blackened pits and sand and blood, and Eve knelt beside the bed, bringing his hand to her cheek, to her face, and holding it tight. *Thor. Oh, Thor.*

Adam was dead.

Even staring at Thor, at his pocked face and what was left of his hair, she couldn't help but think of it. Adam had gone in her place, and he had died. Died because of her. To protect her. Elah had lost her father, Lars had lost his uncle, she had lost—she had lost him.

"I didn't say goodbye."

"To have done so would have been to send him without hope," Raphael said, behind her. He was helping Lars, who worked his magic with nothing more than a scowl and an intense concentration. Raphael only served as his guide. Showing him the anatomy of a god, healthy and whole and alive.

But Adam was dead. Too far gone for even Lars to mend. She knew it even before Athena brought his broken body back. And if she'd been on earth when it had happened, she wouldn't have survived the shock. Asgard had separated them just enough. Enough that she couldn't sit in his mind, that she couldn't hear his thoughts, sense his presence. It had cushioned the blow. But now what? They had been tied to one another for so long. They had been part of one another from Creation, and now he was gone. And she didn't know. She didn't know if he could ever be reborn.

If the venom of Jormungand shattered souls, how could Adam ever live again?

"Thor will live, Eve," Raphael said, his hand resting gently on her shoulder. "And I will see that Lars does not exhaust himself. In the meantime, perhaps you should rest."

"Rest." She knew what would happen if she went to bed, and it wouldn't be restful. "I'd rather not, if it's all the same to you."

"As you wish, of course," the Archangel said.

"What I wish doesn't matter, now," she said, closing her eyes. "It won't bring Adam back. It won't change how all this has ended."

"But it *is* ended, all the same," Raphael said gently. "And it would not have been, if not for your brother's will. Athena said she left him barely conscious. Weak, but alive. That by all rights, he should not have had even the strength to draw his knife. And yet, Michael is dead. Poisoned because of Adam's determination. His last sacrifice. And the world is safe."

"But it will never be whole."

"Are you so certain?" Raphael flicked his fingers, and Eve's gaze shifted along with his. Lars, tracing his father's features, drawing them again and again with a fingertip. The pockmarks of Thor's face had softened, and his eyebrows were full again, his hairline clean of venom-burns. Thor's chest rose and fell more steadily, his heartbeat, when she checked the pulse at his wrist, steady.

"It's okay, Mama," Lars said, looking up at her. "I fixed him. He's just sleeping now."

Eve let out a breath of her own, pressing a kiss to his palm. *Thor. Thor, please. Please wake up.*

The hand she held twitched, and then tightened. His eyelids trembled. Slitted open. Just the smallest crescent of blue and white and the barest curve of his lips.

Hjartað mitt. My love.

Tears blurred her eyes. Choked her throat. "You're alive."

Thor gave a rattling sigh. *By the grace of your son.*

Your son, too.

His eyes were smiling. *Our son.*

"Come along, Lars," Raphael said, taking his small hand. "Let's give your mother and father some peace, shall we?"

"Adam?" Thor croaked. "Athena?"

"Athena is fine," Eve said, swallowing. "Adam—"

Thor's hand cupped her cheek, slipped into her hair. He pulled her in, drew her onto the bed beside him, cradling her against his side. "My love."

He had to be a damn hero, she sniffed, the tears running free, now that she was in his arms. *He had to be a hero instead of a cad, and I never told him, Thor. I never got to tell him I loved him. I loved him for it.*

Thor kissed her forehead. *He knew, Eve.*

How could he? she sobbed. *How could he have known when I denied him for so, so long?*

He stroked her hair, smoothed it. *Because he knew you.*

Elah knew me, too.

Not the way Adam did.

She closed her eyes, thinking of the last weeks they'd shared. How kind he'd been. How understanding. How much he'd done, just for her. For Lars. To protect them both.

He'd never stopped trying to protect them.

He died a good death, Eve. The bravest of deaths.

I'm going to miss him forever.

Thor kissed her again. And even though he didn't say it, she knew he would too.

❧

Eve spent the next day sitting at Elah's bedside, waiting for her to wake. She might not have had the power to command the Archangels, but Raphael and Gabriel hadn't argued when she'd insisted on being the one to tell her daughter about her father's last act. Michael's death. Jormungand's defeat. Eve stared at the sword in her lap, the blade she'd feared for so long. It didn't look like much, just then.

Sheathed, it had no flames, no fire. And the scabbard itself, Thor had promised, would keep Surt's spirit snared. Eve traced the runes absently, thinking still of Adam. Had God realized what would become of him? Had He envisioned her brother's death, when He'd brought him to life, in the Garden? Known just how he would die?

"No."

She lifted her head to see Lucifer at Elah's bedside, though when he'd entered, how he'd arrived, she wasn't certain. "What?"

"The answer to your question," Lucifer said, not meeting her eyes. "Elohim might have hoped for certain outcomes, but he rather preferred to be sssurprised, when it was possible."

"Is that why you're so . . ."

"Perverse?" Lucifer offered.

Eve shrugged.

"Perhaps, in part."

"What's the next outcome?" Eve asked, too tired to be anything less than direct. "What other games does he want you to play with us?"

The snake man sighed. "I sssuppose it was too much to hope that you might consider the bright side of all this."

Her fingers tightened around the scabbard. "My brother is dead. My daughter grievously injured. Half of my family doesn't even remember who I am."

"You have your son, hale and hearty. Your husband returned to you. Your daughter lives, freed from the influence of her enemy. The ssserpent is defeated and the world will heal. Perhapsss the other half of your family might be healed as well."

"My Lions?" she breathed, her heart constricting. "Truly?"

"Where there is a will, there is alwaysss a way."

"But Elah said—"

"What his father's lightning disrupted, your ssson might yet save."

Eve rocked back in her chair, hope filling her heart for the first time in what felt like years. Her family. Her family whole again, aware of themselves, of their place in the world. Elah's punishment finally undone, all these years later. "What about Adam?"

Lucifer's jaw tightened, and he looked away. "It is one thing to heal a living thing, another to piece together a soul, torn to bitsss and scattered across the expanse of the void."

Her vision blurred, her eyes misting even as her throat closed. She remembered the void. Remembered being whole inside it. One with God. She had even yearned to return to that place of safety, of eternity and contentment. But that wasn't what Lucifer had described. That wasn't Adam's fate at all.

"You can't even promise me he has peace, can you? After everything he suffered, everything he sacrificed, he won't even have the satisfaction of an afterlife. Does it bring you some twisted pleasure to tell me this? When he died in my place? When it should have been me?"

His yellow eyes widened. "No!"

"Then why?"

"I—" he swallowed. "It is my curse to ssspeak without thought for the pain my words may cause. I meant to give you solace, some sssmall comfort in your grief. Forgive me, please."

She closed her eyes, drawing from the strength of the tree, of Asgard and Elohim, and nodded. Alone, she couldn't. Forgiveness required more than she had to give when guilt weighed so heavily upon her heart. She didn't deserve his solace, his comfort.

She deserved the cruelty of the truth.

"I doubt that Adam would agree," Lucifer said wryly. "He would sssay you had suffered pain enough for eternity, and deserved no more on his account."

She shook her head, slanting him a look of irritation. She was beginning to understand the frustrations she must have caused her DeLeon family when she lived among them, even if she hadn't been half so cavalier about dipping into their thoughts. But Lucifer wasn't wrong. And she had wasted so much of Adam's time—their time together—with anger and pain, dwelling on it and wallowing in it, thinking she had forever to forgive him. Thinking the next lifetime would be as good as this one. And he had been so patient. So willing to give her as many days, as many weeks, as many lives as she needed. They had both taken their immortality for granted.

But not anymore.

She didn't intend to waste even one more hour with recrimination, with anger, with blame.

If he had lived, still, he'd appreciate that.

❧

"Mama?"

Eve straightened. Lucifer had left some time ago, leaving her with her thoughts and her vigil. She set the sword against the bedside table and reached forward, taking Elah's hand in both of hers, gathering her strength, her will, to meet her daughter's eyes.

"Is the world safe?" Elah asked softly, her voice rough from disuse. "I can't—it doesn't feel right."

"The world is safe," Eve promised. "It's just that you're in Asgard, now. It was the safest place. And then we didn't want to move you until you'd woken. What you're feeling, all that love and peace and wholeness, it's coming from the Tree of Life. Thor's Yggdrasil. You needed it."

"Michael," she said, turning her face away. Somehow, even saying his name had wilted her. "I should have died."

"Lars healed you," Eve said, trying to keep the strain from her voice, struggling to keep her sorrow buried. "But it was a near thing, honey. All of it."

"Father always said he wasn't—" She swallowed something that sounded like a sob, and Eve squeezed her hand. "He wasn't good enough for me."

Eve's throat thickened. They had both warned her. But she had been so young. Too young, when Elohim had taken her and given her into Michael's care. And maybe when he'd been without the sword, Elah had been right to disregard their fears. Eve wanted to believe that. She wanted to believe that Michael had at least been good to her daughter for some brief moment in time. That he had deserved the loyalty she'd shown him, even if Elah's affections had lingered too long. Blinded her to what he was.

"Your father's discernment rarely failed him, so long as he didn't have to apply it to himself. Michael was always difficult, always took too much pleasure in his duty, but none of us knew this was why. Even Gabriel and Raphael didn't realize the significance of the sword, how it had twisted him."

"I put that sword back in his hand, Mama."

"He could have refused it. Ought to have confessed himself, after Elohim took it from him the first time. For that matter, Elohim should never have given him that sword at all. If your Grandfather didn't know any better, I'm not sure how you could."

Elah shook her head. "I should have known. He was mine. All of it was mine, and I should have known."

"Maybe so," Eve said, because as painful as it was, sometimes cruel truths were necessary. Sometimes Lucifer's words were the most important, no matter how she might resent them in the moment.

"Maybe if you had trusted in us, things would have been different. Maybe it would have forced Michael to reveal himself that much sooner, before you had a brother with the power to save you. Maybe we would've all died, together. If you had suspected him as an enemy, maybe you would have been quicker to respond, to act, and he would have been unmade before he struck you, and Jormungand would have been the only battle we had to fight.

"And maybe if I had humored you, if I had tried to forgive your father a little bit sooner, tried to forgive *you* sooner, it would have changed things, too. But we both made our choices, Elah. We all made our choices. And no matter how long we live, how many lives we experience, there will never be any guarantees that the choices we make will be the right ones. We just have to do our best in the moments we're given."

Elah's gaze slid away. "I don't know how you can sit there and not blame me for everything. For all this suffering, all this destruction. You and Daddy, you never would have let this happen to the world if it had been yours."

Eve would have laughed, if it hadn't hurt so much. "As much as I loved the man your father became, if Elohim had entrusted him with the world at Creation, Adam would have been just as happy to watch it burn as to rule it. By comparison, you showed an admirable restraint."

She smiled. "He told me to be better than him."

Eve swallowed against a hard lump of grief. "I think it's safe to say you managed that much."

Elah was watching her now, a small vertical crease forming between her eyebrows. How many times had she seen that expression on Adam's face? Her heart ached at the knowledge that she'd never see it again. But she wouldn't put that blame on her daughter. Wouldn't let Elah take it upon herself. It was the least she could do to honor Adam.

"Mama," Elah said slowly. "What happened while I was sleeping?"

Eve dropped her gaze, staring at her hand, at Elah's.

"Mama, please."

She took a breath, steadied herself. "Your father—Adam—he went with Thor to lure Jormungand. He knew it was dangerous, but he said—he said it was only fair. That it was his turn. Michael attacked him after. During."

"No." Elah's fingers twisted around hers, an echo of pain shaping the denial.

Eve met her eyes, held them. Held her hand as fiercely as Elah held hers. Because it was the two of them now. It was the two of them, and Eve wasn't going to let her go again. As long as she'd had Adam, it had been—it had been different. Elah could be mad at her, furious at her forever, but she'd never be alone. But not now. Not anymore.

"He killed him, honey. They killed each other."

And then, through her tears, through Elah's, she told her everything.

Everything that was left.

CHAPTER FIFTY-ONE
Thor

❧

When he was well enough, he went to the world tree. His mother's tree. Elohim's tree. He sat heavily upon the bench, even journeying so short a distance by lightning had exhausted what strength he had. Most of his wounds were more superficial than severe, and none of them, individually, had been mortal. All together, however, with so much venom in his lungs, and even more in his blood, he had been fortunate to survive. Wouldn't have, if not for Lars.

His son.

His true son, by Eve, with all the power and glory that came with it. The son Odin had denied him, so long ago. And how his father would resent it, now! To think, if he had only embraced Thor's love for Eve, accepted her as his choice after Sif had betrayed him, Odin might have had more power over this world, over Elohim, than he had ever dreamed of.

Thor closed his eyes, breathing in the sweetness of Yggdrasil, always in bloom, always fruiting, always rich with life and brimming with peace. The source of so much of his comfort when he had been forbidden from Eve.

"Mother, why didn't you tell me?" All the years he had been here while Elohim still lived, and he had never revealed himself, never given him any sign of their relationship. Now, he would never know why. "Was it because of my father? Because of me? I longed for you, for your love, for the acceptance Odin could never give me. Why did you not give me some sign? Even that you still lived at all!"

"Maybe it was me."

He opened his eyes. Strange that he hadn't realized Eve had joined him. He must have been weaker than he realized, not to feel her presence. And Lars, too, laughing with Grani as they chased the goats. It did not seem they would ever tire of the game.

"The gods have played me for a fool so many times, why shouldn't Elohim have used me then, too? To gift you, through me, with some measure of His love, His Grace, His warmth and welcome?"

Thor grunted, shifting slightly on the bench to make room for her. "It is not quite the same as a mother's love."

"And meeting you was not the same as having my father's support." She sat beside him, but hugged herself. He wished he had the strength to read her mind, for since Elah had awoken, Eve had kept a careful distance from him. "We both thought He was gone, dead. Maybe by bringing us together, He hoped it would make up for the absence."

"And what of Adam?" Thor asked. "Did he not deserve some solace, too?"

Eve's jaw tightened, and he regretted the question at once. It was thoughtless to speak of her brother. Her lover. It was only that it seemed so easy to forget he was gone, that he would never be reborn again. It seemed too impossible to be true when Adam had plagued him for millennia. A strange emptiness filled him at the thought.

"Adam couldn't miss what he didn't remember," she said after a moment. "And when he did remember—" she stopped. Swallowed hard.

Emotion filled the air, thick between them, and the tree responded, rustling its leaves until an apple fell from the branch nearest them. An offering, Thor supposed, to help them heal. A shame he couldn't bring himself to reach for it.

Eve cleared her throat. "I wish I had asked him about those first days, with Elohim. But I thought we'd have so much more time."

That she loved Adam was no great surprise. She had loved Adam before, faults and all, and there had been no reason, knowing her spirit as he did, to think she would not love him again, given the space to heal. And now that Adam was gone it was natural that she would love him all that much more fiercely. Likely, in part because she had held herself back while he lived. But Thor ached for some small reassurance. Some sign she did not regret what they shared, now. What she had chosen at Adam's expense. Who she had chosen.

"It would not be the same, I know, but perhaps Raphael or Gabriel might share their memories of that time. With both of us."

"Perhaps." Eve leaned forward, picking up the apple from where it had fallen, and offering it to him. "In the meantime, I came to call you back to your bed. You are far, far too ill, yet, to be wandering Asgard, and if you're not careful, you'll attract the attention of your physician."

She nodded beyond him, and he followed her gaze. Lars was running to join them, Grani following at his heels like an oversized dog.

"Did you see?" he called excitedly. "Did you see me an' Grani jump the well?"

"Maybe you should limit your practice to fences and stone walls, love," Eve said warmly, catching him in her arms. "We don't need any more broken bones or bruises with half of Asgard already healing from some injury or another."

Lars wrinkled his nose. "Not *half*, Mama."

"Near enough," she said, pulling him into her lap. "

Lars turned wide eyes on Thor. "Can't *you* say?"

He laughed, though it made something in his chest pull uncomfortably. "I know better than to cross your mother. And she isn't wrong, you know. You're nearly the only one left without a scar, and you'll have to fight for all of us if any more monsters stir. Best not to take unnecessary risks in the meantime."

"I guess," Lars agreed, his solemn face scrunching. "But maybe after you're fixed better?"

"Maybe then," Thor said, ruffling his hair. He glanced up at Eve, catching the crinkles of unvoiced laughter in the corners of her eyes and the press of her lips, keeping her from smiling. "But only if your mother agrees."

"Please, Mama?"

She kissed the top of Lars's head. "We'll see."

And they sat there, the three of them. His new little family, together at last. He closed his eyes and tipped his head back against Yggdrasil's trunk. *Let it last, please. If you grant me nothing else, let it be this.*

What God has joined, Eve said softly, and when he lifted his arm, she slid beneath it. She and Lars, tucked against his side.

The leaves above rustled again, and to his ears, it sounded like a promise.

❧

"It was here," Athena said.

The ground was still blackened, after all this time.

"Here," she said, again, and the angels descended, Hera's tree suspended between them. Hera's tree, stolen from Elohim, from the ashes of the Garden.

Thor must have seen it. How many times had he been to Olympus? He'd even spoken to Zeus in Hera's menagerie, seen the dragon guarding it. Somehow he'd never made the connection, never realized how similar it was, or even that it existed at all.

Eve let out a shaky breath at his side, her hand wrapped around her daughter's, and an Asgardian apple in her other fist. A golden apple, from the Tree of Life. From Yggdrasil. Thor held Lars in his arms, and Raphael held Adam, his burned and broken body shrouded in silk.

"He would have appreciated it," Eve said. "He spent so many of his lives trying to get it back. He should have it now. Everything."

"Daddy didn't care about the Garden," Elah said. "Not anymore. The only thing he cared about—"

"I know," Eve said.

Raphael laid the body down, and the angels settled the tree at his head. There was no digging. Elah had only to flick her fingers and the ground opened, or perhaps it rose up, pulling both down, rooting them into the earth.

Eve stepped forward, setting the apple down over his heart before he disappeared altogether. "Thank you," she said, so softly Thor almost didn't hear the words.

And then Adam was gone.

For as long as they'd been enemies, Thor had no need to feign his own grief. Adam had given up his life for Eve, for Elah, for Lars. Even for Thor, himself. And for everything Adam had done in the North Country—for the world itself—the man had deserved better. More.

He'd deserved to see the fruits of his labor. The world made whole. Lars grown and Eve happy, at peace with her daughter, with her life, and with the choices Adam had made for both their sakes, the choices she had made, as well.

"I should've fixed him, somehow," Lars said, his brow furrowed. "It woulda made Mama happier, if I had. But it was like the spaceship, and it wouldn't fix *right*."

Thor shook his head. "There wasn't anything you could have done, Lars. Not for his body. But maybe, someday—when you're all grown up, and have more time to learn—maybe you might be able to do something for his spirit, hm?"

Eve came back, her eyes meeting his. *Elah wants some time alone. And I—I should call Hilda. Go back to the North Country and see what I can do. Adam wouldn't want everything to fall apart because . . . because.*

He offered her his hand. *I'll do what I can to help. Raphael and Athena, too. If you'll let us.*

He'd like that. Her fingers laced through his. *I would, too.*

The hard knot around his heart unraveled slightly. He'd feared she would blame him, in her grief. Push him away. Push both of them away. But since that afternoon beneath the tree, she had warmed, and they had both begun to close the distance that had stretched out between them. To allow his help in settling Adam's affairs seemed the final step, the final acceptance, even if they had not healed the rift completely, and there was no resentment, no hesitation in her mind at all.

Adam never did anything he didn't want to do, Eve said. *This was his choice. And he went out in style. One final everlasting proof he had changed that neither of us could ever doubt. The stupid hero.*

Now who's the mind reader?

She almost laughed, a ripple of amusement flitting through her mind. *I missed you.*

I never left you, not in spirit.

But now you're here.

Forever, Eve. Adam and Lars gave us eternity. If you still want it.

Eve's fingers tightened around his. *Always.*

It was exactly what he'd hoped she would say.

EPILOGUE

Lars

❧

Lars hesitated at the entrance to the Redwood Hall, a shiver of memory slipping through him at the familiar scent of mulch and earth and a hint of soft pine. Almost twenty years later, and he still remembered that day more clearly than any two-year-old had any right to. The Goddess crumpling, his mother's sharp cry of fear and pain, and his uncle's silent heartbreak to see his daughter broken, dying.

His uncle.

"Knowing your father, I would never have guessed you'd dither in doorways," Elah said, her soft, musical voice only sharpening his memories. Adam picking him out of his mother's arms, grinning, laughing, chiding his daughter for her manners.

He gave himself a shake, dragging his gaze to the Goddess. To his sister, standing off to the side, with her rainbow-black hair, and brilliant hazel eyes. Seeing her struck something—she was more beautiful than he remembered. Maybe because he'd always looked at her through a child's eyes before now. He'd never come here alone, rarely come here at all, truthfully. But then, those first years, after Thor had slain Jormungand, he hadn't seen much of his sister. His mother had gone to see her often enough, but Lars had always stayed with his father. They'd go to Asgard together, spending the day in the old, empty halls, and Thor would try to explain. About Elah and Eve, and how hard it was for them to go on. How they grieved, still, for Adam. How important it was, that he not forget the uncle he'd lost.

Lars swept her a bow. "My father was more concerned that I know my place, I think, than anything else. And coming here this way—I hope I haven't overstepped."

Elah held a broad, green leaf in her hand, twisting it idly between her fingers. "You've grown up, Lars."

"I should hope so." He smiled, focusing on the leaf to keep himself from staring at the rest of her. She was beautiful, glowing like electrum. "Sometimes, my childhood felt as though it lasted an eternity. And it's such a pleasure to have proper control over my strengths. Mother said it was good for me, adolescence, puberty, all those years of awkwardness, but I'm not certain I believe her."

Her lips curved. "All our mother's grace, and all your father's confidence. An unfair advantage."

"Over anyone but you."

She laughed. "I can't imagine you came all this way just to flatter me."

He hadn't. But somehow, it seemed right. Natural. His mother had insisted on raising him on earth, teaching him to be human more than a god. To love humanity, respect them, as well as Creation itself, and of course his very presence on earth had helped to heal it, allowing Elah to draw upon his strength and his power, while he fixed the little things that impinged on his awareness. He hadn't been able to resist, really, even if he hadn't truly realized what he was doing until much later.

"Forgive me," Lars said, almost on reflex. He'd learned the lesson of love, no question, but he'd never felt entirely comfortable with any of his mortal friends, pretending to be something less than he was. With Elah, he didn't have to wear a mask. She'd see straight through it, even if he tried. "You're right, of course. It wasn't my intention to trespass on your time."

She shook her head. "It isn't a trespass, Lars. We've spent so little time together, and we *should* know one another. Better than this. I just—I didn't want Mother to think I was trying to interfere. After everything else. And my father." Her voice caught, her gaze dropping to the leaf in her hands. "My father would have wanted that for you. For her."

He cleared his throat. "It's because of your father, actually, that I've come. It isn't something Mother would ever agree with, of course, but my father thought—well. He suggested that if it weren't questionable, it would hardly be fitting. And Mother's morals and ethics are all well and good, but sometimes even she bends her own rules."

Rambling. He was rambling now. He pressed his lips together, impatient with his own foolishness. And Elah's forehead had creased, as if he'd said something to offend her . . .

"Thor's insight has always been fascinating," she said slowly. "But I'm not sure I understand."

"I believe I know how to bring him back," Lars said, stepping forward. "It might take a little time, and certainly it will require some orchestration, on both our parts, but he doesn't have to stay dead, Lady. Not forever."

The leaf dropped from her hands, fluttering to the mulch of soft, red needles, and her eyes. If he had thought them brilliant before, it was nothing to the light that filled them now. Hope and trepidation and excitement all warred among themselves in those depths, drawing him in, begging him for more.

"How?" she breathed.

Lars smiled. "That's the beauty of it. Just a little matchmaking, a few nudges, here or there, and a dash of love. A distillation of the pieces of him floating across half the earth in a billion different lines, and a healing touch. It's like how Mother was always born with greater frequency into the populations that already carried her blood. We just need to give it a little bit of help. Concentrate his essence just a little bit more. It was the venom, Father says, which shattered his soul, but if we pull the pieces of him that are left back together, the bits of his spirit ought to be drawn home and I can mend it. I'm all but certain."

She must have reached for him while he spoke, for he found himself holding her hand, her perfect, tapered fingers wrapped tightly around his. She smelled like her redwoods, all delicate pine, with a hint of geranium beneath.

"Just tell me when and where and who," Elah said, joy making her glow all the brighter. "And I promise you, Lars, if this works—" she bit her lip, stopping herself, and he had to resist the urge to lift his hand, to brush his thumb across her cheekbone, flushed pink and lovely.

He hadn't the right. And he would have pulled back then, because he had no right at all even for this small intimacy, no matter how beautiful she was, but her grasp firmed, and she looked up at him from beneath lashes, swept low, and he couldn't. He couldn't refuse her anything. Not as long as she looked at him like that.

"I'm so sorry, Lars," she said softly. "I'm so sorry I ever doubted you. I never should have. Not you, not Mother. I—I'd like it very much if you could stay. We're brother and sister, after all, and I feel as though I hardly know you."

He ducked his head, catching her eyes, and he hoped she could see what he hadn't the words to say. All these years, and she'd been so mysterious, so distant, but he'd never resented her. Never for a moment imagined himself slighted. Sister or not she was Goddess. His Goddess, as much as anyone else's. But he hadn't been sure what to expect when he came to see her. Even with his father's encouragement. Certainly, even in his wildest dreams, he hadn't expected her warmth, her obvious affection.

"Well," he said, offering a small half-smile. "If we're going to bring your father back, I don't see that I have much of a choice, really. We'll have to work together closely to get everything just right. You're likely to be sick of me before we're through."

But Elah returned his smile, almost shyly. "I don't know. All your mother's grace and your father's confidence—I'm beginning to think you'll make for rather charming company. It might be fun to have a brother around."

"I'll do my best not to disappoint," he promised.

She dropped her gaze, seeming to stare at their hands. "I'm glad you're here."

He squeezed her hand, enveloped in both of his. It wasn't just that he had come, he knew, or even the reason why. It was that he lived at all, to come, to offer her some small hope. Or not so small, as the case may be.

"I'm glad, too, Lady."

"Elah," she said. "You're my brother, remember?"

Lars bowed over her hand, and let her go. He hadn't come here just to flatter her, after all, even if he could have been content to hold her hand for eternity. Absolutely absurd, not to mention forward of him, when they'd barely spent a week's worth of hours in one another's company, before now. So he pushed all the rest away, and reminded himself of his purpose. It wasn't as if he wouldn't have plenty of time to spend examining the complexity of feelings that threatened to tangle around his heart while they worked.

It wasn't as though they wouldn't have eternity, later, too.

"Shall we start in the British Isles? Mother mentioned to me once that his last line, before you, had settled there. If we can find them, it might be the best place to begin."

And Lars thought, somehow, that when they managed to bring Adam back at last, the two of them together, brother and sister, and maybe, if he were very lucky, more—his uncle would approve.

Novellas in the Fate of the Gods series by Amalia Dillin

TEMPTING FATE

A Fate of the Gods Novella: Book 1.5

Mia's lived in her sister's shadow long enough. Now that Abby is getting married to a Frenchman, Mia scents freedom. In fact, Jean DeLeon, the groom's too-charming cousin, seems like the perfect place to start. But the House of Lions is full of secrets, and what started out as an exciting fling is quickly becoming more frustration than fun. Mia wants answers, or she wants out, and it isn't like she doesn't have other options. Ethan Hastings, for example. Tall, handsome, and gray eyes like nothing she's ever seen before. The fact that Jean seems to hate him is just a bonus. *(This e-novella takes place during the events of Forged by Fate.)*

TAMING FATE

A Fate of the Gods Novella: Book 2.5

Ryam DeLeon may have saved Eve from burning at the stake, but their hasty marriage is off to anything but a smooth start. As tensions in the town grow, Ryam knows if he and Eve cannot find common ground, their first Christmas may be their last.

❧

ABOUT THE AUTHOR

Amalia Dillin began as a Biology major before taking Latin and falling in love with old heroes and older gods. After that, she couldn't stop writing about them, with the occasional break for more contemporary subjects. Her short stories have been published by *Daily Science Fiction* and *Birdville* magazine, and she's also the author of the FATE OF THE GODS series and *Honor Among Orcs*, the first book in the Orc Saga. Amalia lives in upstate New York with her husband, and dreams of the day when she will own goats—to pull her chariot through the sky, of course.

Find her online at AmaliaDillin.com,
or follow her on Twitter @AmaliaTd.

NEW AND FORTHCOMING WORLD WEAVER PRESS TITLES

Beyond the Glass Slipper
Ten Neglected Fairy Tales to Fall In Love With
Some fairy tales everyone knows—these aren't those tales.
Edited by Kate Wolford

Shards of History
Fantasy
Only she knows the truth that can save her people.
Rebecca Roland

The King of Ash and Bones
Breathtaking four-story collection
Rebecca Roland

Opal
Fantasy fairy tale retelling (YA)
White as snow, stained with blood, her talons black as ebony...
Kristina Wojtaszek

The Haunted Housewives of Allister, Alabama
Cleo Tidwell Paranormal Mystery, Book One
Who knew one gaudy Velvet Elvis
could lead to such a heap of haunted trouble?
Susan Abel Sullivan

The Weredog Whisperer
Cleo Tidwell Paranormal Mystery, Book Two
The Tidwells are supposed to be on spring break on the Florida Gulf Coast,
not up to their eyeballs in paranormal hijinks... again.
Susan Abel Sullivan

Heir to the Lamp
Genie Chronicles, Book One (YA)
A family secret, a mysterious lamp,
a dangerous Order with the mad desire to possess both.
Michelle Lowery combs

Specter Spectacular: 13 Ghostly Tales
Anthology
Once you cross the grave into this world of fantasy and fright,
you may find there's no way back.
Edited by Eileen Wiedbrauk

Specter Spectacular II: 13 Deathly Tales
Anthology
Coming in 2014
Edited by Eileen Wiedbrauk

Far Orbit: Speculative Space Adventures
Science fiction in the Grand Traditon—Anthology
Edited by Bascomb James

Glamour
Stealing the life she's always wanted is as easy as casting a spell. (YA)
Andrea Janes

Cursed: Wickedly Fun Stories
Collection
"Quirky, clever, and just a little savage." —Lane Robins, critically acclaimed author of MALEDICTE and KINGS AND ASSASSINS
Susan Abel Sullivan

Fae
Anthology of Fairies
Edited by Rhonda Parrish

A Winter's Enchantment

Three novellas of winter magic and loves lost and regained.

Experience the magic of the season.

Elise Forier Edie, Amalia Dillin, Kristina Wojatszek

The Devil in Midwinter

Paranormal romance (NA)

A handsome stranger, a terrifying monster, a boy who burns and burns…

Elise Forier Edie

Legally Undead

Vampirachy, Book One

A reluctant vampire hunter, stalking New York City as only a scorned bride can.

Margo Bond Collins

Ailen Ways

Darci Salazar Mystery, Book One—*Coming 2015*

The trick to working with drug-addled aliens is not to lose your head…

David J. Rank

Blood Chimera

Blood Chimera, Book One

Some ransoms aren't meant to be paid.

Jenn Lyons

Blood Sin

Blood Chimera, Book Two

Everything is permitted… and everyone has their price.

Jenn Lyons

Virgin

Young Adult Paranormal

Coming March 2015

Jenna Nelson

He Sees You When You're Sleeping
A Christmas Krampus anthology
Coming Holiday 2014
Edited by Kate Wolford

* * *

For more on these and other titles
Visit WorldWeaverPress.com

* * *

World Weaver Press
Publishing fantasy, paranormal, and science fiction.
We believe in great storytelling.

35614912R00239

Made in the USA
Lexington, KY
17 September 2014